TENDER TAMING

"My lord, please—"

"Aye, I will. Think you I don't know how to please a woman?"

Lyon's mouth touched her throat, his tongue bathing the pulse there, sliding down the valley between her breasts. She shuddered as she felt the heat of his breath against her breast. Ariana cried out his name, so seldom uttered from her lips, the entreaty implicit in her quavering voice.

"Lady, lady," he groaned, his own plea rich and deep. "You send me to perdition."

"What are you doing to me? Mercy, my lord."

"I promised no mercy, Ariana." He was too hungry for her to let her pleas sway him. He would make her welcome him as her husband, her conqueror. He would tame her.

THE LION'S BRIDE

CONNIE MASON

LEISURE BOOKS NEW YORK CITY

A LEISURE BOOK®

December 1995

Published by

Dorchester Publishing Co., Inc.
276 Fifth Avenue
New York, NY 10001

Printed in the United States of America.

To all my wonderful readers who continue to buy and enjoy my books.
Your faith in my writing is greatly appreciated.

THE LION'S BRIDE

Prologue

Northumbria, England, 1067

Ominous blood-red fingers stroked the dark underbelly of dawn, heralding a new day, one fraught with impending disaster. Ariana of Cragmere had seen it in a vision. Even if the messenger had not arrived from the bastard Conqueror, she would have known full well what to expect.

She stood now on the parapet of her father's fortress, a tiny figure outlined against the scarlet dawn. A man of foresight, her father, Nyle of Cragmere, had built a fortress on his land employing the French design of motte and bailey instead of erecting a manor house like those of other English land barons. The fortress, one of the few in all of England, proved an effective deterrent to invaders in the highly volatile border lands of Northumbria.

Ariana peered fixedly into the murky dawn, watching, waiting, her face grim. When she first received word of the deaths of her father and three brothers at the Battle of Hastings, she had known this day would come. The Conqueror had acted swiftly after his victory, dispossessing Saxon nobles of their lands and replacing them with Norman knights who had fought at William's side and remained loyal. Ariana knew it was only a matter of time before William the Bastard turned his eyes north, to the rich holdings in Northumbria, and brought them into his fold.

"He comes! The Lion comes!" The warning came from Keane, Ariana's seneschal, who was keeping watch nearby.

Ariana turned her head sharply, sending a swirl of silver-blond hair cascading around her slim shoulders. Narrowing her green eyes against the brilliant, blood-red dawn, she saw the Lion materializing magically in the void where the horizon met the rich Northumbrian soil. He was mounted on an enormous black stallion, advancing slowly toward Cragmere. Abruptly the sun broke through the clouds, sending a shaft of golden light down upon his bronze helmet. The reflection near blinded her.

"Look, he brings his army!"

Ariana frowned. Her faithful seneschal hadn't exaggerated. A veritable army of retainers and mercenaries stretched out behind the Lion, all armed and garbed in chain mail. She made a low sound of disgust deep in her throat. Surely he didn't expect a fourteen-year-old girl with a mere handful of knights and retainers to resist, did he?

With rapidly beating heart, she watched him approach, this fierce warrior whom the Conqueror valued enough to reward with the richest demesne in the land. His bronze helmet was buckled in place, and his nose guard hid his face. Over his leather tunic he wore a long coat of scalelike chain mail that immediately identified him as one of the notorious Norman "fishmen." In his left hand he carried a five-foot oval shield of steel, so heavy and cumbersome that he had to support at least a part of its weight with a broad strap that looped around his shoulder. A pair of seven-foot, steel-tipped lances sat upright in a socket at the horse's flanks, and he carried a battle sword in his right hand, a long double-edged weapon that only a barbarous giant could wield effectively. His show of force was as unnecessary as it was galling.

"He looks fearsome and dangerous, does he not, my lady?" Ariana gave a startled gasp as the witch Nadia appeared at her elbow. " 'Tis said he's a bastard like his master, William. And young. At two-and-twenty years, 'tis rumored he's as fierce a warrior as William, and just as brave. 'Tis said he saved William's life on the battlefield when he was but ten and eight. The Lion of Normandy earned his title performing feats of bravery few men would dare."

"More's the pity he wasn't slain on the battle-field," Ariana replied spitefully. "Cragmere is mine. William has no right to take it from me and give it to another."

"Ye are but a child; ye cannot keep it safe from northern invaders. Scotland's king has ever his eye on Northumbria. Malcolm would not hesitate to take Cragmere by force from a defenseless girl."

Ariana sent Nadia a blistering look. "Whose side are you on, Nadia? What are you doing here? I do not recall summoning you from your hut in the woods. Mayhap the great Lord Lyon of Normandy will not tolerate a witch living on his newly acquired demesne."

Ariana did not mean to hurt the old crone, but she could not call back her impulsive words. She had always known that Nadia was a witch, and that she lived in the woods outside the fortress and moved freely between forest and keep. Women consulted her when they wanted to conceive and couldn't, and when they had conceived too soon after a previous child and wanted to end the pregnancy. Nadia was knowledgeable in both white and black magic, 'twas said, and cast spells that could send humans into perpetual darkness.

Ariana knew most of the rumblings to be false and had in truth grown quite fond of the old woman, whose knowledge of herbs and plants had cured many of Cragmere's sick. Throughout the years of her young life Ariana had learned much from the old woman. Nadia was also one of the very few who knew that Ariana had the gift of Sight.

Ariana's ability to "see" things had manifested itself at an early age, but few knew of her special gift. Except for Nadia, of course, who seemed to know everything. Her mother had known too, of course, and had advised her before she died to guard the gift well, for there were some who would brand her a witch. Ariana had taken the advice to heart.

"The great Lord Lyon of Normandy fears no one, least of all the witch of Cragmere," Nadia answered. "Nay, Ariana, I am here to protect ye from the great beast. Look yonder"—she pointed a bony finger at the rapidly approaching horsemen—"he is well-named, is he not?"

Ariana studied the approaching rider with growing dismay. He did indeed resemble the predator after which he was named. He sat tall in the saddle, appearing invincible in full armor. Despite the concealing nose guard, she could well imagine his fierce countenance, mayhap scarred from previous battles.

Lyon of Normandy rode his charger to the very portal of Cragmere and stopped, gazing in appreciation at the fortress that was now his by right of conquest. The keep, built upon a motte, was surrounded by a square moat and guarded by a barbican. It was the first such fortress he had seen in all of England, though they were quite common in Normandy. It was a rich reward indeed, one he would never dream of possessing had he not saved the life of William of Normandy during one of his early campaigns in Maine.

As a landless bastard, Lyon had little hope of marrying an heiress, let alone becoming lord of such a grand demesne. The taint of bastardy clung tenaciously and had sunk deeply into Lyon's nature. It had embittered and hardened him.

Lyon saw at a glance that the tower was well fortified, built to repel marauders from the north, and he was well pleased. The fortress lay in a wide, shallow valley, through which the Humber River flowed. The main tower was protected by a drawbridge, and by machicolations below the battlements, while smaller rectangular towers, pierced with loopholes at either corner, made it a veritable stronghold. He had ridden through the nearby village earlier and saw that the serfs and freemen appeared to be prospering.

Lyon lifted his gaze upward, his eyes narrowing on a small, pale face gazing down at him from the parapet atop the main tower. His charger pranced restlessly beneath him as he bowed slightly, amused when the tiny figure ducked out of sight behind the battlement. Abruptly he wheeled his horse toward the drawbridge and removed his helmet, waiting for the bridge to be lowered. The glint of sunlight on his glistening black hair was nearly as blinding as it had been upon his bronze helmet.

Keane, Ariana's steward, turned to her, his

eyebrows raised. "My lady?"

"Aye," Ariana said sourly, "lower the drawbridge. I will go down and greet the new lord of Cragmere, though I'd prefer to put a knife in his heart."

" 'Ware, Ariana, 'ware," Nadia warned in a voice made raspy with age. "The Lion be not yer father or brothers, who held ye in great esteem. He be the Conqueror's man, never forget it, and the Lion will obey William in all things. Do not overset him."

"I will do what I must," Ariana said with a wisdom beyond her meager years. "I will leave Cragmere and go to my betrothed, Edric of Blackheath."

Ariana was waiting for Lyon in the inner bailey courtyard when he rode over the drawbridge and through the curtain wall. His charger danced to a halt before her and he dismounted, laid his shield across the pommel, and slipped his sword into a noose at the side of his saddle. He bowed with solemn mockery, more than a little surprised to find a slightly built maid, whose immature figure had not yet ripened into womanhood. William had not told him the heiress was so young.

He spoke in understandable albeit accented English. "I was told you were young, Lady Ariana, but did not expect to find a child barely out of the nursery."

"Old enough to recognize an enemy, Lord Lyon," Ariana shot back. "You have come to steal my land."

Lyon stared at her, recognizing immediately the promise of great beauty, of depth and fire. One day Ariana of Cragmere would possess grace of form and beauty of face few women could claim. Presently she was naught but a belligerent child whose green eyes flamed with intense hatred.

"Nay, demoiselle, neither an enemy nor a usurper. I vow to protect your demesne from invaders. Even as I speak, Scotsmen gather on the borders to claim your land. King William is wise. He knows that a mere girl cannot protect valuable holdings such as Cragmere. King William, in his generosity, has gifted me with Cragmere and charged me with its protection. 'Tis a great honor he bestows upon me."

"Norman invaders killed my father and brothers," Ariana retorted. "The Conqueror is your king, not mine. What, pray tell, does he intend to do with me? Toss me out to live with the serfs?"

" 'Ware, Ariana," Nadia warned as she sidled up beside Ariana, "lest ye find yerself helplessly caught in the Lion's snare."

Ariana paid her no heed as she continued to glower at Lyon. She was too enraged over losing her home and her inheritance to note that Lyon was a well-favored young man with hair as dark as a raven's wing and eyes as blue as a cloudless sky. His face was finely sculpted, his features classically handsome, yet hard and stern. Years of war and fighting had stolen the softness of boyhood. Living with the stigma of bastardy had only served to hone his fighting skills.

"Your tongue is sharp for one so young, demoiselle. Many fell at Hastings. Think you that William does not grieve for all those who died?"

Ariana sent him a scornful look "William is a depraved Norman beast and you are his cub."

Her words scalded him. She would have quailed before him had she known how close to the surface his temper lay. If she were anyone but a child she'd not live to see another day. He knew of few men who would dare taunt him so. Instead of replying, he turned abruptly and said to his lieutenant, "Where is the priest? Send him forth."

Beltane the Bold, a handsome young knight and Lyon's liegeman, wheeled his mount and rode off in search of the priest who had accompanied them on the journey from Londontown.

"If you have need of a priest, we have our own here at Cragmere," Ariana said. "I will summon him."

"Nay, demoiselle, William has sent his own priest for the occasion."

A frisson of apprehension shot down Ariana's spine. "What occasion is that, pray tell?"

"The occasion of our wedding, Lady Ariana," Lyon said blandly.

Ariana gasped, shocked to the roots of her silver hair. William's messenger had said nothing about a betrothal or wedding. He'd merely informed her that Cragmere had been given to the Lion of Normandy, a loyal Norman knight, as

19

reward for his faithful service, and that he would arrive soon.

"Nay, I am already betrothed to Edric of Blackheath. We are to wed when I turn sixteen."

"William has decided to set aside the betrothal and give you to me, though truth to tell I have little use for a wife, now or ever. Nevertheless, William wishes for us to wed, and so we shall."

The color drained from Ariana's already pale features. "Nay." The word was a breathy whisper, shaky and unsure. All her life she had known she would marry Edric and had grown comfortable with the knowledge. Edric was a fine young man, one she liked as a friend and felt certain she could learn to love. "I am to wed Edric, lord of Blackheath since the death of his father at Hastings."

"Edric has sworn fealty to William," Lyon said, experiencing an unaccustomed and puzzling pang of pity for the slender little maid whose life had been torn asunder by the Conqueror. "He will not gainsay William. Few men dare. As a reward for bending to William, Lord Edric was allowed him to keep his lands."

Ariana's unfeigned shock surprised Lyon. Didn't the little maid realize that wealthy heiresses become pawns in William's political plan to replace Saxon noblemen with faithful Normans? She could have been given to an older man, hardened by too many years in William's service, who would ill-use her. With him as a husband, she would be free to do as she pleased, for he would not be home enough to disrupt her life. "Edric has raised no objection to William's desire to see us wed."

Ariana's green eyes flared with disbelief. "You lie!"

"Nay. Lord Edric has sworn fealty to William, just as I said. Where is that priest?"

"Here, my lord Lyon. Have you told the maid? Is she agreeable to the wedding?"

Dressed in unrelieved brown, the rotund priest darted a glance at Ariana, frowning when he saw her mutinous expression.

"She has no choice, Father. We will wed in the chapel in one hour."

Ariana recoiled from him in abject horror. "Nay."

"Aye. One hour." He strode past Ariana into the keep, shouting for the steward to show him to the master's bed chamber. Everyone in his path scurried aside, none brave or foolish enough to challenge the Lion of Normandy.

"Whatever will I do, Nadia?" Ariana asked shakily as she watched Lyon disappear into the keep.

When the old crone did not answer, Ariana turned to look at her, stunned when the old woman appeared to be in some kind of trance. After a lengthy pause, Nadia opened her rheumy eyes and spoke in a toneless voice that sounded as if it were coming from some distant place.

" 'Ware the beast, Ariana. If ye succeed in taming him, ye must 'ware yer heart. I see dark days ahead, aye, and years too. But wed him ye must. Yer future is with the Lion."

A small cry of denial slipped past Ariana's lips as she turned and fled inside the Lion's den, toward her destiny.

The wedding was a farce. When Ariana withheld her response to the wedding vow, Lyon spoke in her stead, and she could do naught about it. William had ordered her to wed the Lion and William was king and she his vassal. She gained small satisfaction from the fact that she had refused to change her clothing, appearing in the chapel at the appointed time in a well-worn tunic and surcoat that had seen better days.

She cared not at all that Lyon hadn't bothered to don wedding finery either, merely removing his chain mail for comfort's sake. He looked every bit the fierce warrior, Ariana thought dimly. His broad shoulders and thick chest stretched the material of his long leather tunic, and his stride was so long that its narrow skirt was slit at the sides to allow him greater freedom of movement.

His tight-fighting chausses of unbleached wool revealed long, muscular thighs, and his strong, sturdy legs were encased in knee-length Norman pedules, or sock boots. His short cloak of rough black wool was open and held together by an unusual broach fashioned of gold and precious gems, leaving his sinewy arms free. His waist was belted in wide leather, into which was tucked a dagger of the finest steel with curved blade and jeweled hilt. That and the ornate gold broach were his only ornamentation. Both were gifts from William.

The deed was done. The moment the priest pronounced them husband and wife, Lyon turned to Ariana and affected a stiff-legged bow. " 'Tis done, my lady." He offered his arm. "I will accompany you to your chamber."

Nadia, who had stood unobtrusively in the corner during the ceremony, suddenly thrust herself forward to block Lyon's path.

"Nay, my lord, ye cannot bed her! 'Twould not be seemly. She is slow in maturing and has not yet begun to bleed. Ye cannot get an heir from her."

Ariana felt as if the floor had opened beneath her and she had dropped into hell. Embarrassment clawed at her, turning her pale face to dull red.

Lyon sent Nadia a look of unbridled disgust. "Think you I would bed a child? Nay, wretched crone, I merely accompany my lady to her chamber so she may pack her clothing."

"Pack?" Confusion sent Ariana's brain spinning. "Where are we going?"

"I must make haste back to Londontown. William returns to Normandy soon for his wife and children and I am to accompany him. You will abide with the nuns at St. Claire Abbey, where the good sisters will teach you humility and obedience. You will be safe there."

"Nay." Her voice shook with dismay. "I cannot live the cloistered life. I would die of bore-

23

dom. I will remain at Cragmere and see to its running in your absence."

"I'm leaving my own man, Sir Guy, in charge of Cragmere in my absence, and enough seasoned soldiers to protect the keep from invaders. I spoke to your seneschal, and he assures me that matters will go on as before. When William no longer has need of my good right arm, I will return and take my place as lord of Cragmere."

"What about me?"

He sent her an assessing glance. "Someday I may have need of a wife. Until that day arrives, you will bide at the abbey."

Ariana rounded on him, her eyes blazing with fury. "Norman bastard! Butcher! I'd rather rot in the convent than become your wife."

With a toss of her silver head, she swept past him and up the narrow stone steps that curved a path to her chamber in the north tower. Lyon's intent blue gaze followed her up the stairs, his expression thoughtful. One day, he reflected, the feisty little maid would be a hot-blooded wench ready and eager to be bedded. He hoped he'd be the one to unleash and nurture those passions when that time came.

When he thought of another man coaching her in the ways of love, he was overcome by blinding jealousy. A possessiveness he'd heretofore thought impossible in one of his temperament and calling smote him fiercely. He felt an unaccountable need to hasten the years to a future day when his innocent young bride was ready to taste the heady pleasures of the flesh.

Chapter One

William's Tower, Londontown, 1072

William the Conqueror had built his tower immediately after riding victoriously into Londontown in the year of our Lord 1066. He built it of earth and timber at the southeast corner of the old Roman city walls. He built it to command the River Thames as well as the city, and to keep an eye on his conquered subjects.

The Lyon of Normandy watched the Conqueror drum his fingers on the table in a manner that clearly revealed his state of agitation. Lyon had no idea why he had been summoned to wait upon the king's pleasure but assumed it was because his men and arms were needed to quell yet another uprising within the kingdom. In 1068, William had broken the back of the

25

revolt that began with the attack and slaughter of three thousand Normans, who formed the garrison at York, by disgruntled Saxons in Western and Southwestern England. William had reacted swiftly. He entered York and ravaged the whole country as far as the Tees.

As always, Lyon had ridden at William's side, wielding his sword with terrible vengeance. Once the uprising had been put down, William turned his sights to castle building and devising ways to hold his conquered land from invaders, while Lyon continued to ride wherever he was needed on William's behalf.

William acknowledged Lyon and beckoned him forward. Apparently he had something pressing on his mind. " 'Tis time for the Lion to return to his den. I have need of you at Cragmere. My spies tell me that King Malcolm of Scotland is conspiring with deposed Saxon barons. Malcolm is ever greedy and eager to extend his borders into England, and there are those within the kingdom who plot with him."

Lyon stared at William thoughtfully. The Conqueror was often pensive these days, aware that his was an army camped in a hostile land, holding the population down by castles constructed at key points. Saxon resistance died hard.

"You wish me to take up residence at Cragmere? Have you no longer need of my arm and my sword?"

"I know where your arm and your sword are should I have need of them. Nay, Lyon, you will be of more use to me at Cragmere. 'Tis time you produced an heir to hold the Northumbrian land in England's name after we are both gone. Have you seen your bride since you left her at the abbey? Or inquired after her?"

"Nay," Lyon said, recalling with alacrity that willful child the king had commanded him to wed. "You gifted me with rich lands but gave me a child as bride. I do not bed children."

"I had no inkling the Cragmere heiress was so young. But men often take brides younger than she."

"Not I. I prefer bedding women who know what they are about."

"Women like Lady Zabrina? 'Tis time you stop wasting your seed on your mistress and produce an heir for Cragmere. None of your bastards can inherit, and you know how I frown on infidelity. Your bride is ten and nine now and ripe for bedding. In truth, some would consider her past her prime."

Lyon laughed harshly. "I have no bastards. I am careful not to produce children. I would not have them suffer the same cruel prejudice you and I experienced as bastards of noblemen. As for my lady wife, she detests me. Her Saxon roots run deep."

"Nevertheless, she is your wife, the only woman who can bear your legitimate heirs. Need I say more?"

"I will do as you command, sire, albeit with misgiving. My wild Northumbrian rose has sharp thorns and a viper's tongue. Though only fourteen at the time, she subjected me to the vicious edge of her temper from the moment of our meeting. I pray the good sisters have subdued her wild nature and taught her the humility and obedience desirable in a woman."

William suppressed a smile. Though only seven and twenty, Lyon was a formidable fighter, feared and respected by the enemy. Strong of arm and body, with a handsome countenance to match, Lyon had had his pick of willing Saxon women since their arrival on English shores. Yet William had never seen him react to a woman as he just did at the mention of his own lady wife.

St. Claire Abbey, 1072

Ariana slipped out the door into the dark shadows surrounding the abbey. The night was moonless, the shadows deep. Not a soul stirred within the graceless yellow stone building. The nuns retired early and arose early, leading an austere life devoid of outside influence.

Ariana moved stealthily along the wall to the postern gate, where a small, vine-covered grilled door led to the outside world. Unfortunately Ariana did not have the key and had not been able to secure one, but she was grateful for this small link to the outside. Without it she would have gone mad. And without Edric, who had discovered this little-used door, she would have been completely shut away from important events unfolding in the world beyond cloistered walls.

Thoughts of Edric brought a smile to Ariana's full lips. Edric had found a freeman's daughter, a young woman who worked within the abbey, willing to carry messages to her for a small coin. Shortly after her arrival at the abbey, Ariana had been more than a little shocked when a servant girl from the village pressed a scrap of parchment into her hand. Having learned to read with her brothers, Ariana slipped into her tiny cell and quickly scanned the contents of Edric's message. He had instructed her to meet him at the postern gate when the moon reached its zenith that night.

That first meeting had been brief. Ariana rejoiced in the fact that Edric hadn't abandoned her, and still wanted her. He told her he had secretly joined forces with some of the northern barons who had sought sanctuary with King Malcolm in Scotland. Their mutual cause was ridding England of Norman domination. Although Edric had sworn fealty to William, he was willing to betray that vow in order to free England and claim Ariana. His reward for joining forces with Malcolm was the king's promise to have his bishops set aside Ariana's marriage to Lyon so she could wed Edric. All this Ariana learned on subsequent nocturnal visits from Edric. For Ariana, those visits were precious and came all too infrequently. Usually many months passed between Edric's visits.

Ariana took special interest in Edric's tales of the Conqueror's activities and the daring feats attributed to her husband. It wasn't as if she cared what happened to Lyon. Far from it. The beast had left her to languish at the abbey. To her knowledge, he had never during all that time inquired about her well-being. If she never saw Lyon again it would suit her just fine. Edric had told her of the gossip linking Lyon with the wealthy young widow, Lady Zabrina of York. Afterward Ariana had seethed in cold rage. For all she cared the Lion could take a dozen mistresses and sire even more cubs. She was no longer a child but a woman full grown. If Lyon cared nothing for her, Edric did, and proved it by waiting patiently for her when he could have married another.

"Ariana, is that you? Thank God you received my message. I have something important to tell you."

Ariana was startled to find that she had reached the postern gate so effortlessly. Edric was there waiting for her and had heard her light footsteps. She pushed aside the vines and peered through the grill.

"I am here, Edric. Why have you waited so long to return? I feared you had forgotten me."

"Nay, my lady, I would never forget one so fair. I have been to Edinburgh, conferring with King Malcolm. If all goes well, you will soon be free and we can be together as our fathers wished."

"You have news of an uprising? I hear nothing behind these walls. I hate it here. The abbess says I am willful and disobedient. My knees are raw from the hours of penance I must do to atone for my sins, and my back is black and blue from canings. I curse the day I was brought here and despise the man who consigned me to this hell."

"The Lion has become a powerful man in England," Edric said. "William thinks highly of his skill. He is ever at William's side. You are his countess but he acknowledges you not. He is an arrogant bastard."

"I am his chattel; he can ignore me now that he has my demesne. I wish I were free of him."

"Amen," Edric concurred solemnly. He grasped her fingers through the grill. "I have always loved you, Ariana. That is why I came as soon as I learned that Lord Lyon . . ."

His words hung in the air as a woman's stern voice echoed through the darkness. Ariana stepped back in alarm as someone thrust a torch into her face. "Go away, Edric, quickly. We are found!"

Edric melted into the darkness, upset that he'd been interrupted before telling Ariana that her husband was on his way to claim her.

"Who are you talking to, you wicked girl?" The abbess's voice carried an ominous note that did not bode well for Ariana.

"No one," Ariana lied, darting a glance at the grilled door, relieved to see that Edric had melted into the darkness. "I couldn't sleep, so I came out to get some air."

"Liar!" The abbess's arm snapped forward, delivering a stinging blow to Ariana's face. Ariana reeled backward. "I distinctly heard a

31

man's voice. How long has this been going on? You are a sinful hussy."

Ariana's jaw lifted in stubborn defiance. "There is no man. I am meeting no one."

Clutching the torch tightly, the abbess thrust it toward Ariana. Ariana retreated until her back came into contact with the cold wall.

"I was nearby when I saw Tersa place a note into your hand. I knew immediately that you bore watching." She snorted in disgust. "Tersa is a simple girl, unable to bear up under questioning. She revealed everything. I was told that you have been in contact with a man since entering the abbey. Tersa knew not the man's name but admitted that she has carried messages to you for the price of a coin. I am quite certain the man is not your lord husband."

"Nay," Ariana persisted. "Mayhap the poor girl spoke out of fear, telling the story you wished to hear."

"And mayhap Tersa told the truth. Fear not, the girl is no longer at the abbey. She has been severely punished and sent back to her father's hut. He has promised to see her wed to a stern widower with six children in need of a mother."

Ariana suffered a pang of guilt over the poor girl's plight. "The girl did naught wrong. I did naught wrong."

"You are wed to a great man, or have you forgotten the vows spoken before a priest?"

"Aye, I am wife to the Lion, but against my will."

"Such is the plight of all women. They wed

where they are told, regardless of their own wishes. Why do you think women choose a cloistered life over marriage? Nay, Lady Ariana, you are no different from hundreds of other young women across our land. Obviously your husband values you little. If he did, he would not entrust you to our care and promptly forget you. You are a countess of little account. You must follow our rules or suffer the consequences."

Ariana stiffened. "I have felt the sting of the cane before."

The abbess gave her a vicious shove. "Go to your cell and pray for your sins. Punishment will take place after matins, before the entire congregation. In the entire history of St. Claire Abbey there has never been one as disobedient as you in our order. When your husband learns of your shameful behavior, he will punish you severely. But I will save him the trouble."

Ariana turned and fled to the tiny cubicle that had been her prison for five long years. She could expect little mercy from Lyon were he here. He had Cragmere, a title, and a mistress; he did not need her.

Shortly past matins, Lyon approached St. Claire Abbey. The church bell still echoed with the last resounding peel. He pulled the bellcord at the front gate and waited for it to open.

Inside the dimly lit chapel, Ariana knelt before the altar, her back arched, her arms raised protectively over her bent head. The abbess stood over her, wielding the cane with dexterity while several dour-faced nuns watched, their faces slack and expressionless.

Ariana stifled a gasp of pain as a particularly vicious blow struck her between the shoulder blades. She would die before she gave the abbess the satisfaction of hearing her cry out. Each blow served only to deepen the hatred she felt for the man who had thrust her into this hell. From somewhere in the dark recesses of the abbey, Ariana heard a bell chime, but it barely registered on her brain. She was too steeped in misery to think past the next blow.

Lyon chafed impatiently at the abbey gates, thinking seriously of breaking the door down to claim his wife if he must. Wife . . . He had spared little thought for the spirited little maid he had deposited at the abbey five years ago. He smiled in remembrance. Her sharp tongue had torn him to bits during their journey to the abbey. His relief had been enormous when he left her in the capable hands of the stern abbess. He sincerely hoped that five years of strict control and proper guidance had subdued his child-bride's fiery disposition. He fully expected to find a vastly changed Ariana of Cragmere. Instead of a viper-tongued termagant, he had visions of a demure, sweet-tempered, submissive woman.

Just when he thought he'd have to use force on the iron gate, it swung open on rusty hinges. A thin woman draped in unrelieved black appeared in the opening, cowering before the huge knight standing before her garbed in full armor.

"Men are not allowed inside the abbey," she said in a high-pitched voice that bespoke her fear.

"I am Lyon of Cragmere. I have come for my wife," Lyon thundered, pushing the door wide. The timid nun gave a squeak of alarm and scuttled aside. "I would speak with the abbess."

The nun glanced uneasily over her shoulder and swallowed nervously. "The abbess is—unavailable."

"I will wait inside for her."

The nun looked warily at the half-dozen armed men accompanying Lyon and stepped aside. "As you will, my lord. I will show you to the reception room, where you may wait. Alone," she added. "Your men may not enter."

"My men will wait without."

Lyon waited for the nun to scurry in front of him so he could follow her inside the abbey. The halls were silent; no one was about, which seemed strange to Lyon. But as he was ignorant of convent life, he pushed aside his reservations. The nun led him past the chapel with undue haste. Following close behind, Lyon's steps faltered. The strange noises coming from inside the chapel were vaguely alarming. Suddenly it dawned on him. The steady "whack, whack" could not be mistaken by anyone familiar with the various instruments used to administer punishment. Obviously some hapless creature was being beaten, and quite severely. Lyon

couldn't imagine one of these holy women doing anything sinful enough to warrant a severe
punishment. Curiosity got the better of him. He
stopped abruptly outside the chapel.

"No! You must not go in there." Lyon's guide
had seen him hesitate before the chapel and
sought to distract him. But her vehemence only
made Lyon more determined.

" 'Tis the chapel, is it not?" One curved eye-
brow rose in inquiry. "Mayhap I wish to pray."

"M-mayhap," the nun stuttered, "but 'tis not
advisable for you to enter right now."

Ignoring the woman, Lyon pushed inside. A
hundred candles flickered around the altar. The
scene was a tableau straight from hell. A group
of black-clad nuns, their white wimples casting
winged shadows on the dark walls, looked like
vultures surrounding their victim. The victim,
Lyon saw, was a small woman garbed in drab
gray, her head covered with a white cloth. She
knelt before the altar, her back bent beneath the
savage blows delivered by the abbess, who
wielded a thick cane with obvious glee.
Throughout the beating the woman uttered not
one cry, and Lyon felt a jolt of pity for the poor
creature. He wondered what terrible sin she
had committed to warrant such punishment.

Aware that he had no business interfering,
Lyon turned to leave. But he hesitated a moment too long, for in that short span of time the
headcloth slipped from the victim's head. Lyon
gave an involuntary gasp. On only one other occasion had he seen hair that particular shade of

pale blond. Not really blond, not even gold, but spun silver, so fine and lustrous it nearly blinded him. She turned her face toward him and he paled, recognizing that little pointed chin, those high cheekbones, stark now in her rigidly controlled face.

Ariana of Cragmere.

It had been five years since he'd seen her, and suddenly he recalled everything about her. The stubborn tilt of her straight little nose, those high cheekbones, her wide lips, more lush and red than he remembered, those emerald green eyes, that splendid hair. By the rood, what was going on?

"Hold!" The abbess's arm, poised to deliver another blow, halted in mid-air. Every eye focused on Lyon as he strode boldly toward Ariana and the abbess.

"Lord Lyon," the abbess said with a hint of fear. The Lion was a powerful lord of the land, much revered by King William. It was unfortunate that he'd chosen this particular time to visit. "What brings you to our humble abbey? You should have waited in the reception room for me. My business here is nearly finished. The doorkeeper was remiss in allowing you entry."

"God's blood, madam, what are you doing to my lady wife?"

Still on her knees, Ariana peered around her shoulder, too steeped in agony to grasp the significance of Lyon's appearance. To her befuddled mind, he looked like a magnificent savior, all silver and gold, standing over her in splendid fury. She closed her eyes and swayed. Her Sight, which had occurred rarely since entering the abbey, suddenly came upon her. She trembled as the dark aura swirling around Lyon blotted out everything and everyone in the chapel. She perceived him as a ravaging storm, composed of all the elements—wind, rain, and lightning—fierce and uncompromising in its intensity. She knew in an instant that so overwhelming a force would be quite capable of destroying anything that lay in its path.

Lyon saw Ariana sway dangerously and scooped her up in his arms scant moments before she crumpled to the hard stone floor. She cried out once as her bruised back came into contact with his mailed arm, then she went still. Her eyes were glazed. Darkness hovered around Lyon like an invisible curtain and she saw herself being drawn into that darkness, suffocated by it. Then the specter of death appeared, grinning at her, and she knew no more.

"God's blood, you have killed her," Lyon cried in alarm. "Her eyes roll in their sockets and her flesh is as cold as death. She lies like a stone in my arms."

" 'Tis naught, my lord," the abbess said, waving aside Lyon's alarm. " 'Tis a quirk of hers, naught else. It has happened before, and she quickly revives."

"Is Ariana ill?" Remorse softened his features. He'd believed St. Claire Abbey to be a safe haven for a young girl in need of direction, else he would have found another place for his child

38

bride. "Why wasn't I told?"

"Nay, my lord, your lady wife enjoys perfect health. As I said before, 'tis but a quirk."

"I will take her to her room so that she may rest before we depart."

The abbess indicated that Lyon was to follow her. "This way, my lord." Lyon carried Ariana the length of several narrow hallways before the abbess stopped before a cubicle, one of many lining the corridor. She opened the door and Lyon glanced around the bleak cell in disgust.

"Is this what I paid good coin for? A dark cell with naught but a cot and chair and one window?" He blasphemed fluently, frightening the nun so badly that she paled and crossed herself.

Lyon approached the cot, carefully placing Ariana on her stomach. She grunted but did not awaken. With grim purpose, he grasped the neckline of the threadbare tunic and ripped downward.

"My lord, what are you doing?"

The abbess stood over him, her face dark with disapproval.

"I wish to inspect the damage to my lady wife's back. She must be treated if she is to travel on the morrow."

The abbess frowned. To lose Ariana of Cragmere now would mean a considerable loss of income. "You are taking her away? I assumed you had placed her here permanently. You have contributed to her upkeep most generously throughout the years."

"I am taking Lady Ariana home to Cragmere." Ignoring the holy woman's annoying presence, Lyon carefully peeled away the edges of Ariana's tunic, baring her back. Light from a single candle fell upon the bed, revealing the full extent of the damage. "Jesu," he hissed softly.

The bruises on Ariana's back had already turned purple. The abbess must have known exactly how much pressure to apply, for nowhere had she broken the tender skin. But there were welts aplenty from the tops of her shoulders to the small of her back, where her buttocks began. Lyon took careful note of yellowing bruises left from previous beatings.

He rounded on the abbess, his calm deceptive. "What did she do to deserve such severe punishment?"

"Your lady wife is disobedient and irreverent. She accepts neither authority nor direction. She is willful and stubborn, the very traits you despaired of when you brought her here. You bade us rid her of those unworthy traits and mold her character. But alas, those are the least of her sins."

She drew herself up imperiously and glared down at the unconscious Ariana. Her next words were delivered with righteous condemnation. "My lord Lyon, it grieves me to say that your lady wife has been secretly meeting a man under the cover of darkness."

Lyon's dark brows rose sharply. "Does the man have a name? How is it possible for them to be together? I thought the gates were locked at night."

The abbess shrugged. "So they are, my lord. I cannot say for certain that Lady Ariana left the enclosure, or if the man entered, but she did meet him. One of the village girls carried messages between Ariana and the man. As for his name, you'll have to ask your lady. She would not say." She turned to leave. "I'll send some salve to soothe her back."

Ariana stirred and groaned. Her back was on fire. This was the worst beating she could recall in the five years she'd been at St. Claire. Had her sin been so grave?

"Do not move. The abbess is sending something to soothe your back."

That voice! She recognized it immediately. Low and dark and vibrant with inflexible power. She hadn't been dreaming. Lyon was actually here; she hadn't imagined him. The object of her hatred was standing before her, more powerful than ever, bigger than she remembered, bigger than life . . . and handsome . . . sweet Mother, so handsome she had to remind herself that he was the devil incarnate. Then she recalled the vision she'd had of him and shrank back in fear.

Death.

So vivid. She had no idea whose death she had envisioned, but there was no mistaking the dark specter.

"Why are you here?"

"I'm taking you home to Cragmere. William has need of a strong man to protect the borderlands against King Malcolm."

"You were ever eager to do the bastard's bidding."

Lyon gave her an oblique look. "And you, my lady, have not lost the sharp edge of your tongue. From the condition of your back, I'd venture to say the abbess has not been as tolerant as I of your willful nature."

Lyon stared at her back, and Ariana was suddenly aware that he was looking at bare skin. The heat of his gaze struck her forcibly, and she struggled into a sitting position. The torn edges of her tunic parted even farther, sliding down one shoulder and revealing the rounded white top of a breast. If Lyon had questioned whether Ariana was a woman full grown, he no longer doubted. Before she hastily covered her bared flesh, he caught a tantalizing glimpse of a well-formed, pink-tipped breast.

"I am no longer a child, my lord. And I fear my tongue has grown sharper with age."

" 'Twould seem you speak the truth. On both scores," he added, staring purposefully at her breasts. "William has the right of it. 'Tis time I settled down and produced an heir for Cragmere. But first, lady, tell me who it is you meet in the dead of night."

His voice had taken on a cold sharpness that sent chills slithering down her spine. She should have known the abbess would delight in telling Lyon of her terrible sin, though she was guilty of naught but speaking to Edric through the grill.

"The abbess is mistaken. There is no man." Wild horses couldn't drag Edric's name from her.

Lyon stared at her. She was lying. He could tell by the way her green eyes refused to meet his. "Have you taken a lover?"

Ariana laughed mirthlessly. "A lover? 'Tis folly you speak, my lord. The abbess is the only one who can unlock the gates. I cannot sleep and sometimes stroll the grounds at night."

"Time will tell if you are lying," Lyon said cryptically. "If I learn you have dishonored your marriage vows, you'll find yourself back within these walls so fast your head will spin."

"I have never wanted to be your wife."

He glared at her. "You will be my wife in all ways, lady. You will share my bed and bear my children. You will obey me and swear fealty to me. And, my lady wife, you *will* be faithful to me."

Her eyes grew wide as she considered all that his words implied. She might be forced to bed with him, and obey him in some things. And it went without saying that she'd not dishonor marriage vows spoken before a priest, but never—ever—would she swear fealty to a Norman beast.

Her expressive green eyes conveyed her thoughts as clearly as if she had spoken them aloud.

"Aye, my lady wife, everything I have said will come to pass."

"Mayhap, my lord," she said sweetly, "and mayhap not."

Chapter Two

Ariana sat her horse stiffly as she left the abbey the following morning. Her stiffness was due partly to the beating she had received from the abbess the night before and partly from not having ridden for many years. It had been a very long time since she'd sat a horse and gloried in the freedom it afforded her. Just being outside the abbey gates sent her senses soaring.

Ariana cast a surreptitious glance at Lyon, riding a short distance in front of her. He had camped outside the abbey walls with his men last night after he had seen to her comfort. He had come for her shortly after chapel this morning, leading the horse she was to ride back to Cragmere. She observed him silently now, deeply unsettled by the shattering effect he had on her. She hated him, of course, this Norman conqueror, yet she could not help but admire many things about him. He had the lean look of a predator, a man who'd worked his body long and strenuously.

His arms bulged with ropy muscles and his legs, stretched across his huge destrier, were as sturdy as the trees in the forest. He could kill her with one stroke of his mighty hand, and no one would say him nay. She longed for the day this intruder would be vanquished along with his cohorts, and England would once again belong to the Saxons. She prayed it would be soon.

The expression on Lyon's hard face did not change as he waited for Ariana to catch up with him. He noted how the drab gray tunic she wore failed to hide the lush curves of her ripe body. He grimaced in distaste at the pristine white headcloth hiding the magnificent mass of silver hair. Who would have thought that the wild little creature he had taken to St. Claire Abbey five years ago would develop into an enchanting temptress?

Had she really taken a lover? he wondered dimly, or had the abbess fabricated the whole story? It seemed highly unlikely that Ariana had engaged in a forbidden love affair while confined behind the formidable walls of St. Claire. Yet stranger things had happened. There was only one way to tell, and in his own time Lyon would learn for himself whether Ariana had dishonored her marriage vows. If he found her ruined, he'd send her back to the abbey, where she would spend the remainder of her life doing penance for her sins.

As they approached the sprawling village flourishing outside the abbey walls, Ariana's gaze wandered over the busy scene, savoring the sights and sounds she encountered along the narrow, crowded streets. It had been far too long since she'd experienced this kind of freedom, enjoying the wind and the sun on her face and the company of people other than dour-faced nuns. She sniffed appreciatively of the air, redolent with the scent of the rich foodstuffs she remembered from her childhood. Her mouth watered.

Suddenly a young woman darted out from nowhere, tugging at Ariana's reins and plucking at her skirt. "My lady, 'tis I, Tersa."

Ariana stared down at the girl, recognizing her, despite her swollen and bruised face, as the servant who had carried messages between her and Edric. Appalled, Ariana gave a cry of dismay. "Tersa, what is amiss? Who hurt you?"

"I beg you, sweet lady, take me with you. Let me serve you and your lord."

Lyon frowned with impatience at the poorly dressed woman whose lank blond hair hung in matted strands down her back. He reined in beside Ariana. "Who is this woman, lady? Do you know her?"

Ariana gave her answer careful thought. Evidently the abbess had not told him the name of the woman who had carried Edric's messages. " 'Tis but a servant from the abbey. She

47

wishes to serve me at Cragmere."

He looked at her more closely. "Who has beaten you, wench?"

"My father, my lord," Tersa said timidly. "He wishes me to marry Doral, a widower with six children. Doral has already buried three wives, and I do not wish to be the fourth."

" 'Tis a woman's lot to marry where her father wishes," Lyon declared.

"Is it a woman's lot to be beaten into submission?" Ariana asked with a boldness that startled but did not surprise Lyon.

"Aye, if she is willful and disobedient." His words held a hint of warning that Ariana found offensive.

"If you beat me, my lord, I will ask Nadia to place a curse on you. Mayhap you did not know that Nadia is the witch of Cragmere."

Lyon gave her a grin that lifted and lightened the dark contours of his face. "Think you I fear a witch? Nay, my lady, 'twill take more than that to stay my hand if you do something to deserve punishment."

Ariana glared at him. He had adroitly brought the subject around to her, hinting at her secret meetings with Edric. Lyon would never know whom she had been meeting, Ariana vowed, for she would never tell him.

"My lady, please take me with you."

"Tersa, go home!" a stern voice commanded. Tersa turned to face her father, a brutish man with fists the size of ham hocks. She flinched as he threatened her with them.

"Do not strike her again," Ariana said with quiet authority. Lyon sat back and watched, amazed at her audacity. His lady wife had more mettle than any woman of his acquaintance. Certainly more than was proper or admired in a wife.

"My daughter is none of your concern, my lady," Tersa's father said.

At this point, Lyon saw fit to interfere. "Are you freeman or serf? What is the problem here?"

"Freeman, my lord. I am called Balder. My daughter is promised to Doral, the blacksmith. He has need of a wife and mother for his children." Balder thought it prudent not to volunteer the information that Tersa had been sent in shame from the abbey for violating the rules. Tersa's sins would not reflect well upon him and perhaps lose him a son-in-law if Doral was to learn of Tersa's shameful actions. "Tersa objects to marrying Doral, but she will agree soon enough." His clenched fists gave silent testimony to the kind of persuasion he intended to use in order to change Tersa's mind.

Though Lyon believed in obedience, he did not condone senseless beatings. What he had told Ariana moments before had been more warning than threat. There were other ways to keep his wife in hand than administering beatings.

"My lord," Ariana said. "I wish Tersa to serve me. Can we not take her with us to Cragmere?" She asked it so sweetly that Lyon was momentarily distracted by her seductive smile and honeyed voice. Did he know this temptress at all? He shook his head and his senses returned.

"There are servants aplenty at Cragmere."

"I want Tersa." The service Tersa had performed for her these past five years deserved a reward. Ariana couldn't bear to see Tersa given in marriage to a cruel man who might abuse her. She had already been abused enough by her brutish father.

"What say you?" Lyon asked Balder, who stared from Tersa to Ariana to Lyon with a puzzled look on his slack features.

"You want my daughter to serve you?" What man, Saxon or Norman, hadn't heard of the Lion of Normandy or his brave deeds? 'Twould be an honor, Balder thought, to have his daughter so well placed in the household of so great a lord. Still, he should gain some reward for allowing Tersa to leave.

"Aye," Lyon said, "my lady wishes it, and it pleases me to grant her wish."

Balder licked his thick lips in gleeful anticipation of what this might mean in terms of hard coin. Or mayhap he could earn favors from so great a lord.

"I am loathe to part with my oldest daughter, my lord," Balder whined. "I set great store in Tersa. Her mother depends on her help."

Lyon felt naught but loathing for Balder. He knew exactly what Balder was hinting at and decided to put an end to it. "How much do you want for your daughter, Balder? I will buy her for my lady wife."

Balder blinked rapidly. "God's blood, my lord, I didn't mean . . ."

"Aye, I know what you meant." Lyon dipped into the pouch hanging from his belt and removed a small silver coin, tossing it to Balder. Balder caught it deftly, studied it a moment, nodded, then said, " 'Tis enough." Turning on his heel, he left without a word to his daughter—no farewell, no advice, nothing. It was clear he was already planning how to spend his windfall.

During all of this, Lyon barely spared Ariana a glance. He was puzzled and somewhat embarrassed by his easy acquiescence to his wife's whim. Not known to be overly indulgent of women, he had no idea why he had granted Ariana's request so readily. Perhaps it was Tersa herself he felt compassion for, but that thought made him distinctly uncomfortable, for neither was he known as a compassionate man. He was a hardened fighter, a staunch defender of William of Normandy and all he held in his name.

Surprised by Lyon's uncharacteristic capitulation, Ariana watched open-mouthed as Lyon beckoned to Beltane, his lieutenant, and bade him take Tersa up before him on his destrier. Bending to the girl, Beltane scooped her up with one thickly muscled arm and sat her before him. Then Lyon gave the signal for them to proceed.

"Thank you, my lord," Ariana said with more

warmth than she'd exhibited toward Lyon at any time since she'd known him.

"The only thanks I require, lady, is the name of the man you met secretly at the abbey." He searched her face. "I will have it, you know, for I am seldom gainsaid." Then Lyon kneed his mount, abandoning her to her own devices as he rode ahead. Sir Beltane came up to ride beside her.

"I will serve you faithfully, my lady," Tersa said, leaning sideways to speak with Ariana. "I will be forever grateful to you."

"I ask only that you speak not of my years at the abbey, for I do not want to be reminded of that unhappy time."

Tersa did not have to be told not to mention the abbey, or speak of the messages she had carried to Ariana from a man who was not her husband. Wild horses could not drag that information from her even though she felt a certain loyalty to Lord Lyon for rescuing her from a desperate situation.

They stopped briefly at noontime to eat the meat pies purchased at the market in the village. Ariana selected a spot away from Lyon's men and sat down beneath a thick-limbed oak tree. Lyon joined Ariana as she nibbled at the delicious fare, having tasted nothing quite as good in more than five years. The plain, unappetizing food at the abbey left much to be desired.

"You are quiet, Ariana," Lyon said, using her

given name for the first time. "Do you contemplate your sins?"

Ariana fixed him with a baleful glance. "I fear my sins will bore you, my lord. There is scarce occasion to sin behind thick walls."

"Yet you found occasion, did you not, my lady? The abbess was most distressed by your behavior."

"I'm sorry if I do not please you, my lord. Mayhap you can get the priest to set aside the marriage since it was never consummated."

Lyon frowned. "Nay, Ariana, we are wed and we will stay wed. And when we reach Cragmere, I will have the truth from you. Our marriage will be consummated, never fear, but not until your woman's flow commences. Only then will I know you are not carrying a bastard."

Dull red crept up Ariana's neck. Lyon's blunt language had shocked her. They might be husband and wife, but she hardly knew the man. Nor was she accustomed to the company of men, having lived in virtual seclusion these past five years.

"I am no longer a child, my lord, easily controlled or cowed. 'Tis a pity you do not believe me."

"Aye, Ariana, a pity indeed," Lyon repeated, grasping her arm and pulling her hard against him. "Unfortunate for you if I learn you have betrayed me."

She stared into his blue eyes, seeing her reflection. He was so close that she could feel his breath upon her cheek and see the dark stubble growing on his newly shaven face. The metal links of his mail pressed against her breasts, making her aware of the massive strength of the man beneath the armor, and her breath caught in her throat. This man, this Norman enemy, had the right to use or abuse her body in any way he saw fit. She had no idea if he'd be brutal or loving, though all indications pointed to the former. She had no one to rely upon for help except her own ingenuity. And mayhap Edric. Thank God for Edric.

Lyon lost himself in the compelling green depths of Ariana's eyes, mesmerized by the hint of something deep and defiant that he found there. He felt exhilarated as he had never been before. She challenged him—aye, challenged him and defied him—but he would tame her. First he would subdue her spirit, then her body, making her want him, need him. He grew hard just thinking about it. Perhaps he should have brought Zabrina with him to ease his loins until such time as he knew for certain his "innocent" bride was not carrying a bastard.

Damn that abbess, he thought sourly. She had no idea the damage she had done by putting ideas about Ariana into his head. But he would have the truth of it—aye, the whole truth. He pulled her closer, staring at her lush lips, wondering if they had tasted passion or if he'd be the first to sample them. The temptation was too great. Placing a finger beneath her stubborn little chin, he lifted her lips to his. A small gasp exploded from her chest when she felt the weight of Lyon's mouth pressing against hers, teasingly at first, as he ran the tip of his tongue along the seam of her lips, then more forcefully as his tongue nudged her lips apart and thrust inside.

Ariana's mouth gaped open in shock, giving Lyon unlimited access to the sweet depths within. Ariana had had no idea a man's mouth could arouse such unholy feelings in a woman. And when she felt his hands knead her breasts, she nearly swooned.

Lyon plundered the sweetness of Ariana's mouth, aware that the boldness of his tongue had shocked her. Secretly he rejoiced, for he would have been angry had she proven adept at kissing. And yet that small doubt remained. And as his hands plundered the womanly roundness of her breasts, he felt himself responding almost breathlessly to this woman who was his wife, this woman who knew him as an enemy.

This woman who might even now be carrying another man's child.

Did another man claim her love? That thought sent him into a blind rage and he thrust her away, his face dark and threatening. "Mount your horse, my lady. I would that we reach Cragmere by nightfall." Rising abruptly, he stalked away.

Ariana stared at him in dismay. He was the enemy, a Norman butcher, just like his king. How could he touch her as he did and make her feel shameful things? Were they shameful? Or were those virtues of chastity, humility, obedience, purity, and modesty taught by the nuns naught but reflections of their austere lives? Were their teachings meaningless ideals which no woman could live up to?

Sir Beltane appeared at Ariana's elbow to help her mount. She glanced over at Tersa and saw that she was already mounted atop Beltane's destrier, staring at the handsome knight with barely disguised adoration.

"I am to accompany you the rest of the way to Cragmere, my lady," Beltane said respectfully. "My lord Lyon is riding ahead."

Ariana nodded curtly. No matter how polite or respectful this man might be, he was still a despised Norman. She wanted nothing to do with any of them.

Lyon dug his heels into his destrier's flanks, fleeing from the newly aroused demons plaguing his mind and body. For years he had given Ariana little thought. If the truth be known, his horse held a higher place in his esteem than did his lady wife. Whenever he pictured her in his mind, he saw naught but a belligerent child who had tried his temper sorely. Never in his wildest imagination had he envisioned a haughty beauty with shimmering silver hair, lush red mouth, and ripe body. Five years had wrought a miracle. Unfortunately, one thing had not changed—her hatred for Normans.

Lyon paused before the drawbridge and stared up at the keep, pleased with his new holdings. Not really new, for he had been lord of Cragmere for five years, but his service to William had kept him away from his demesne during those years. He had seen many changes during that time. Great fortresses had been constructed at strategic points throughout the land, staunch guardians of William's might and power.

He hailed his men standing guard on the ramparts and waited for the bridge to be lowered, then he rode past the barbican into the inner bailey. He saw the strange horses immediately and reined in sharply. He recognized neither the colorful trappings nor the men milling about in the courtyard. When a serf hurried up to take his reins, he said harshly, "I see we have visitors."

"Aye, my lord," the serf said, pulling his forelock. " 'Tis Lord Edric of Blackheath. He waits within the hall."

"Edric," Lyon repeated slowly. The man Ariana was to marry before William set aside the betrothal. He was now Edric's liege lord but had seen little of the man these past five years. Edric had sworn fealty to William, sent his allotment of knights to swell William's army, but otherwise kept himself close to his border estates. If he recalled correctly, Edric had never married.

The smoky dimness of the hall stung Lyon's eyes as he stepped inside. A half dozen or so men slouched at a long table—quaffing tankards of his best ale, no doubt. The seneschal, Keane, stood nearby as one serf refilled the mugs and another set down platters of meat and bread. Obviously his hospitality was not lacking.

Edric rose from the bench the moment he saw Lyon striding toward him. He stared at Lyon with undisguised hatred and jealousy, until he remembered his reason for being here. Then he composed his handsome features into more pleasant lines.

"I give you greetings, my lord," Edric said as Lyon strode forward. "I have heard great things about the Lion of Normandy. 'Tis time we met, since we are neighbors and you are my liege lord. When I heard you'd returned to take up residence at Cragmere, I thought 'twas time I presented myself to you." He glanced past Lyon expectantly, and when no one appeared, he seemed disappointed. "I have not had the opportunity to extend felicitations to you and your lady upon your marriage. But I forget," he hinted slyly, "you have not seen Lady Ariana in as many years as I. Does she still abide at St. Claire?"

"You seem well versed on the subject of my lady wife," Lyon said with dark suspicion.

" 'Tis no secret you deposited her at the abbey after your marriage. Five years will have wrought miracles in her appearance. By the by," Edric said with mock nonchalance, "have you brought your mistress with you to Cragmere?"

"You are uncommonly knowledgeable for a man who rarely shows himself at court," Lyon grumbled.

"I may not frequent William's court, but I have ample access to court gossip," Edric said. " 'Tis common knowledge Lady Zabrina was bereft when you were ordered to Cragmere to protect your holdings against invasion by King Malcolm."

Lyon stared at Edric, seeing a golden man with uncommon good looks. No wonder Ariana had wanted to marry him. He was everything that he, Lyon, wasn't. For starters, Edric was legitimate and had inherited his title. He had fought at Hastings and earned praise from his Saxon cohorts. Lyon thought it odd that he had capitulated so easily when ordered to swear fealty to William or lose his lands.

Strangely, Edric had offered only token protest when he lost his betrothed to Lyon. Had Lyon been in his place, he would have fought to the bitter end to keep Ariana and Cragmere. No wonder he didn't trust Edric. The man was too passive, too accepting of the vagaries of fate. What mischief was he planning?

" 'Tis passing strange that you should appear at Cragmere on the very day I arrive home with my lady wife. Is there some pressing business you wish to discuss with me?"

Edric sent him an oblique look. "I heard you were returning to Cragmere today, and since I was passing this way I decided to stop and pay my respects. You have been absent from Cragmere many years. I did not know Lady Ariana would be with you. Where is she, my lord? I had not the chance to wish her felicitations upon her marriage. She is well, I trust." His words were in the form of a challenge. If Lyon had harmed Ariana, he would pay dearly.

Lyon's answer was forestalled when Ariana walked through the door, having arrived with the rest of the party. She took one look at Lyon and Edric, and her heart plummeted down to her toes. What was Edric doing here? Did Lyon suspect that she had been in contact with Edric during her years at the abbey?

Composing her face to conceal her apprehension, Ariana smiled and said, "Lord Edric, what brings you to Cragmere? Is all well at Blackheath?"

Edric's intense gaze settled on Ariana's face. It was the first time he'd seen her in the light of day in more than five years. When he saw her at the abbey, thick vines and a grilled door separated them, and darkness made it next to impossible to see more than vague shadows. She was breathtaking, he thought as his gaze traveled slowly down the length of her body and back. Ariana had shown great promise as a child; as a woman she was fairer than any other of his acquaintance. His jaw tightened, thinking that such great beauty was wasted on the Lion of Normandy. Ariana belonged with him, Edric, a true Saxon nobleman, not with a Norman invader.

Lyon stared from Ariana to Edric, his brow furrowed in intense concentration. He sensed something pass between them but knew not what. Did Ariana still want Edric? From the look on the Saxon lord's face, Lyon deduced that Edric had more than a passing interest in Ariana. He wanted her.

Suddenly Lyon knew . . . he *knew*. The abbess hadn't lied. Ariana had indeed been meeting a man . . . Edric of Blackheath.

"My lady wife is tired from her trip, Lord Edric," Lyon said smoothly. He summoned Keane, who was hovering nearby. "Escort Lady Ariana to our bedchamber."

Keane bowed. "Welcome home, my lady. 'Tis indeed good to have you back at Cragmere where you belong."

"Thank you, Keane. I am most happy to be home." She turned to Lyon. "I am not tired at all, my lord. Lord Edric has not answered my question; pray let him continue while I quench my thirst." She reached for a flagon of ale and smiled at Edric. "Is all well at Blackheath?"

"Blackheath prospers, my lady," Edric said, keeping a wary eye on Lyon, who looked as if he was about to explode. Ariana had certainly lost none of her mettle while cloistered at St. Claire, and he hoped she didn't suffer for it. Lord Lyon didn't appear the type of man to be overly indulgent of his wife. And the way he was glowering at her now made Edric aware of the tension between the two.

"Excuse us, Lord Edric," Lyon said lightly. "My lady wife doesn't realize how tired she is." Ariana yelped in dismay as Lyon swept her from her feet and into his arms. "Please continue to partake of our hospitality while I see to my wife's comfort."

Ariana opened her mouth to protest, saw the look on Lyon's face, and quickly changed her mind. His jaw could have been carved in stone so tightly was it clenched, so stern and inflexible was his expression. He said nothing as he strode from the hall and up the narrow stone staircase that led to the solar on the second floor of the keep. Unlike most keeps of the period, in which the master chamber was a leather-curtained cubbyhole off the hall, Ariana's father had built his keep with a solar and sleeping chambers above the huge room where his knights and retainers slept on pallets on the floor.

"My lord, put me down," Ariana said as she shoved ineffectually against his mailed chest. "I did not think even Normans could be so rude."

Lyon said nothing, continuing up the winding staircase until he reached his bedchamber and shoved inside. Then he set Ariana on her feet and glared down at her. His voice was deceptively calm when he spoke.

"Doesn't it seem strange to you that Edric should turn up here now, on the very day I bring you home to take up residence at Cragmere? I find it more than strange. I find it suspicious."

Ariana swallowed visibly. "Strange? Suspicious? What is strange or suspicious about a neighboring lord calling upon his liege lord?"

"Think you I am stupid, my lady? I know Lord Edric is the man whom you have been seeing secretly. One has but to look at his face and know that he still wants you."

"Nay, my lord!" Ariana denied vehemently. " 'Tis a lie. I—"

"Cease, Ariana!" Lyon thundered. "Fear not. I will not kill your lover. Confess now and I will spare his life . . . and yours."

"If you kill us, you will be taking innocent lives," Ariana said in a voice fraught with fear. She knew so little about this great Norman warrior, and knew even less of what he was capable. He looked ready to explode, and Ariana decided it prudent to tell the truth. Lies did not come easily to her. " 'Tis true that Edric came to me at the abbey, but we met behind locked gates. We never even touched. We talked; naught else passed between us. Lord Edric thought of me while my own husband forgot I existed. If not for King William, you would have left me at St. Claire to rot into old age."

God's nightgown, she was lovely when aroused to anger! Lyon thought as he stared at Ariana. He felt his groin tighten with wanting. Her cheeks bloomed red against white, her green eyes flashed like precious emeralds, and her chest rose and fell in anger.

"You were naught but a child when we wed— what would you have me do with you?" Lyon countered with a calmness he didn't feel. "From our first meeting, I knew you were no meek and biddable girl. I hoped the good nuns would teach you humility and obedience and all those other virtues you lacked."

Refusing to back away from him, she raised

her chin and held her ground, though she wanted to turn and run away as fast as she could. "I will cower before no Norman invader. I speak the truth. Edric came to me because he was concernced for my welfare. He kept me informed of current events." She sent him a sardonic look. "The good sisters did not deem it necessary to regale me with tales of your brave deeds."

"Edric was once your betrothed. Do you still want him? 'Tis folly if you do, for I'll not set you free. You are my wife, Ariana, and until I learn differently, I will pretend you are still an innocent."

Reaching out, he grasped her arms, pulling her flush against him. "You tremble, my lady. You are wise to fear me."

Ariana couldn't seem to stop the tremors that shook her body. It wasn't fear, exactly. 'Twas Lyon's nearness, his male scent, the overwhelming aura of power that exuded from his every pore. She sensed the dark power emanating from him and fantasized about it.

Feared it.

Was both attracted and repelled by it.

"Pretend all you want, my lord, 'tis the truth," Ariana declared as she stared into the compelling heat of his eyes. Never had a man looked at her like that. She saw her reflection in the hot centers of his eyes, and her heart pounded out of control.

Lyon felt his control snap. Ariana was so close that her enticing scent, her softness, even her stubborn resistance, all combined to send him over the edge. He wanted her! God's nightgown! He wanted this belligerent little wildcat with a fierceness that defied logic. More than he'd ever wanted Zabrina, and he had been more than satisfied with his mistress.

His hands slid through her hair, lifting her face to his. Silken strands of pale silver flowed over his fingers as he lowered his head and covered her lips. His mouth moved restlessly over hers, tasting, teasing, his passion soaring. Then abruptly he unleashed his desire as he deepened the kiss, thrusting his tongue past her lips and into her mouth. Ariana whimpered against his mouth as his tongue thrust and retreated and his hands sought her heaving breasts. When he drew away, he was panting as hard as she was.

" 'Tis but a sample, Ariana, of what to expect as my wife. There is passion in you, and that pleases me."

"A pity you do not please me, my lord," she said bluntly. "You have the manners and finesse of a wild boar."

Chapter Three

Lyon bristled in splendid anger. The moments it took to regain his breath allowed him time to grasp the waning shreds of his temper . . . just barely. "You liken me to a wild boar? If you were a man I'd split your gullet for that insult."

"If I were a man, I would not be in this position," Ariana flung back at him.

Lyon's anger began to fade. When she raised those beautiful green eyes to his, there was infinite courage and vulnerability in their compelling depths, and with a jolt of emotion that left him shaken, Lyon realized that he wanted Ariana desperately. He wanted her body, certainly, but he wanted her heart as well. He shook his head to clear it of such distressing notions. That kind of thinking was dangerous and likely to bring him more heartache than he had ever known.

"Your position is enviable, my lady," Lyon said with deceptive calm. "You are a countess. Your husband is a powerful man in William's court and our lands prosper. Fortunately, I am strong enough to hold them against marauding Scotsmen and disgruntled Saxon lords."

Ariana searched his face. There was something wild and raw about him that intrigued her. He exuded confidence and arrogance and, aye, dignity, though she hated to admit it.

"I was a countess before the Norman invaders killed my father and brothers and stole my land," she informed him coolly. "You want a wife no more than I want a husband."

"Yet we are husband and wife and must make the best of it. Provide me with heirs and swear fealty to me, and I will neither complain nor treat you harshly."

"Swear fealty to a Norman pig? Never!" Ariana said it with such venom that Lyon felt as if the sharp edge of her tongue had pierced his flesh.

The blue of his eyes seared into her. If she had angered him before, it was nothing compared to the rage he felt now. Pinning her arms at her sides, he lifted her bodily and tossed her onto the bed. She bounced once and then settled into the soft surface, realizing she had gone too far this time. Would she never learn to curb her tongue? When she dared to look up at him, he had shed his mail and was glaring down at her.

"You will swear fealty to me, lady," Lyon said as the bed groaned beneath his weight.

"Nay."

His eyes blazed into hers. His head dipped and she closed her eyes. Then his lips touched hers. She tried to twist her head away, but his strength was overwhelming. His mouth was forceful upon hers, his tongue a thrusting sword against her lips. A moan of protest came from deep within her chest. His tongue entered her mouth and found hers, drawing upon it. Thrusting more and more deeply into her mouth. Hot, slick, wet, she prayed for the strange fire in her belly to go away.

She felt his hand slide over her breast, his fingers pulling at her nipple before exploring further—her waist, her hips, her buttocks. His large hands cupped, teased, learned her body as he continued to kiss her. His hard body and mouth promised no mercy as he plundered her ruthlessly, his anger still hot and fierce.

"Do you force me, my lord?" Ariana cried when she felt his hands beneath her tunic, slowly lifting it to bare her tender flesh to his touch.

Lyon's head rose sharply. "Force?" The word left a bad taste in his mouth. His anger had nearly destroyed his resolve not to take Ariana until her woman's time had commenced. "Nay, lady, when I take you, it won't be by force."

With great reluctance, he lifted himself to his feet and pulled her with him, shoving her to her knees before him. "Swear, my lady, swear fealty to me on bended knee. I am your lord. You owe me your loyalty."

Though she would surely suffer for her defiance, she could not swear loyalty to a man who had come with the invaders, taken the lives of her family, and stolen her lands. She clamped her lips tightly together and remained silent. Closing her eyes, she waited for his blows to fall, aware that he had every right to beat her. Most men would. Tense seconds turned into minutes, and when nothing happened, Ariana opened her eyes and glanced upward through a fringe of silver. The chamber was empty but for her. Collapsing with relief, she let several minutes pass before she rose shakily to her feet and sat on the edge of the bed.

" 'Ware, my lady, 'ware the Lion. Have ye learned naught in five years?"

"Nadia!" Ariana cried with relief. "Where did you come from?"

"From below, my lady. Yer door was open. I passed Lord Lyon on the stairs, and he looked fit to kill. What did ye do to him?"

Ariana flushed and looked away. "I refused to swear fealty to him."

Nadia came closer and looked her over carefully. "I see no bruises. Did he hurt ye?"

"He didn't touch me, Nadia. I expected a beating but . . ." Her words fell away.

"Does he know about Lord Edric?"

Ariana gasped in surprise. "How did . . . No one knows about Edric. How could . . ."

Nadia gave her an enigmatic look. "I know

many things, Ariana. I see many things. Do ye still have the Sight?"

Ariana glanced at the open door before answering. She couldn't afford to be overheard. "Aye, though it happened rarely at the abbey."

"What will ye do, Ariana? The Lion will kill both ye and Edric if he knows about yer meetings at the abbey."

"He already knows, Nadia, and I still live. 'Tis passing strange, Nadia, but at times Lord Lyon seems almost gentle. And at other times I fear him greatly. He is so big, so . . . so male . . . so Norman. His temper is fearsome. I fear he will kill Lord Edric. Will you go down to the hall and listen to what's being said? When Edric leaves, search him out and tell him I would speak with him in private. I fear for his life."

Nadia stared at her narrowly. "Is there something yer not telling me, Ariana? Is Lord Lyon going to find a virginal wife when he finally beds ye?"

Ariana flushed. "Aye, Nadia, I've done nothing to be ashamed of."

"God be praised," she said fervently. "I would not wish to be in yer place were it otherwise. Be forewarned, my lady, 'tis said the Lion is no gentle man."

Nadia left as silently as she had arrived.

Ariana lay down on the bed and closed her eyes. It had indeed been a long day, and she was tired. Hungry as well. She briefly considered going down to the hall and finding something to eat but could not bring herself to face Lyon again. Soon she drifted into sleep.

Lyon entered the hall in a rage. Not only had Ariana defied him but Edric was still there, sitting at the table with his men, partaking of his hospitality. He approached the Saxon lord warily. He briefly debated killing the man outright for his perfidy. But for William's sake he had to tolerate Edric, for the man had been a faithful subject since the day he'd become the Conqueror's man. Personally, Lyon didn't trust the man despite the fact that Edric protected the Borderlands against invaders.

"Will you and your men spend the night, Lord Edric?" Lyon asked without enthusiasm. "The hall is large and we have pallets aplenty."

"Nay," Edric said, rising abruptly. There was nothing more he could do for Ariana at this time. He had come to see for himself that she had not been harmed after the abbess caught her at the postern gate. His timing had been incredibly bad, and he was sorry he had caused Ariana problems.

"I must return to my manor. Tell Lady Ariana I will return soon to see how she fares."

"You need not concern yourself with my lady wife. Are you implying that I might harm her?" Lyon asked tightly. He might yet kill the bastard if he continued to annoy him.

"I imply nothing, Lord Lyon. Lady Ariana and I have known one another many years, when she was but a child and I her betrothed. Her father is dead, and I feel a certain responsibility toward her."

"I absolve you of that responsibility," Lyon returned shortly. "What I do with my wife is my business, but rest assured, she will not suffer at my hands as long as she remains obedient and docile."

Edric laughed harshly. "You do not know Ariana very well, my lord, if you think she is meek and submissive." Lyon's dark visage gave credit to Edric's words. "Ah, I see you *do* know her. Well, then, my lord, I bid you good night." Bowing slightly, he turned and strode from the hall, his men hard on his heels.

Edric had just mounted his horse when a wraithlike figure slunk out of the dark shadows and grasped his reins. "My Lord, 'tis I, Nadia. I have a message from Lady Ariana."

Edric glanced furtively behind him, saw that the door to the hall was closed and moved deeper into the shadows. "What is it, Nadia? What does Ariana want of me?"

"She wishes to speak to ye privately, Lord Edric, but greatly fears the Lion."

"Tell your lady I will arrange something, but I must go now before I arouse suspicion. I must pretend to be William's faithful subject for a time yet." Leaving Nadia in the shadows, he rode through the gate and across the bridge toward Blackheath.

Lyon drank late into the night with his men, quaffing mug after mug of strong ale, but nothing was potent enough to dispel the image of his lady wife, her green eyes flashing, her pouting lips swollen from his kisses. Briefly he considered taking one of the maidservants to his bed, but his discerning eye saw no one to compare with his fiery bride, no one who affected him in quite the same way. He tried to recall Zabrina and her passionate embraces, but not even that image could drag his thoughts from the wild bundle of femininity waiting for him upstairs in their bedchamber.

When the last of his men sought their pallets beside the fire, Lyon staggered to his feet and made his way carefully up the torchlit staircase. A single candle guided him to the box bed as he stumbled inside the dimly lit room. Ariana's sleeping figure made only a slight dent beneath the blanket. She did not awaken when he removed his boots, chausses, and tunic and flopped down beside her atop the covers, clad only in his baggy, round-necked shirt. She let out a soft sigh when he rolled over and pulled her into the curve of his body.

Accustomed to the early hours kept by the nuns, Ariana stirred with the dawn. She felt warm and cozy, much warmer than she could ever remember being in her cold cell at St. Claire's with naught but a threadbare blanket to ward off the chill. She burrowed deeper into the warm cocoon, coming fully awake when she butted against hard, unyielding flesh and bone. She stiffened and pulled away. When she tried to rise, she felt the thick band of Lyon's arm spanning her waist. Holding her breath, she carefully removed it and slipped from bed. Standing back, she stared down at her husband with a strange, inexplicable yearning.

His mouth was slightly open and he was snoring softly. He was barely covered by his shirt, his bare legs sprawled atop the covers. The baggy garment had shifted upward, exposing his thighs and a portion of one buttock. Ariana looked away. She had never considered a male beautiful before, but that was the only word that came to mind as she admired the awesome strength of Lyon's magnificent body. Even in sleep he exuded power. She felt shame for thinking such unseemly thoughts. Edric, a true Saxon, was every bit as handsome and powerful as Lyon, yet she did not tremble in his presence or gape shamelessly at him.

Lyon watched Ariana through slitted eyes, feigning sleep. What was she thinking? he wondered. Did he meet with her approval? Did she think him as pleasing in appearance as Edric?

"If you continue to look at me like that, I won't be responsible for my actions."

Ariana started violently. "I—I thought you were sleeping."

"I was until I felt your eyes on me."

She turned abruptly, embarrassed to have been caught staring at him. "I am needed in the kitchen. Now that I am home 'tis my duty as mistress to take over the reins of the household. I go now to bathe in the bathing chamber." A huge wooden tub installed in a separate chamber behind the kitchen was one of the luxuries her father had caused to be built into the keep.

"A wife has more important duties," Lyon reminded her softly as he lifted himself gingerly from the box bed and shook the cobwebs from his head. "But you will learn those things soon enough. Come, we will bathe together." He donned his tunic, took her hand, and led her from the chamber. Aghast, Ariana tried to hang back, but his superior strength soon won out as he forced her to keep up with him.

The serfs were just beginning to stir in the wooden building behind the keep that housed the kitchen as Lyon and Ariana strode past them into the bathing room. A well had been dug in the chamber to provide fresh water and a giant hearth kept the room warm at all times. Huge pots of water had been set to boiling long before dawn expressly for the lord and lady of the manor's bathing pleasure. Lyon set to work immediately, emptying buckets of hot and cold water into the tub. When the temperature was to his satisfaction, he turned to Ariana with a flourish.

"After you, my lady."

Ariana froze. Did he actually intend to bathe with her?

"Come, my lady, don't be bashful."

With slow, deliberate motions he removed his tunic, then his shirt, having already removed his chausses before he lay down to sleep. Before Ariana turned and fled, she had a fleeting glimpse of a broad expanse of back and tautly muscled backside. His laughter followed her out the door.

Accompanied by Tersa, Ariana bathed later, after Lyon rode from the keep with several of his knights to inspect the village and peasant huts. With winter coming on roofs would need rethatching and wattle and daub would have to be replaced. As lord of the manor, it was Lyon's duty to see that the villeins working his land were producing as they should; he was also responsible for collecting rent from the freemen who had saved enough money to purchase their land. It was the way the feudal system had worked since the Conqueror's invasion of England.

After Ariana bathed, she invited Tersa to use the tub, seeing that the girl was none too clean. Tersa accepted with alacrity, for in truth she preferred cleanliness to filth. When the maid emerged from the tub, Ariana was amazed at how lovely the girl was once all the dirt was removed from her body. Her hair was the color of ripening wheat and her skin flawless beneath the grime. Together they went to the storeroom to look for material to make new undertunics and surcoats for both of them.

"Think you Sir Beltane will find me beautiful?" Tersa asked shyly as she combed the snarls from her hip-length hair with her fingers.

Ariana appeared at a loss for words. "Do you wish him to think you beautiful?"

"Oh, aye, my lady. He's the finest knight in all the land, I vow. And handsome, too. Much too good for me."

"You are a Saxon, Tersa, too good for a Norman pig. Find someone more worthy of you."

"Aye, my lady," Tersa said, lowering her eyes respectfully. She couldn't help how she felt about Beltane. Saxon or Norman, she wanted him, though she knew her feelings would come to naught.

From the stores of material, which no one had touched in five years, they selected pale blues, greens, and deep rose for Ariana's surcoats, and soft linen for undertunics. For Tersa, Ariana passed over the grays and browns usually worn by serfs and selected brighter colors and finer fabrics. With any luck, they would both have something decent to wear within a matter of days.

When Lyon returned to the keep later that day, a fine meal was waiting for him. The mainstay dishes of fish, fowl, and beef were supplemented with vegetables, fruit, and bread baked from finely milled white flour, a delicacy only the wealthy could afford. There was beer, wine, and ale, which the men quaffed with gusto. Ariana sat on the dais beside Lyon, sharing his trencher.

"You are to be complimented, lady," he said sincerely. " 'Tis a fine meal you've set before my men and me."

"I know my duty," Ariana replied.

Lyon's dark brow rose sharply. "Not yet, lady, but you will."

Ariana tried to summon a curt reply, but suddenly her tongue refused to work and her head began to spin. Lyon's face receded, and a dark void opened up beneath her. With a sigh she slid effortlessly into it. Then the vision began. She tried to stop it but could not.

Lyon stood in the center of a thick gray mist. His chest was bare, his torso covered with blood. A faceless warrior stood before him, a deadly pike aimed at Lyon's heart. And Ariana was there too, standing off to the side, almost obscured by the mist. She felt herself floating, without substance or weight. And then, to her dismay, the faceless warrior turned to her with a silent question. Though the warrior had not spoken, Ariana knew he was asking if he should drive the pike into Lyon's heart. The decision was hers.

Lyon's life.

Or his death.

She opened her mouth to speak, but her voice had no substance, no sound. She shook her head, clearly unable to decide between life and death. In that timeless interval, as the warrior awaited her answer, Lyon seized the pike, spun around and flung it at Ariana, piercing her heart cleanly. Strangely, there was no blood. Then the vision slowly disintegrated. Lingering fingers of mist surrounded her as she stared down at the place where the pike had pierced her. Then came the pain—deep, penetrating, trenchant in its intensity.

Had her indecisiveness caused her own death? Her hesitation had wrought more pain than she could bear. She felt it keenly. She opened her eyes, struggling to escape the agony, and saw Lyon bending over her, a concerned look in his eyes. She saw that she was no longer in the hall but reclining on her own box bed.

"Do you do that often, Ariana?" His voice was cautious and wary.

"Do what, my lord?"

"I've never seen anything like it. 'Twas not a simple swoon, was it, lady? Your eyes rolled back in your head, and you appeared to have stopped breathing. I feared you had left us. I carried you to our chamber and summoned the priest."

Ariana tried to sit up. "I do not need a priest."

Lyon pushed her back down. "Tell me. Tell me what happened."

She bit down on her lower lip, unwilling to answer his blunt questions. "I—I wish to see Nadia."

The priest poked his head into the room. "Did you summon me, my lord?"

Lyon stared at Ariana and saw the fear in her eyes. "Nay, Father, send the witch to me."

"The witch? You want to see Nadia? 'Tis an abomination she practices, my lord. Her black magic cannot help Lady Ariana."

"Nevertheless, I would see her."

"I am here, my lord."

79

The priest started violently when Nadia shoved past him into the room. She seemed to appear from nowhere. Did her spirit dwell in every nook and cranny of the keep, appearing and disappearing at will? He made a sign to ward off evil and scuttled away.

"It has happened again, has it not, my lady?" Nadia asked cryptically. "It has frightened ye."

"What has happened?" Lyon demanded to know. "God's blood, woman, will you tell me what this is all about?"

Ariana shuddered. "I can't recall ever being so frightened. It—it was like judgment day, only worse, for I was the judge."

"For the love of God," Lyon thundered, "I demand to know what is amiss with my lady wife."

Nadia brushed Lyon aside with a wave of her hand. " 'Tis not for me to say, my lord." She gave Ariana a piercing look. "Ye may as well tell him, Ariana. He'll find out sooner or later, for 'tis bound to happen again."

Ariana gazed at Lyon from beneath lashes the color of moonbeams. Nadia was right. It would likely happen again and Lyon would know that she was different without being told. He might think her crazed.

"I have the Sight, my lord."

Lyon stared at Ariana as if she'd just grown two heads. He wasn't normally superstitious, but he had a healthy respect for the supernatural. If the truth be known, it made him more than a little uneasy.

"Does she speak the truth, old woman?" he asked Nadia harshly.

"Aye, my lord, Ariana has the Sight. As a small child, she could see things before they happened. Her mother and I tried to keep it from the villagers and peasants so they would not fear her or accuse her of witchcraft. The visions come upon her without warning, like it did at supper tonight."

Lyon backed away from Ariana cautiously. "What did you see, my lady?"

Ariana's mouth went dry. "Naught of importance." How could she tell him about her vision when she didn't understand what she'd seen? She had hoped Nadia would help her interpret it. If only Lyon would leave them alone.

"Naught of importance?" Lyon repeated, not at all convinced.

"Aye. Afterward I have difficulty remembering exactly what I've seen. Like now. All I recall are swirling mists and dark shadows."

Lyon searched her face and then nodded, apparently satisfied. "I will leave you with Nadia. I do not believe in such things."

Ariana watched him stride from the chamber, relieved that he did not seem overly concerned about her Sight.

"What has frightened ye, Ariana?" Nadia asked once they were alone. "What did ye see?"

Ariana rose from the box bed and began pacing. "The vision itself was frightening, but what it implied was even more so. Oh, Nadia, my vision implied that Lyon's life lay within my keeping. How could that be? Am I to be his executioner? I never wanted him for a husband, and Lord knows I hate all Normans, but I do not want to be the one who must decide whether or not he lives." Then she told Nadia everything she remembered of her vision.

Nadia was thoughtful for a long time. " 'Twas a powerful thing you saw, Ariana. You say you could not decide whether or not to spare Lyon's life. Mayhap 'tis a sign that something strong and powerful binds ye to Lyon of Normandy. Or mayhap 'tis a warning of danger to ye if ye let him into yer heart."

"I despise the man!" Ariana spat venomously. "My heart is in no danger where Lyon of Normandy is concerned."

"Time will tell, my lady, time will tell," Nadia intoned dryly.

"Oh, go away, you're no help at all," Ariana said crossly. "What kind of witch are you if you can't interpret my visions?" When Ariana turned to challenge the old woman, Nadia had slipped out as silently as she had arrived.

When Lyon returned to their chamber later that night, Ariana was already sleeping. He did not awaken her as he removed his clothing and slid into the box bed beside her. In the dim light of the candle's golden glow he studied her face, wondering what manner of woman he had wed. He didn't believe in witches or supernatural power, but a frisson of fear slid down his spine when he thought of her ability to "see" things before they happened. It wasn't normal, and he vowed to keep Ariana's strange ability from public knowledge lest she be branded a witch and burned at the stake.

Troubled by what he had witnessed earlier, Lyon tried to sleep but could not. He still wanted Ariana despite her many faults. She was disobedient, strong-willed, sharp-tongued, and exasperating. Counterbalancing those negative qualities were her incomparable beauty, courage, and sensuous nature, of which she seemed blissfully oblivious. Her lack of wifely qualities was compensated for by her desirability.

The more Lyon learned of Ariana, the more he was convinced that she and Edric of Blackheath had done nothing more than meet clandestinely, just as she had said. Of course, that in itself was a punishable offense, for she was a married woman and had no business meeting a man in the dark of night without a suitable chaperon. To Lyon's way of thinking, that could mean only one thing. Ariana still wanted Edric, preferred him to her lawful husband. Which came as no surprise. Edric was a Saxon while he, Lyon, was a Norman, a man who had invaded her country and killed her menfolk. It was entirely possible that he had cut down her father and brothers with his sword in the heat of battle, recognizing them only as the enemy.

Ariana sighed and moved against Lyon in her sleep, destroying all thought of slumber. He moaned, growing instantly hard. God's blood, he'd been wed over five years and still hadn't consummated his marriage! He knew he'd vowed not to take her until she'd given him proof that she did not carry a bastard, but he was no monk. Bedding his wife was his right, his duty—and he wanted her!

With a will of their own, his arms slid around her waist, pulling her into the curve of his body. Ariana awoke with a start. Her eyes flew open. "Wha . . . what are you doing?"

She cried out in dismay as his powerful arms lifted her to lie on top of him. Her soft breasts were crushed against the hard slab of his naked chest. His thighs beneath her felt like granite. All of him was hard, too hard, his hands, his mouth, that man part of his body that probed relentlessly against her softness. The masculine lines of his face looked as if they had been hewn with an ax. His long black hair curled wildly at his nape, making her suddenly eager to run her fingers through it. The planes of his face were stark with desire, the cheekbones prominent, the jaw square, bold, and arrogant.

More spellbinding even than his over-whelming masculinity were his ice-blue eyes, dangerously compelling in that dark, riveting face. They could either freeze or incinerate a person with one brief look. His intimate glance gave his words unmistakable meaning.

"You are my wife."

Ariana swallowed visibly. "I am well aware of that."

"We have not had our wedding night. After five years 'tis my due. I am not a patient man." He stared at her lush lips, so irresistible in the misty, candlelit room. Fierce wanting turned him hard as marble.

Ariana's eyes widened, feeling him swell against her. "But you said . . ."

"I've changed my mind, Ariana. I want you. If I find you other than virginal, I can still send you back to the abbey."

"I . . . I don't want you. Please, don't . . ."

A blaze within him burned, incredibly swift, dangerously hot.

His expression grew fierce and his arms tightened. "Is it Edric you want?" She opened her mouth in denial, but he forestalled her answer. "Nay, do not tell me. It matters not. You cannot have him. One day, I vow, you will pay homage to me. You will beg me to bed you. If you even think of betraying me with any other man, I will lock you in the tower where you can repent of your sins in leisure. You are my wife. I will bed you when it pleases me, and you will welcome me."

"I will welcome you as England welcomed the Conqueror."

When she would have said more, his lips captured hers. The kiss was like the soldering heat that joins metals. She expected cruel ravishment of his mouth but found instead a burning temptation.

Chapter Four

Lyon changed positions, rolling Ariana beneath him. She felt his heavy-lidded gaze on her and raised her eyes to him. His expression was stark with desire. His thick-muscled limbs were a brace around her, his mouth forceful upon hers. His hands tore away the last barrier of clothing between them.

"My lord, please—"

"Aye, I will. Think you I don't know how to please a woman?"

His mouth touched her throat, his tongue bathing the pulse there, sliding down the valley between her breasts. She shuddered as she felt the heat of his breath against her breast. He blew on her nipple, watching intently as it puckered and peaked for him. When she felt the pressure of his tongue laving it, she cried out in confusion. What was happening to her? She moaned deep within her throat, protesting his handling of her, her hands winding into the linen sheets on the bed. Then his mouth captured a nipple, tugging upon it, sucking, drawing from it until she thought her soul would leave her body.

She cried out his name, so seldom uttered from her lips, the entreaty implicit in her quivering voice.

"Lady, lady," he groaned, his own plea rich and deep. "You send me to perdition."

"What are you doing to me? Mercy, my lord."

"I promised no mercy, Ariana." He was too hungry for her to let her pleas sway him. He would make her welcome him as her husband, her conqueror. He would tame her.

He slid down the length of her, his hands moving around to cup and lift her buttocks. She felt the slide of his rough tongue against her thighs and she thought she would shatter into a million pieces. Bucking, writhing, she tried to escape his brutal grip, but he held her fast. She felt the earth shaking beneath her as the intimate thrust of his tongue, hard, probing, entered her. Sliding deeper, retreating, teasing, tormenting, taking her to a place where it no longer mattered that she was Saxon and he Norman.

Her hands grasped the sheet in desperate abandon as she felt the length of him slide upward again, settling against her, his mouth finding hers. She tasted herself on him and nearly swooned.

He lifted his head, his blue eyes searing into her.

"I implore you, do not force me, my lord," she whispered shakily.

"I would rather seduce you, Ariana. 'Tis your choice. Force or seduction. Name it, lady, but do not ask me to stop."

Ariana closed her eyes and shuddered. Her ache had no name. She only knew that Lyon had caused it and she wanted it to go away. Was he capable of gentleness? Possibly. Of cruelty? Surely. Of making her want him? She feared it was so.

"Force!" she lied. She was too proud to admit that a Norman could make her tremble with wanting. If he took her, she wanted him to know that it was against her will.

He stared at her and then laughed. "Force, lady? I fear you would not like it. Nay, Ariana, you are ripe for seduction."

Despite her plea for force, his hands were amazingly gentle as he swept her against him, exploring her body boldly, stroking her sensitive skin with the rough pads of his strong fingers. She cried out as those same strong fingers delved into the moist crevice of her womanhood, stealing her breath away. He stared intently into her face, watching those magnificent green eyes darken with her first real taste of passion. He smiled, overjoyed at the heady thought that she hadn't lied. She truly was untouched. No one could feign that kind of innocent response.

Ariana was panting now, feeling things she

had never imagined, not in her wildest dreams. She felt Lyon's fingers searching for something hidden within the intimate folds of her flesh and gasped in dismay when he found what he was looking for. She arched wildly against him as he stroked and teased the tender little bud, then stifled a shriek when he thrust a finger inside her.

"You weep for me, Ariana," he said, savoring the soft, elusive scent of her as he released her juices. She felt her own wetness down there and wanted to die with embarrassment.

His fingers stretched her, readying her for the final assault upon her maidenhead. Then she felt the fullness of his sex at her entrance, probing, hot, marble-hard. He pushed it in a fraction, his control hanging by a mere thread. He was so damned hot that he wanted to shove himself to the hilt and thrust to completion. She had asked for force, but something inside him balked. This wasn't a serving wench, accustomed to rough handling; this was his wife, the future mother of his children. He knew how to be rough, but he'd rather have Ariana pliant and eager beneath him.

He pushed himself more deeply inside her, keenly aware that she was still a virgin. Not that he needed proof, for he'd already surmised that she was untouched. Ariana gasped and bit her lower lip, feeling herself stretch and fill with him. Suddenly, inexplicably, he felt regret at having to hurt her.

"This is going to hurt," he told her. "You're so

small. I know of no way to make it otherwise."
He went deeper still, butting against her
maidenhead. Ariana paled and whimpered.

She knew so little about sexual matters. She
could feel his rod pushing inside her and wondered if she could take his great size. There was
pain, just as he'd said, though still bearable and
not intense enough yet to quell the pleasure of
his foreplay. Just when she thought she might
be able to stand it, Lyon flexed his hips and
thrust sharply forward, breaking cleanly
through the barrier. She screamed, digging
bloody grooves into his back, rebelling against
the agony of his entrance. He held rigidly still,
waiting for her pain to subside.

"The worst is over, sweeting," Lyon crooned,
smoothing silver strands of damp hair from her
face. He wanted to thrust so desperately that the
effort to lie perfectly still, waiting for her to ad-
just and accept his size, brought beads of sweat
to his forehead.

He moved very slowly at first, caressing her
from the inside, soothing her torn flesh. Though
she still felt considerable pain, the sensation became almost pleasant. Just when she felt the
urge to writhe up and meet his easy strokes, his
thrusting became a tempest. Rotating his hips
in wild rhythm, Lyon felt the crescendo of climax rising within him, fierce, debilitating, faster, ever faster . . . He felt his body constrict. He
knew he was going too fast for Ariana, but there
was no help for it. His need for her had driven
him beyond the point of human endurance. He

realized that she would receive no joy from this mating and vowed to bring her pleasure the next time.

Ariana felt his body harden and tense, heard the harshness of his breathing in her ear, his hoarse cry, felt the wet splash of his seed spill inside her. In seconds he fell beside her. The slickness and heat of his body scorched her inside and out.

She leaped up, furious, hating him for what he'd done, for how he had made her feel, hating herself for enjoying it until the very last, when he had hurt her.

"Norman bastard!" she spat venomously. Unfortunately, she didn't get far. His incredibly long arm reached out, curling around her wrist and drawing her back down beside him. His face was dark and forbidding. He looked like a devil. Nay, more like a wild animal—untamed, aroused, dangerous. He looked like a lion. His intense masculinity overwhelmed her.

"Aye, I'm a bastard, I do not deny it. I know you think yourself too good to wed a Norman bastard, but one day you will realize how wise William was to give you to me. The whole of my life, I've had to live with the shame of my bastardy, but no longer. Now I have the land that I've always coveted and a fine fortress of my own. And a wife whose bloodlines are flawless. Our children will become the rulers of this land. They will be the defenders of England and perpetrators of William's legacy."

"Mayhap I will give you no children," Ariana

declared sourly, rubbing her wrist, which bore the marks of Lyon's strong fingers.

His eyes narrowed dangerously. "You can't possibly know that. Has your Sight revealed something to indicate that you are barren? Are you a witch?"

She recoiled in fear. "Nay, I am no witch. My visions rarely concern myself, only others."

"How comforting," he intoned dryly. Suddenly his mood changed. He swept her with a look that scorched her, making her aware that she stood before him gloriously naked. "What we just did wasn't very enjoyable for you."

"Am I supposed to enjoy it?"

"Aye, lady, and you will, I swear it."

"Not if it doesn't happen again. Mayhap I conceived already. Then you need not bother again."

"And mayhap you didn't. Even if you did conceive, there is nothing to say we shouldn't continue to do this for our own pleasure."

"For *your* pleasure," Ariana corrected. "I would be surprised if any woman enjoyed what we just did."

Amusement lurked in his ice-blue eyes. "You are mistaken. A diligent man can bring any woman to pleasure, and I am most diligent."

He pushed her down on the bed, rose, lit another candle from the flame of the one now nearly burned down to a nub, and found the water jug. He poured out a generous portion into a bowl, picked up his shirt and returned to sit beside her. Ariana watched him warily, not knowing from one minute to the next what he might do. When he dipped the tail of his shirt into the bowl and spread her legs, she let out a ragged cry of protest.

"Nay!"

Before she could leap up again, he pressed the wet shirt between her legs. When he took it away it was streaked with blood. Ariana's eyes bulged. "You've wounded me mortally!"

"Nay, 'tis normal. The bleeding isn't profuse and will stop anon. I was gentle with you even though you said you preferred force. The next time it will not hurt, I promise you."

"I do not think it will improve. Mayhap you're not very good at this. Think you we need do this very often?" she asked hopefully.

Lyon laughed aloud, the sound rich and deep. "I've had few complaints on my performance. Most women think me quite adept."

"Aye, mayhap your mistress enjoys what you do. I understand Lady Zabrina is quite lovely."

Lyon's expression hardened. "What do you know of Zabrina?" Ariana bit her lip and looked away. "Nay, let me guess," Lyon said, comprehension dawning. " 'Twas Edric who told you, was it not? Forget Edric; you cannot have him. I am your husband, our marriage has been consummated, and I intend to make love to you every night, twice a night, three times a night, if it pleases me."

Ariana sent him a look of utter disbelief. "Think you I am stupid? That is not possible."

Lyon gave her a wicked grin. "Is it not? I am

young and lusty. Allow me but five minutes rest and I will fill again." Grasping her hand, he guided it to his staff. Heat flooded his groin, and his rod filled and lifted. With a will of their own, her fingers curled around it, testing its strength. A low groan escaped him; his great body shuddered as her hand tightened involuntarily around his engorged sex. Sheer, stunning bliss swept over him.

"Jesu!" His cry startled her, and her fingers fell away instantly. But the damage had been done. He wrenched her from the bed and lifted her high into the air, settling her atop him. "What say you to a ride, lady? I made a vow and I intend to keep it. Before the dawn creeps across the sky, you will be satisfied."

"Or dead," Ariana whispered fearfully.

He brought her mouth down to meet his. His fingers laced into the silk of her hair as he kissed her deeply, probing the fragrant cave of her mouth with his tongue. He began to touch her, stroke her, his fingertips like butterflies dancing over her flesh. He licked her breasts, gently nipped her shoulders, her throat, explored her intimately, igniting that tiny spark inside her she thought dead.

Her heart spasmed fiercely, as if seized by lightning, and she began kissing him back, clutching at his shoulders, running her hands through his dark hair, never so desperate to touch, to taste, to hold, to experience. Surely her senses had left her, Ariana thought as she felt a heady burst of some dormant emotion inside her. The Lion had invaded her country, stolen her land, and forced her into marriage. She hated him, yet her traitorous body was responding to his loving with shivers and moans and little cries of pleasure.

"I'm coming into you, sweeting," Lyon panted harshly as he raised her buttocks and pushed inside her. The fit was tight but there was no barrier to hinder him this time. He slid full and deep into her moist warmth. Ariana braced herself for the pain and was pleasantly surprised when naught but a feeling of fullness resulted.

She clung to him mutely, following her body's dictates as she met his thrusts. A fever filled her, conveying itself to Lyon as he drove into her fiercely, compelled by the terrible need she had awakened in him. He couldn't recall losing control like this with any other woman he had bedded. When he feared he would spill prematurely and leave her unfulfilled again, he slipped a hand between them and stroked the tiny bud of her passion with a calloused thumb, swiftly catching her up to him.

Suddenly she was caught in a stormy tempest that seemed to crash and vibrate around her in wave after wave of intense pleasure. Her head spun; her body felt as if it no longer belonged to her. It was as if a wild creature possessed her as her very first climax burst upon her. Thunder crashed, and stars fell from the sky. Then she seemed to die a little. When she came to her senses, she lay shivering against the slick length of Lyon's bronzed body.

"What happened?"

Slowly reviving from the most violent and exciting climax he'd ever known, Lyon waited for his breathing to return to normal before replying. "I kept my promise. Do you still think me unskilled?" His amused gaze slid the length of her flushed body.

Ariana blushed and looked away, suddenly embarrassed by her abandoned response to his loving. "Mayhap I was mistaken." Suddenly she noted the slant of the sun in the sky. " 'Tis daylight, my lord. I've duties to attend to."

"We will bathe together, Ariana. Come." He gave her his hand. She wanted to resist, but his eyes compelled her. When she placed her hand in his, Lyon smiled inwardly. He would tame her yet, he vowed as he handed her her tunic and slipped into his own. Once she was sufficiently tamed, he reflected, she would become the docile wife he desired.

Ariana donned one of her new tunics and surcoats, finished this very morning. It felt wonderful to wear something attractive that did not abrade her tender skin, she thought as she smoothed the material over her hips and thighs. The linen undertunic felt soft and supple against her bare skin, and the surcoat of blue damask trimmed in ermine was most elegant. It was surely worthy of a countess. She had even pinned an elaborate jeweled broach to her shoulder. Her mother had possessed many fine pieces of jewelry, which now belonged to her.

She wondered if Lyon would notice, then scoffed at such an outlandish notion. Lyon cared for nothing but his land, his king, and sexual gratification.

Before leaving the chamber, she slid a shy glance at the bed, recalling all the incredibly erotic things Lyon had done to her the night before and how he'd made her feel. Though she'd fought him as well as her own body, in the end he'd had his way. He had made love to her twice, and again in the bathing chamber with the water splashing wildly around them and on the floor. There had been no way to gainsay him, for he'd quickly broken down her barriers. This morning she was sore, 'twas true, and her body ached in places she'd never been aware of before, but she could not say he had hurt her unduly. Verily, she had been surprised by his gentleness.

Flushing with the memory of last night and this morning, Ariana composed herself and left the chamber. An excited Tersa met her on the stairs.

"My lady, I have something of great import to tell you, but 'tis for your ears alone." She looked furtively behind her, her expression fearful. "If Lord Lyon should hear, he will punish me. And I do not wish Beltane to think ill of me."

Perplexed, Ariana stared at Tersa, noting her great agitation. "Come into my chamber, Tersa. Lord Lyon went hunting this morning before matins and I don't expect him back till night-fall."

Once inside the room, Ariana waited for Tersa to impart her important news. She didn't have long to wait, for Tersa started speaking immediately, her voice low and intense.

"He's here, my lady. He wants you to meet him in the garden behind the kitchen. He says to tell you that he will be by the back curtain wall behind the grape arbor."

"Who is here, Tersa? You speak in riddles."

" 'Tis he, the man who paid me to carry messages to you when you lived at the abbey. I've learned since that he is Lord Edric of Blackheath. I didn't recognize him at first because he wore a hooded tunic. He stopped me in the village and asked me to give you a message."

Ariana's heart stopped. She wanted to speak with Edric, but dared she meet him secretly, knowing how Lyon would react? She had seen Lyon's gentle side when he made love to her and was aware that he had a violent side, one that hadn't been fully revealed to her. She had unleashed only a small portion of it when she'd called him a Norman bastard.

"Thank you, Tersa. Fear not, neither Sir Beltane nor Lord Lyon will hear of this from my lips."

Tersa's relief was immediate. She hated being disloyal to Lord Lyon after he had made it possible for her to escape marriage to

Doral. But her first loyalty was to her lady. "Will you meet Lord Edric, my lady? He is a great lord, and handsome, too, but not as handsome as Lord Lyon . . . or Beltane," she added shyly.

"I will think on it, Tersa," Ariana said softly. "Go now, there is much to be done today. Keane mentioned that it is candlemaking time and he will need your help."

Ariana scarce noted Tersa's departure. Her mind whirled in indecision. Lyon was conveniently gone from the keep for the day; 'twould be a perfect opportunity to meet Edric without anyone knowing. Lyon was cunning—he would strike when one least expected it—and loyalty to her Saxon roots demanded that she warn Edric to be on his guard. Right or wrong, she decided to slip out to the garden to meet Edric before Lyon returned to the keep.

Edric lounged against the curtain wall, secure in the knowledge that he could not be seen behind the tangled vines of the grape arbor. He didn't know if Ariana would come, but he prayed she would. It tore him apart to think of her at the mercy of the Lion of Normandy. With any luck he would free her from her odious marriage and make her his. His ruminations were disturbed by the rustle of leaves. Ariana.

"Edric, where are you?"

"Here, my lady." Edric's soft whisper drew

her to his concealment behind the arbor. He caught her hands and drew her to him. "I feared you would not come."

"I cannot stay long, but I had to warn you."

"Warn me? Where is the danger?"

" 'Tis Lyon. He knows about our secret meetings at the abbey. I do not know what he will do. I fear he is biding his time."

"I do not fear your husband, Ariana. Besides," he said with supreme confidence, "I have sworn fealty to William. My knights and retainers fill the ranks of his army. Killing me would displease King William."

Ariana frowned. "Are you truly William's man? I thought . . ."

Edric's expression grew fierce. "Nay, Ariana. I am Saxon, never doubt it. I despise the bastard Conqueror and all his minions. I feign loyalty for a purpose. One day soon Saxon lords who lost their lands will rise up in rebellion. When the time arrives, I will join them. I am in contact with King Malcolm. He has generously placed men and arms at our disposal. I swear you will soon be free from your detestable marriage, and I eagerly await the day you will become my wife. You are the reason I never married all these years. I am waiting for you, my lady."

Ariana was impressed by Edric's fervor even though she saw no possible way to cut the ties that bound her to Lyon. "I fear that will never come to pass. 'Tis folly to think on it."

"It will come to pass if you help bring down the Lion. Without the Lion, Cragmere is ripe for attack from Malcolm. The man is too strong, too well guarded. His death must come from within. 'Tis why I seek your help, Ariana. You are close to him; you sleep in his bed. Will you do this for us?"

Ariana stared at Edric in abject horror. "You want me to kill Lyon? Nay, you ask too much. I despise all Normans and 'tis true I never wanted to be Lyon's wife, but I have not the stomach to kill him with my own hands, or cause his death."

Edric's eyes narrowed. "What has he done to you, Ariana? Have you sworn fealty to the man?"

"Nay! Never that!" she denied vehemently.

"Do you care for him?"

"Certainly not!" she declared emphatically, though in truth her answer was not so simple. Lyon of Normandy was an enigma, a law unto himself. He was like no other man. She recalled vividly his strong hands, so capable of cruelty yet gentle upon her body. Though she'd given him plenty of reason, he had never struck her or been intentionally cruel.

Edric smiled complacently. "I thought not." Watching Ariana intently, he dipped his hand inside his pouch and removed a small vial filled with a greenish-gray liquid. He took her hand and placed it in her palm, squeezing her fingers around it.

"What is this?" She stared at the murky green

liquid inside the vial, praying it wasn't what she thought it was. Unfortunately her greatest fear was realized.

" 'Tis poison," Edric said softly. "Very potent, very swift. A drop or two is all that is needed."

"Poison!" The word hissed between her teeth in an explosion of shock and disgust. "Whatever am I to do with it?"

Edric gave her a look of utter disbelief. "Ariana, my lady, think how bereft William will be if the Lion is disposed of. Without Lyon's strong arm to defend his lands, Northumbria will be ripe for invasion. Think what it will mean to us."

Ariana tried to give the vial back to Edric. "I . . . I cannot, truly I cannot."

Edric shook his head, refusing to accept the vial of poison. "Keep it. You are Saxon. Your heart will tell you what to do."

"I cannot!"

"Aye, Ariana, you must. Think of your father and brothers, who were killed by bloodthirsty Norman invaders. Think of your land and how it was taken from you, of those years you spent behind cloistered walls. Think how the Lion's death will help bring about freedom for England."

She couldn't think. She couldn't breathe. Edric's words whirled around inside her brain, drowning her in confusion. Slowly she backed away from him, then turned abruptly and ran back inside the keep. Yet no matter how hard she tried, she could dislodge neither Edric's words nor his logic from her mind.

Jesu! He wanted her to poison Lyon. Edric's terrifying words reverberated in her brain as she climbed the stairs to her bedchamber. Numbly she sank down onto a bench and opened her hand, appalled to see that she still clutched the vial of poison.

She could not do it; truly she could not.

Chapter Five

Ariana glanced nervously at her clothes chest, imagining she could see through the wood where she had hidden the vial of poison beneath her clothing, and feared Lyon would be able to see it too. Since Edric had given it to her three days before, her life had become a living hell. She felt disloyal to her Saxon heritage for lacking the courage to do as Edric asked, but killing Lyon took more courage than she possessed. He was her husband, whether she like it or not, and in truth he had not been cruel to her.

For the last three nights, Lyon had crawled into bed exhausted from his toils. Having been an absentee landowner for five years, he had found much at Cragmere to occupy his time and energy. Yet despite his weariness, each night he had reached for her, finding renewed vigor in the mysteries of her body as he slowly and methodically brought her to the point where she wanted him desperately.

She had fought against his seduction, resisting vigorously, until her body betrayed her and she melted against him in surrender. He knew he would prevail and had rejoiced in his mastery over her. Afterward the hate and resentment reasserted itself within Ariana, and she vowed it would not happen again. But it did.

Lost in thought, Ariana started violently when Tersa entered the chamber, her gaze darting about furtively. When she saw that Ariana was alone, she shoved a note into her hand. Ariana stared at her for the space of a heartbeat, then carefully unfolded the small sheet of parchment.

"Where did you get this?"

"A young lad thrust it into my hand when I was walking through the inner bailey. I've never seen him before. He said it was for my lady, then he disappeared."

"Thank you, Tersa, you may go now."

"Aye, my lady." Tersa curtsied and left the chamber while Ariana read the note.

The note held but one sentence. "Do not fail me." It wasn't signed but the initial E was scrawled across the bottom of the message. Edric!

Ariana's hands began to shake as she glanced again at the chest where the poison reposed— so tempting, so deadly. Without warning, the door opened and Lyon burst into the chamber. Ariana was so dismayed to see him in their chamber at this time of day that she dropped the note, a horrified expression on her face as it fluttered to the floor and settled at Lyon's feet. Lyon's eyes narrowed when he saw her blanch, her eyes fixed on the small sheet of parchment lying at his feet. When her frozen limbs thawed and she reached for it, Lyon was there before her.

"What is this, my lady?" he asked coolly as he quickly scanned the note. When it became clear who had written it, he swept her with a look of cold contempt.

" 'Tis n-n-nothing, my lord," Ariana stammered, searching her mind and finding it lacking a plausible excuse.

"You call a note from your lover nothing?" He shoved the note into her face, his expression dark and dangerous. He had arrived home in a lighthearted mood, thinking to indulge his wife and take her riding. Now suddenly he found himself on the verge of doing violence. "The initial scrawled on the bottom tells me 'tis from Lord Edric."

"I have no lover," Ariana denied vehemently, unable to deny that the note was from Edric.

"Nor will you ever," Lyon replied tersely. "What does Lord Edric want of you? What mischief are you planning, wife?"

"No . . . no mischief, my lord."

"Then explain what it means."

Ariana swallowed visibly and shook her head. "I cannot, my lord."

"Cannot or will not?"

" 'Tis the same. Beat me if you will, but I can tell you nothing. The message is as much a mystery to me as it is to you," she lied, albeit not very convincingly.

Lyon glared at her, his expression fierce, his mood growing darker by the minute. Ariana was his. How dare Lord Edric try to take her from him. If not for King William, he would go to Blackheath and slit the bastard from gullet to groin.

Ariana looked all innocence and wide-eyed vulnerability standing there, defying him, mocking him. Did she think him stupid? She knew what the message meant and would rather suffer a beating than reveal it to him. She had no idea how her green eyes, misty with fear yet boldly rebellious, challenged him, attracted him, made his body grow taut and his groin harden. Even her stance, firm little breasts thrust forward, shoulders back, fists clenched at her rounded hips, excited him. God's blood, he wanted her! Wanted the lying little witch.

"I will give you one last chance, Ariana," he warned. "Tell me what the message means and swear fealty to me, and you will not be punished. Continue lying and withholding your loyalty, and you will be punished severely. Ten lashes with a whip should prove sufficient to improve your memory and gain your loyalty."

Lyon's threat had no substance, though Ariana did not know it. He would never beat a woman, let alone his own wife, but he hoped the threat of a beating would frighten her sufficiently to loosen her tongue. When he saw her face whiten and go slack and her body slump, he knew he had succeeded. But he had yet to see the full measure of her courage. Ariana quickly recovered, regaining some of her former spirit.

"Beat me, my lord, if you wish, but I will never swear fealty to you. I repeat, the message is a mystery to me. I know not what it means."

The harsh planes of Lyon's face darkened as he fought to control his temper. Ariana's blatant defiance was beyond belief. Ten lashes would fell even the strongest of men and likely kill a frail woman like herself, yet she would rather take the punishment than betray her would-be Saxon lover or swear fealty to a Norman bastard. Unless he left the chamber immediately, he couldn't guarantee that he wouldn't carry out his threat so fierce was his anger. Damn Ariana for her stubbornness!

"Mayhap you need time to think on your punishment," he said once his rage had cooled enough to speak coherently. Didn't she know he'd rather be exploring her lovely body with his hands and mouth than marring it with a whip? "I will leave you to contemplate your choices. I will return later to hear your answer."

Ariana waited with bated breath for Lyon to leave, her body numb, her mind filled with nameless terror. She had survived the canings administered by the abbess but suspected they were tame compared to the pain inflicted by a rawhide whip wielded by a man with Lyon's strength and vigor. Would she survive? What alternative did she have? Telling Lyon about the poison would doubtless earn her punishment even more severe. Or mayhap death. Thank God he had not found the hidden vial. Suddenly Ariana realized that Lyon had not left, that he was still staring at her.

"What . . . what is it, my lord?"

He said nothing, but merely stared at her, his ice-blue eyes kindling into twin flames. When he reached for her, she gasped and retreated a step. He stalked her, grasping her arm and hauling her hard against him.

"You bewitch me, Ariana. What black magic do you work on me? You deserve a beating but instead I find myself eager to taste your lips, to explore your tempting flesh."

His lips smashed down on hers. His kiss was not gentle, nay, it was punishing and angry, yet beneath the anger Ariana sensed a softness, a giving that could not be denied. She was forced to endure the harshness of his mouth as he pried her lips open with his thrusting tongue. Lyon knew he shouldn't have touched her, not yet, not while his anger was still full-blown, but he couldn't help himself. Where Ariana was concerned he had no control. She drove him to the brink of madness and beyond.

Ariana's knees buckled, and she had to cling to him to keep from falling. Lyon responded by sweeping her from her feet and carrying her to the box bed. He didn't bother to undress her or himself. He merely shoved her tunic and surcoat up to her waist, lowered his chausses and braies and fell atop her. She felt his hands upon her, exploring her most intimate places, doing all those things that made her mindless with need. She cried out in protest, twisting away from the hot thrust of his staff. She would rather suffer a beating than be brought low by the male domination of his body.

He pushed into her, sinking full and deep, his climax only seconds away. His anger had driven him to this, he lamented, stealing his will and destroying his resolve. Loving was not meant to be punishing, but God help him for he could not help himself. His mute plea seemed to bring a measure of calm as his lips softened and his hands gentled. But it was too late. He could feel his climax building and knew he was giving Ariana no pleasure, yet he couldn't hang on long enough to do so.

Ariana braced herself as his hips pounded against her and his mouth ravaged hers. She gained small comfort from the fact that he'd never know how desperately she wanted to respond, how splendidly alive he made her body feel. Then she felt him stiffen and cry out, and knew instinctively that it was too late for her. He had exacted punishment from her body in a humiliating way, though it wasn't what he intended. Leaving her unfulfilled and aching was nearly as bad as a whipping.

How she hated the Norman bastard!

But did she hate him enough to poison him? At this moment she did.

Lyon spilled his seed and immediately rolled off of Ariana. He had eased his sexual frustration but gained no pleasure from their mating. He felt deep shame for what he had done. He would rather have her moaning and writhing beneath him, eager for his pleasuring, her hands hot upon his flesh, her lips open and welcoming. Unfortunately it was too late now to repent. If he did, Ariana would take it as a sign of weakness and 'twould be impossible to maintain discipline within his marriage. Nay, he would express no regret, show no mercy. Let her think this was but a prelude to the beating he'd promised.

Lyon pushed himself to his feet, adjusted his chausses and braies and stared down at Ariana. Her stricken expression brought a wave of remorse, but he hardened his heart.

"I will return for your answer, lady. Swear fealty to me now and explain the note and we will forget this unpleasantness. Continue this foolhardy silence and you will most assuredly regret it. I do not wish to beat you but will do so if I must." When she remained mute, he turned abruptly and strode from the room, praying he had frightened her enough to drag the truth from her, for never could he bring himself to scar her lovely flesh.

Ariana stared at the door, arms and legs obscenely sprawled, skirts bunched in disarray at her waist. She ached. She burned. She hated. Oh, how she hated! The Norman bastard had humiliated her beyond repair. If she had the means, she would kill him . . . Kill him . . .

She froze, recalling the vial of poison still in her possession. Kill Lyon. Aye, he deserved to die. He intended to beat her when he returned. Ten strokes with the lash. She'd not last beyond five. Then he would have Cragmere and be free to wed a woman of his own choosing. Was that what he wanted? Was that why he had ordered ten lashes instead of a less severe punishment?

She lifted herself from the bed, her mind numb as she recalled Edric's words. "Do not fail me." As if in a trance, she walked to the chest. Her eyes were glazed as she lifted the lid and rummaged inside for the vial. She found it easily, raising it to the light and staring at the murky liquid with something akin to horror. Who would think something so innocuous looking could be so deadly?

She turned and searched the chamber, her gaze settling on a wine flagon Tersa had left earlier. It was Lyon's habit to pour himself a goblet of wine before retiring. Sometimes he even insisted that she join him. As if in a trance, she walked to the wine. Her movements took on a dreamlike quality. She was trembling from head to toe as she uncorked the tiny vial of poison and held it poised over the wine.

Nay, she couldn't do it! No matter how much she hated her Norman husband, something deep and undeniable existed between her and

Lyon. An emotion hovering somewhere between hate and love. Between heaven and hell. An emotion that had no name. Lyon tormented her endlessly and gave her more pleasure than she'd ever known.

He was going to beat her, the devil within her goaded. Mayhap even kill her.

She hated him. He deserved to die for what he had just done to her. He had used his great man tool to punish her.

She tilted the vial. Two round drops fell into the wine, spreading across the surface. She halted the flow and gently shook the flagon. Then, very carefully, she tipped the vial to allow two more generous drops to disappear into the fragrant dark wine. Recalling Edric's words about the potency of the poison, she carefully replaced the stopper and shoved the vial into a hidden pocket in the seam of her surcoat. She was beyond thinking now, beyond the ability to reason as she returned to the bed, sat down, and folded her hands in her lap. She was still in the same position when Lyon returned two hours later.

Ariana looked up when she heard the metal scrape of the door closing behind him. Lyon stood just inside the room, holding a coiled whip in one hand. She jerked in revulsion. Did he intend to lash her here, in their bedchamber?

Lyon's eyes narrowed upon Ariana, as if trying to read her thoughts. Then abruptly his gaze left her, fixing on the wine flagon sitting on a small table beside the bed. Ariana paled, wondering if he somehow sensed what she had done. He loosed the lash, dragging it behind him as he walked to the bed and stopped scant inches from her. Ariana's eyes remained downcast, fearing they would reveal her guilt, fearing she would blurt out what she had done if she looked too deeply into his ice-blue eyes.

"Do you swear fealty to me, my lady?" Lyon asked softly, too softly. "Will you tell me the meaning of Lord Edric's message?"

"Nay." Still she refused to look at him. "I cannot." She bowed her head, waiting for his terrible vengeance.

Lyon stared down at her. Her neck was white and childishly vulnerable. A single wisp of hair curled at her nape. Lyon had an overwhelming longing to touch it, but he dared not. He wondered, knowing what he now knew, if he could ever trust her. Her silver hair, falling about her face and shoulders like a shining halo, belied her black heart.

"Are you prepared to take your punishment?" His hand tightened on the whip. Ariana flinched.

Her eyes were glassy, her face slack with fear as she rose and presented her back. "Aye, my lord." Her voice quivered. "Should I have the misfortune to die beneath your whip, bury me beside my father and brothers." She clenched her fists and waited in stoic resignation.

"I thirst," Lyon growled suddenly. "Mayhap wine will fortify my stomach for what I must do."

Jesu! Ariana felt the color drain from her face. She whipped around, saw Lyon pour a goblet of wine, and the horror of what she had done struck her full force. Her hand flew to her mouth. Nay! Nay! She didn't want Lyon dead! He was too young, too vigorous, too vital. She must have been mad to attempt something so contemptible, so utterly despicable. What had she done? He lifted the goblet to his lips and Ariana cried out, at the same time leaping forward to knock it from his hand. She lunged for it and missed. A few drops of the dark liquid spilled over the rim onto her surcoat, leaving a blood-red splotch against the pale blue of her tunic.

Lyon looked at her as if she had just lost her mind. "If you wished a drink, wife, you had but to ask. Here," he said, offering her his goblet, "I will share mine with you."

Ariana stared at the wine in horror. Was this how her life would end, writhing on the floor in the throes of agony, poisoned by her own hand? So be it. She took the goblet in both hands, stared over the rim one last time at the man whom she might have loved under different circumstances, and carried it to her lips.

Suddenly the goblet flew from her hands, spilling upon the walls and floor. "Little fool! You would have died, and for what? For a cause that is lost? For a man who would use you for political reasons?"

"Who told you?" she asked in a shaky whisper. He should have let her drink the poisoned wine; it would save him the trouble of killing her himself.

"The witch."

"Nadia? How did . . ." Her sentence fell off. Nadia knew everything that went on inside the keep. But why would she tell Lyon?

"Ask me not how she knew. She stopped me on the stairs as I was coming to our chamber. She uttered but one sentence. She told me to 'ware the wine.' It took only a moment to realize what she meant."

"Nadia," Ariana repeated dully.

"Nadia," Lyon confirmed. "Where is the poison? Or have you used it all in the wine?"

It was far too late to deny the obvious; Ariana removed the vial from her pocket and placed it in Lyon's hand. He stared at it a moment, then picked up the flagon of wine and walked to the arched window. With an oath on his lips, he uncorked the vial and spilled the contents of both the vial and the wine flagon out the window. When he turned to face her again, his expression was stark and frightening.

Ariana realized that she had acted recklessly, in the heat of passion, and at the same time she knew that she would never have allowed Lyon to drink the poisoned wine. Despite the threat of severe punishment, she would have told him about the poison and stopped him from drinking it, even if she died at his hands for her sin. She faced him squarely now, her face pale, her head held high. Never would she show fear to the Lion of Normandy.

"I am ready for my punishment, my lord," Ariana said, meeting his eyes with unflinching courage.

"Take off your clothes."

Ariana shook slightly but did as he bade. When she stood before him, naked and vulnerable, she glanced up at him. With the handle of the lash he sketched a circle around each breast, then dragged it across her nipples. When they hardened into points, his eyes narrowed and his heart pounded. Ariana sucked in her breath as he drew the handle down her stomach and into the fluffy blonde hairs covering her mound. When he thrust it between her legs, she cried out in alarm.

"Turn around," he ordered harshly. He was becoming painfully aroused but refused to let it distract him. Once again she did as he asked, presenting her backside. " 'Tis a pity to mar all that lovely white flesh."

The lash handle moved again, this time over the firm mounds of her buttocks. They tautened—from fear, he supposed—but the reflexive motion was highly arousing. Her thighs were long and supple, her calves sleek; he recalled how they felt wrapped around his waist as he plowed her sweet belly. He grew harder. She dared a glance over her shoulder and saw him standing there, the lash slack in his hand, his eyes smoldering cauldrons of hot desire.

"I am ready, my lord. I cannot stand this waiting."

"Sweet Jesu, I cannot! Ten lashes will kill you.

Mayhap you're carrying my child." He swung her around to face him, trying to keep his gaze from fixing on her firm, coral-tipped breasts. " 'Tis Lord Edric's doing, is it not? He gave you the poison, did he not? I have no idea how or where your meeting took place, but I vow 'tis your last. I will have you watched night and day. If someone in my household is disloyal to me, he will be punished, no matter who he is. As for your oath of fealty to me, I want it not from a woman who has proven herself untrustworthy."

He grasped her arm, his grip brutal. "I warn you, lady, do not try me again. The next time I will not be so forgiving." Whirling on his heel, he stormed from the chamber, dragging the lash behind him.

Ariana stared at the door for several minutes, scarcely able to believe that she had escaped punishment. She expected Lyon to change his mind and return at any moment, this time wielding the whip with a vengeance. When she realized that he was not coming back, she slid to the floor in a dead faint.

Ariana had no idea how long she had lain on the floor, so great was her misery. Finally, she picked herself up and began dressing, her motions slow, her mind and emotions suspended. She was still stunned that she had entertained the notion, albeit briefly, of poisoning Lyon. He had come so close to drinking the wine, aye, so close. Yet not really close at all, for Nadia had forewarned him.

As if her thoughts had conjured up the witch, Ariana saw Nadia standing just inside the room. Ariana started violently. The woman was indeed a witch. She appeared and disappeared without being seen or heard.

"Ye are well, my lady?" Nadia asked. Her bright eyes bore into Ariana with compelling intensity.

"You should have considered my state of health before you told Lyon about the poisoned wine," Ariana charged. "I had not thought you a traitor, Nadia. How did you know?"

"Nay, Ariana, no traitor. Ye know I see things others cannot. 'Tis not Lyon's time to die. Cragmere has need of him."

Ariana felt a jolt of remorse. "I would not have let him die. Did your vision not tell you I would not have allowed Lyon to drink the wine? You know that Lyon had every right to kill me for what I attempted, do you not?"

"My visions are not always clear. I would not have warned the Lion if I believed he would have harmed ye. On yer wedding day I warned ye to 'ware the Lion, my lady. Ye did not heed me. Cragmere's safety now depends on the Lion. Yer own life depends on him. 'Twould not serve had ye killed him as Lord Edric wished. Once Malcolm of Scotland gets his hands on Cragmere, he will betray both ye and Edric."

"You know nothing, witch!" Ariana cried, denying that which she already suspected. "I do not need Lord Lyon to protect me or my land."

"Heed me well, my lady. Ye need the Lion,

just as he needs ye. If ye betray him again, he will be forced to deal harshly with ye."

"Spare me your advice. Since when have you become a staunch defender of my husband? You hate Normans as much as I do."

"Times change, Ariana, and ye must change with them. I have seen things ye would not believe." Her eyes turned glassy and her voice lowered into a toneless drone. "The Normans are here to stay. William the Bastard rules our land with an iron fist, and all who oppose him will fall beneath his mighty sword. He deals harshly with his enemies. Yer future lies with the Lion. Yer children will be vassals of William the Bastard. All these things will come to pass."

Ariana covered her mouth with the back of her hand to stifle a cry of dismay. Was Nadia right? Did she belong with Lyon? Nay! What about her own visions? One of them had already come to pass. She had been given the choice of life or death over Lyon, and she had chosen to let him live. At the last minute, she had sought to divert the poisoned wine from his lips, thus giving him life. She closed her eyes, recalling the specter of death she had envisioned hovering above Lyon. She had felt the coldness of the tomb upon her flesh. Was it her own death or Lyon's her vision had foretold? When she opened her eyes to challenge Nadia, the witch was gone, having left as silently as she had appeared.

Ariana paced the chamber. Her stomach growled hungrily, making her aware that she had eaten no midday meal and it was now the supper hour. She debated whether to go down to the hall to sup with Lyon and his men or to order a tray. Taking her courage in hand, she decided to test the waters. Lyon had said nothing about confining her to her chamber, and she'd be damned if she'd wait timidly for his approval to move about freely in her own home. Breathing deeply to still her wildly beating heart, she opened the door and peeked into the hallway. The whisper of voices drew her gaze to a dark corner, where two people were intimately entwined. When they broke apart, she wasn't overly surprised to see Tersa and Sir Beltane. She shut the door soundlessly and waited for them to leave.

Scant minutes later, Tersa entered the chamber. "Oh, my lady, please forgive me for causing you distress."

Ariana's brow furrowed. " 'Tis not your fault, Tersa."

"I should never have delivered Lord Edric's message. How did Lord Lyon find out? Did you tell him 'twas I who—?"

"Nay, Tersa, rest easy. Your name was not mentioned. Lord Lyon learned of it from . . . never mind, 'tis not important how he learned about it."

Tersa relaxed visibly. "Nevertheless, I'm sorry I carried the messages. 'Twas disloyal of me. Lord Lyon has been nothing but kind to me."

Ariana groaned. Was everyone except her enamored of her husband? "Do not fear, Tersa, I will not mention your name," she said, recalling Lyon's words about punishing anyone in his household who proved disloyal. "You must do nothing to anger him; 'tis too dangerous."

Tersa licked her lips nervously, cast a furtive glance over her shoulder, and asked, "You must have angered Lord Lyon greatly. I know not what the message from Lord Edric said, but Lord Lyon ordered a guard placed at your door. Beltane told me he is to watch you during the day, while Lord Lyon is occupied with other duties. He did not hurt you, did he, my lady?" Her concerned gaze swept the length of Ariana's body, looking for bruises or other signs of injury.

Ariana recalled the whip and how he had taunted her with it, wondering anew why he hadn't beaten her when she so richly deserved it. If Lyon wished to kill her, there was no one to gainsay him.

"Lord Lyon did not harm me, Tersa. But I do not know what the future holds for me. He does not trust me."

"He must love you a great deal," Tersa said dreamily. "My father would have slain my mother had he discovered her meeting secretly with another man. He is a generous man, my lord Lyon."

"Love me?" Ariana laughed derisively. "There is no love between me and Lord Lyon. Come, Tersa, I hunger. I will not starve myself because Lyon has placed me under guard."

*　　*　　*

Lyon stared morosely into his mug of ale, feeling Ariana's absence beside him keenly. He had not forbidden her to leave the chamber, but he doubted she had the courage to appear in the hall to partake of the evening meal.

Poison! Jesu! She had attempted to kill him. It mattered not that she had tried to prevent him from drinking the poisoned wine at the last minute. What mattered was that the intent was there, fueled by a man who would take his place in her bed once her legal husband had been disposed of. The man was as good as dead, Lyon vowed. He would risk William's wrath, lay siege to Blackheath, and slay the Saxon bastard.

Suddenly a hush fell over the hall. Lyon drained the mug of ale in one gulp and looked up just as Ariana swept into the room. No one, except for Beltane, suspected that she had tried to poison him, yet all were aware that she had done something reprehensible to cause Lyon to place her under guard. Her own people feared for her, and Lyon's knights knew not what to make of the situation.

Ariana felt curious eyes follow her as she took her place at the head of the table next to Lyon. She did not flinch or lower her head, but kept her eyes fixed on something in the distance as she slid into her chair.

Motioning for a serf to refill his mug, Lyon took another long draught of ale, then carefully set the mug down. "I did not think you would join us, lady."

"I did not think you wished me to starve, my

123

lord," Ariana replied with forced calmness.

"Mayhap you wish to poison my ale," he said in a voice for her ears only.

Ariana paled visibly. "I . . . I would not have let you drink the poison. I could not have done it."

"So you say."

"You know 'tis true. I tried to stop you. I do not want your death on my hands." She lowered her head. "I do not want your death at all."

Lyon stared at her. "'Spare me your false sentiments, my lady."

"What are you going to do to me?"

"Mayhap, after I'm sure you're not increasing, I'll send you back to the abbey. If you are increasing, I'll wait until our child is born before sending you away. And you can forget about Lord Edric. If fortune shines on me, I will present Lord Edric's head to you in a basket."

Bile rose in Ariana throat and she clasped a hand over her mouth. "Bastard!"

"Aye, I freely admit it."

"You are an animal, a heartless Norman beast."

"So I have been told. How do you think the Lion earned his name?"

Chapter Six

Ariana tried to flee the hall the moment her stomach was sufficiently full. Never had she felt such overwhelming rejection. Everyone in the hall seemed to be staring at her, accusing her of unspeakable things. She excused herself and started to rise from the chair, when the condemning weight of Lyon's hard hand fell upon her arm.

"Are you leaving so soon, my lady?" he asked with cool disdain.

"I—I grow weary," Ariana replied, glancing at him through lowered lids. In the flickering torchlight, his profile appeared harsh and arrogantly masculine. And he was big, overwhelmingly big.

"Go then and await my pleasure. Tomorrow I lay siege to Blackheath, and the need for a woman is always fierce within me before battle." His hand on her arm relaxed, and she pulled free.

Ariana stared at him for the space of a heartbeat, then turned and fled. Lyon watched her disappear into the north tower, his expression brooding, his eyes dark with an emotion he refused to acknowledge. When a villein ushered in a messenger from the king a few minutes later, Lyon was still staring after Ariana and had to force his attention to the messenger.

Unrolling the thin sheet of parchment, Lyon read the message, slammed his fist on the table, and spat out an oath. "God's blood! The king orders me to Londontown. He is calling a meeting of the Witenagemot. And since I am a baron and major landholder in the north, I am required to attend the council meeting," he told Beltane, who stood at his elbow while he read. "He asks that I bring Ariana with me."

"What of the siege, Lord Lyon? The men were looking forward to attacking Blackheath. It has been a long time since we've ridden to battle."

Lyon frowned. "We ride to Londontown, Beltane. William commands it. Tomorrow we will prepare for the journey and leave the day after that. The Witenagemot convenes in two weeks. You will ride in my escort. Choose the men you wish to leave behind to guard the keep."

"Aye, my lord. I fear your lady will balk at visiting the Norman stronghold."

"Aye, I know that. At least there is no one for her to conspire with in Londontown."

* * *

Ariana was sleeping when Lyon entered their chamber much later. He undressed quickly and slid into bed beside her. He felt the scorching heat of her body through her thin shift, and his response was immediate and violent. God's toenails! Was he to suffer through life wanting his own wife with a need that was tormenting to both body and soul? He didn't want to need anyone with such consuming fury, especially a faithless woman who hated him with every fiber of her being. Not all women hated Normans, he consoled himself. His mistress Zabrina couldn't get enough of him. With mixed feelings, he thought about seeing Zabrina again in Londontown. His cold, haughty wife might look down her nose at him, but Zabrina would welcome him.

"Wake up, lady," Lyon said, giving Ariana a little shake. "Wake up and greet your husband."

Ariana woke with a start, dismayed to find Lyon's hand on her thigh. She groaned in protest. Hadn't he punished her enough? " 'Tis late," she complained. "What do you wish of me?"

"Merely to talk. Your body holds no appeals for me," he lied. He'd rather test his body to the limit of its endurance than let her know how much he still wanted her. How desperately he yearned for her to come willingly into his arms and open to him with eager acceptance.

Ariana heaved a sigh of relief. The last thing she wanted was for Lyon to turn her body into a mindless mass of writhing, quivering flesh, burning for his touch. "What more is there to say, unless it is to convince you to abandon your plan to lay siege to Blackheath?"

"William has summoned us to Londontown; there will be no siege."

Ariana blinked up at him. No siege? God had heard her prayer! But Londontown? The very thought made her shudder with dread. "Londontown!" she said harshly. "I do not wish to go."

"Your wishes do not count. William commands it. He is calling a meeting of the Witenagemot and I am to attend. He requests that you accompany me; his queen wishes to meet you. You will like Matilda; she is a saint among women. You have tomorrow to pack and prepare for the trip. We will leave the following day."

" 'Tis not enough time to prepare!" Panic colored her words. She didn't want to meet the Conqueror or his queen, no matter how saintly the woman. She hated William. Hated all Normans. She'd never been to Londontown. The court was a wicked place, she'd heard, despite William's efforts to keep it moral.

"It will have to suffice," Lyon said grumpily. He was trying his best to ignore the drugging effect her closeness had upon him. Jesu! She had tried to poison him—how could he still want her? "Go to sleep; 'tis late."

* * *

When Ariana awoke the next morning, Lyon was gone. She arose hastily, mentally tallying all that needed to be done before leaving on their journey to Londontown the next day. The very thought sent her senses reeling. In Londontown she had no friends, no one to protect her from Lyon and the Conqueror. At least at Cragmere she was surrounded by those she had known as a child, and Edric was near at hand should she need him. In Londontown she would be surrounded by despicable Normans.

Ariana's thoughts skidded to a halt when Tersa entered the chamber to help her dress. "Good morrow, my lady. Lord Lyon bade me help you pack for your trip." Her cheerful manner did not set well with Ariana, whose own mood was dark and unsettled.

"You seem unusually cheerful this morning, Tersa. Is Beltane the cause of your happiness?"

"Lord Lyon said I am to go to Londontown with you," Tersa said gleefully. "Isn't it wonderful? Londontown! It must be a grand place. I never dreamed I'd actually see it one day. And Beltane is to go, too," she added shyly. "I'm grateful to Lord Lyon for including me."

The corners of Ariana's mouth turned down. Lord Lyon said. Was the entire household becoming enamored of her husband? He had stolen her home, and now he was stealing her people. "I'm glad you approve of my husband," she said with brittle sarcasm. "I am perfectly capable of dressing myself. But if I am to make a good showing at court, I must be properly clothed. Summon women from the village. There must be chests of my mother's clothing around somewhere in the keep that can be altered to fit me. I have only this day to put together an adequate wardrobe."

The day progressed with alarming speed. There was so much to do and so little time. Ariana indeed found several chests of her mother's clothing, which needed little or no altering. Some of the more elegant surcoats were trimmed in ermine and other precious furs, and Ariana felt certain she would be as well turned out as any lady at William's court. She also found jeweled girdles, broaches, and pins among the clothing.

By the end of the day her chests were packed and nothing remained to be done except bid her people good-bye. She had no idea how long the council would meet or when they would return, but she trusted Keane to keep things running smoothly at Cragmere in their absence.

Ariana had caught no more than a passing glimpse of Lyon the entire day. She knew he had much to do to prepare for their trip and was grateful for his absence. She had escaped the whipping he had promised but not his wrath. Punishment took many forms, and there was no doubt in Ariana's mind that Lyon would find another way to make her life miserable. Why in God's name had she ever considered poisoning Lyon? Why had she listened to Edric? She had never wanted Lyon's death. She might have refused to swear fealty to him, but he was still her husband. He had goaded her into doing something despicable, something she'd regret the rest of her days.

Ariana entered her bedchamber, too tired to sup in the hall with Lyon and his knights. The room was dimly lit; only firelight from the hearth relieved the darkness beyond. She sat down on the bed to await the tray she'd ordered, her mind in a turmoil. She had no idea what to expect in Londontown, surrounded by the enemy. Fear of the unknown turned her thoughts inward. Then, without warning, the room began to spin around her. Swirling mist surrounded her, and when it cleared she was no longer in her chamber.

Her vision revealed a large hall filled with many people—men and women in fine dress, laughing and conversing. She saw a dark man, solid and compactly built, wearing a crown. And she saw Lyon. Hovering behind Lyon was a woman of enormous beauty, richly dressed and bejeweled. She was simpering up at him, her eyes dark and inviting. Ariana sensed her own presence, though it lacked substance, as if she were merely an onlooker, invisible to those assembled in the hall. Then Ariana perceived a dark, threatening aura in the room. The dark specter drifted aimlessly, then paused briefly to hover directly over Lyon. Abruptly the specter turned and moved in Ariana's direction, growing darker and more threatening.

Danger!

She saw it clearly.

An enemy awaited her at court.

She sensed it with every fiber of her being. She screamed and slid effortlessly into unconsciousness, ending up on the floor beside the box bed.

Lyon walked slowly toward the bedchamber, wondering if he'd find Ariana asleep. Lord, he wanted the little vixen! As busy as he had been this day, he'd still found time to fantasize about her, to picture her tempting little body, her perfect breasts spread beneath him to feast upon. He recalled vividly how tight and hot she felt as she took his staff inside her and closed around him. He felt guilt over giving her no pleasure yesterday, but she had driven him too far into lust. He couldn't wait. He hadn't meant to bed her at all. Even after she had attempted to poison him, he wanted her. He had taken her first in anger, then in lust, then with a swift gentleness he was hard put to explain.

Standing just inside the room, Lyon gazed about the dimly lit chamber. He did not see Ariana at first, and a jolt of fear burst through him. He had been mistaken to place no guard on her today. He knew she didn't want to go to Londontown. Did she so fear the trip to the Norman stronghold that she would run away? He'd put nothing past the little witch. Not as long as Edric was waiting for her with open arms.

Then he saw her.

She was lying on the floor beside the bed, pale and unmoving. He flew to her side and dropped to his knees. He called her name softly and grew alarmed when she did not respond. He shook her gently, but she remained deeply sunk in unconsciousness. He stared at her for a moment, his gut churning with indecision. What should he do? Should he summon the priest or . . .

The witch.

Aye, the witch. He rose abruptly, intending to call out for a servant to summon Nadia when he felt a presence behind him. The hair rose on the back of his neck and he turned abruptly. Nadia was standing by the door, her gaze intent upon him. "I will take care of her, my lord."

Lyon started violently. "How did you know?"

Her eyes were inscrutable. "I have my ways. Leave us, my lord. I know what to do."

Lyon glared at her. "Think you it is another vision?"

Nadia mumbled something unintelligible, then urged him toward the door. "Go, my lord. Yer lady will come to no harm at my hands. I will call ye when Ariana has revived."

Reluctantly Lyon left the chamber, but he did not go far. He remained outside the door to await Nadia's summons.

Nadia knelt beside Ariana, removed a vial from her pocket, pulled out the stopper, and held it beneath her nose. Ariana coughed, sputtered, and slowly opened her eyes.

"What happened?"

"The Sight came upon ye, Ariana. Ye have never reacted so violently before. What did ye see?"

Ariana shuddered. "Danger," she whispered

shakily. "I have an enemy at court."

"Aye."

Ariana sent her a guarded look. "You know?"

"Aye, I saw it too. I came to warn ye. 'Ware the dark lady, Ariana. 'Ware her lies and spiteful ways. She means ye harm."

"Do you know her name?"

"Nay. I know naught save she is fair to look upon. 'Ware her black heart and 'ware yer friends who would lead ye astray."

Ariana rose shakily to her feet. "Why should I trust you after the way you betrayed me to Lyon? You have become the Lion's pawn."

"Nay, Ariana, I am still faithful to ye. 'Twas for yer own good that I told the Lion about the poison. Ye need Lyon. Cragmere needs him. Ye would gain naught from his death and lose much. Mayhap even Cragmere."

Ariana's mind whirled in confusion. Her vision had given her much to ponder. Was the danger at court to herself or to Lyon? And what of the beautiful dark woman she had seen? Was she the same treacherous lady Nadia warned her about? Could she even trust Nadia?

"Go now, Nadia, I wish to be alone. My vision was frightening, and I need to think on how to protect myself and Lyon." She did not think it strange that she would wish to protect Lyon.

"Yer husband waits without."

"Lyon is here?"

"He found ye, my lady. I said I would summon him when ye were yerself again. I fear he grows impatient."

As if to prove her words, Lyon stuck his head inside the door. "How is she, Nadia?"

"I am well, my lord," Ariana said, forestalling Nadia's answer.

"Heed my words, Ariana," Nadia whispered as she sidled past Ariana and out the door. "'Ware the dark lady." Lyon closed the door firmly behind Nadia before turning back to Ariana.

He searched her face, noting her paleness and the rapid rise and fall of her breast. "You don't look well. What happened?"

" 'Tis naught, my lord."

He didn't believe her. "You had another vision. What did you see?"

She turned away to stare into the hearth. The fire etched bewitching patterns upon her face, and Lyon was struck by her ethereal beauty. She seemed as elusive as a mist, as mysterious as a fairy spirit. For the briefest moment he was frightened by her power to "see" things. Then he shook his head to clear it of such disturbing thoughts. Ariana was but a woman, weak in all the ways women were weak.

Ariana gnawed her bottom lip as she considered her answer. Would Lyon believe her if she told him she sensed danger at court? Nay, she doubted it. He was too arrogant to pay her the slightest heed. Yet . . . yet her vision had been so real, the danger so fearful.

"Tell me, lady, what did you see?" His soft words held a core of steel. He would not be satisfied until she revealed her vision.

Ariana whirled on her heel to face him. "There is danger at court, my lord. An enemy awaits us there."

Lyon searched her face, not at all convinced. He tried not to laugh. "Who is this enemy, Ariana?"

She looked away. "I . . . I do not know."

"Your enemy or mine?"

"I . . . Mine, I think. Or mayhap the danger is to both of us, I know not. Please, my lord, do not go to Londontown. Tell King William that you cannot attend the council. Tell him you must oversee the harvest. Tell him anything. I fear that evil is afoot in Londontown."

Lyon scoffed derisively. "Only friends await us in Londontown. Men with whom I fought and lived for many years. My king awaits in Londontown. No evil, no danger."

"William is not my king," Ariana said earnestly. "Go then without me. I care not to mingle with Normans. My vision—"

"Your vision is but a figment of your imagination. No danger awaits us in Londontown. Unless," he added ominously, "you have sent word to Lord Edric about our plans to journey to Londontown. Is he planning some mischief?"

Ariana recoiled as if slapped. She supposed she deserved that. "Nay, my lord, why would I tell Lord Edric? You accuse me unjustly."

Lyon paced back and forth before Ariana. She watched him warily, aware of his low regard for her. He was dressed in tunic and chausses, his feet encased in soft leather boots. The bulging muscles of his thighs reminded her of his strength and virility and the set of his shoulders gave hint to his implacable will and determination. She imagined how he must look to other women and understood immediately that there would be more than one kind of danger at court. Nadia had already warned her of another woman.

"I do not frighten easily, Ariana," Lyon said gruffly. "I will overcome any imagined evil that awaits us in Londontown."

"What of me, my lord?" Ariana asked softly. "What if the danger is to me?"

Lyon's smile was not reassuring. "Think you I cannot protect you?"

"I do not doubt your prowess with weapons, my lord, but what if other evil is afoot? Evil you cannot fight with weapons?"

"You speak in riddles, Ariana. A strong arm is all that is needed against one's enemy. Were you not so fanciful a creature, you would recognize the logic of my words. I do not believe in visions, nor any other kind of spiritual phenomena. 'Tis time we prepared for bed. We leave with the dawn."

Lyon stripped quickly and slipped into bed while Ariana stood with her back to him. She heard the bed protest his weight, then whirled around to face him. "Is there nothing I can say to change your mind?"

"Nay," Lyon said, growing weary of the subject. "I must answer William's summons." Deliberately he turned his back on her. He feared that if he watched her bare her lovely flesh, he'd lose control. His body wanted to love her, but his mind utterly rejected the notion of making love to a woman who wished him dead.

Would she really have stopped him from drinking the poisoned wine? he wondered, not for the first time. How badly did she want Edric? He already knew the answer. Badly enough to kill her husband. He mocked himself for a fool. There were no surprises where Ariana was concerned. She hated Normans. She hated him. She wanted him dead and would have succeeded had the witch not interfered.

Lyon felt the bed shift slightly as Ariana eased into bed and moved as far away from him as possible. Just as well, he thought as he composed himself for sleep. He didn't want to need any woman to the point that it made him weak. He didn't want to confront feelings better left unexplored, but he could not purge them from his mind. It defied all rationality that a man of his firm will and strength could want such a treacherous woman.

All that nonsense about danger awaiting them in Londontown irked him. He didn't believe in visions. He believed in strength and courage and survival. He believed in William and in England. And he believed in himself.

The heat of her body tormented him. It seemed to follow him no matter how he arranged his body. He could leave the bed and seek his rest elsewhere, he supposed. Or he could take what was his and use Ariana as she was meant to be used. As God intended.

He reached for her, dragging her into his arms.

His lips found hers. Before she had fully awakened, her body rose up to meet his.

She had been seduced from sleep, and it was too late to quell the clamoring of her body, the quivering of her flesh, the aching response he wrung from her. She wanted to deny him. To lie passive beneath the magic of his touch, unmoved no matter what he did to her.

But the harsh demand of his mouth and hands wooed her, excited her, made her tremble with anticipation. His touch renewed her craving for that indescribable sensation of yearning, seeking, reaching, attaining that ultimate plateau where only Lyon could take her.

He touched her in a vulnerable place and she cried out, losing the battle that had never really begun. This time he did not deny her the pleasure she craved.

The next morning, Ariana was waiting beside her horse as a rosy dawn crept over the horizon. She had broken her fast in the hall, barely finding the strength to eat. She was exhausted. It sickened her to recall how Lyon had reached for her in the night and how eagerly she had turned to him. Once again he had used her, though this time he was careful to give her extraordinary pleasure. Afterward he had shoved himself off her and turned away, his rejection hurting more than she cared to admit. Filled with bitterness, she had finally fallen asleep. Tersa had awakened her before dawn. Lyon was already gone, the place where his body rested cold to the touch.

" 'Tis time, lady," Lyon said as he approached Ariana.

He placed his hands on her waist and lifted her easily into the saddle. Then he mounted his destrier and rode beside her through the gate, past the barbican, and over the drawbridge. A dozen men fell in behind them, followed by a cart bearing supplies and equipment for camping outdoors when no lodging was available to them. Obviously Lyon intended for them to travel in comfort.

The first night was spent at a Norman keep. Lord Alain, who had fought beside Lyon at Hastings, resided in a grand manor that had once belonged to a powerful Saxon lord. Early in his reign, the Conqueror had rewarded his loyal men with manors and titles that had once belonged to Saxons, thereby gaining him lands and people faithful to his cause. If not for William's largess, men like Lyon would still be landless knights without hope of title or property. Ariana had experienced personally William's penchant for granting land and wives indiscriminately. She had been one of his first victims.

Pleading exhaustion, Ariana retired directly after the evening meal. Lord Alain had a Norman wife, and Ariana could not bear the simpering, gloating woman who made it abundantly clear that the only reason a rebellious Saxon was allowed beneath her roof was because of Lord Lyon. Ariana went to sleep alone and awoke alone, much to her vast relief.

There was a sameness to the days and nights as they traveled south to Londontown. Most nights they found lodging at various manors and keeps, or in towns which they passed through. When they entered York, she saw for herself the destruction wrought by William and his army against defiant Saxons who resisted Norman rule. For miles around, crops and villages had been burned and cattle and people slaughtered. Ariana pitied the people who had risen in protest of William's rule, for he had been ruthless in his punishment.

"William is a cruel man to have wrought such destruction upon the people," Ariana said sadly as she rode through the devastated land.

"Cruel to those who resist his rule," Lyon responded harshly. "If he didn't put down all rebellions with relentless severity, the country would be forever torn by strife."

"Are there any Saxon nobles left?" she asked contemptuously.

"Very few," Lyon answered honestly. "Most have been dispossessed in favor of Norman knights. Those who are left have been demoted in rank, like Lord Edric. In order to keep their lands, they were required to pay homage to William."

"Aye," Ariana said with scathing contempt. "Some of our noble Saxons roam the country without homes or property. Common people can no longer hunt in the forests for game. William has declared all forests royal territory and our people must find food elsewhere or starve. They are required to pay exorbitant taxes in districts where a Norman was killed by unknown assailants. Do you wonder why Normans are hated and reviled?"

Lyon's face remained impassive. He was well aware of William's relentless cruelty when forced to uphold his laws, but he also knew of William's kindnesses. He was loyal to those who served him, kind and generous to his friends, and religiously faithful to his wife. He was a moral man, who sought to impose his code of honor upon his court with little or no success. He was a rough warrior, a bastard like himself, who had fought and fought hard for all he owned and held in his name.

"You do not know William as I do," Lyon said with waning patience. "He must be ever vigilant, ever protective of his conquered lands. Aye, he has rewarded his followers with land and titles, but each of them, myself included, is required to provide the king with a sufficiency of men practiced in the art of fighting on horseback. Each baron must be responsible for a certain number of fully armed knights to fill his army."

"I do not wish to know William at all," Ariana declared disdainfully as she turned her horse to join Tersa, riding at the rear of the party.

From that day until they reached Londontown, Ariana avoided Lyon's company. One or another of his knights usually rode beside her while Lyon rode ahead with Beltane. At night Lyon usually slept with his men in the hall of the manor where they passed the night, and during the day he didn't appear eager to resume conversation. Which suited Ariana just fine.

One day well into their journey, Lyon motioned for her to join him. She hadn't spoken privately with him in days, and it was obvious that he had something on his mind.

"Londontown lies before us, my lady," he told her. "Barring mishap, we should reach the gates tomorrow."

Ariana greeted the news with welcome relief. She had been in the saddle more than ten days and was weary to the bone, though in truth the journey hadn't been excessively difficult. The pace Lyon set had been neither overly strenuous nor challenging.

"I will not be unhappy to part company with my horse," she commented dryly. She knew he wished to say more and waited.

"I expect you to act with decorum in Londontown. We will abide with William in his tower. The king is not an unkind man and holds women in great esteem. Unless," he added by way of warning, "they are undeserving of his regard.

"When William sanctioned our marriage, he hoped we would find happiness together. I do not intend to tell him about the poison incident, for he would be most aggrieved. And I'd advise you to keep a civil tongue when speaking with William. Most people at court don't trust Saxons, especially those from the Borderlands."

"Most Saxons don't trust Normans," Ariana retaliated.

"Ariana . . ." His expression hardened. "I will have your promise that you'll act with proper respect. There are many Saxons at court; mayhap you will find your stay not quite as burdensome as you imagined."

Suddenly Ariana recalled her vision and Nadia's warning. Londontown and William's court was a dangerous and inhospitable place where dark undercurrents and potent enemies awaited them . . . or her. She began to shake as fearful images built in her mind. Images without faces or substance.

Lyon saw her tremble and frowned. "Ariana, what is it? Are you having another vision?"

Ariana shook her head. "Nay. I do not need a vision to know that danger exists at court."

"There is no danger," Lyon said, his tone patronizing. "And if there is, I will protect you. Now, my lady, I will have your promise that you will behave like a dutiful wife while in Londontown."

She searched his face, noting a subtle change in his expression. She was startled to find a hint of pleading in the clear blue of his eyes. And something else, something so elusive and undefined that she almost missed it. But the rapid beating of her heart told her she hadn't been mistaken.

She offered him a shy smile, the first she had willingly given. The effect upon Lyon was immediate and startling. Her lovely features were illuminated with splendid radiance, transfixing him. His heart thudded so fiercely within his breast, he feared it would burst through his rib cage. If she would but smile at him like that all the time, she would have him groveling at her feet. That thought was not comforting.

"Aye, my lord, I will be most dutiful, as long as I am not forced to endure William's company too long."

Chapter Seven

William's tower, started shortly after the conquest, sat on a little hill on the northern bank of the river Thames in the southeast corner of the old Roman city walls. The first stage, built of wood on an earthen mound and surrounded by a ditch, was an imposing structure situated in the heart of Londontown. It held a commanding view of both the river and the city. The tower itself was surmounted by a palisaded rampart.

As they approached the city, Ariana could see the outline of Westminster Abbey in the distance, which had been finished in 1065 by Edward the Confessor. Also in various stages of construction were three great fortresses surrounding Londontown, all ordered to be built by William as "protection against the fickleness of the vast and fierce populace," as he phrased it.

Ariana and Lyon rode through the old Roman gate in silence, Ariana too enthralled by the teeming population scurrying to and fro through the narrow streets and alleys to offer comment. Street sellers appeared on every corner, hawking wares of all kinds. A variety of smells wafted to her on the breeze, some pleasant, others not so pleasant.

They traveled the streets with little fanfare, knights and noblemen being a common sight in Londontown. Many rich and noble families resided in the city, all bent upon their own pleasure and enjoyment while the common people struggled to put food on their tables.

"The tower lies directly ahead of us," Lyon said as he directed Ariana past a crowded marketplace sporting more peddlers than she had ever seen gathered in one place.

Ariana swallowed hard and nodded. Soon she'd be in the Norman stronghold, a lamb among lions. And her husband was the fiercest lion of all. Fear seized her. Would she recognize the danger awaiting them? she wondered. Or would it come without warning, when she least expected it?

Lyon smiled, transforming his brooding features. His smile was beguiling, and Ariana stared at him in awe. If he smiled at her like that very often, she'd be reduced to a gibbering idiot.

Lyon noted the tightness around Ariana's

mouth and sought to ease her fears. "Forget that nonsense about danger, Ariana. No one will harm you here. I am well loved by William, and he will love you also."

Ariana blinked. William love her? She doubted it. "I do not wish to be loved, or even liked, by your Norman king, or by any other Norman."

"Not even by one Norman?" he asked, hinting at their passionate encounters in the dark of night.

Ariana blushed and looked away. "Nay," she lied. She heard a rumbling sound and realized that Lyon was laughing. She knew he was remembering those nights when he reached for her and she responded with aching desire.

"We shall see, lady," he said cryptically, "we shall see."

Cries of welcome greeted Ariana and Lyon as they rode through the palisade surrounding William's tower. Apparently her husband was easily recognized and well liked, just as he'd said. Villeins took their horses when they dismounted, and William's seneschal met them at the entrance.

"Welcome, Lord Lyon. King William is anxiously awaiting you and your lady. He is preparing for tomorrow's meeting of the Witenagemot now but will greet you in the hall tonight. Come, I will show you to your chamber."

" 'Tis good to be back, Royce," Lyon declared. "How fares William?"

"Well, my lord, well indeed since his lady wife has arrived from Normandy."

They entered a large hall, and Ariana looked around in awe. More than twice the size of the hall at Cragmere, the chamber was crowded with people wandering aimlessly about in various pursuits. Many were noblemen who had been summoned to attend the Witenagemot. The men were richly dressed in fur-trimmed tunics and brightly colored chausses. The women looked like flower gardens in their colorful surcotes and sparkling jewels. There was a hum of curiosity when she and Lyon entered the hall, followed by Tersa and Beltane the Bold.

The Lion of Normandy was hailed with affection and respect by both men and women alike. Their progress through the hall seemed to take forever, and Ariana tried not to recoil in revulsion when they were greeted effusively by Lyon's friends in their native French, the language of the court. How she wished the floor would open up and swallow her. How she wished she was back at Cragmere, where she felt safe among people she had known since childhood. These Normans were the same men who had killed her father and brothers, stolen land and titles from Saxon barons, and threatened those who resisted Norman rule.

From the corner of his eye, Lyon noted that Ariana seemed to be having difficulty coping with so many Normans in one room and decided against introducing her to any more of his friends. There would be plenty of time for that later, he reflected, after they had shared the evening meal with William and she saw that the king meant her no harm. Realizing that he would be kept in the hall greeting friends longer than he'd like, he quietly told Royce to take Ariana to their chamber. When Royce bade Ariana follow him, she looked at Lyon for direction.

"Go with Royce, Ariana. He will see that you have everything you need. I will join you when I can. Why don't you rest before meeting William tonight? We are to sit with him at the high table." He did not need to add that she would be on public display all evening.

Ariana nodded gratefully. Never had she felt such an overwhelming need to escape. She felt suffocated by Normans. They stared at her in open curiosity, which did little to allay her fears. Worse yet were the leering looks directed at her by men, as if she were fair game. And the women. Their close scrutiny and open hostility made her feel like a sacrificial lamb. Her vision had been lacking in scope. She had not just one enemy at court; she had many.

Following close on Royce's heels, Ariana looked back over her shoulder at Lyon as she passed from the hall. What she saw made her halt in her tracks. A dark, riveting beauty broke away from a group of people and headed directly for Lyon. With a delighted squeal, she threw herself into his arms, pressing her curvaceous little body against his intimately. The breath slammed from Ariana's chest, and she stifled her cry of dismay with the back of her hand.

"Do not look back, my lady," Tersa hissed as she nudged Ariana forward. "Do not give these Normans something to gossip about."

"Who is that woman?" Ariana asked softly.

"Beltane told me she is the Lady Zabrina, a widow of some means. She is William's ward. The king is looking for a proper husband for her, one to further his political needs."

Zabrina! Lyon's mistress.

Not waiting to see how Lyon responded to the woman's enthusiastic greeting, Ariana turned and hurried after Royce. Tersa followed close behind.

Royce led them up a winding staircase and through many passages, finally stopping before a door similar to others in the cavernous tower. Ariana wondered how she was expected to get from one place to another without becoming lost.

"I trust you will be comfortable here, my lady," Royce said, swinging open the door. "Queen Matilda picked it out herself. There is a footman stationed nearby should you want for anything. Your serving woman can sleep with the other servants on the floor above when she is not serving you." He bowed low. "My lady." Then he took his leave.

" 'Tis grand, my lady," Tersa said as she inspected the sumptuous chamber. A huge box bed dominated the room, which sported a stone hearth stretching across one entire wall. Woven tapestries hung along the other walls. A woven carpet on the floor was a luxury she did not have at Cragmere. It felt soft and luxurious beneath the soles of her shoes.

"Aye," Ariana said sourly, still thinking of the woman who had thrown herself into Lyon's arms. "The king taxes the poor so that he may live in luxury."

"Do you wish to bathe, my lady? I will see if I can find someone to carry water up to you."

"Aye, a bath would be wonderful."

After Tersa left the room, Ariana walked to the tall, arched window and gazed down upon the river Thames. She watched boats sailing up and down the heavily traveled waterway and tried hard not to think about Lyon and Zabrina together. Was he with her now, privately renewing their friendship? Was he kissing her? Was he telling her how very much he missed her, how desperately he wanted her? Jesu! She could not bear it.

Lyon was anything but pleased by Zabrina's public show of affection. His gaze followed Ariana as she walked from the hall, then stopped to look back at him. Her dismay had been visibly apparent when she saw Zabrina rush up to him and wind her lovely white arms around his neck. By the time he'd escaped her clinging grasp and stepped away, Ariana had turned and fled up the winding staircase.

"Behave yourself, Zabrina," Lyon hissed as he held her away from him.

Zabrina sent him a beguiling smile. "You must forgive me for forgetting myself, my lord," she whispered coyly. "I've missed you most dreadfully."

Lyon sent her an amused glance. "I doubt that, Zabrina. Have you found no one at court to console you during my absence?"

"None to compare with you, my lord." Her full red lips turned downward into a charming pout.

" 'Twas not well done of you, Zabrina, to act so brazenly with my lady wife present."

Zabrina glanced disparagingly at Ariana's departing figure, her violet eyes dark with scorn. "Everyone knows how little you care for your wife and how the king had to force you to claim her from the convent. It should not matter to you if she sees us together. If she doesn't already know, she will hear soon enough that you and I are . . . more than just good friends. When can we be together again? I burn for you, Lyon. Will you come to me tonight?"

Lyon frowned. Had Zabrina always been so bold, so blatantly wanton? He searched her face, well aware of her vibrant beauty, the richness of her dark hair, the sensual promise of her unusual violet eyes, the lush fullness of her mouth. And he saw something else he'd never noticed before. There was a wicked gleam in her eyes that could only be described as greedy. The sensual pout she affected with such success now appeared avaricious and bold.

His gaze traveled downward over her tempting little body. Her purple velvet surcoat was magnificent, elaborately embroidered along the hem and sleeves with gold thread and trimmed in ermine. A golden girdle encased her narrow waist, heavily encrusted with jewels, and her veil was of the finest silk, held in place by a gold circlet embellished with a variety of gems. He admired the circlet and pictured it on Ariana's silver-blond tresses.

Lyon did not have to wonder about the treasures that lay hidden beneath Zabrina's finery, for he'd seen them more times than he could count. He was intimately familiar with every lush curve of her body, knew where she liked to be touched, how to make her hot and eager for him. She had been married at thirteen to an old man, a Saxon nobleman, who conveniently died after three years and left her enormously rich. Lyon had no doubt that Zabrina had taken many lovers before William's conquest of England, for she was a hot-blooded wench who knew well how to please a man.

When William learned that Zabrina was a wealthy young widow in possession of vast lands, he made her a ward of the crown and seized her lands in the name of England. She met Lyon at court after his return from Normandy in 1069 and had been his mistress ever since. Evidently she didn't share Ariana's hatred for her Norman conquerors.

Zabrina glowed under Lyon's slow perusal. She knew him so well. The colorless girl he'd married could not hold a candle to her own vibrant beauty. She imagined that the little nun had run away screaming the first time Lyon tried to bed her. The wench couldn't possibly satisfy a lusty man like Lyon, she thought disparagingly. And Lyon was the only man who could completely gratify her own sensual nature. She had tried many men in his absence and had been dissatisfied with them all. Now that he was back in Londontown, she fully intended to have him in her bed again. She knew William wouldn't like it, but if they were discreet the king need not know.

"Will you come to me tonight, my lord?" Zabrina repeated in a voice ripe with promise. "You will not be sorry."

"Nay, lady, not tonight," Lyon said, surprising himself. A month ago he would have taken her with or without an invitation and enjoyed her with gusto. He knew her so well but had never loved her in the same way that William loved Matilda. The nights spent in Zabrina's bed were memorable and immensely pleasurable, but he had never felt the urge for a permanent relationship.

"Soon, my lord," Zabrina said heatedly. "Make it soon. I will be waiting." She sent him a look that scorched his skin, then turned and walked away, her hips swaying provocatively.

"Lady Zabrina was most insistent," Beltane said.

"You heard?" Lyon asked his lieutenant. He wasn't surprised to find Beltane standing at his elbow. He and Beltane had been together a long time; they shared both good and bad times.

"Aye, I heard. What of your lady wife? Will you take up with your mistress while at court?"

"Mayhap," Lyon replied honestly, "and mayhap not. 'Tis naught for you to be concerned about."

Beltane gave him a disapproving look, which surprised Lyon, for Beltane was his staunchest champion.

"What's amiss, Beltane? Why do you disapprove? You have never questioned me before."

"That was before I knew Lady Ariana."

Lyon snorted disgustedly. "The lady tried to poison me."

"Tersa says her mistress would never have allowed you to drink of the potion. Mayhap you pushed her too far."

Lyon scowled. "And mayhap my lady wife wished me dead so she could wed another. Go, Beltane, and see that the men are quartered comfortably."

With a curt nod, Beltane turned and strode away, his passage noted by many. Tall, blond, and muscular, his rugged good looks attracted the eye of more than one fair maiden.

Lyon approached the chamber Royce had directed him to and opened the door. It swung inward on silent hinges and Lyon stepped inside. He paused on the threshold, his heart hammering in his chest, mesmerized by the sight of Ariana at her bath. He stared intently at the soft curve of her elegant neck and back

156

as she leaned forward to rinse the soap from her hair. Tersa stood behind her, holding a linen bath cloth in readiness for her mistress to emerge from the tub. Lyon moved silently across the carpet, signaling Tersa to leave quietly as he took the cloth from her hands and positioned himself at Ariana's back. Tersa took one look at Lyon's fierce expression and fled.

"Oh, there is soap in my eyes, Tersa. Hand me the cloth, please." Her eyes tightly closed against the sting of soapsuds, Ariana held out a slim, white arm.

"Lift your face, my lady, so I may wipe the soap from your eyes."

Ariana started violently. She hadn't expected Lyon back so soon. She'd thought him pleasurably occupied with Lady Zabrina. Slowly she opened her eyes, dashing away the suds as she stared incredulously at Lyon. He bent and cupped the globe of her breast. Ariana cried out softly, splashing water over the side of the tub as she tried to escape the warmth of his caress.

"Nay, stay, Ariana, I will join you," Lyon said as he began stripping off his clothing.

Panic seized Ariana. "I am finished, my lord. You may have the tub to yourself."

She started to rise, but Lyon placed a hand on her shoulder, holding her firmly in place as he stepped into the tub and eased himself into the water. He slid down behind her, spreading his legs and bringing her into the vee of his body. Water overflowed the tub and sloshed onto the floor.

"Where is Tersa?" Ariana asked breathlessly.

"I sent her away."

He searched beneath the water, his hand brushing the slick folds of her womanhood. Ariana stiffened, feeling her flesh swell beneath his caress. His fingers grew bolder, more purposeful, thrusting inside her. Ariana cried out.

"Stop, please stop!"

Lyon smiled without mirth. "You do not really want me to stop, do you, my lady?"

Ariana could not move, could not speak. It had become nearly impossible to understand his words when he pulsed naked and hard against her bottom and his fingers surged forcibly inside her aching flesh.

He nipped at her neck, then licked it to soothe the hurt. His tongue was rough and hot and maddeningly thorough. While his one hand was busy below, he circled her breast and teased her nipple with the other. She bit her lip to keep from crying out her pleasure. But when he half turned her so he could take her breast in his mouth, she finally heard herself moan. He lifted his head, his face close to hers.

"Tell me you want me, my lady."

Ariana's eyes were glazed. It was all she could do to keep herself from reaching for him, clinging to him. "N . . . nay, I do not want you." The lie nearly strangled her.

He bent his head and took her other breast in his mouth, laving it with his tongue, rolling the nipple between his teeth while he found the tender nub of flesh at the opening of her thighs and gently rotated it with the rough pad of his thumb.

"Tell me you want me, my lady," he repeated. His voice was rough and broken as he manipulated her with his thumb.

Ariana knew an intense pleasure—and an intense need. Her fingers opened, curling around his biceps. Her eyes were wild, her breathing harsh.

"My lord . . ."

"Lyon. Call me Lyon. Open your sweet lips and say my name."

Ariana stared at him blankly—at his eyes, his mouth—and knew a need both fierce and hot. He half-smiled and half-grimaced, nearly stretched now beyond the limits of his endurance. "My name, Ariana. Say it."

"Lyon." Then more loudly. "Lyon!" She would say anything he asked if only he would continue to touch her.

"Jesu!" he cried as he surged to his feet with Ariana in his arms. He seemed not to care that water sloshed on the floor and dripped from their bodies as he carried her to the bed.

He laid her down gently, belying the fierce desire churning inside him. Then he knelt down beside her, bent low, and thirstily lapped the water clinging to her breasts and belly. He paused a moment to look into the vivid green pools of her eyes, then lowered his head and continued to feast on her succulent flesh, moving down her body toward a sweeter reward than he'd ever claimed. She began to whimper mindlessly, thrashing from side to side.

"My lord. Oh, Lyon, please."

"Aye, Ariana, I will please you. When you say my name so prettily, how can I deny you?" His mouth slid down the slick expanse of her flat belly, through the bright golden fleece guarding her womanhood, his tongue parting the dewy folds of swollen, aching flesh.

The moment his tongue touched her intimate parts Ariana arched wildly and cried out. "Lyon—oh, no, please, you must not."

"Aye, Ariana, I must," came his muffled reply. "You will like it, I promise."

Ariana tried to formulate a reply, but all reason left her as Lyon's tongue and mouth worked their magic upon her. Her head fell back and she was lost to all coherent thought. He stroked her until her pulse accelerated madly, until her heart pumped furiously and she moaned in helpless surrender. When she felt his finger ease into her and work in rhythm with his tongue, she arched violently upward. Placing a hand on her stomach to anchor her in place, he continued his tender torment, lashing her ruthlessly with the wet roughness of his tongue.

His white-hot breath spread liquid fire; her whole body began to vibrate. The splendor coursing through her was nearly unbearable. Her climax came abruptly and savagely. The muscles of her stomach tightened and she arched upward into the heat of Lyon's mouth, crying out as undulating waves of pure bliss consumed her.

Rising over her, Lyon watched Ariana's face and thought her more beautiful in the throes of climax than he'd ever seen her. Her face was flushed, her body alive and pulsing, her green eyes glazed with passion. As the final tremors passed through her, he lowered himself atop her until he rested above her on his elbows. Looking into her eyes, he rubbed the heavy head of his shaft against her swollen nether lips.

" 'Tis my turn, lady," he whispered hoarsely.

He pushed himself inside her, the wet heat of her desire welcoming him. His hips arched downward as he cupped her buttocks, pulling her up to meet his thrust. The size of him hurt her. He was larger than she remembered. At the height of his penetration she cried out, fearing she could not take all of him. But the discomfort lasted only a moment as their bodies locked together in magnificent union and he began to move, sliding in and out, her moistness easing their joining.

He heard her cry of pain, felt her muscles contract around him, and feared he had hurt her. He deliberately slowed his pace, willing himself to harness his driving need, and was surprised when Ariana's arms came around him and she arched upward to meet his thrusts. The pleasure she gave him was so great that he felt close to heaven. Lusting for the sweet taste of her, he kissed her pale face, her neck, her white breasts, so very close to him. When he caught her lips with his, the drumming in his ears was so loud that he did not hear her cry out his name when she climaxed a second time. But he felt it shudder through her and gave up his own seed in a tremendous outpouring of searing, liquid heat.

Lyon collapsed atop her, the sweating wall of his chest pressing against her breasts. When he heard her gasp for breath, he immediately rolled his weight off her. His own rasping breath sounded harsh and grating in the silence of the room. He glanced at Ariana and saw that she had scrambled as far away from him as she could get, her face turned away, one hand covering her eyes. He stared at her in consternation, wondering what there was about the little witch that tempted him so. He could have had Zabrina, whose passion was familiar to him, but he had declined, preferring to bed his own wife. Ariana pleased him beyond anything Zabrina could have done. Ariana was all sweet innocence and melting desire, a combination he seemed unable to resist.

He hadn't intended on bedding Ariana when he'd first entered the bedchamber. But seeing her in her bath, flushed from the warm water and sweetly inviting, had moved him in ways he couldn't explain. He didn't want to need her so desperately, but he couldn't help himself. He had no control where Ariana was concerned. His feelings for Ariana were sown not in his mind, but in the chambers of his heart. He knew he wasn't thinking rationally, but what he felt defied rationality. He could not put a name to his feelings, nor did he want to.

He reached out and touched her. "Lady."

"Do not torment me again, I beg you." How could she respond so wantonly to a man she hated? She felt too much shame to look him in the eye.

Lyon scowled in dismay. Did she still hate him so much? Was it so difficult to accept that he was her husband and he gave her pleasure?

"You can deny that I gave you pleasure if you dare." He gave her a mirthless smile. "But I would not believe you. Your breathless sighs and cries of delight tell me otherwise. Your hot sheath weeps for me and your white arms and legs cling to me. You want me, Ariana. Think you I do not know of such things?"

Ariana's arm flew away from her face and she glared at him. "Aye, you know of such things, my lord. You know how and where to touch me to make me cry out. You know ways to give me pleasure that make me blush. I doubt not that Lady Zabrina appreciates all the things you know. Compared to her I am an innocent."

His scowl grew fiercer. "You know naught."

"Zabrina is your mistress. Think you I do not know about her? Why aren't you with her now? I give you leave to go to her."

Lyon laughed harshly. "You give me leave? Ariana, if I wanted Zabrina, I would not ask your leave. Nay, lady, 'tis you I wanted. I thought I made that clear. If not, mayhap I should try harder to convince you." He dragged her into his arms.

"My lord. Lyon," she amended when he sent

her a dark look. " 'Tis late. The king is expecting us to sup with him."

Ariana could not have cared less about meeting William. What she didn't want was for Lyon to create that indescribable wanting inside her that turned her into a mindless pawn, his to do with as he pleased. What manner of man was he to make her into someone she neither recognized nor liked? Conflicting emotions warred inside her. She hated Lyon, didn't she? How could she hate him and desire him at the same time?

"There is plenty of time for what I have in mind, lady," he whispered huskily. "I would rather lie between your sweet thighs than feast at William's table, bountiful though it may be. Open to me, sweeting, and I will take you to Paradise."

His voice, low, coaxing, lulled her once again into doing his bidding as she opened to him and tasted Paradise, just as he promised.

Chapter Eight

Ariana looked about her nervously as she and
Lyon entered the great hall later that evening.
From the cacophony of voices drifting through
the narrow passages, it sounded as if everyone
had already assembled in the hall. Her stomach
was clenched tightly, and it was impossible to
steady her erratic pulse. She had no desire to
meet William, no desire at all. The Conqueror
was the most feared man in all of Christendom.
If rumors could be believed, he was a ruthless,
brooding man whose violent temper and relentless severity made people quake with fear.

The moment their entry was noted, a hush
fell over the hall. People turned in their direction, whispering behind their hands, their eyes
avid with curiosity. William, who was seated at
the high table on a dais, noted their entrance

immediately and stood up to greet them.

Ariana felt like a volcano about to erupt, and she came to a sudden stop. William's commanding presence was more powerful, more imposing than she'd imagined. He was built like a bull, a very strong bull, with barrel chest, legs like oak trees, and arms three times the size of hers. He looked as if he could wield a broadsword or mace with equal ease.

His hair was dark, like Lyon's, and his eyes keenly intelligent. She had the distinct feeling that he looked into her heart and found her lacking. His hair was shorn in the Norman manner, his face clean-shaven. By contrast, his queen was a small woman with a sweet but determined expression. Ariana could tell at a glance that the woman was quite capable of ruling Normandy in William's absence, as she had done for the past several years.

"Lord Lyon," William greeted in a booming voice. "I am truly aggrieved to call you back to Londontown so soon, but your presence is sorely needed at the council tomorrow." His penetrating gaze settled on Ariana, disconcerting her. "I am pleased you brought your lady wife with you. The years in the convent have been most kind to her. Ariana of Cragmere is a fitting bride for the Lion of Normandy." He slapped Lyon on the back and winked broadly. "Did I not tell you the time was ripe to claim your bride?"

Lyon appeared amused by William's words. "Aye, sire, 'twas long past time. Once again you were right." He gazed at Ariana. "Ariana of Cragmere pleases me greatly."

Ariana gasped, stunned by Lyon's bold pronouncement. Fortunately, she regained her composure in time to drop a curtsy to William. Had the king known her well, he would have guessed that the rosy flush creeping up her neck had nothing to do with embarrassment and everything to do with her hatred for Normans, including her husband. How dare Lyon lie so brazenly before all these people? She was well aware that Lyon had to be forced to claim her from the convent. He lusted for her, surely, but that didn't alter his feelings where she was concerned. He still held her accountable for conspiring with Edric to poison him.

William grasped Ariana's shoulders and pulled her to her feet. Then he presented her to his queen. Matilda was most gracious, and Ariana could not help liking her. Nevertheless, she was more than grateful when Royce pointed out their seats at the high table. Lyon took his place at William's right, while Ariana was seated next to Matilda. William and Matilda's sons Robert, who was destined to rule Normandy, and William Rufus, who had been promised England, were also seated at the high table.

Throughout the interminable meal, consisting of many courses including fish, meat, fowl, vegetables, and rich desserts, Lyon and William engaged in lively conversation. They appeared at ease with one another, like old friends. They both imbibed freely of the excellent wines and ales served by English servants, few of whom understood French, which was now the official language of England.

Ariana had learned French at the abbey but used it infrequently, for Lyon spoke to her mostly in English. She had to think carefully as she conversed with Matilda.

"I am pleased that you and Lord Lyon are happy in your marriage," Matilda confided. "William was worried that Lord Lyon would not settle down to it. Lyon seemed disinclined to claim you from the convent until William ordered him to do so. With unrest rife in the Borderlands, William needed a loyal baron in the north. Many of the dissident Saxon lords fled to Scotland after their lands were seized by the crown and are plotting with Malcolm to overthrow William's rule. William seriously doubts that all those Saxon lords who swore fealty are loyal to us. Poor William, so great a burden he bears."

Poor William, indeed, Ariana thought as she interpreted Matilda's words. The man was a tyrant. What did he expect? Aloud she said, "Have you forgotten that I am Saxon, madam? I do not wish to anger you, but I will not lie about where my loyalty lies."

Matilda sent her a shrewd look. "I would think less of you if you did not defend your countrymen. But you are married to a Norman now and owe fealty to your husband. A wife obeys her lord husband in all things. You are still young and have much to learn about marriage and trust between husband and wife. William hasn't always been an easy man to live with, but we have managed quite well throughout the years."

Ariana did not appreciate the lecture, though she supposed Matilda meant well. "I will think on your words," she said demurely.

Matilda searched Ariana's face, apparently satisfied by what she saw. "You care for Lyon, don't you, my dear? 'Tis obvious he cares for you."

Ariana frowned. Where in the world did Matilda get that idea? "Nay . . . that is . . . we hardly know one another." She lowered her head, pretending great interest in her food as Matilda turned to speak with the king.

Ariana stared at her trencher without appetite. She felt like a fish out of water in this Norman stronghold. Then she made the mistake of glancing at the noblemen, knights, and highborn women seated at long tables placed perpendicular to the dais. Her gaze settled on a woman who occupied a seat well above the salt.

Zabrina.

Zabrina's expression was hateful, malicious, and filled with resentment so potent that Ariana drew back in alarm. It took little imagination to realize that she had met the faceless enemy of her vision. Only the enemy now had a face as well as a name.

Supper was finally over and entertainment was brought in. A place was cleared in the center of the hall for the jugglers and acrobats, followed by a harpist and minstrels. After the entertainment, the men and women broke up into groups to play chess and other board games. Ariana took that as an excuse to escape to her chamber. But when she looked around for Lyon, he was nowhere to be found. She doubted she'd be able to find her way back to her chamber alone, so she went in search of Royce.

Lyon watched the minstrels with great pleasure. He wished he had been seated closer to Ariana, for he hadn't been able to speak with her during the entire meal to learn what she thought of William and Matilda. He wondered if she and Matilda had found common ground, since they seemed to be conversing quite easily. He started violently when he felt someone touch his shoulder. He turned abruptly, cursing beneath his breath when Zabrina whispered into his ear, bidding him to follow her into a curtained alcove, where assignations sometimes took place.

Lyon shook his head, denying her request, but she was most persistent. Rather than make a scene, he nodded his acquiescence, waiting until the entertainment ended and William's attention was centered elsewhere before disappearing into the curtained enclosure.

"God's nightgown, Zabrina, this is madness! What do you want of me?"

"You know what I want, my lord," Zabrina purred seductively. "Have I not made myself clear? 'Tis you I want, Lyon." She stepped closer and closer still, until her breasts pressed against his chest and her white arms circled his neck. "I'm mad for you, my lord. You promised that your wife would not change things between us."

"You are a bold wench, Zabrina. My lady wife . . ."

"That drab little mouse is a colorless, vapid creature who can't possibly know how to satisfy a virile man like you."

Ariana colorless? Vapid? Lyon thought her beauty every bit as vibrant and seductive as Zabrina's. Ariana was brightness and light. She was the sun, the moon, and the stars. Zabrina was darkness. She was the velvet temptress of the night, whose promise lay in all that was forbidden. He stared at Zabrina, mentally comparing her to Ariana and finding her lacking. He searched for a subtle way to break off their liaison without seeming too cruel. She had given him much pleasure during their passionate relationship. Not long ago she had been all he wanted, all he could have asked for. But that was before . . .

Ariana.

"Zabrina, this isn't going . . ."

Whatever he was going to say died in his throat when Zabrina pulled his head down and kissed him with a fervor born of desperation. She clung to him tenaciously, molding her body against his until he was forced to put his arms around her to keep both of them upright.

On her way out of the hall, Ariana passed a small curtained alcove, giving it little thought.

Then the sound of voices coming from within caught her attention, and she tried to ignore them. She wasn't so innocent that she didn't know what was taking place inside. The voices were those of a male and female, the woman's voice impassioned, the man's harsh and grating. Thinking it none of her business, she moved on. Until she recognized the man's voice. Lyon! She came to an abrupt stop, staring at the curtain as if she expected it to part of its own accord.

Inside the alcove, Lyon managed to break off the kiss and remove Zabrina's arms from around his neck. "Zabrina, we are risking William's wrath by meeting in secret like this. You know how he feels about infidelity in marriage."

"Fie on William," Zabrina said recklessly. "I care only how *you* feel, my lord. Do you burn like I do? It has been so long. Kiss me again, my love."

Lyon held her at bay. " 'Tis too dangerous, Zabrina. The hall is crowded. We risk exposure."

"Come to my room tonight," she invited. Her voice was a seductive whisper, made husky with desire. "Send your little mouse to her bed alone and come to me."

"Zabrina . . ."

"I will not leave until you promise," Zabrina said with a hint of iron will.

Wishing to escape the intolerable situation, Lyon decided it would be expedient simply to agree. He had to disentangle himself from her without causing a scene. It wouldn't do for them to be seen in a compromising position. Not only would he earn William's wrath but he would also provide fodder for the gossip mill. It had never mattered before, while he and Ariana were living apart, virtual strangers to one another, but now that they were living as man and wife, William would not condone his carrying on with his leman in public. The court was notorious for its gossip, and he imagined everyone was waiting breathlessly for the next scandal to develop.

For some unexplained reason, Lyon felt no compulsion to resume his affair with Zabrina. He might have told her he'd visit her chamber tonight, but he had no intention of doing so. On the contrary, he'd simply ignore her and hope she got the message.

"Aye, Zabrina. I will come to your room tonight, but you must go now before either of us is missed."

Zabrina gave him a radiant smile. "I will be waiting, my lord."

Ariana had heard enough. She turned and fled as quickly as her legs could carry her, out of the hall and down a dark passageway. She had no idea where she was going, or how to reach her chamber, but hoped to find a servant who would give her directions. When she heard footsteps behind her, she hastened her steps, fearing Lyon had noted her absence and come looking for her.

"Ariana, wait!"

Jesu! She couldn't face Lyon. Not now, not

after hearing him agree to an assignation with Zabrina. Just the thought of him and Zabrina together made her want to retch.

"Ariana, hold! 'Tis Edric."

Edric? What was Edric doing in Londontown? she wondered as she darted a glance over her shoulder to confirm his identity.

"Edric, I can't believe it's you!" She nearly collapsed in relief as she waited for him to catch up to her.

"What happened?" Edric asked with concern. "I saw you run from the hall and followed. Where is your husband?"

"Naught happened," she lied. "What are you doing in Londontown?"

"William summoned me for the Witenagemot. Though demoted in rank, I still control strategic Borderlands. I am to sit on the council. It must be an important meeting, for I've seen many prominent lords tonight, both Saxon and Norman."

Ariana glanced furtively over her shoulder. "We must talk, Edric. Lyon knows about the poison. He was preparing to storm your demesne when we were called to Londontown."

Edric blanched. "How did he find out? Why didn't you give him the poison?"

" 'Tis a long story."

Grasping her arm, he pushed her into the nearest room and closed the door. Fortunately it was a deserted anteroom. "Now, tell me what happened. I've been hoping to hear that the Lion had mysteriously expired."

"I was so angry at Lyon, I put the poison in his wine, but at the last moment I could not let him drink. I tried to knock the wine cup from his hand but he already knew it was poisoned and offered it to me to quench my thirst."

"Sweet Jesu . . ."

"I felt such overwhelming guilt that I would have drunk the poison myself, but Lyon would not permit it. I . . . I know not why."

"What did he do? He could have killed you—'twas his right—or beaten you senseless. Or locked you away for the rest of your life."

"He did none of those things," Ariana said. "He threatened to beat me but did not. I do not understand him. Sometimes I fear him and other times . . ." Her sentence fell off as she recalled those tender moments when he held her, loved her, told her how well she pleased him.

His face grew hard. "Who told him?"

"Nadia. She saw it in a vision and warned Lyon not to partake of the wine. I refused to tell him where I got the poison, but he is not stupid. He guessed immediately. He swore to storm Blackheath and kill you. I fear for your life. You must leave Londontown immediately."

Edric searched her face. "I will not leave without you, Ariana. You are no longer safe with the Lion. His punishment may be slow in coming, but it will come. He dare not do anything to me without incurring William's wrath. William needs loyal men to hold the Borderlands in England's name. I have sworn fealty to him. He trusts me as much as he can trust any other

Saxon lord who supports him with men and arms. No one but you knows I conspire against William and his Norman rule. All that I learn in council meetings will be reported back to Malcolm."

"You play a dangerous game, my lord," Ariana whispered, fearing for Edric's life. "Spying can result in death."

"Better to be dead than exist under Norman rule," Edric said bitterly.

"When I leave Londontown, I want you to come with me," he urged. "Malcolm will have your marriage annulled on grounds that our prior betrothal is still valid in Scotland."

Ariana opened her mouth but could not speak. Her mind told her one thing and her heart another. She remained mute, unable to find it in her heart to leave Lyon and marry Edric. She was fond of Edric, and would never betray him, but she didn't love him. That thought brought a frown to her face. If she didn't love Edric, did that mean that she loved . . .

Lyon.

"Hark, someone comes," Edric hissed. With great relief, Ariana heard the voices grow dimmer. Whoever it was had passed them by.

"It isn't safe here," Edric said as he cracked open the door and peered into the passageway. "We will speak again soon. I'll get a message to you somehow." He stepped into the dark passage and quickly disappeared.

Ariana made her way back to the hall, since she had no idea how to get to her chamber. She saw Matilda motioning to her and went to join her.

"Where have you been, Ariana?" Matilda asked curiously. "Your husband has been looking for you. 'Tis obvious he misses you."

Ariana nearly laughed aloud. She seriously doubted Lyon missed her at all with Lady Zabrina so eager to oblige him in every way.

"I . . . I visited the garderobe, madam," she lied, "and got lost on the way back."

Matilda laughed. "You will soon learn your way around. You should have asked a servant to show you the way."

"There you are, my lady." She was startled to find Lyon standing over her, his smile beguiling. "I've missed you."

Missed me indeed, Ariana thought ruefully as she glared up at her handsome husband. The sight of him nearly took her breath away.

"Are you ready to retire? You must be weary after traveling so great a distance from Cragmere to London. I will see you to our chamber." His face was composed, his voice pleasant, but Ariana sensed something . . . something she could not identify. Or was it his hooded eyes that made her wary?

"Do you leave us already, Lord Lyon?" William asked. "The night is still young."

"I will return, sire. First I must see to my lady wife's comfort. I have promised a game of chess to Lord Fitz Osbern."

Ariana rose, making her obeisance to both king and queen. Lyon took her arm and es-

corted her from the room. Was he walking faster than necessary? she wondered uncertainly.
Was he holding her arm more tightly than the
occasion warranted? He did not speak until
they reached their chamber and he had closed
the door firmly behind them.

"Edric is at court," he said without preamble.
"William summoned him to attend the Witenagemot. Where were you earlier? I searched
the hall for you."

Ariana's heart pounded furiously against her
rib cage. Should she confess that she had seen
and spoken with Edric, or should she pretend
ignorance? She decided that pleading ignorance was wiser.

"I was visiting the garderobe, my lord. I did
not see Lord Edric."

Lyon searched her face. So far he had no reason to doubt her. Conversely, he had no reason
to trust her. "Do not lie to me, lady. I have not
forgotten that you and Edric conspired together
to poison me. Unfortunately, I cannot exact retribution from Edric here at William's court.
William does not condone murder among his
subjects and that's exactly what I plan."

"You accuse falsely, my lord," Ariana insisted
doggedly. "I acted on my own. And you well
know I would not have let you drink the poison."

"I know no such thing. Nevertheless, I give
you fair warning, lady. Keep away from Edric
of Blackheath. I do not trust him. Remember
your marriage vows."

Ariana laughed harshly. " 'Tis you who should remember our marriage vows, my lord. Unlike you, I intend to remain faithful to mine. Though unwillingly wed, in the eyes of the church and God we are legally joined."

"And you think I do not intend to remain faithful?" Lyon asked evenly.

"Can you? Is it even in your nature to do so? Zabrina is a lovely woman. I cannot compare with someone of her beauty and—and"—she bit her lip, searching for the right word—"passionate nature."

Lyon grinned in genuine surprise. "You think not? I am well pleased with your passion. 'Tis true Zabrina and I have been lovers in the past, but that was before our marriage was consummated."

Ariana blinked at him. Did he think her a naive child? She had heard them planning an assignation this very night. "I care not what you and Lady Zabrina do," she declared hotly. "You may go to her tonight with my blessing. That *is* what you planned, is it not?"

Suddenly Lyon's features lifted, as if he'd just learned something of great import. "You're jealous!"

"Nay!" Ariana denied vehemently. "You may bed whomever you please as long as it isn't me."

"May I indeed, lady?" He laughed and Ariana felt her composure shatter. "It pleases me that you are jealous. I can handle your jealousy better than I can your hatred. Nadia might not always be around to warn me of attacks upon my life."

A rosy flush blossomed on Ariana's cheeks. She supposed she deserved that. "I most certainly am *not* jealous, my lord. 'Tis just that I do not wish to become a laughingstock at court. Your Norman friends are eagerly anticipating a scandal involving you and Zabrina."

"What will you do if there is a scandal, Ariana?"

She gave a careless shrug, refusing to look at him. He knew as well as she that he had an assignation with Zabrina this very night. Why must he lie about it? Didn't he realize that she didn't care? Or did she care too much?

"I think you do care, Ariana," Lyon said with sudden insight. "I can feel your jealousy; I can taste it. Why would you be jealous if you hate me so much?"

"I told you, I'm not . . ."

Her words ended in a squawk of surprise when Lyon pulled her into his arms and covered her mouth with his hard lips. He kissed her fiercely, rapaciously, his tongue seeking the sweetness of her mouth. He kissed her until she grew dizzy, until her legs turned to rubber, until her arms rose up to clasp his neck in sweet surrender. Her body grew liquid, and a melting sensation deep within her core burst into white-hot flame. When his hand found her breast, seeking out the turgid nipple, she wanted to scream in sweet pleasure.

"Not jealous, you say?" Lyon taunted, teasing

her nipple with the rough pad of his thumb. "Would you care if I did this to another woman?"

"If it pleases you," she lied shakily. She could tell he did not believe her.

Sweeping her from her feet, he carried her to the bed and sat down with her on his lap, burying his face in the fragrant hollow of her neck. She felt his tongue begin a slow slide down her neck, darting with thrilling results into the pink shell of her ear. She shivered, willing herself not to respond and failing miserably. With swift, deft fingers he removed her girdle and surcoat and tossed them aside. Her undertunic followed. Then he sat her astride him. He stared at her breasts, at the golden gate of Paradise between her legs, and hardened instantly. She felt his shaft push against her bottom. She squirmed, nearly destroying his composure.

"Please, my lord, I am tired. 'Twas only this afternoon when we . . . when we . . ." She blushed furiously. He was like a stallion, ever ready, ever willing. He could bed her now and still find the strength to please Zabrina afterward.

Her words gave him a moment's pause. Was he being unreasonable in his demands? The long journey from Cragmere had been hard on her, and he had already bedded her once today. He wasn't normally a man who lacked control, he reflected, but with Ariana his willpower went out the door. She was but a weak woman; perhaps her words had merit. Abruptly he plucked her from his lap and placed her on the bed. Before he stood up and straightened his clothing, he could not stop his natural instinct to bend down and kiss her pouting nipples, which he did quite thoroughly.

"Sleep well, my lady," he said, sending her a wicked look that mocked her. He knew well that he had aroused her, just as he had been aroused. "I will leave you to your rest."

Pulling a cover over her nakedness, Ariana sat up in bed. "Where do you go?" She knew but still felt the need to ask.

"Why, to play chess, of course. 'Twill likely be a long night. A *very* long night," he added mysteriously.

"Aye," Ariana replied bitterly. "I wish you joy of her."

Lyon frowned. "You speak in riddles again, lady. Whom do you wish me joy of?"

"Lady Zabrina, of course. She must be wondering what is keeping you. You do have an assignation with her, do you not?"

Lyon stared at her curiously. "Have you had another vision? What makes you think I have an assignation with Lady Zabrina?" Her visions made him uneasy.

"I do not need a vision to tell me that you intend to take up where you left off with Lady Zabrina." Her voice dripped with contempt.

Instead of being angry, Lyon smiled.

"Methinks you care more than you wish to admit." Still smiling, he strode out the door without a backward glance. He wanted to stay and make love to her, to whisper to her softly words that told of her allure, her innocent seduction, the web of intoxication she spun.

He bit down savagely on his lip to stop his train of thought. This was the same woman who had tried to poison him, who wished him dead so another man could claim her.

Yet the thought that Ariana was jealous gave him a strange joy. Mayhap, he thought cunningly, he could use that jealousy to turn Ariana's hatred into an emotion more pleasing to both of them.

Chapter Nine

The Witenagemot, for hundreds of years one of the most sedate of councils, was in an uproar. Lyon sat at the council table watching William's reaction to the protests of both Norman barons who had been granted prestigious titles and native English lords who had sworn to support the conquering monarch. Their voices were raised in unison, shouting and cursing. Norman and Englishmen alike forgot their jealousies and hatred as they glared at King William, who was carefully polishing his helmet on his sleeve as he sat at the head of the long council table.

Of all those present, only Fitz Osbern, the Earl of Anglia, and Lanfranc, the new Archdeacon of Canterbury, were calm as they sat back in their chairs, waiting for the storm to subside. At last the great lords exhausted their supply of expletives and William glanced at them with cool disdain.

"As I was saying, I am instituting a new policy, effective immediately. From this day, this very moment, all land in England, every acre of streams, fields, and forests, is property of the crown."

Once again pandemonium reigned until William rose majestically, eyeing each of the men coolly. Some of the barons fell silent beneath his glacial glare, and a few looked sheepish. Earl Edwin bit his thumbnail and Giulio of Tuscany stared at the floor. Lyon wasn't overly surprised by William's proclamation. He'd had an inkling it would come to this.

"Members of the nobility will be the King's caretakers and will guard his property against invaders and poachers," Lanfranc explained. "They will use it as their own, and the crown will take no more than a just and reasonable tax from them."

"I'll decide eventually just what the rate of taxation will be," the King interjected, "and you can be assured of my fairness in the matter. Do I hear discussion on the subject?"

William paused, gazing out at each of the lords in turn, and when no one replied, he smiled. "Thank you. I guarantee that none of you will find the policy a hardship."

The truth was, William was a very stern and violent man, so no one dared do or say anything contrary to his will. He put barons who had acted against his will in fetters. He expelled bishops from their sees and abbots from their abbacies; he put thanes in prison and did not even spare his own brother, Odo, a powerful bishop in Normandy who had an earldom in England. Odo even now was languishing in prison at William's order. No one was safe from his wrath.

At the far end of the table, Lanfranc stood up again. "If I may speak freely, Your Majesty? It occurs to me that the lords have a right to know your reasons for the policy. England was disunited before King William's reign. Without a sense of unity, any country will perish, and His Majesty asked me to recommend ways of building our English strength. The Earl of Anglia"—he nodded at Fitz Osbern—"helped me formulate the plan of achieving this unity by placing all land under the protection of the crown."

Fitz Osbern picked up where Lanfranc left off. "I know you are all in agreement," he said, before anyone could protest. "Our next task, a difficult one to be sure, is to find out precisely what lands there are and to determine their exact boundaries."

"That could take years," Lord Morcar complained.

"You will find," the king added craftily, "that your own positions will be strengthened by my policy."

"How so, sire?" Lyon asked curiously.

"I shall hold each of you responsible to me," the king said vigorously. "In the same way, each of the lesser nobles will come directly under the jurisdiction of his immediate overlord. In other words, Lord Lyon, Lord Edric and other lesser Northumbrian noblemen will come directly under your jurisdiction. You will be not only their liege lord, but the absolute and final authority in your own realm."

Lyon's gaze sought and found Edric's, his expression dark and forbidding, promising retribution for past transgressions.

"Your authority in your realm will naturally be subject to my approval and veto," William added by way of warning.

"Naturally," Lyon echoed, wondering if William guessed how greatly he despised Lord Edric.

"The merits of the King's plan are so obvious that we should vote without delay or discussion," Fitz Osbern said smoothly. " 'Tis a waste of time to discuss something so beneficial to England."

"I do not ask for a vote of confidence," William said in a booming voice. "Instead, I suggest that anyone who objects shall make his views known to the rest of us. Do I hear any protests?"

His gaze moved slowly up and down each side of the table, so challenging that the barons and earls who might have had the courage to express their convictions or doubts remained discreetly silent. No man wanted to stand alone against the ruler who had become the most powerful sovereign of his age. They had been outmaneuvered, of course, but there was no longer a choice. The nobles would have to obey and make the best of the situation.

The meeting adjourned when William remarked loudly, "From this hour forward, all land in England is property of the crown. So be it."

Lyon started to leave with the others, but William asked him to remain.

"What think you about my proclamation? Not all agree with me, I know, but most feared speaking out against me. 'Tis just as well. I will have my way."

"I agree," Lyon said after careful thought, " 'tis necessary for the sovereign unity of England. I imagine the barons will come around in time. 'Tis not for me to judge you. Without your good graces, I would not be Lord Lyon, or possess so grand a keep as Cragmere, or such vast acres of Borderlands."

"Or a wife," William reminded him. "You seem well pleased with Ariana of Cragmere. Her beauty is being widely remarked upon at court. Matilda liked her immensely."

"Aye, I am pleased with Ariana. What man wouldn't be? Unfortunately, my lady wife still thinks of me as the enemy. Placing her in the abbey with the nuns did nothing to tame her fiery nature or quell her rebelliousness."

William eyed him with amusement. "Can the Lion not tame his lioness? Fie, Lord Lyon, I doubt not you will have your lady wife eating out of your hand in no time. Fill her belly with your babe. I've never known a woman who wasn't mellowed by motherhood."

"Mayhap I will," Lyon said, warming to the idea. Watching Ariana swell with his child would please him. " 'Tis most unnerving to live with a wife who wishes you dead."

William frowned. "Surely not, Lyon."

Lyon's expression grew fierce as he recalled Ariana's attempt to poison him. " 'Tis nothing I can't handle, Your Majesty." He wisely decided to keep his near brush with death from William, all too aware of the king's penchant for swift retribution. William would likely banish Ariana to the abbey for life if he learned of her attempt to poison him. Nay, he decided, he would handle the situation himself. He'd rather have Ariana in his bed than locked away in some remote convent. As for Edric, he'd find a just punishment for the Saxon lord.

"I have missed you, Lyon. Do not be so swift to leave us after the Witenagemot. It would please Matilda and me if you and your lady stayed with us for a time."

"Thank you, sire. We will remain a short time, but as you well know, there is much unrest in the Borderlands. Malcolm conspires with deposed Saxon lords against your rule. We must be ever vigilant. I greatly fear that disgruntled lords in the North have joined his cause and plan to march on us."

"Aye, I am aware of Malcolm's machinations, and of those Saxon lords who connive behind my back. The day approaches when I will be forced to march into Scotland and put Malcolm in his place. Before his subjects and God, he will bend his knee and swear fealty to me."

Ariana could tell by the look on Lyon's face when he entered their chamber that the meeting of the Witenagemot had been anything but serene. He appeared tired. His face was haggard and shadowed. She wondered if Zabrina was the cause of his exhaustion, for she hadn't seen him since he'd left her so abruptly the night before. Since he'd failed to return to their chamber, she assumed he had spent the night in the bed of his mistress. She would have been surprised had she known he had played chess far into the wee hours of morning, then slept at the table with his head resting on his arms.

"Has the Witenagemot been adjourned?" she asked as he removed his leather jerkin and tossed it over a bench.

"For now," Lyon replied. "There are still some matters to be discussed."

"I was in the hall when some of the barons came from the meeting. They seemed most aggrieved. Some were shouting and gesturing angrily."

" 'Tis William's proclamation. He declared all the lands of England, every acre of it, property of the crown. In effect, every member of the nobility will be the king's caretaker, owing him just and reasonable taxes for the use of his property."

Ariana sucked her breath in sharply. "Jesu, no wonder the nobility was angry. 'Tis robbery!

Not only has he stolen the land of widows and heiresses like myself, but of all men. He is a tyrant without equal."

Lyon's voice held a note of warning. "Hush, Ariana, 'tis treason you speak. 'Tis for the good of England."

" 'Tis for the good of William," Ariana charged. "What of lesser lords, like Edric?"

Lyon sent her an inscrutable look. "Each of the barons holds jurisdiction over the lesser lords. I am now Edric's overlord. I have complete jurisdiction over him. Do not concern yourself with Edric of Blackheath—I will see that he gets everything he deserves."

The way he said it made Ariana's skin crawl. "There will be much unrest over this new policy of William's."

"He will handle it."

"Ever the Conqueror's defender," Ariana said dismissively. "When can we leave, my lord? I do not like living among Normans."

"William wishes us to remain at court for a time. There is still a week of meetings, then we shall see. Relax, Ariana, and get to know Matilda. She can be a good friend to you if you'd allow it. Are you ready to sup?"

Ariana had no desire to sit on display at the high table as she had done the night before. "Mayhap I'll ask Tersa to bring a tray up from the kitchen. Rubbing elbows with your Norman friends does not appeal to me."

"You will accompany me like any good wife and eat and smile as if you enjoyed it," Lyon told her. "In time you will become accustomed to Norman company, though in truth there are as many Saxon lords as Normans here tonight. If you are worried about your appearance, there is no need." His appreciative gaze traveled the length of her trim form and back, pausing briefly at her full breasts. Her surcoat was of deep yellow damask, embroidered in gold at the sleeve and hem. The links of her jeweled girdle spanned an impossibly narrow waist and her silver-blond tresses were covered with a silken veil. "You look quite fetching, my lady."

His compliment stunned her. Rarely had he commented on her appearance. The only time he appeared pleased with her was when he was making love to her.

"Come, my lady," he said, grasping her arm and guiding her from the room. "I am hungry and thirsty after the long meeting."

Royce met them at the entrance to the hall, ushering them to their seats. Ariana was relieved to learn they weren't required to sit at the high table tonight. But her relief was short-lived when Royce seated them between Zabrina and a leering Norman lord who appeared to be far gone in his cups. To her chagrin, Lyon seated himself next to Zabrina.

Zabrina leaned around Lyon, looked directly at Ariana, and said, "We have not met, my lady. I am Lady Zabrina, a good—uh, an intimate acquaintance of your husband's."

"And I am Lord Eustace," the man beside Ariana interjected smoothly. He touched her arm in a manner far too intimate for her liking. "This must be my lucky day. 'Tis not often I find myself seated beside so lovely a lady. Lord Lyon is a fortunate man."

Ariana slid her gaze to Lyon, wondering what he thought of the obnoxious Lord Eustace. Did her husband care that the drunken lord touched her without her leave? She was annoyed to see that Lyon was paying little heed to her or to Lord Eustace. He appeared deeply engrossed with Zabrina, adoring her with his eyes as she fluttered long dark lashes and postured before him in brazen invitation. What made the whole thing outrageous was the fact that every eye in the hall seemed to be focused on them, waiting, watching Zabrina's bold display and evaluating Lyon's reaction. Ariana did not know about the bets wagered on whether or not Lyon had taken up with his mistress again.

From the corner of his eye, Lyon saw Ariana's shuttered expression and suppressed a grin. Evidently she had noted his preoccupation with Zabrina and didn't like it. She was jealous, all right, he thought gleefully. And if she was jealous, that meant she cared enough about him to resent his attention to his former mistress. If he could raise that kind of reaction in her by merely speaking with the dark-haired beauty, what would Ariana do if she thought he was bedding Zabrina? Would she realize that her feelings for him were not really hatred? Would she admit that she . . . That she what? Cared for him? Wanted him?

Aye, all of those, Lyon reflected. He wanted Ariana to want him, to care for him.

To love him more than she loved Edric of Blackheath.

His eyes narrowed in amazement. Love. Where did that thought come from? Could he make Ariana love him?

"Where were you last night?" Zabrina hissed into his ear. "I waited till the candles sputtered and died."

"I was engaged in a chess game with Fitz Osbern. We played so late that I slept in the hall rather than awaken you."

"You were with *her*," Zabrina accused him hatefully, "your wife."

"Nay," Lyon denied, though it was where he had actually wanted to be.

"Come to me tonight." She spoke louder this time, and Lyon knew she meant for Ariana to hear. "I will wait as long as need be. Do not be late, my lord."

"My lady, you do not eat," Lord Eustace said as Ariana toyed with her food. "Is the food not to your liking?" Deliberately he speared a choice morsel from his trencher and held it to her lips.

Ariana pushed it aside. "I have no appetite, my lord." Her appetite had left her when she heard Zabrina and Lyon arranging another assignation. Had the woman no scruples?

"No appetite, my lady?" He took another healthy draught of wine, wiped his lips with the back of his sleeve, and burped crudely. "A pity.

But fear not, I have appetite enough for both of us." He leered at her and grasped her hand. "Your husband appears engrossed with the beautiful Lady Zabrina. Mayhap we should adjourn to another part of the tower where we can become better acquainted."

Ariana pulled her hand away with such force that she nearly fell from the bench. Finally Lyon seemed to recall that he had a wife and looked at her. "What is amiss, my lady?"

"Mayhap Lady Ariana would prefer Saxon company," Zabrina purred spitefully. "She does not try to conceal her hatred for Normans. Does she wear claws in bed, Lord Lyon? 'Twould be a pity to mar such flawless flesh as yours. I have always been partial to your hide, my lord. All of it." She stared pointedly at his loins, leaving no doubt as to her meaning.

Lyon's face contorted into a grimace, as if he had eaten sour grapes. The little bitch, he thought. She was deliberately goading Ariana.

Ariana gritted her teeth and forced a smile. "Forgive me, Lady Zabrina, but I thought you were of Saxon birth."

"I do not bear grudges, my lady. 'Tis far more rewarding to embrace the enemy with open arms than to fight him."

"And open thighs," Ariana muttered sarcastically. "I hope the King finds you a husband soon before you wear out all the men at court." Lyon nearly choked on his food, praying that no one had heard Ariana's words. But Zabrina heard, as did several others seated nearby, and she flew into a rage.

Leaping to her feet, she screeched like a banshee and tried to claw Ariana's face. "The little bitch insulted me, my lord—punish her." Only Lyon's swift action saved Ariana as he grasped Zabrina around the waist and held her at bay. Titters broke out around them, and the gossip mongers were already whispering behind their hands. Tonight there would be more than one kind of entertainment to savor as the clash between the Lion's wife and his mistress was told and retold with relish.

Royce, drawn to the table by the ruckus, blanched when he saw a furious Zabrina trying to escape from Lyon's arms and Ariana's smug smile as she danced out of reach.

"My lady wife has no appetite, Royce," Lyon said tightly. "Please escort her to our chamber."

"Aye," Zabrina crowed spitefully. "Send your lady wife to her chamber. Tonight I vow you will find more pleasure in my bed than hers."

Lyon sent Zabrina such a rebuking glare that she clamped her lips tightly shut and looked away. She didn't need to say any more; she'd already gotten her point across. At least now Ariana knew where she stood in her husband's affection.

Ariana stared at Lyon. Dismissed! He had dismissed her like a naughty child. Didn't he care that Zabrina had goaded her until she felt called upon to retaliate? Didn't he care that now the entire hall was aware of how little he thought of his wife?

"I bid you good night, my lord, Lady Zabrina," she said sweetly. She would rather die than show Lyon how desperately he had hurt her. His protective instincts toward his mistress made a mockery of their marriage. Holding her head high, she swept from the hall with the regal grace of a reigning monarch.

Lyon thought he'd never seen Ariana more magnificent. Her incredible green eyes flashed with jealous rage, her breasts heaved most enticingly, and her hair danced around her face like errant moonbeams. Sweet Jesu, he wanted her! If jealousy was the only emotion to which she responded, then he'd employ it with relish. Never had he experienced such an overwhelming desire to have a woman look upon him with desire, with . . . love.

The feisty little Saxon had truly bewitched him. To the point where he wanted no other woman. He could have happily strangled Zabrina for falsely implying before everyone present that they had resumed their relationship. Regrettably, she failed to realize that their affair was over. He had been more than a little shocked, and at the same time inordinately proud, of the way Ariana had stood up to Zabrina. His lady wife was no meek little mouse. She had given Zabrina as good as she received—nay, better.

*   *   *

Connie Mason

Ariana paced her chamber in a fine rage. Tersa watched her warily, realizing there was no placating her mistress. Whatever had happened in the hall must have upset Ariana greatly. She had stormed into the chamber calling her husband every foul name she could think of. What she called the Lady Zabrina didn't even bear repeating. It worried Tersa to see her mistress in such high mettle.

"Do not fash yourself, my lady. No man is worth upsetting yourself over. Besides, it couldn't have been that bad."

Ariana whirled on her. " 'Twas bad enough, Tersa. I as much as called Lady Zabrina a whore before everyone in the hall. You should have seen the look on Lord Lyon's face. There is no escaping his punishment this time."

Tersa blanched. "Oh, my lady, say it is not so! Beltane says that Lady Zabrina has powerful friends at court. What did she do to earn your wrath?"

"What did she do!" Ariana repeated at the top of her lungs. "I'll tell you what she did. She acted like a brazen slut with my husband. She admitted that he had shared her bed last night and that it would happen again."

"But that's not true, my lady!" Tersa denied. "I saw Lord Lyon in the hall last night, playing chess with Fitz Osbern."

Ariana shook her head in vigorous denial. "He did not sleep in our chamber last night, Tersa. I can only assume that he went to Lady Zabrina."

198

"Oh, my lady, Lord Lyon would not do such a thing. I do not believe it is so."

"What don't you believe, Tersa?"

Lyon stood in the doorway, feet spread wide apart, hands on hips. He looked magnificent . . . and terrifying. His expression was utterly ruthless, his blue eyes dark and intense.

Tersa emitted a little squeal of fear and stuttered hopelessly as she tried to speak, but couldn't.

" 'Tis all right, Tersa, I won't eat you. You may go. I wish to speak to my lady wife in private."

Ariana's knees turned to jelly. "No! Stay, Tersa."

Lyon's gaze remained fastened on Ariana, but his words were for Tersa. "Leave, Tersa. Now!"

Sending Ariana an apologetic look, Tersa turned and scurried from the room, closing the door firmly behind her.

Ariana lifted her chin and glared at Lyon. "I will not apologize, my lord."

Lyon sent her an inscrutable look. "I have not asked you to apologize."

Surprised, Ariana searched his face for a hint of softening. "You may beat me if you wish, but I refuse to stand by and let your mistress insult me. Have you no conscience? You made a laughingstock of me before your friends. They all know you are sporting with Lady Zabrina beneath my nose. I do not wish to be laughed at or pitied."

Lyon chuckled ruefully. "I doubt anyone here pities you, Ariana. More likely they pity Zabrina. I had no idea you had such sharp claws. I should make you jealous more often. You were magnificent."

Ariana blanched. "Is that what you think? That I am jealous? Nay! Nay! 'Tis not so. You could plow Zabrina's belly every night and twice on the Sabbath for all I care. You could bed—" When Lyon continued to grin at her, she clamped her mouth tightly shut.

Sweet Jesu. She sounded like a jealous shrew. She sounded as if she truly cared. She'd die before she'd give Lyon the satisfaction of knowing how deeply he affected her, how much it hurt knowing he shared his bed with another.

"If my lady wife didn't make clear the depth of her hatred for me, I would have no desire to bed another," Lyon said accusingly. "We are wed, Ariana. Can we not find common ground and make the best of this marriage? Must we always be at odds with one another? Must I always fear that you will try to poison me again? Can you not forget that it is Edric you love?"

Ariana stared at him, perplexed. What made him think she loved Edric? "I never wished you dead, my lord. You need not fear poison again. Do not ask me to forget that you are Norman, or that your kind stole my land and killed my family. Aye, we are wed, but as long as you continue to bed Zabrina, there can be no common ground for us. I will not share you with your mistress."

"What if I were to tell you I will renounce Zabrina?"

"I would not believe you. What if I were to say I do not love Edric of Blackheath?"

"I would not believe you."

"Then we are at an impasse, my lord."

"Mayhap I can convince you that I speak the truth."

Ariana felt the blood drain from her face. If he touched her, she'd go up in flame. In truth, where Lyon was concerned, she was a weak-willed creature unable to resist his seduction.

"Don't touch me. Please . . ."

"Do you fear me, Ariana?"

"Nay. Aye, I fear what you do to me, how you make me feel."

He reached for her. "Those are things you should welcome, not fear. You enjoy it when I make love to you."

He kissed her, slowly, thoroughly, relishing the sweet taste of her as his tongue slid past her teeth into her mouth. His arms tightened, bringing her flush against him from groin to breast. He swallowed her gasp and the moan that followed, relentlessly pursuing her tongue with his in a duel that inflamed his senses. His hands glided upward, cupping her breasts, squeezing, then downward, molding the sweet mounds of her buttocks, pulling her against his hardening body.

Ariana felt as if the earth had opened beneath her and she was falling into a bottomless pit. With tremendous effort, she managed to pull away from him. "Is this your idea of punishing me for insulting your mistress? If it is, I'd rather you beat me."

"Punishing you is not what I have in mind, Ariana. You have my word that I will never again take you in anger. When I love you, it will be for our mutual enjoyment. I promise never to defile your sweet body, or employ sex as a means of punishment. On this you have my solemn vow."

Lyon had given her more than she dared hope for. During their marriage, he had made few concessions. She wanted more. "What about Lady Zabrina? Do you promise faithfulness in our marriage?"

Aye, aye, aye, Lyon wanted to shout. But he did not. Though he had no intention of bedding Zabrina, giving her a little attention certainly couldn't hurt his cause with Ariana. If it roused Ariana's jealousy and made her more aware of him as a man, then he'd carry the ruse a little further by making her think he was still enamored of Zabrina.

"Marriage is a new concept to me, Ariana," he said plaintively. "We must both accustom ourselves to it. Mayhap it will take a little time to completely purge Zabrina from my system. I cannot promise absolute fidelity, but I will try my best. If you were to come to me willingly, without argument, I might find it less difficult to forget Zabrina."

Ariana's response startled him. Just when he thought he had bested her, she surprised him. "Take all the time you need, my lord. When you have purged her from your system, I will help you find another mistress more to my liking." Her dulcet tones did not deceive him. "And if you'd like, I'll let you choose a lover for me. A Saxon, of course, for I could not abide another Norman beast in my bed. I've already had a Lion and found him not to my taste."

Lyon's face puffed up with rage. The little witch! How dare she mock him! Her tongue was sharper than a double-edged sword. "So, I am not to your taste," he ground out through clenched teeth. "I am very much to Zabrina's taste."

"Then go to Zabrina!" she challenged.

"God's blood! I do not want Zabrina. Is that what you wanted to hear?"

Ariana smiled serenely but said nothing, merely staring at him. His eyes gleamed dangerously and his brow appeared permanently furrowed. Even his anger was magnificent, she thought, too entranced to feel fear.

"Dammit, Ariana, do you enjoy baiting me?" He gave her a shake that rattled her teeth. "Answer me! 'Tis you I want, not Zabrina. What do you say to that?"

"Do you see Zabrina's face before you when you make love to me?" she asked boldly.

"Nay. Do you see Edric's face when I'm loving you?"

"Nay. I see you, my lord, only you."

"Ah, Ariana, sweeting, I do not wish to fight with you. Forget Zabrina. Forget Edric."

Ariana would give her soul if Zabrina and Edric would disappear from the face of the earth, but she feared she asked too much. Lyon was a Norman, a man too weak to resist a woman like Zabrina despite the best of intentions. And she was a Saxon, a woman who would always remain loyal to her heritage.

" 'Tis not so simple, my lord," Ariana whispered shakily. She lifted her head, staring into the torrid depths of his eyes, drawn by his powerful allure.

"Sweet Jesu, Ariana, you drive me mad with desire."

Chapter Ten

Nothing had prepared Ariana for the pleasure and excitement Lyon's words gave her. She had expected unrelenting anger, not an affirmation of the attraction they shared. He wanted her; she recognized desire in the smoldering blue of his eyes. And Lord help her, she wanted him. Her feelings for Lyon had nothing to do with logic and everything to do with emotion. If she didn't say something, and quickly, he'd have her on her back and he'd be taking her to that place where she was his completely, to do with as he pleased.

Her mouth went dry as he touched her breasts. "Zabrina is waiting for you, my lord."

"Let her wait." His hands dropped to her buttocks, bringing her closer. She felt the heat of his flesh, the hardness of his loins, and moaned in protest of her body's surrender. His nearness made her senses spin.

If only she could trust him.

Her mind whirled as he released the clasp on her surcoat and pushed it past her shoulders. It caught on her hips and clung. Lyon fell to his knees before her, gathered the material in his hands, and tugged. It pooled at her feet and he stared at the pale flesh revealed through the thin linen of her undertunic. He buried his head in the fragrant cradle of her loins, kissing and nipping through the flimsy barrier of cloth.

"Take it off," he whispered hoarsely. His hands moved up her sleek flanks, dragging the material with them.

Just as Ariana moved to obey, a loud pounding sounded on the door. Ariana jerked in awareness, the madness of the moment and the unexpected interruption bringing her abruptly to reality.

"My lord, I have a message for you." The voice on the other side of the door sounded insistent.

"Unless it's from the king, I do not wish to be disturbed," Lyon growled in a tone that would have sent the bravest of knights fleeing. Obviously the man outside the door was made of sterner stuff.

"Please, my lord, 'tis most urgent."

Rising from his knees, Lyon flung open the door, his expression so fierce that the messenger shoved the slim sheet of parchment into his hands, then turned and fled as if the devil was nipping at his heels. Lyon slammed the door shut with a loud bang. Curious, Ariana moved to his side as he read the note. All she saw was the spidery handwriting and Zabrina's signature before Lyon turned his back, deliberately blocking her view.

"What is it?" Ariana probed.

Lyon folded the note, slid it inside his tunic, then spun around to face her. He looked angry. "Something has come up and I must leave. Wait for me, my lady. We will continue this later."

"Does Lady Zabrina grow restive?" Ariana asked frostily.

"Good night, my lady," Lyon replied, refusing to deny or acknowledge her accusation. Ariana stared at the door in splendid anger, then picked up a wine decanter and hurled it against the panel, watching in satisfaction as it trailed a blood-red puddle to the floor.

Lyon knocked discreetly on Zabrina's door and it opened immediately. Grasping his arm, she pulled him inside, closing the door behind him.

Lyon glared at her coolly. "This had better be good, Zabrina. What is of such vital urgency that you'd summon me from my bedchamber?"

"Did I interrupt something?" Zabrina asked sweetly. "I guarantee you won't be sorry."

"That remains to be seen. Tell me what you wish to say. The hour grows late."

"Sit, my lord." She led him to a chair and handed him a goblet of wine that had already been poured. "Quench your thirst first."

Lyon drank deeply, then set the goblet down. "What hoax is this, Zabrina? Didn't you do enough damage at the table tonight?"

Zabrina gave a long-suffering sigh. " 'Tis no hoax, my lord. I have information that will prove of great interest to you."

Lyon stared at her. "Out with it, lady, I have little taste for games."

"Not even if the games involve your lady wife?"

With the swiftness of a lion, he grasped her arm in a brutal grip, "What are you saying, lady?"

"Lyon, please, you're hurting me."

Immediately he released her, but his expression remained fierce. He took another deep draught of wine to cool his temper. "Explain yourself."

Zabrina gazed at his empty cup, smiled, and said, "You are aware, of course, that I have powerful friends at court."

"Aye." His eyes narrowed, wondering what she was hinting at.

"I overheard something tonight that I think you should know."

He waited.

"Lord Edric of Blackheath is plotting with Malcolm of Scotland against William. He is at court rallying Saxon lords to his cause."

" 'Tis no more than I expected," Lyon muttered darkly. "Why are you telling me this? Why don't you go to William with your suspicions?"

"You are Lord Edric's liege lord, are you not?"

"Aye, so William has told me."

" 'Tis why I came to you first. I overheard him speaking with a Saxon baron whom I do not wish to betray. He is a special friend," she said coyly. "If I tell the king, I will have to reveal names and William will have the man's head."

"So you wish to save your lover but not Lord Edric."

"Edric is a spy. After the council adjourns, he is going straightaway to Scotland to give Malcolm the names of those Saxon barons he can count on when he invades England. I am telling you because your lady wife is involved."

His voice grim, he said, "You think Ariana is a spy? Explain yourself."

"Mayhap not a spy," Zabrina amended, "but I overheard Lord Edric tell my friend that he and Lady Ariana would soon be together as they were meant to be. Apparently your lady wife has knowledge of Edric's plan and is in cahoots with him. If she objected, she would have told you that Edric connived at court with Saxon lords."

Lyon felt as if the earth had just opened up and swallowed him. Did Zabrina speak the truth? Did Ariana intend to leave him and take up with Edric? His head ached and his eyes felt heavy. Did Ariana hate him so much? Sweet Jesu . . . He tried to rise but his knees buckled beneath him. What was the matter with him?

Zabrina was beside him immediately, supporting him as he leaned heavily against her. "The news of your wife's disloyalty has affected you badly, my lord. Come and lie down. I will help you forget that faithless bitch William married you to."

Zabrina's words sounded as if they were coming from a great distance. What was happening to him? His legs quivered and his head spun dizzily. Zabrina eased him onto the bed and his eyes drifted shut. He heard someone shouting at him but could not make out the words.

"Damn you, Lyon, don't you pass out on me!" Zabrina spat out a vile oath. "The alchemist swore the potion would make you amorous, not render you unconscious." She shook him to no avail; he was out like a light. Perhaps she had spilled too much of the potion into the wine. Sighing in exasperation, she stripped off her clothes, then with great effort rendered him as naked as she. After admiring the long length of his splendid body, she crawled onto the bed beside him, placing his arms around her and snuggling close. She felt confident that when he awoke he would be eager to engage in the explosive sexual pleasure they had enjoyed in the past.

Sleep would not come to Ariana. She imagined Lyon in Zabrina's room, intimately entwined, kissing Zabrina in the same way he kissed her, in the same places. Never had she been so humiliated. Zabrina had but to summon him and he went running into her arms. The woman was without morals. Just when Ariana was beginning to come to grips with her feelings for her Norman husband, he demonstrated once again how little she meant to him. She should have listened to Edric. She should have . . .

A furtive knock on the door and a husky whisper startled Ariana from her dark thoughts.

"Ariana, open quickly. 'Tis Edric."

Edric! If someone saw him at her door and reported it to Lyon, Edric would be a dead man. She flung the door open and Edric stepped inside, glancing furtively down the passageway before closing the panel behind him.

"What is it, Edric? What is wrong? You shouldn't be here. What if Lyon returns and finds you? He could come back at any moment. How did you know I'd be alone? God's blood, do you harbor a death wish?"

"Cease, Ariana. Lord Lyon will not return any time soon."

Ariana frowned. "How do you know?"

He gave her a sardonic smile. "I saw him go into Lady Zabrina's room a short time ago. The lady's reputation for bedroom antics are legion. I've never sported with her myself, but I must admit the prospect is tempting. I anticipate that Lord Lyon will enjoy many long hours of pleasure in her arms."

"What is it you want, Edric?" Ariana asked, too upset by his words and Lyon's defection to be civil. Edric only confirmed what she suspected. Lyon had gone to Zabrina knowing his own wife was eager and willing to give herself to him. He had left her without a backward glance, without a thought to her feelings or emotions.

"I'm leaving Londontown. I fear that William is a breath away from finding out that I am spying for Malcolm. If some of the Saxon lords I spoke with take it into their heads to tell William, I could hang for treasonous activity against the crown."

"Oh, Edric, you must go immediately. Some of the Saxon lords attending the council support William. Will you go home to Blackheath?"

"Nay, I go to Abernethy. Come with me, Ariana. Malcolm's bishop will annul your marriage so you'll be free to wed me. I cannot leave you here with *him*."

Ariana drew back in alarm. "Nay, I cannot. He is my husband."

"How many times does the bastard have to humiliate you before you'll come to your senses? Do you wish to see for yourself how he honors his wedding vows? Come," he said, grasping her hand and pulling her toward the door. "I will show you where your husband bides this night."

Ignoring her protests, Edric pulled Ariana out the door, checked to see if anyone was about, then dragged her down the darkened passageway, deserted at this time of night. Light from the wall sconces guided their steps to Zabrina's chamber, which was on the same floor and several doors down the curving passageway. Edric stopped abruptly, held his finger to his lips, and pushed her in front of him. Then he eased open the chamber door, not too surprised to find it unlocked.

"The brazen hussy does not care who sees them together. Look," he hissed into her ear, "Is that not the great Lion of Normandy in bed with his naked leman?"

Ariana tried to look away but couldn't. Lyon's powerful form was easily recognizable in the diffused glow of candlelight. Even in repose he was magnificent. Tears sprang to her eyes when she saw Zabrina draped around Lyon, her naked buttocks gleaming whitely in the glowing mist of candlelight. Before she turned away in disgust, she noted that Zabrina was tightly clasped in Lyon's arms. A sob caught in her throat as she turned and fled to the safety of her chamber. Edric followed close on her heels.

"Ariana, I did not mean to hurt you," Edric said when he caught up with her. "Lord Lyon is unworthy of you. Come away with me, my lady. Meet me behind the mews tomorrow after vespers. I will have a horse for you, and provisions for our journey."

Confusion and hurt warred within Ariana. Lyon did not deserve her loyalty. Yet he was her husband, legally wed before God. Sweet Jesu! She needed time to think.

"I . . . I don't know. Leave me. I must think."

He kissed her hand fervently. "I will be waiting behind the mews." Then he turned and left.

Ariana slipped inside her chamber and leaned against the door, trying desperately to forget what she had seen in Zabrina's room.

Should she confront Lyon with what she saw? she wondered dully. Nay, for he would accuse her of spying. Should she flee north with Edric and try to make a life for herself in Scotland without Lyon? Would Lyon come after her? That thought brought a harsh laugh to her lips. Lyon would probably be glad to be rid of her. Doffing her clothing, she crawled into bed, pulling the blanket over her head to muffle her heartrending sobs.

Lyon lifted his head and searched the room. He was confused and disoriented and groggy. His gaze drifted to the windows, noting the scarlet dawn slowly coloring the eastern sky. He groaned. Funny, he couldn't recall seeking his bed last night. He must have imbibed more of the king's potent wine than he'd thought. He shifted slightly, aware of a solid weight resting against him. A soft feminine weight. A pleasing weight that made him smile and harden.

God's blood! Had he made love to his wife last night without even remembering? "Ariana . . ." Her name fell softly from his lips as his hands made a slow perusal of her naked curves.

Zabrina stirred and stretched sinuously beneath his searching caress. "Ah, Lyon, I've been waiting for you to awaken. It has been so long . . . so very long . . . Love me, my fierce lion, love me."

"Zabrina!" Lyon jerked upright, groaning as his head protested the sudden movement. He pushed Zabrina away rudely. "What in all that's holy are you doing in my bed?"

" 'Tis my bed you're in, my lord, not the other way around." Her coy smile did nothing to improve his memory—or his temper.

"How in the hell did I get here?"

"You came to my room, do you not recall?"

His brow furrowed in deep concentration. "Aye, a message. You summoned me. You had something of great import to tell me."

"Aye, about Lord Edric. Do you remember now?"

"I remember," Lyon said slowly. "Then everything went blank."

"Mayhap the wine was too strong, my lord. But not too strong to dull your senses. You were magnificent, Lyon." She gave a sigh of sublime ecstasy. "I nearly died of pleasure." She tried to push him onto his back and mount him. "I would taste of that pleasure again."

Lyon pushed her aside and leaped to his feet, looking down at her with something akin to disgust. "If I made love to you, I would remember it. What did you put in the wine, Zabrina?"

"You accuse me wrongly, my lord," Zabrina said contritely. "Mayhap you drank too deeply. But fear not, it did not affect your performance."

"Cease!" Lyon roared as he gathered up his clothes. "I will hear no more."

"What about Lord Edric? What of the treason he and your wife plan against William?"

"I will take care of it," Lyon said dully. His head ached too ferociously to think clearly.

Later, after he had time to consider everything Zabrina said, he would look into Zabrina's charges. Acting before he had the facts would destroy what small ground he and Ariana had gained in their relationship.

Ariana tossed and turned the night away, seeking some course other than the obvious one. She had just fallen into a deep sleep when Lyon arrived back in their chamber. She looked so appealingly innocent compared to Zabrina's flamboyant beauty that he wanted to awaken her and make love to her until she begged for mercy. But he didn't. Instead, he pulled up a bench and sat beside the bed, watching her sleep. Were she and Edric conspiring together? he wondered. Did she know that Edric was Malcolm's spy? Was his wife playing him for a fool?

Admittedly he'd been at fault for seeking to make Ariana jealous. It was not well done of him. Lord knew he no longer wanted Zabrina in a sexual way. He was too bewitched by his own wife to desire another woman. He hadn't wanted it to happen, never expected to harbor such tender feelings for the acid-tongued little vixen. But somehow she had bewitched him. He'd never let her go, never!

Ariana stretched and opened her eyes, suddenly aware that she was not alone. "Lyon!" She gasped in dismay and sat up, hugging the sheet to her naked breasts. "What are you doing here?"

216

His eyes glowed midnight blue. "This is my chamber, remember?"

"I'm surprised *you* remember," she said coolly.

"What's that supposed to mean?"

"Did you enjoy Lady Zabrina last night?"

"What makes you think I was with Zabrina?"

"Do me the honor of not insulting my intelligence. She summoned you and you went running to her bed."

Lyon tunneled his fingers through his dark hair, searching for the right words. "I wasn't exactly *with* Zabrina last night."

She stared at him in open derision. "Were you or were you not in Zabrina's bed last night, my lord? Did you or did you not enjoy your leman last night?"

"The answer is not as simple as it sounds. I was in her bed, but I did not enjoy her in the way you imply."

All she heard was Lyon's admission that he had been in Zabrina's bed. At least he had not tried to lie about something she had seen with her own eyes.

Her skepticism struck him forcibly. "Ariana." Her name left his lips in a ragged growl. "You're mine. No man will ever have you but me. Do not even think of leaving me."

Ariana stared at him in consternation. Did he suspect that Edric had asked her to flee with him?

"Forget Edric of Blackheath. He plots treason. Naught good can come of it. Tell me what you know about his plans."

Ariana's eyes widened. "Naught. I know naught."

"That's not what I've been told."

"Your leman is mistaken, my lord. She *is* the one who told you, is she not?" She wondered how Zabrina came to the knowledge that Edric was at court soliciting support for King Malcolm.

Lyon stared at her, his eyes liquid with desire. He shifted to the bed, reaching out to trace a finger over the downy softness of her cheek. She stiffened but did not recoil, emboldening him to carry the caress further. His finger moved downward, along the proud column of her neck, past her collarbone, coming to rest on the erect tip of one breast. His hand opened, fully encompassing the sweet, firm mound; he stroked it, his touch light and teasing. Ariana emitted a low gasp of startled pleasure. He played her body like a fine instrument, knowing just where to stroke her to give the most pleasure.

He stared at her mouth, conjuring up images of passion and pulse-pounding pleasure. A trifle too large, he had to admit, but its lush redness suited him perfectly. Her magnificent green eyes, her mane of silver hair spilling over her shoulders and back, her high, pronounced cheekbones, all combined to make her unique among women. His woman.

Ariana suffered his perusal in silence, fearing to speak, to move, to break the spell that held them in thrall. The sexual tension stretched taut between them. The very air seemed to hold its breath. He stared at her lips so intently that she imagined him kissing her, thrusting his tongue into her mouth, then taking his kiss further, to taste the ripe little fruits of her nipples.

She felt a quick light brush of his lips on hers. A touch of fire. Suddenly breathless, she inhaled sharply. Heat radiated from her mouth and spread down her throat. His hand scraped across her taut nipples and little shivers raced down her spine. She drew back in alarm. How could she let him do this to her? He flitted from bed to bed as effortlessly as eating or breathing.

"D-don't. Don't do this to me. You confuse me."

"You're my wife, Ariana. I want you." He pushed her down onto the soft surface of the bed, pulling the sheet from her nerveless fingers and pinning her in place with the weight of his body.

"Did your leman not satisfy you?" Her voice shook with anger—an anger directed not just at Lyon but at herself as well. At this moment she wanted him with a fierceness that went beyond anything she'd ever felt before. It was humiliating, debasing, especially after he'd just lain with his mistress.

"I did not make love to Zabrina," Lyon reiterated.

Ariana opened her mouth to call him a liar and his mouth took hers in a long, lingering kiss. A shock rippled through her as his tongue slid across her teeth and delved into her mouth. As if unable to get enough of her, his lips turned forceful and his tongue thrust demandingly. Suddenly the lure of his appeal destroyed all the barriers she'd erected against him. If she had to leave him this very day, she wanted to taste once more of the sublime pleasure she'd found in his arms. She wanted to feel him inside her, touching her soul, ravishing her with his searing passion.

She closed her eyes and melted against him, surprising Lyon. He expected her to fight him, to curse and rage at him, not this sweet surrender. His arms tightened convulsively, realizing that he'd never known a more perfect peace. The need to possess her body and soul was a sickness inside him, one he had no wish to cure. He had married this child-woman reluctantly and discovered that she enchanted him.

Ariana needed no words to tell him that she wanted him. Her body ached for his touch, inside and out. Against the softness of her flesh she could feel the hard arousal of his sex. She reached down between them and touched him. He nearly flew off the bed.

"Wait," he gasped, "let me get out of these clothes." His shirt, braies, chausses, and boots left him in an economy of motion and he posed proudly before her, magnificent in his nudity. Staring deeply into her eyes, he took her hand and placed it on his pulsating shaft.

She closed her fingers around him. An exclamation exploded from him. She grew bolder, stroking the hardness of his shaft, touching the softness of his sac while teasing his chest with the tip of her tongue, tasting the saltiness there.

"God's blood, enough!"

She emitted a cry of surprise when he slid down her body, his tongue and mouth pausing along the way to worship her breasts, to suckle her nipples, to explore the tempting indentation of her navel. Intense, satisfying pleasure spiraled through her. Then his mouth found her core, pressing open the soft petals with the tip of his tongue. Ariana gave a keening wail, her hands grasping his dark hair as he plied the rough heat of his tongue to her tender folds.

The room spun crazily around her; her breath came in great rasping sighs and her body arched to meet the bold conquest of his mouth.

"Lyon, please, I cannot bear it!"

The wet penetrating lash of Lyon's tongue was the only answer she received. But by then no answer was necessary. She climaxed powerfully, arching upward, her body trembling as intensifying waves of pleasure vibrated through her. Lyon waited until the last tremors left her body before rising to his knees and plunging into her. He stroked furiously, then slowly subsided, wanting to bring her again to pleasure before spilling his seed.

She placed her hand on his back and stroked him; his skin felt warm and vibrant beneath her fingers. She touched his face, memorizing the hard line of his jaw, aware that they would never be together again like this.

"Ah, sweeting, you please me greatly," Lyon whispered between clenched teeth.

He was holding on by a mere thread, so close to exploding inside her, so very close. She stroked his mouth. He pulled her fingers away and roughly kissed her face, her lips, her throat, the movement of his hips almost frantic now. When he felt her quicken beneath him and catch her breath, he jerked his hips back and forth frantically, pounding inside her, carrying her along on the wings of his passion.

"Come with me, my love. Aye, that's the way. Move just so. Ahhh."

He rocked her and lifted her with his wild thrusts. Her legs came up to grasp his hips, bringing him deeper. She felt slick and hot as he slid in and out, measuring her progress, until he felt her convulse and tighten around him, heard her scream softly into his ear. Then he held her bottom with both hands, melding them together. He bucked, stiffened, and cried out her name. He held her until the world stopped spinning and settled down around them.

Ariana opened her eyes, waiting for the mist to clear. Lyon was still embedded deep inside her, watching her, his eyes dark and intense. He moved slightly, feeling the slickness of his seed and reluctant to leave her silky tightness.

"Mayhap I put my babe inside you," he said, dropping a kiss on her lips.

Please, God, no, Ariana prayed silently. Not now, not when she planned on leaving him. She knew now that she loved this incredible man and could not, would not, share him with another woman.

"If 'tis God's will," Ariana murmured, carefully averting her eyes lest Lyon suspect she was lying. Under any other circumstances she'd love and cherish a child of Lyon's, even though she knew he'd demand that his offspring be raised in the Norman tradition, loyal to the Conqueror.

Reluctantly Lyon pulled out of her and rolled to his feet. "Rest. 'Tis early yet. I go now to bathe. William has called another meeting of the council today and I am required to attend."

He gathered up clean clothing from his chest, then turned to look at her, his eyes dark and probing. "When I return we will speak of Edric and what you know of his plotting against William. I cannot go to William with falsehoods against those who support him unless I can prove treason."

"You wish me to betray my own countryman?"

"I am your husband. Your loyalty belongs to me."

"I am your wife, yet you betrayed me with Lady Zabrina."

Exasperated, Lyon said, "I told you I did not bed Zabrina."

"I . . . saw you."

"You saw me? Jesu! You spied on me!"

Her chin rose stubbornly. "Aye." The cords rose in his neck and she knew fear, but she did not cower before him. "I had to know if you and

Zabrina . . . I peeked into Zabrina's chamber and saw you lying with her."

"You spied on me!" he repeated, his voice low and menacing. "You did not trust me."

"Nay. Should I?"

"About as much as I trust you," he said, recalling the incident with the poison. "You will swear fealty to me. Now!"

"I swear loyalty to no Norman."

He glared at her. "If you betray me, you will be sorry, my lady."

Having given that warning, he turned and stormed from the chamber.

"Good-bye, Lyon," Ariana whispered softly. "Good-bye, my love."

Chapter Eleven

Ariana entered the hall in a state of agitation, still undecided about leaving Lyon. If she left, she knew she might never see her beloved Cragmere again. Just because Edric said that many northern barons had joined forces with King Malcolm of Scotland was no guarantee that the combined forces were enough to drive the Conqueror from English soil. The Conqueror was a canny fighter and a brilliant tactician. With men like the Lion of Normandy at his side, he would be a formidable foe.

The hall was not as crowded as it had been the night before. Most of the barons were still sitting in council with William, leaving only their knights and several women to partake of the noon meal. Ariana selected a seat below the salt, where she wouldn't be noticed, but unfortunately one woman noted her presence and moved unerringly in her direction.

"Lady Ariana, how fortunate to find you alone." Zabrina seated herself beside Ariana with much pomp and ceremony. When her skirts were settled around her to her satisfaction, she turned a false smile on Ariana. "I've been hoping for a word in private with you."

"I cannot imagine why," Ariana said coolly.

"Come now, my lady, we both know your marriage to Lord Lyon is not a love match. He left you to languish in a convent with little concern for your welfare. He thought so little of you, he scarce mentioned you during all the years of your marriage."

"Why would he mention me when he had you to succor and comfort him?"

"Just so," Zabrina said complacently. "Lyon and I have been on intimate terms many years, and I see no reason for our relationship to cease just because William has ordered Lyon to get an heir on you. *Are* you with child yet?" Her violet gaze passed assessingly over Ariana's slim figure.

Ariana paled. She had known, of course, the reason Lyon had finally claimed her, but to hear it put so bluntly shamed her. Did the entire court know that Lyon looked upon her as a brood mare?

"Nay, I think not."

Zabrina seemed to be holding her breath for she let it out slowly after hearing Ariana's answer. "Mayhap Lyon finds bedding you a chore," she taunted.

"Has he told you that?" Ariana challenged.

"Nay, but it does not take a seer to know that you cannot tolerate your Norman husband. Perhaps that's why my Lord Lyon invited me to Cragmere." It was a vicious lie, but Zabrina felt little guilt over telling it. She was jealous of Ariana. Had she known Lyon before William gave Ariana to him, she would have convinced the king to wed Lyon to her instead of the little colorless mouse he now called wife.

Ariana gasped, shocked to the core. Would Lyon actually bring his leman to her home? He wouldn't dare! But he would dare, and she knew it. Lyon would dare anything. If he wanted his leman at Cragmere, he certainly wouldn't hesitate to bring her there.

"Come if you will," Ariana said with cool disdain, "but you will find no welcome. I'm surprised William has not yet found you a husband."

Zabrina gave Ariana a shrewd smile. "William is looking for a man who is both loyal and capable of defending my vast holdings. The king has full control and benefit of them now. Why should he be in a hurry to lose the wealth those lands produce? One day the right man will come along, but until that time I am free to share friendship with whomever I choose. Lord Lyon is a powerful lover, and I do not wish to give him up."

Brilliant color fled up Ariana's neck and

cheeks. Had the woman no shame, no morals? Did she want Lyon badly enough to travel to Cragmere and share him with his legal wife? If Zabrina came to Cragmere at Lyon's behest, Ariana vowed she'd not be there to welcome her.

"I suddenly find I'm not hungry," Ariana said as she rose abruptly from the table.

It was true. Gorge rose in her throat, and if she didn't leave immediately she feared she'd spew forth her insides. She had just reached the door when she saw Lyon and some of the other lords enter the hall, having come directly from the council room. Her heart plummeted when she saw Zabrina rush forward to greet Lyon, laughing up into his face with the guile of a courtesan. When Lyon placed his arm around Zabrina's waist and pulled her close, Ariana turned on her heel and fled to the safety and peace of her chamber.

Lyon spied Ariana the moment he entered the hall. The council had been dismissed briefly for the noon meal. He watched as she rose somewhat unsteadily and headed for the circular staircase, unaware that Zabrina was making straight for him. When Ariana paused in the doorway and looked back at him, Lyon was momentarily distracted as Zabrina literally bowled him over. Instinctively, an arm curled around her slim waist to steady her. When he turned back to look for Ariana, she had already fled up the staircase. With a vicious snarl, he shoved Zabrina away.

"What are you doing, lady? Isn't it enough

that you drugged me last night?"

Zabrina's eyes widened in mock dismay. "Nay, Lyon, I would not do such a thing. The wine was potent and you were tired. I cannot count the times you have lain in my bed after imbibing too freely. 'Tis no different now than then."

"Is it not?" Lyon asked evenly. His voice was calm—too calm, Zabrina thought as she retreated a step. "Ariana is no fool. Nor is William. At council today William told me he has found you a husband. He says it is a most advantageous match."

Zabrina blanched. "A husband! Who? Tell me the man's name."

"William did not confide in me. You will have to hear it from his lips. He seemed pleased with his choice. He was quite vocal in stating that our liaison must cease forever. While it has been enjoyable, it is no longer advisable for us to share more than innocent friendship. I have Ariana and you will have a husband on whom to lavish your affections."

The news, while not a complete surprise, nevertheless did not please Zabrina. From the very first day she'd met Lyon, she'd wanted him for her husband, but could think of no way to rid him of Ariana of Cragmere. Protected as she was at St. Claire Abbey, there was no way that Ariana could come to any harm. So Zabrina had contented herself with being Lyon's leman, hoping that Ariana would sicken and die before the king betrothed her, Zabrina, to another. But fate was not kind to her. William had ordered Lyon to retrieve his bride, take her home to Cragmere, and found a dynasty.

"Do you think I'll be satisfied with any man the king chooses for me?" Zabrina spat harshly. "You have not heard the last from me, my lord!" Turning on her heel, she swept away with the regal grace of a queen.

When Tersa arrived later in Ariana's chamber to see to her needs, the maid found her packing. She gave Ariana a hard look, then asked, "Where do you go, my lady? Are we returning to Cragmere?"

"I . . . I cannot tell you," Ariana said, refusing to look Tersa in the eye.

"Oh, my lady, you're not going to do anything foolish, are you? Pray tell me 'tis not so."

Ariana stopped her packing to look at Tersa, her expression melancholy. "I cannot remain here while my lord Lyon beds his leman. I am no lackwit to meekly accept that my husband prefers another woman in his bed."

Ariana had thought it out carefully. If Zabrina was coming to Cragmere, then she, Ariana, would not be there to suffer the humiliation of being replaced by her husband's mistress. Edric had offered her a way out, and though it wasn't a perfect solution, she had no alternative.

"Oh, my lady, Lord Lyon would not . . ."

"Aye, Tersa, 'tis true. Lord Lyon wants me no more than I want him. He will be most happy to be rid of me."

Tersa gave her a dubious look. "I will pack the rest of your clothing so it can be sent on to Cragmere. When do we leave?"

Ariana shook her head. "I go not to Cragmere. And 'tis best if you do not accompany me."

"Not accompany you! You jest, my lady. Do I no longer please you? Have you found another maid to replace me?"

Ariana grasped Tersa's hands and pulled her down beside her on the bed. "What I tell you must go no further than this room, Tersa. Do I have your vow?"

Tersa's doelike eyes looked troubled. "Aye, my lady, you have my word."

"Lord Lyon has asked Lady Zabrina to bide with us at Cragmere. 'Tis more than I can bear. I do not intend to return to Cragmere while Lyon cavorts with his leman beneath my very nose."

"I cannot believe that of Lord Lyon. 'Tis your home. What will you do? Where will you go?"

"Lord Edric has asked me to go—away with him," Ariana confided. She said nothing about Scotland, or the annulment of her marriage, for she doubted she would actually agree to an annulment once in Scotland.

"Away! You would leave Lord Lyon? You love him, my lady! How could you leave him for Lord Edric?"

"Nay, I do not love Lyon!" Ariana denied vehemently. Her hands flew to her cheeks, which had turned a vivid crimson. Were her feelings so apparent?

"Deny it all you want, my lady, but I know better. Lord Edric is a handsome fellow, but he cannot hold a candle to my Lord Lyon. Beltane says the Lion of Normandy is the bravest knight in all the land. Does Lord Lyon know you care for him?"

"Care for him? Nay," Ariana scoffed, "I do not care for him, and he cares for no one save for his king, his horse, and his leman. He will be relieved to be rid of me."

"You are not thinking clearly, my lady," Tersa admonished. "Leaving with Lord Edric now would give Lady Zabrina free rein with your husband. And Lord Lyon will be most aggrieved when he learns you have left him."

Aggrieved was putting it mildly, Ariana thought ruefully. Lyon would be absolutely livid. He would hate her, perhaps even petition the king to dissolve their marriage.

"I know what I must do," Ariana said, her mind clearly made up. "And you must keep my secret."

"You cannot go alone. I will go with you."

"Thank you, but nay. You would not wish to leave Sir Beltane. I believe he cares for you. I am safe with Edric. We have known one another for many years. I was once his betrothed."

Tersa was torn by indecision. The thought of parting from Sir Beltane was painful, but allowing Ariana to travel alone with a man not her husband was equally repugnant.

Ariana recognized the maid's dilemma immediately. "I will be fine, Tersa, truly. I ask only that you tell neither Lord Lyon nor Sir Beltane where I have gone until I am well away from Londontown."

Tersa gulped in fear. All Lord Lyon had to do was level a black look on her, and she'd spill everything she knew. "Take me with you, my lady, please. 'Tis not seemly that you travel alone with Lord Edric. Besides," she admitted sheepishly, "Lord Lyon will have information from me before the day is out, he is that determined."

Ariana recognized truth in Tersa's words. Still, she would rather not involve the maid in her problems. "Take to your bed after I leave, Tersa, and do not show your face until absolutely necessary. Plead illness, contagion, whatever it takes to avoid Lyon and Sir Beltane. Will you do that for me?"

Tersa gave reluctant agreement. "Aye, my lady. When will you leave?"

"Tonight, after vespers. Lord Lyon will no doubt play chess or other board games with his cronies till very late. Then he will go to his leman. If I'm lucky, he won't find out I'm missing until morning, or possibly evening if he's tied up with the King's business. By that time you'll have taken to your bed with a mysterious illness."

"Are you sure, my lady? Mayhap Lord Lyon will give up his mistress for you."

Ariana laughed harshly. "And mayhap pigs will sprout wings and fly. Lady Zabrina has her clutches too deep into my husband's hide."

"Go with God, my lady."

"And you," Ariana said sadly.

Lyon watched Ariana warily throughout the endless meal, wondering at her evasiveness, her unnatural stiffness, her lack of response to his attempts at conversation. When he had last seen her that morning, they had parted on less than friendly terms, but before their argument they had been the closest of lovers. Jesu, she was magnificent. Her response to him had been wild, abandoned, and completely spontaneous. Did she fear answering his questions about Lord Edric? Did she fear implicating her countryman in a treasonous plot against William?

"You are quiet tonight, my lady," Lyon said as he offered her a drink from their shared cup.

Taking the cup without a word, Ariana drank deeply of the fine French wine William favored at his table. "What do you wish to hear?" she asked as she carefully set the cup down on the table between them.

"The truth," Lyon said. "Is Lord Edric involved with traitors?"

Her eyelids swept downward, shielding the incredible green of her eyes. "I know not. You must ask Edric."

"Aye," Lyon said sourly, "mayhap 'tis best."

Forcing a lightness she did not feel, Ariana asked, "Do you go to your leman tonight?"

Lyon sent her a speculative glance. "Do you want me to?"

She shrugged. "I care not." She dared not tell

him how much easier it would be for her to leave if he sought Zabrina's bed tonight, despite the pain of imagining him in his leman's arms.

Lyon stared at her, wondering if Ariana was jealous or if she truly did not care. He hoped it was the former, for he was beginning to care too much for the contrary little witch he had married. After they returned to Cragmere, away from Londontown and the Normans she despised, he hoped to repair things between them. Given half a chance, the spark she ignited within him could grow into a raging inferno. Even now he felt the burning need to carry her up to their chamber and make love to her, endlessly, tirelessly. . . . These feelings were so new to him that he was at a loss to explain them.

"If you care so little," Lyon said airily, "then perhaps you should not wait up for me tonight." He didn't exactly say that he was going to Zabrina, but the look on Ariana's face told him it was exactly what she thought. She was wrong. He was meeting privately with William in his chambers tonight, where they would talk and play chess until the wee hours of morning. He intended to tell William this night that he and Ariana would leave within the week. He was more than anxious to get back to Cragmere, where he would endeavor to make Ariana forget all about Edric of Blackheath.

Excusing himself politely, Lyon left the table immediately following the meal. Ariana watched until his broad back disappeared through the door. A moment later Edric approached, saw that no one was close enough to overhear, and said for her ears only, "Tonight, my lady. I will be waiting behind the mews. Do not fail me this time."

After Edric's terse message, Ariana spoke pleasantly to Queen Matilda, waited a decent interval, then quietly left the hall. There were so many people in the huge room that she felt certain no one saw her leave. Nor was anyone around when she came back down the stairs later and made her way outside. There were few people about in the inner bailey as she hastened through the darkness to the mews, dressed in her warmest clothing and carrying a cloth valise. She voiced a silent prayer as she groped her way to the deserted building and saw the outline of two horses. Edric stepped out of the shadows to greet her.

"You've come," he whispered, pulling her into a dark corner and taking her bag. "The horses are ready. Let me help you mount." He lifted her easily into the saddle.

"How will we get past the guards without being seen?"

" 'Tis all taken care of, my lady. Palms were greased. A small postern gate was left unlocked this night. What did you tell Lord Lyon?"

"I told him nothing. He is with his leman."

"Ah, the lovely Lady Zabrina. She will keep him pleasantly occupied till we are well away. This way," he said, grasping her reins and leading both horses through the darkness, keeping well to the shadows.

No one challenged them as they rode through the gate and away from William's tower. Away from Londontown and away from Lyon, Ariana thought with a pang of regret. The man she loved, the man who didn't care a fig about her, the man who thought more of his leman than he did his own wife.

The farther away they got from Londontown, the greater were Ariana's misgivings about what she had done. Going off with another man was an irresponsible thing to do. In effect she was cutting her ties, for after this Lyon would doubtless wash his hands of her and ask King William to annul their marriage. The thought was not comforting.

They had reached the outskirts of town when Ariana realized that she must have been insane to leave with Edric. She had been so upset over Lyon and Zabrina that she hadn't been thinking coherently.

"Edric, wait." She reined in her horse.

"What is it, my lady?" He wheeled in beside her, grasping her leading reins to steady her horse. "The city is behind us. Fear not, we will stay at safe houses during our journey north. No one will betray us."

"You don't understand," Ariana said breathlessly. "I . . . I cannot go. 'Tis wrong. No matter what Lyon has done, I am his wife. 'Tis cowardly of me to leave. What . . . what if I am carrying his child?"

Edric's jaw hardened. "I should have killed the bastard before he defiled you."

"He did not defile me, Edric. I am his wife and have been for these past five years."

"His wife, aye," Edric spat bitterly. "Child or no, Malcolm will instruct his bishop to annul your marriage so you and I can wed. If you are increasing, I will raise the Lion's babe as my own. That much I promise."

Without waiting for a reply, he yanked on her horse's leading reins, forcing her to hang on to the pommel or be dashed to the ground.

"Edric, please. I've changed my mind. I don't want to go to Scotland. I belong in England with Lyon."

This time she wasn't going to be talked into doing something she would regret. Trying to poison Lyon had been the worst mistake of her life. This was almost as bad. If she was fortunate, she'd be safely back within William's tower before Lyon even missed her.

"Too late, my lady," Edric said tightly, "I cannot let you go back. I want you for my wife, Ariana. Nothing has changed that. You were betrothed to me long before Lyon arrived in England."

Ariana's answer was lost to the wind as they sped at breakneck speed along the rutted road. It was midnight dark and they were traveling at such a fast clip that she feared she'd be killed if she fell or tried to jump from her horse's back. All she could do was hang on for dear life and pray Edric would come to his senses and listen to her plea to return her to Londontown and Lyon.

A myriad of emotions raced through Ariana's mind on her wild flight through the black night. She wondered why she had listened to Zabrina's cruel words, why she had allowed them to send her fleeing into the night. She felt hurt and betrayed. How could Lyon make such tender love to her, then turn around and invite Zabrina to bide with them at Cragmere? Obviously one woman was not enough for him.

She should have remained in Londontown, she knew that now. She should have stayed and demanded that Lyon give up Zabrina. She never should have listened to Edric. She wanted Edric as a friend, not as a husband or lover. She didn't want her marriage to Lyon annulled. Why couldn't she have swallowed her pride and fought for what she wanted? She wanted Lyon, God help her. Against her will she had fallen in love with her husband, a Norman, a man who had come with the Conqueror and stolen her home, her demesne—and her heart.

Would Lyon understand and forgive her when she returned? she wondered dismally. Would she be able to return at all? Obviously Edric was determined to take her to Scotland, but she was just as determined to return to Lyon.

Toward dawn, Edric said, "We're far enough away from the city to stop. There is a safe house nearby where we can pass the daylight hours. We'll travel by night until we reach Scotland."

Ariana did not know the name of the household where Edric stopped, nor was she told.

Ready to collapse, she was shown directly to an empty bedchamber while Edric remained behind to speak privately with the Saxon lord who was obviously one of the dissidents conspiring against William.

A tray of food was brought almost immediately, and Ariana ate ravenously. Despite her exhaustion, she made secret plans to sneak away and return to Londontown after she had refreshed herself. It might mean stealing a fresh horse, but she shoved her guilt aside. Desperate times called for desperate measures. Unfortunately, Ariana's plans went awry when she tried to leave her chamber and found the door locked from the outside.

Dawn was just moments away when Lyon entered the bedchamber he shared with Ariana. William had been in a talkative mood and engaged Lyon in conversation until mauve streaks appeared on the eastern horizon. He gave Lyon leave to return to Cragmere within the week, admonishing him to keep his eye on the situation arising in Northumbria. Edwin and Morcar, northern Saxon lords, were still unsubdued and defiant.

"I fear an uprising is brewing in the Borderlands," William had confided to Lyon. "King Malcolm is restive and has gathered strength from dissident barons. 'Tis possible that Edric of Blackheath supports Malcolm and will come to his aid should fighting break out. You are the one man in the North I can trust, Lyon."

Lyon debated telling William what Zabrina had said earlier but decided against it. It appeared as if William already knew what was brewing in the North. If he mentioned the conversation he had had with Zabrina, it would implicate Ariana, which he didn't really want to do.

"I am your man, sire," Lyon returned ardently, "ever willing to do your bidding."

"Seek your bed, Lyon. I fear I have kept you overlong." They clasped arms and parted.

Lyon entered his chamber quietly so as not to awaken Ariana. The morrow would be time enough to tell her that they would return to Cragmere within the week. The light from a single candle spilled across the bed, revealing an undisturbed expanse of counterpane. Lyon froze as he stared at the unoccupied bed. His gaze probed outward, sweeping the room as far as the light permitted. He called her name softly. When he received no response, he picked up the candle and carefully searched out the darkened corners of the chamber.

"Jesu!" The word left his lips in an explosive burst of air. Where in the hell had Ariana gotten herself to? He knew she was angry at him, but where could she have gone? Tersa would know, he thought as he turned and stormed from the chamber.

"I have a fever, my lord," Tersa called through the closed door when Lyon awakened her a short time later. "I dare not infect you."

"I care naught about infection," Lyon thundered ominously. "Tell me where my lady wife has gone. Is she with you?"

Tersa was glad Lyon couldn't see her quaking behind the closed door. "She is abed, my lord."

"Nay, she is not."

"I have not seen her since she sent me to my bed hours earlier. You must pardon me, my lord, I am not well. I . . . I know nothing, nothing. . . ."

Lyon doubted Tersa was as innocent as she pretended. Still, if the woman was ill, it would be heartless of him to badger her. Nay, he would turn the tower upside down if he must, but find Ariana he would.

Turn the tower upside down was exactly what Lyon did. When he failed to find Ariana or learn where she had disappeared to, he again sought out Tersa, bringing Beltane with him. This time he pounded on her door until the woman appeared, looking pale and frightened.

"I ask you again, Tersa, where is my lady wife?" He was frantic with worry. Obviously Ariana hadn't returned to Cragmere, for she had taken none of their retainers with her. And she wouldn't have been so stupid as to travel that great distance alone and unprotected.

Tersa looked from Lyon to Beltane, wanting to lie to neither of them but determined to obey her mistress. She cast her eyes downward. "I do not know, my lord."

Lyon's face grew red with rage. He would get the truth from the woman if he had to beat it out of her. Aware of Lyon's tenuous hold on his temper and fearing for Tersa's well-being, Beltane pulled Lyon aside and whispered frantically into his ear.

"Let me try, my lord. Tersa will talk to me. I will convince her that she must tell us where to find your lady wife."

Lyon gave Beltane a hard look. "Very well, you may try. Impress upon her the importance of finding Lady Ariana. If you fail to convince her, I have no recourse but to use force."

Beltane blanched. He cared for Tersa and did not want to see her hurt. Lyon retreated down the passageway while Beltane returned to where Tersa stood in the doorway, looking like a frightened rabbit.

"You must tell us what you know," Beltane pleaded softly. "Lord Lyon has searched every chamber in the tower, with no luck. As you well know, Lady Ariana is nowhere to be found. You do know where she is, do you not?"

Tersa shook her head.

"Tersa, I do not wish to see you hurt. Lord Lyon will not hesitate to beat the truth from you if you continue pretending ignorance." He pulled her gently into his arms, smoothing the hair from her forehead. "Mayhap your mistress is in danger. Would you wish her harm?"

"Oh, nay," Tersa breathed shakily. With Beltane's arms around her she could hardly breathe, let alone think. "I am sure my lady will come to no harm."

"How do you know?"

"Lord Edric would protect her with his life."

The moment the words were out, her hands flew up to cover her mouth. She had not meant to reveal so much, but Beltane was looking at her with such tenderness that her will deserted her.

"Lord Edric?" Beltane repeated. "Lady Ariana is with Lord Edric?" His words were loud enough to carry to Lyon.

A chill went through Lyon. He'd always known Ariana wanted Edric. "Tell me what you know, Tersa," he demanded tightly. The planes of his face were stark with anger and resentment, his eyes cold and condemning.

Tersa looked up at Lyon and went limp with fear. She had promised to keep Ariana's secret, but how could she when faced with a furious Lyon? Tersa seriously doubted that anyone, man or woman, could hold out for long against the Lion of Normandy.

" 'Tis true," Tersa whispered through white lips. "Lady Ariana left with Lord Edric."

Lyon spat out a violent curse. "I will kill him. Where have they gone?"

Tersa swallowed visibly and shook her head.

"Come, Tersa," Beltane said, "tell Lord Lyon what he wants to know. If you tell the truth he will not harm you."

Tersa licked moisture onto her dry lips. "I do not think she really wanted to go, my lord. 'Tis my belief that you forced her to leave."

Lyon's brows flew upward. "I? I forced her to leave?"

"Aye," Tersa said, gathering her courage. "She

told me you had asked Lady Zabrina to bide with you at Cragmere."

"Nay, I did not! Lady Zabrina lied. I will find Ariana and set things right. Where did Lord Edric take her?"

"I do not know, my lord. Truly, I do not know."

Chapter Twelve

"I will kill him, sire," Lyon said with deadly calm. "Lord Edric has fled Londontown with my wife." He paced before the king, his face stark with anger and something else, something raw and undefinable. "Surely you must know by now that Lord Edric spouts treason."

"Calm yourself, Lyon, and tell me what has happened. Has Lord Edric kidnaped your lady wife?"

Lyon flushed and looked away. "As you well know, sire, Ariana has little love for Normans. Our marriage thus far has not been a tranquil one. Ariana had contact with Lord Edric during her years at the abbey without my knowledge. If you recall, they were once betrothed. Lord Edric still desires Ariana for his wife."

Deep in thought, William stroked his chin.

"So you think your lady wife went willingly with Lord Edric?"

"I did not say that," Lyon claimed. "Ariana is . . . vulnerable. Bringing her to court was not a good idea. There are certain things . . . I am not entirely blameless. Lady Zabrina is quite determined, and I thought to make Ariana jealous. I realize my mistake now. Ariana is a proud woman."

William gazed at Lyon intently, his eyes narrowed in disapproval. "Did I not tell you to cease wasting your seed on your mistress and get an heir upon your wife? Think you I have not observed you and Zabrina together since your arrival in Londontown? Well you know that I do not condone immorality among my subjects."

Lyon whirled in mid-stride. "I have not been unfaithful to Ariana since our reunion. I told Zabrina our affair was over, but she refuses to accept the inevitable. I told her I no longer require a mistress."

William was pleased with Lyon's apparent sincerity. He smiled, replacing his normally dour expression with one of rare amusement. "Can I assume you care for your lady wife?"

"Assume what you like," Lyon growled, refusing to admit something so personal, something that not even he knew for certain.

The smile did not leave William's face. "I see," he said slowly. "Where do you think Lord Edric took Lady Ariana?"

"To Blackheath, possibly, but I can't imagine

him doing so. His manor cannot withstand an attack by my superior forces. Do I have your permission to slay him once I have found him?"

William slanted Lyon a shrewd look. "Nay, I have other uses for Lord Edric. I need him in the North. Lords Edwin and Morcar are gathering support in their effort to drive me from England. They will strike first in Northumbria. Possibly with help from Malcolm."

"Lord Edric cannot be trusted," Lyon protested. "He has already demonstrated his disloyalty."

"He has sworn fealty," William persisted.

"His Saxon roots run too deep. Replace him with a Norman you can trust."

William considered Lyon's suggestion and then shook his head. "Nay. Edric has a loyal following among the Border lords. I need their support. If I replace Edric, I may have a small rebellion on my hands. And right now there is enough trouble brewing in the Borderlands without asking for more."

"Mayhap Edric is deeply embroiled in the trouble," Lyon qualified.

"Mayhap he is, but I have devised a plan to bring him back to the fold. I intend to reward him with rich estates and a wealthy wife. Not some old hag, mind you, but a young, beautiful woman with lusty appetites."

"Jesu! Nay, you do not mean . . . You are speaking of Zabrina, of course."

"Aye, the Lady Zabrina. Her lands and wealth are extensive. The monies from those lands have enriched my coffers immeasurably since I made her my ward, but now I must think of England and what is best for the country. 'Tis a great honor I bestow upon Lord Edric, one I do not think even he can refuse."

The shrewd devil, Lyon thought, suppressing a grin. What man could refuse both Zabrina and great wealth? Lord Edric was not a rich man. His demesne was not as large as Cragmere by half. He suspected that one of the reasons Edric wanted Ariana was to enrich his own holdings. But rewarding Edric when he deserved to be punished did not sit well with Lyon.

"Forgive me, sire, but I cannot like what you intend. Edric of Blackheath has been a thorn in my side far longer than even I knew. He conspired against me at Cragmere, using Ariana as his pawn. If not for Ariana's conscience and the good graces of an old witch named Nadia, I would be dead."

"I will make a concession," William granted. "If Edric of Blackheath has harmed your lady wife in any way, you may kill him in mortal combat. Otherwise, inform him of the betrothal between him and Lady Zabrina and act as witness to their marriage."

"Witness their marriage!" Lyon exploded, the full impact of William's words finally sinking in. "But that would mean . . . Nay, sire, surely not."

"Aye," William nodded sagely. "You will take Lady Zabrina with you to Blackheath. Keep in mind that I expect you to restrain your lusty passions while providing escort to Lady Zabrina. 'Twill be difficult for Lord Edric to refuse my offer with Lady Zabrina available for an immediate wedding. The betrothal agreement is even now being prepared. I will inform Lady Zabrina shortly of my decision to wed her to Lord Edric."

"She will not be pleased," Lyon predicted. Nor will I, he thought but did not say. Not that he cared who Zabrina wed. What galled was the knowledge that he could not kill Edric. If the Saxon had harmed Ariana, he thought fiercely, or forced her, he'd kill him with or without the king's permission. And mayhap send Ariana back to the abbey if he learned she'd willingly given herself to Edric of Blackheath. The thought of Ariana in another man's arms made him physically sick.

"Wed Edric of Blackheath!" Zabrina exploded. Her eyes were tiny pinpoints of violet fire. "Nay!"

William remained unmoved. "Why not, pray tell? The man is young, reasonably handsome, and in possession of all his teeth."

She sent a malevolent glare at Lyon, who was standing quietly behind William. He braced himself for her vindictive diatribe. He didn't have long to wait.

" 'Tis your fault, Lord Lyon! You put the king up to this. I had no hand in driving away your precious wife. You did it all by yourself."

Lyon's jaw stiffened but he said nothing, too

much of a gentleman to shame a lady before the king.

" 'Tis my decision and mine alone that you wed Lord Edric," William said sternly. Zabrina knew enough to hold her tongue. William was a rigid disciplinarian with a short fuse. He was known to unleash his temper with dire consequences. "The betrothal agreement has already been drawn, signed, and sealed."

"Does Lord Edric know of this *honor* you bestow upon him?" Zabrina asked with scathing sarcasm. "If I am not mistaken, Lord Edric has run off with Lord Lyon's wife." She slanted Lyon a superior glance, as if to say that he couldn't even manage his own wife.

"Nay," William admitted, "but he will as soon as Lord Lyon finds the scoundrel. 'Tis my hope that the match will please him. I have need of supporters in the North."

More than you know, Zabrina thought but did not say. There was endless intrigue at court, and a good deal of it involved northern barons and the Borderlands.

"I will be anxious to learn of Lord Edric's reaction when he hears you have betrothed us."

"You will learn of it firsthand, my lady," William informed her. "You are to accompany Lord Lyon to Blackheath. You will be present when the betrothal is announced, and it is my wish that a marriage ceremony be conducted immediately."

"Is that your final word, sire?" Lady Zabrina asked. If she was to travel with Lyon, it wouldn't be as bad as she had first thought. She had many days in which to work on Lyon. If she could entice him into her bed, perhaps he wouldn't give her up to Lord Edric after all. Besides, Edric wanted Ariana. Mayhap they could agree upon some kind of trade that would make everyone happy.

"That is my final word, my lady. How soon can you be ready to leave for Blackheath?"

"I will need several days, sire. There are bags to pack, personal belongings to prepare, and many other tasks too numerous to count."

"I wish to leave immediately, sire," Lyon protested forcefully. "Lord Edric has my wife and I fear for her life."

"I doubt Lord Edric will harm your lady wife," William said after careful thought. "It appears to me that a misunderstanding has developed between you and your lady. Lady Ariana has known Lord Edric all of her life and trusts him. Doubtless she is anxiously waiting for you to come after her. A few days' delay will work to your advantage, making her more eager for you when you arrive at Blackheath."

"If she is at Blackheath," Lyon muttered beneath his breath, none too pleased with William's decision. He thought the king was taking the situation much too lightly. There was a distinct possibility that Edric was taking Ariana to Scotland, where English law could not reach him.

*   *   *

"Edric, I insist you release me," Ariana said, growing angrier by the minute.

Finding herself locked in the room that first day had been the final insult. Nothing she had said since had gotten through to Edric. When she refused to mount the next evening, he had tossed her bodily onto her horse's back. And when she tried to jump off, he found a rope and lashed her wrists to the pommel. And that was how they had traveled during their whole journey.

"Edric, you must listen to reason," Ariana pleaded when Edric continued to ignore her.

"It will all work out for the best, my lady, you'll see. You're angry now, but when your marriage to Lord Lyon is annulled, we will be wed and all will be well. Soon the Conqueror and the Lion will be driven from English soil."

"Then England will be ruled by King Malcolm," Ariana taunted. "Is that what you want?"

Edric frowned. Somehow he had imagined England under Saxon rule again. "Better that than Norman rule."

Ariana had no reply. She was no longer certain that Norman rule wasn't the best for England. England had been conquered by the Danish and ruled by them for many years. In 1052 King Edward the Confessor had first offered his crown to Duke William of Normandy, then injudiciously to Harold, Earl Godwin's son. Angry at the loss of England to Harold after Edward's death, William had marched into England and defeated Harold at Hastings, claiming England for himself.

Ariana hated to admit it, but William seemed to be uniting England under one rule. William was harsh and ruthless to those who did not obey him, but she could not recall one instance where William had demanded a man's death as punishment for a crime.

"Untie me, Edric."

He gave her a soulful look. "Soon, my lady, but not yet. Mayhap when we reach Blackheath and my knights join us on our journey north to Abernethy. With our great numbers, you will have no opportunity for escape."

Ariana felt a surge of renewed hope. Blackheath was close to Cragmere. If she could get word to her men at Cragmere, they would come for her and keep her safe until Lyon arrived. But would Lyon come for her? Her rashness was ever getting her into trouble. Mayhap she was too much trouble and Lyon would happily forget her. With Lady Zabrina at his beck and call he had little need for a wife. If only he cared for her a little, she thought resentfully. If only they could start over from the beginning.

Lyon readied his men and arms, eager to leave Londontown the minute Zabrina's baggage was loaded into a wagon, which would follow at a more sedate pace. But fate conspired against him. He was felled by a mysterious malady hours before they were to leave. The illness swept through William's tower, infecting nearly everyone within, spreading like wildfire throughout Londontown. First came the fever, then alternate bouts of retching and emptying of the intestines. After that a debilitating weakness left its victims with little energy. Even turning over in bed became an impossible chore. Lyon had been dosed, purged, and bled by the king's own physician as he lay listless and unresponsive.

After a week he began to mend, albeit slowly. Just when he felt strong enough to mount a horse, Zabrina was struck down. Though few died from the strange malady, everyone, including the king's family, fell victim to its symptoms. A full three weeks passed before both Lyon and Zabrina were recovered enough to leave on their journey north.

With each passing day, Ariana began to fear that Lyon had indeed forgotten her. Their journey had been necessarily slow, since they traveled mostly at night. Lyon would have had plenty of time to catch up to them had he wanted to. When they finally reached Blackheath, Ariana perked up noticeably. Perhaps now she could find a way to send word to Cragmere. But once again fortune deserted her. After a few hours rest, they were off again for Abernethy with an impressive escort of Edric's knights.

Nearly back to his full strength, but thinner and paler, Lyon drove his knights through the countryside with one thought in mind. Finding

Ariana. Nearly a full month had passed since she'd left with Edric and anything could have happened in that time. Did she love the Saxon lord? he wondered. Did she think about her legal husband at all?

Had she given herself to Edric of Blackheath?

"My Lord Lyon," Zabrina called out as they rode, "if you do not call a rest, I will expire from exhaustion. Have pity. I am recovering from an illness and cannot take this terrible pace."

For the most part, Lyon had ignored Zabrina. He had no inkling of Zabrina's plans to seduce him, else he would have taken more care to remain out of her reach.

Lyon halted abruptly, bringing his escort of twelve trusted knights to a stop. He knew Zabrina was right, for some of his own knights had been infected with the same malady and looked quite peaked.

"There is a manor house not too distant. We will ask succor for the night. Lord Denton will be most eager to offer his hospitality when he learns the beauteous Lady Zabrina rides in our party." He spoke in jest but knew it was doubtless true. Illness had not dimmed Zabrina's vibrant beauty.

Lord Denton, an elderly bachelor, was most happy to welcome Lord Lyon and his party. Lyon and Zabrina were given spacious chambers and the knights were quartered with Denton's own men. After a copious repast fit for a king, a game of chess, and a shared bottle of fine wine, Lyon retired to his chamber. Zabrina had already sought her bed after charming a thoroughly smitten Denton. Lyon felt a twinge of anger when Denton casually mentioned that he was a lucky man to have the Lady Zabrina as traveling companion. He also said, as an aside to Lyon, that he had given Lyon and Zabrina connecting chambers. Lyon decided immediately to make certain the door was locked from his side.

A single candle sputtered in its holder as Lyon entered his bedchamber. True to his word, he locked the connecting door then undressed quickly. He fell into bed with a audible sigh. It Lyon took scant seconds to realize that he wasn't alone. He could have described every charming curve of the voluptuous body warming the bed beside him. He groaned in dismay. It had been too long since he'd bedded a woman, and he felt his body leap in response.

"Ah, my lord, it has been a long time, has it not?" Zabrina fondled the hard length of his staff, cooing in delight when it jerked upright in her hand. "Let me ease you, my lord. I know what you like."

The moist heat of her mouth moved down the length of his body, the roughness of her tongue coaxing him into rigid erectness. He groaned and tried to shove her away.

"Nay, my lord, let me do this for you. Does your lady wife ease you in this manner? You're wonderfully virile, my lord."

He felt her lips circle him fully, taking him deeply. In another minute he'd be entirely at her mercy, ensnared as helplessly as a moth by a flame. Then suddenly the image of Ariana floated before his dilated pupils. She was smiling at him, beguiling him with the sweetness of her expression, the beauty of her face, the lithe suppleness of her body. Her flaxen hair floated around her head like a halo. Her lips were lush and red, her eyes as green as precious emeralds.

He recalled those eyes, flaming with anger. He remembered them soft with passion, and he knew no other woman could ever please him like Ariana. Simply said, he cared for Ariana more than he had realized. Even if she loved Edric, she was his and he would have her back. With a strength born of determination, he lifted Zabrina bodily and set her aside.

"Get out of here, Zabrina, before I lose my temper. If you ever try anything like this again, I will beat you and advise your husband to do likewise."

"My lord, say it is not so! Surely you will not abandon me to Lord Edric."

" 'Tis William's wish."

"Edric has Lady Ariana. And you have me. It is the way things were meant to be. It is the happy solution."

"Happy for whom? Nay, Zabrina, 'tis Ariana I want. You would do well to set your mind to marrying Edric of Blackheath. Go back to your chamber. I want you not."

Her violet eyes glowed with dark menace. "Do you reject me, my lord?"

"Aye. I am married and you are promised."

She flounced from the bed, her naked body a pale blur in the dimly lit room. "Being married never stopped you before. Mark my words, my Lord Lyon. When your lady wife bears Lord Edric's babe, you will regret clinging to a faithless woman." Having uttered those hurtful words, Zabrina bounced from the chamber in magnificent anger.

Lyon thought long and hard about Zabrina's words. It was entirely possible that Edric had bedded Ariana. He'd certainly had plenty of opportunity to do so, given the time that had lapsed since Ariana left with Edric. He cursed anew the sickness that had laid him and most of the court low, wasting precious time. No matter what happened, Ariana was his and Lyon vowed that no other man would have her. Somehow he couldn't believe that Ariana would betray him with another man. If she was forced, he'd deal with it.

Three days later, Lyon's party, fully garbed for battle, rode through the gates of Blackheath unchallenged. A few serfs milled about the yard looking frightened. When Lyon sought to question them, they fled in terror. Finally Edric's seneschal appeared on the steps, literally shaking in his boots.

"Where is your master?" Lyon demanded to know.

The man swallowed visibly. "Not here, my lord."

"Do you know who I am?" Lyon asked, raising

the face piece of his helm so the man could see his face.

"Aye, everyone knows the Lion of Normandy."

"So I am," Lyon conceded. "Now you may tell me where your master has gone. And if he had a lady with him."

Lord Edric had given his seneschal few instructions when he left Blackheath, save to inform him to expect Lord Lyon and hold him at bay as long as possible. Though the man had been a faithful retainer for many years, he did not think it worth his life to lie to the Lion of Normandy.

The seneschal moistened his suddenly dry lips, finding speech difficult when faced with such a formidable foe. "Lord Edric told me nothing of his plans, my lord."

Lyon fixed him with an austere glare. "If you value your life, churl, you will tell me what you know."

"My Lord Edric and his guest stayed at Blackheath but a few hours, my lord. He rode north." He paused, staring fearfully at Lyon before adding, "I heard him mention that he was joining King Malcolm at Abernethy."

"Was the lady with him?" Lyon queried tightly.

"Aye," the man said in a barely audible whisper. His knees shook so hard that he could hear them rattling together. He prayed the invincible Lion of Normandy would not take his wrath out on him, a poor man with a family to support.

Had he known that Lyon rarely punished where punishment was not earned, he would have breathed much more easily.

Lyon and Beltane exchanged meaningful glances. "Do we ride to Abernethy, my lord?"

"Aye," Lyon said, "to Abernethy." His voice was taut with dark undertones. "We will bide the night at Cragmere, since 'tis on the way."

Wheeling his mighty destrier, he rode from Blackheath in a thunder of hooves and clatter of armor.

"We did not expect you at Cragmere, my lord," Keane said as Lyon strode into the hall unannounced. When he saw Zabrina at Lyon's side, his brow rose in disapproval. He waited a moment, and when Ariana did not appear, asked, "Is aught amiss? Where is my lady?"

"A good question, Keane," Lyon replied. "Has Lady Ariana been to Cragmere recently?"

Keane's curiosity turned into alarm. "Nay, my lord, I have not seen Lady Ariana since you left together for Londontown." He bent Zabrina a look that described exactly what he thought of Lyon bringing another woman to Cragmere. "Would you like a chamber prepared for your . . . guest, my lord?"

"Aye, but we do not bide long at Cragmere. We journey to Scotland. Make Lady Zabrina comfortable and see that provisions are made ready for us. We leave at dawn tomorrow."

"The lady too, my lord? Or will she bide at Cragmere during your absence?"

"Lady Zabrina rides with us, Keane. Show her the bathing room and assign someone to help her."

"Aye, my lord. If you will follow me, my lady," Keane said to Zabrina.

Turning away before Zabrina could engage him in conversation, Lyon hastened to his bedchamber. The moment he entered the room, he knew he was not alone. He searched the lengthening shadows, his hand poised above his sword. Nadia seemed to appear as if by magic, staring at him intently with eyes as dark and glowing as burning coals.

"What have ye done to her, my lord? Ariana would not leave ye if she did not have good cause."

Lyon sent Nadia a fulminating scowl. "How did you know Ariana left Londontown? Have you been in touch with her?"

"Nay, my lord, I have neither seen nor heard from Lady Ariana, but she appears in my visions. Ye have driven her from ye and she cries out for ye."

"What nonsense are you spewing, witch!" Lyon roared. "Ariana left with Lord Edric of her own accord."

"I warned her, my lord," Nadia continued, ignoring Lyon's ferocious temper. "I told her to 'ware her heart where ye were concerned."

"What else did you tell her?" Lyon asked evenly. His calm was deceptive and Nadia knew it.

"I told her ye were necessary to Cragmere,

and so ye are. And now I will give ye a warning, my lord."

Her eyes glazed over and her sight turned inward as she wove from side to side, repeating her prophesy in a monotone that raised goose bumps on Lyon's flesh.

"Ariana is no longer yers. Dark forces are at work against ye. I see betrayal, and bloodshed, and aye, mayhap death. If ye live, ye will learn the meaning of love at the cost of yer honor."

Lyon cocked a dark brow. "*If* I live? What do you mean, Ariana is no longer mine? Speak, crone, I wish to know the meaning of your visions."

Nadia let out an unearthly shriek and fell to the floor unconscious.

Cursing violently, Lyon strode to the door and called for Keane. When the man did not appear immediately, he bounded down the stairs, seeking help. He barked instructions to a maid who answered his call and hurried back up the stairs, intending to question Nadia further after she revived. When he reentered his chamber, Nadia was gone.

The following morning, with an escort of a dozen armed knights and Lady Zabrina in tow, Lyon set out for Abernethy.

Chapter Thirteen

A suffocating mist rolled in from the Tay River, obscuring the sun and dewing Ariana's face with sparkling droplets of moisture. Curling tentacles of fog clung to her clothing and hair, enveloping her in a cloud of unhappy thoughts. Weeks had elapsed since she and Edric arrived at Abernethy. King Malcolm had greeted them effusively, along with Edgar the Atheling, Anglo-Saxon heir to the English throne, who with his sister Margaret had fled England after William's conquest. Malcolm had married Margaret in 1069.

Also in attendance were Saxon lords who had fled to Scotland to join forces with Malcolm. Malcolm's dream of expanding his kingdom into England was enhanced by those same English refugees seeking asylum.

Ariana stood at the open window of her chamber, staring at the river through the shifting fog. She had almost given up hope of Lyon coming for her. He probably hated her for the way in which she had left him. She had acted unwisely, she realized, just as she had done so often in the past. Even when she was a child, her mother had despaired of her impulsive nature, but she had been too headstrong to change her ways. The nuns at the abbey had tried to tame her wild ways, too, but only succeeded in pushing her further into rebellion. They had reminded her often that she was an abandoned wife whose husband neither wanted nor cared for her. If she didn't believe it then, she certainly did now.

If Lyon truly wanted her, he would have followed her and Edric to Scotland without delay, Ariana thought dully. Obviously he was glad to be rid of her. She knew she had made some serious mistakes in judgment, one of which was to believe Zabrina's lies.

"Ariana, open the door. 'Tis Edric. I have good news."

Ariana frowned at the closed door. The only good news Edric could give her was to tell her he was sending her back home.

"Ariana, open. I've just come from the king."

Sighing in resignation, Ariana opened the door to her comfortable chamber, admitting Edric. "What is it, my lord? Have you come to tell me I may return to England?"

"Well you know I will not let you go, my lady,"

Edric said, sending her a heated look. "Read this," he said, unrolling a sheet of parchment and holding it up for her perusal. " 'Tis an annulment of your marriage to Lord Lyon, granted by King Malcolm's bishop. 'Tis legal, my lady. Nothing hinders us now. We can be wed immediately."

Ariana drew back in alarm. " 'Tis legal in Scotland, mayhap, but not in England. I do not wish to marry you, Edric."

"At one time you were willing—nay, eager—to become my wife."

" 'Tis true our fathers betrothed us at an early age, and I was quite agreeable, but I was but a child who knew naught of such things. I am a married woman now, joined with Lyon before God. My marriage was consummated, and there can be no annulment."

Edric's jaw hardened. "I care not if the Norman bastard has bedded you—you were meant to be mine. Just as William set aside our betrothal and gave you to Lyon, Malcolm has set aside your marriage and given you to me. If Lord Lyon wanted you, he would have followed us to Scotland. Nay, Ariana, the fearless Lion of Normandy is quite content with Lady Zabrina."

Ariana's cheeks burned with humiliation. The truth hurt. Mayhap she would be better off with Edric, a man she had known since childhood. Except . . . except that she could never love Edric in the same way she loved Lyon. She could never desire Edric as she desired Lyon. She had found paradise in Lyon's arms and the thought of never experiencing the miracle of his love again saddened her beyond measure, beyond endurance.

"Malcolm will announce our betrothal at the evening meal tonight," Edric continued blithely. "The betrothal will not be a lengthy one, owing to our haste. Within a fortnight we will be wed." He grasped her shoulders, pulling her close. "Come, my lady, do not be sad. We will deal well with one another. I will treat you with the honor and love you deserve. You were not meant to be wasted on a Norman bastard."

"Edric, I implore you, return me to Lyon. If you care for me, you won't force me to marry you. I already have a husband."

Edric sent her a scathing glance. "Jesu! You love him! I expected better from you, my lady. Have you no pride? He flaunts his mistress in your face and still you cling to him. Nay, Ariana, your tender pleas do not move me. In a fortnight we will wed. King Malcolm himself extends his blessing and will attend the ceremony. He went to considerable lengths to procure your annulment. I am most grateful to him."

"I do not feel well, my lord. I would like to be alone," Ariana said, turning toward the window to hide her tears. Edric sent her a concerned look, then quietly left the chamber.

Did a woman have no rights? she wondered desperately. Was it her lot in life to be passed from man to man without so much as a by-your-leave? *Lyon, where are you?* she cried out in silent supplication. *Please come to me. I need you.*

Suddenly, without warning, the thick mist outside the window began to shift, and a small clearing appeared at its center. Her eyes glazed over as she stared at the figures forming within the mist-framed vision. She saw Lyon, riding over the moors. Sir Beltane was at his side. Armed and determined, they rode with a purpose. Every instinct told Ariana that they rode to Abernethy. Suddenly her inner sight sharpened, and she saw that a woman accompanied him. Lady Zabrina! She gasped in dismay and fell to the floor in a swoon.

Ariana gained her wits slowly, recalling every nuance of her vision, every hurtful detail. Lyon was coming to Abernethy and Lady Zabrina was with him. For what purpose had he brought his leman? she wondered as she lifted herself from the floor. Did he bring Zabrina to taunt her? To prove how little he needed his wife? To show his contempt for her? Sweet Jesu, how could she bear it?

Lyon saw Abernethy rising in the distance and smiled grimly. He wondered how his lady wife would greet him when he arrived. Not with open arms, he suspected. Nevertheless, he would have her back in his care. Whether she liked it or not, she would have to learn to live without her lover. Should Malcolm refuse to release Ariana to him, he had only to send a messenger to William, who was even now gathering an army to march into Scotland and foil Malcolm's plans to expand his kingdom into England.

William was no fool. He knew what was going on north of the border and had admitted to Lyon that he was preparing to retaliate with men and arms. Edgar the Atheling would never sit on the English throne, William had vowed. Nor would Malcolm of Scotland.

"My lord, I would like a word with you," Zabrina said as she rode up beside Lyon.

"Speak," Lyon said curtly.

"Is that Abernethy ahead?"

"Aye."

"Please, my lord, for all we once meant to each other, I beg you not to deliver me to Edric of Blackheath. There are many suitors more worthy of my hand. If you send me back to Londontown, mayhap I can persuade William to reconsider. Take me to Cragmere and leave your lady wife to Lord Edric—they deserve one another. I will be most happy to bide with you at Cragmere, with or without the king's blessing."

" 'Tis William's wish that you wed Lord Edric, Zabrina," Lyon said firmly. "I asked permission to kill the bastard but was denied that pleasure. Instead, William awarded him a wealthy wife and rich lands. I like it not but recognize the wisdom of William's decision. William needs Edric's support in the north to protect the Borderlands."

"But Edric has already proven disloyal to Malcolm," Zabrina reminded him.

" 'Tis not too late for him to change his mind. William hopes to lure him back over the border with promises of great wealth and a lusty wife. I would prefer killing the man, but I will obey William in this, unless Edric has harmed Ariana. Then I will not hesitate to slay the bastard."

The sun hung low in the western sky when Lyon approached the gates of Abernethy keep. He was challenged immediately by the captain of the guard. In a strong voice Lyon gave his name, stating that he came in peace, bearing a message from King William. Since England and Scotland were not officially at war, Lyon was welcomed to Abernethy, albeit with a marked lack of enthusiasm. Tossing his reins to a serf, Lyon strode boldly into the great hall, where the king and queen and the entire court were partaking of the evening meal. He paused just inside the door, his gaze searching the room for Ariana.

Ariana paid little heed to the murmur of voices, which seemed to swell for no apparent reason. But when people turned to stare at the two strangers poised just inside the hall, she looked up and met the burning intensity of Lyon's eyes. Their gazes collided and clung for the space of a heartbeat, until the corners of Lyon's mouth turned up into a sneer and he forced his gaze along another path.

Ariana groaned in dismay and started to rise to go to him. Edric grasped her arm in a bruising grip, forcing her back into her seat. "Do not make a fool of yourself," he hissed into her ear.

"Are you blind? He has brought his leman with him. Does that not tell you something?"

Sitting on the dais with his queen, Malcolm spoke quietly to his seneschal, who then strode briskly to where Lyon stood, making him welcome with polite words.

"Who are you and from whence do you come, my lord? Do you have business with King Malcolm?"

"I am Lyon of Cragmere," Lyon said in a voice loud enough to carry to Malcolm. "And this is Lady Zabrina. I bear greetings from King William of England."

"Welcome, Lord Lyon," Malcolm said expansively as he motioned Lyon forward. "Sit down and sup with us. I will meet with you and hear King William's greetings in my chambers later."

Malcolm had been expecting the mighty Lion of Normandy to come for his woman. It was why he had applied considerable pressure upon his bishop to grant an annulment of Lady Ariana's marriage to Lord Lyon with the greatest haste. He fully expected a wrathful Lord Lyon to show up demanding the return of his wife, but he had come too late. The annulment had already been granted and the lady was now betrothed to Lord Edric.

Lyon found a seat for himself and Zabrina, and the hall settled down to its usual mealtime chatter. Lyon had chosen their places well. From where he sat he could look across the room at Ariana and Edric. Though he ate with gusto, he watched Ariana from the corner of his eye, noting that while pale, she appeared otherwise unhurt. When he glanced at Edric, he was annoyed by the man's protective attitude towards Ariana.

At length the meal ended and King Malcolm pounded on the table for attention. It was obvious that he had an announcement to make, and his subjects looked at him in eager anticipation.

"I propose a toast," the king said, rising to his feet. All those in the hall followed suit. "To the betrothal of Lady Ariana and Lord Edric. May their union be long and fruitful." He raised his cup and drank noisily.

Ariana found herself the center of attention as cups were raised to her in congratulation. Lyon was too stunned to react. Suddenly Ariana could bear no more. Lunging from her seat, she ran from the hall as if the devil was nipping at her heels. Even within the safety of her chamber, she could still see the utter contempt in Lyon's eyes. Truth to tell, she couldn't blame him. If only she could see him alone, explain how foolish she had been to run away without allowing him the courtesy of answering Zabrina's charges. If Lyon couldn't bear the sight of her, why had he come to Scotland?

All these thoughts and more ran through Ariana's head as she restlessly paced her chamber. Would Lyon believe that she hadn't wanted this annulment? Or would he be pleased to be rid of her? Jesu, if only she could see him, talk to him, make him understand that she had been hurt and driven by pride. She could never tell him she loved him, but at least she could try to convince him that she had never wanted this annulment or the subsequent betrothal to Edric.

Through a haze of shock, Lyon watched Ariana flee the hall. Ariana looked so upset, so utterly miserable, that he wanted to go after her, wanted to hold her close to his heart, to make her love him better than she loved Edric. The announcement of her betrothal had stunned him. He should hate her, but he didn't. She had tried to poison him, had left him for another man, and still he wanted her. He glared ominously at Edric, the man he believed his wife loved. And by William's order he couldn't even slay the bastard.

Lyon paced Malcolm's outer chamber, waiting for the promised interview. In his pouch he carried the betrothal document between Edric of Blackheath and Lady Zabrina that William had given him before he left Londontown. William had also given Lyon another missive to be delivered to Malcolm. Lyon had no idea what it said but suspected it had something to do with Malcolm's intention of expanding Scotland's borders into England.

"His majesty will see you now."

Lyon started violently. He had been so lost in thought that he had not heard the king's man approach.

"Thank you," Lyon said as he approached the open door to Malcolm's chamber. He walked in without knocking. Malcolm was sitting in an easy chair. Queen Margaret was nowhere in sight. Lyon supposed the saintly woman was off by herself somewhere praying.

"Ah, my Lord Lyon. I have been expecting you. You have come to inquire about Ariana of Cragmere, have you not?"

"Aye, sire, I have come for my wife."

"She is no longer your wife."

"By whose order?" Lyon asked with distinct mockery.

Malcolm flushed but held his temper. "An annulment of your marriage has been granted by my bishop. The decree bears my royal seal and is quite legal."

Thunderclouds gathered in Lyon's eyes, making the planes of his face even more pronounced. "Legal in Scotland, mayhap, but not in England."

Malcolm sent Lyon a grim smile. "This is Scotland, my lord. I have betrothed Lady Ariana to Edric of Blackheath. Queen Margaret is planning a great feast for the wedding. If you bide with us a fortnight, you can participate in the celebration."

"Jesu!" Lyon swore violently. He had not thought things would progress so fast. If not for the cursed illness that had laid him low, he would have arrived before an annulment could be granted. He must rethink his position and act accordingly. It would serve little purpose now to show Malcolm the papers betrothing Zabrina to Edric. The situation had grown desperate. He would show the document to Edric and hope for the best.

"You said you had a message from King William," Malcolm reminded him. He appeared anxious to be rid of the tall Norman knight.

"Aye." He reached into his pouch, carefully extracting the message for Malcolm while leaving the betrothal document undisturbed. He handed it over with a flourish. "I will carry your answer when I leave."

Malcolm quickly scanned the message, which was brief and to the point. In a violent burst of temper, Malcolm wadded it up and threw it across the room. "Your king demands that I submit to him. I, King of Scotland. 'Tis outrageous! You may go. There is no answer. Need I remind William that half the English barons have joined forces with me? I have the manpower to drive William from English soil. Nay, I say! I will never swear fealty to the Norman bastard!"

Lyon bowed and left the chamber quickly. Malcolm was working himself into a frenzy, and Lyon realized that he must send a message quickly to William, telling him to expect an attack from the north. He found Sir Beltane in the garrison with his knights. Taking him aside, he quickly explained the situation, charging him to deliver the message to William with all due haste. Beltane left immediately with two knights handpicked for their endurance.

Lyon's seneschal was waiting for him when he returned to the hall. "Your chamber has been prepared for you, my lord."

From the corner of his eye, Lyon spied Edric sitting before the fire, staring morosely into his cup. "I am not ready to retire yet. Bring wine. I will join Lord Edric by the fire."

"Aye, my lord. My name is Gunn. Summon me when you are ready, and I will direct you to your chamber."

"Thank you, Gunn." With slow deliberation Lyon made his way to the huge hearth that stretched across one wall. He took a bench directly across from Edric.

Edric glanced up from his cup. "What took you so long, my lord? I expected you much sooner. Your timing is impeccable. You arrived in time to hear Malcolm announce my betrothal to Lady Ariana. Soon she will be my wife."

Lyon's smile did not reach his eyes. "Over my dead body."

"If that's the way it must be."

Lyon stared at him, holding his temper with admirable restraint. "Has my lady wife shared your bed?"

Edric leaped to his feet, seething with anger. "I would not insult Lady Ariana in such a vile manner. I love her."

"Hmmm, I wonder." Yet despite himself, he believed Edric.

"What is that supposed to mean?"

Reaching into his pouch, Lyon withdrew the betrothal document given to him by William and handed it to Edric. "Calm yourself, Lord Edric, and read how well King William values you. His sentiments are not mine, but I have agreed to deliver this into your hands. If it were up to me, I would slay you."

Edric stared at the document. "What is this?"

"Read it. I think it will please you."

Edric held the fragile parchment close to the fire so he could peruse the words. When he finished reading, he looked at Lyon in disbelief. His shock was evident in his dilated pupils and arched brows. "I cannot believe William would betroth me to the wealthiest widow in the land. Or the most beautiful. God's blood! Lady Zabrina is a worthy catch for any man."

"Aye. 'Tis William's wish that you wed with Lady Zabrina immediately. I am to act as witness to the marriage."

Edric sent him a shrewd look. "Am I supposed to be grateful for William's largess? What of Lady Ariana? Am I to abandon her?"

"Ariana was never yours to abandon," Lyon said evenly.

"She came with me of her own free will. She is no longer married to you."

"I will deal with Ariana. You need only accept the betrothal to Zabrina and claim her enormous wealth and vast lands in England. Upon your marriage you will become one of the richest and most powerful barons in all of England."

"And I would answer to a Norman king."

"Would you rather call Malcolm King of England? Or Edgar the Atheling? One is overly ambitious and the other is weak."

Edric was silent so long that Lyon feared the betrothal was not to his liking. Finally he turned to Lyon, his eyes bright with curiosity. "Does your leman no longer please you?"

"Zabrina is no longer my leman. She hasn't been for a very long time. And for your information, she pleased me well enough."

Edric swallowed visibly and leaned toward Lyon. "They say Lady Zabrina is . . . most accomplished."

Lyon's eyes sparkled with amusement. William was right. Edric was nearly salivating over the prospect of possessing both Zabrina and her incredible wealth.

"Lady Zabrina, in my estimation, will make you a profoundly happy man in more ways than one. I've found her knowledge of giving pleasure extensive as well as extremely satisfying."

A thrill of excitement slid up Edric's spine. He had to admit the betrothal between him and Zabrina offered much: It titillated him, intrigued him, made his mind soar with possibilities. Unfortunately, he was already betrothed to Lady Ariana. He could not abandon her to a Norman beast. Besides, Malcolm relied on his support.

"Tempting though the offer may be, I am already betrothed to Lady Ariana," Edric said haltingly. It was difficult to turn down so generous an offer from the Norman king, but he knew whence it came. William needed his support in the north and was offering him a boon to come back to the fold.

"You refuse?" Lyon asked, clearly shocked.

"Nay, do not give me your answer now. Think about it. Consider what it will mean to you, and mayhap you will change your mind. I warn you, though, no matter what you decide, you cannot have Ariana. She is mine." He rose abruptly. "I bid you good night, my lord. It has been a long day."

Ariana paced the length of the chamber and back again. She stopped and stared at the door, as if expecting Lyon to storm into her chamber and make demands. He did not come, and that worried her even more. She knew Lyon had met with King Malcolm after the evening repast and wondered if they had discussed her. It occurred to her that mayhap Lyon was either pleased with the annulment or too angry to face her. For her own peace of mind, Ariana was determined—nay, eager—to explain that she wasn't a willing participant in Edric's conniving.

Aye, she had left Lyon, but she had attempted to return time and again, only to be thwarted by Edric, who fancied himself in love with her. Since she had run off into the night, she'd had plenty of time to think, and even more time to realize that she truly did love Lyon. She knew now that she should have stayed and fought Lady Zabrina for Lyon's love.

Her expression turned bleak when she recalled that Zabrina had accompanied Lyon to Abernethy. What did it mean? Had he dragged his mistress halfway across England just to flaunt her? If Lyon wanted to hurt her, he had succeeded.

The more Ariana considered the situation, the more she came to realize that she was completely in the dark concerning Lyon's motives for coming to Scotland. If he didn't want her, why had he come? It took little imagination to picture him in Zabrina's bed, mayhap in a chamber close to hers. She closed her eyes against the pain and knew she had to speak to Lyon privately. If he wouldn't come to her, then she had no choice but to go to him. Locating him wasn't going to be easy. Finding him in bed with Zabrina was a distinct possibility, but one she had to face if she wanted to speak to him.

Easing the chamber door open, Ariana peered into the dimly lit passageway. She was just about to step through the door when she heard the heavy tread of footsteps trudging up the stairs. Ducking behind the door, she peered around it as a man appeared at the top of the staircase. He paused, as if to get his bearings, then turned in the opposite direction.

Though she could not see his face, Ariana recognized Lyon from his proud carriage—so powerful, so overwhelmingly virile. She identified him by the incredible stretch of his shoulders, the slimness of his waist, the strong, sleek length of his legs. Before she could consider the consequence of her action, she stepped into the passageway and called his name.

"Lyon . . ."

Following the directions given him by Gunn,

Lyon sought his bedchamber, his mind on Ariana and how he could rescue her from her own folly. He was so engrossed in his thoughts that he very nearly didn't hear the soft whisper of his name. He paused and turned slowly, peering through the murky shadows at the woman outlined in the dim light. At first he thought it was Zabrina, bent on another attempt at seduction. His heart lurched with joy when he recognized Ariana, her bright hair floating about her shoulders like a silver cloud.

"Ariana . . ." He pulled himself together and walked toward her. "You called, my lady?"

"Aye, my lord, I . . ." She hesitated, hardly knowing where to begin. "I would speak with you. 'Tis most urgent. I will not keep you from Lady Zabrina longer than necessary."

Lyon's dark brow arched upward. "You assume too much, my lady." He approached her slowly, his steps deliberate, almost menacing. Ariana shrank back in fear. "Do you fear me, Ariana?"

"Aye . . . nay. I do not know. Should I?"

"Mayhap. Why did you leave me? Have I been deliberately cruel? Though you richly deserved it, have I beaten you? Have I abused you verbally?"

Ariana shrugged and looked away. " 'Tis a long story. I wish to explain."

Lyon glanced toward her partially opened door. "Very well." He grasped her arm, shoved her inside her chamber, and closed the door behind them. "I am anxious to hear what you have to say."

Ariana's tongue flicked out to moisten her lips. Lyon watched, mesmerized, recalling how sweet her tongue tasted, how wantonly it had dueled with his, how soft and lush were her lips. "Did you come all the way to Abernethy on my account? If so, why did you bring your leman?"

Lyon sent her an amused glance. "I thought you wanted to explain, not ask questions. Have you bedded Lord Edric? Is that what you want to explain?"

"Nay!" Ariana denied vehemently. "I did not leave on Edric's account."

"Why did you leave?"

"Because I could not bear the thought of Lady Zabrina biding with us at Cragmere. I am your wife. The humiliation of living with your leman was too much to endure, so I left. I realized too late how reckless it was to run away, how foolish. I should have stayed and fought Lady Zabrina for your affection." She was grateful that Lyon would never know how much her admission cost her pride.

Lyon stared at her in consternation. "What made you think I invited Zabrina to Cragmere? 'Twas never my intention to keep a leman after I collected you from the abbey and installed you as mistress of Cragmere."

Seized by a choking sensation, Ariana forced herself to breathe deeply lest she swoon. Someone was lying, and she prayed it wasn't Lyon.

"Are you all right, my lady?" Lyon asked, obviously concerned at her inability to breathe properly.

"Aye," Ariana choked out on a gasp. "If you did not intend to bring Lady Zabrina to Cragmere, why did you bed her in Londontown? Do not be so quick to deny it, my lord, for I saw you with my own eyes."

"I admit to trying to make you jealous, my lady, but I did not actually bed Zabrina. I went to her room that night to speak with her and 'tis my belief that she drugged me. She must not have known how powerful the drug was, for I passed out immediately. When I awoke and found myself in her bed, I left the moment I regained my senses."

Ariana sent him a look of utter disbelief. "Am I to believe you, my lord? 'Tis almost too much to swallow."

"Did you not ask me to believe that you truly hadn't meant to poison me, Ariana?"

"Aye, but that was the truth," she said heatedly.

"So is this the truth. I would not insult you by bringing Zabrina to Cragmere. I no longer need a mistress. I have a wife."

"A wife," Ariana repeated, wanting desperately to believe him. And then she remembered that she was no longer Lyon's wife. She fixed him with a baleful glare. "Indeed, my lord. Have you forgotten that I am no longer your wife? Your delayed arrival allowed Malcolm sufficient time to set aside our vows. And you still have not explained to my satisfaction why you brought your leman with you," she told him with some bitterness.

He clenched his mouth tightly, his blue eyes glowing darkly as they held hers. "You are my wife, Ariana. No writ will take you from me."

Grasping her shoulders, he pulled her against the unyielding wall of his chest and lowered his head, capturing her mouth in a soul-destroying kiss. "I want you, Ariana. No other woman existed for me from the moment I set eyes on you at the abbey. We have been married five years, legally wedded and bedded. Nothing can change that."

Speechless, Ariana could only stare at Lyon. "I tried to poison you," she reminded him.

"Aye."

"And . . . and I ran away with another man."

"Aye. I know you love Edric of Blackheath, but I will make you forget him."

His words stunned her. Where did he get the idea that she loved Edric? "I am no longer your wife."

He laughed harshly. "You are still my wife, and I intend to prove it."

He kissed her again and she believed him.

Chapter Fourteen

Ah, sweet ecstasy! Lyon's kiss started as a gentle exploration, then quickly escalated to full-scale possession. Ariana throbbed with renewed life, reveling in Lyon's hunger. Not long ago she had despaired of ever experiencing his passion again. Sensation exploded in her loins. Her mind spun dizzily and merged with feeling, consuming her with grinding need. She breathed deeply of the very unsettling, very masculine odor of his arousal, glorying in his nearly frantic lust for her.

He probed her lips with his tongue and she opened her mouth, inviting him inside. He groaned and accepted her invitation, exploring the sweet depths of her mouth. The look on his face was stark need, made utterly ruthless with desire. She closed her eyes and surrendered to his hunger, loving him too much to protest.

She felt the silk of her tunic abrading her nipples as they jutted out to meet his searching fingers. A warm place grew and tingled where her thighs met her hips. And she felt wetness there. She heard him groan over the whisper of material as he hiked her skirts up around her waist. She placed her hand on his neck and felt him quiver. Holding her skirts up with one hand, he probed between her legs with the other. The moist evidence of her desire ignited a wildness in him as he seized her mouth again, thrusting his tongue into it.

"Ah, sweeting," he groaned into her ear, "you're hot and wet for me."

With a fierceness that took her breath away, he unfastened his chausses, backed her up against a wall, and plunged into her. He was so wild for her, he couldn't wait to undress her or lay her upon the bed. She moaned at the exquisite feeling of his penetration.

Lyon went still. "Have I hurt you?" he whispered against her mouth.

"No, no, don't stop."

He rocked her gently upon the marble-hard length of his shaft, covering her face with kisses. "I've dreamed of this all those lonely days and nights of my journey to Scotland. All I could think of was the sweet warmth of your passion and the tightness of your sheath welcoming me inside you."

"What made you so certain I would welcome you?" Ariana gasped as he lifted and rocked her against his thrusting hips.

"I did not know for certain," he admitted.

He slid in and out of her slowly, savoring the silky tightness, groaning in pleasure at the tiny internal contractions squeezing him. The world rocked beneath them, and suddenly all barriers were broken as Lyon moved his hands to grasp her bottom and thrust violently, again and again, clenching his teeth and groaning.

She felt his body pounding against her, felt the trembling of his hips and legs, felt her own body responding to the force of his violent strokes. She felt him grow inside her, stretching her, filling her, driving her to shuddering ecstasy.

It was savage. It was sweet. It was beyond wonderful. Then she felt his body stiffen. He bucked, driving her against the wall, then clenched his teeth and cried out her name. They held each other as the world around them tilted crazily. She felt sticky with his seed. Her legs were cramping and she tried to move away.

"Nay, not yet." He hadn't softened yet, and he slid in and out of her a few more times, enjoying her diminishing shudders. He smiled as she clung to him. "I wish I could stay inside you like this forever."

Ariana thought he meant to do exactly that but finally, reluctantly, he pulled out of her, swept her off her feet and carried her to the bed. Then he undressed her.

"Your body looks golden in the firelight," he said as he gazed at her spread out before him as if she were a tender morsel created specifically for his enjoyment. With feverish haste, he tore off his own clothing and joined her on the bed.

Ariana studied him through slitted eyes, admiring the sleek muscles roping his upper arms, the broad expanse of his chest, the slimness of his waist and firm, muscular legs. She reached out and traced an old scar that bisected his ribs.

He covered her smaller hand with his large one. "An old war wound. 'Tis long healed."

"It must have been a fearsome wound," she whispered with a touch of awe. He was much too young to have so many scars, she thought as she spied yet another running along the upper curve of his hip.

" 'Tis nothing. Fighting wars was how I earned my living. I fought beside William in Normandy, Maine, and Anjou. Then there was Hastings."

His eyes glowed with renewed passion and he touched her breasts, reverently, lovingly, his fingers pulling her nipples into hot buds. He dropped his head and took them into his mouth, first one, then the other, stroking them with the rough wetness of his tongue. Ariana squirmed and sighed. She tried to rationalize her need for this conquering Norman and failed utterly. Love was not rational. How could it be? Its mere definition defied reason. Love was not a product of logic. It was bred and nurtured within the heart.

Lyon was nearly undone by his obsessive

need for Ariana, and the devout love he bore
her. He still ached for her. Yet he knew he must
not surrender totally to his burning desire lest
he lose his sanity. He had to keep enough wits
about him to remove Ariana from the impossible situation she had gotten herself into. But
Jesu, he was still hard for her, still throbbing as
if he hadn't had her just moments ago.

"I want you again, sweeting," he whispered
hoarsely. Abruptly he levered himself from the
bed, drawing a murmur of protest from Ariana.
"I will be back in a moment," he promised.

He returned almost immediately, bearing a
cloth he had moistened with water from the
pitcher sitting on a nearby table. The bed
groaned with his weight as he rejoined her.

"What are you going to do?"

"I made the mess, I shall clean it," he said,
giving her a cocky grin. Then he spread her
knees, and with great gentleness cleansed his
seed from between her legs.

Blushing furiously, Ariana voiced vigorous
protest. "I can do that myself."

"Let me, sweeting, let me . . . There, 'tis
done." He tossed aside the soiled cloth, bent his
head, and placed a kiss on her most secret
place. "You're beautiful there. I never tire of
looking at you." When his head lowered for a
more intimate taste, she gasped, stiffened, and
cried out.

Her spicy scent titillated him. Emboldened,
he lowered himself between her legs, spread her
knees apart, and placed heated kisses along the

insides of her thighs. Ariana was nearly frantic when his lips finally found that place that ached for his attention. She arched wildly against his mouth.

"Jesu, oh Jesu," he chanted, his fingers flexing on her hips. Ariana gasped for air. She was drowning in the liquid heat of his mouth.

"Mercy, my lord," she begged, panting to catch her breath. "Have mercy."

He glanced up but a moment to smile at her before returning to his feast, using his tongue and teeth to tease and torment the tiny button hidden beneath the hood of flesh that was the font of her sensitivity. He allowed her no mercy, no respite, bringing her expertly to the peak of ecstasy before taking her over the edge. Ariana screamed, consigned by Lyon to a seething pit of churning, grinding pleasure. When the last shudders left her body, he rose over her, his face utterly ruthless. He resembled the magnificent beast his name implied, Ariana thought as she gazed into the scalding heat of his eyes.

"Touch me, my lady." His words were a harsh plea—nay, a demand, one Ariana obeyed instantly.

She took him into her hand, steel encased in velvet, reveling in her power over him, loving the way he groaned his need against her lips. She explored the tip, glistening with tiny drops of moisture, unable to resist the urge to bend down and taste him in the same way he had tasted her. Lyon felt the feather-soft touch of her tongue and nearly flew off the bed.

"Jesu! Sweet blessed Jesu! Cease, I want to spill my seed inside you, not waste it on the bedding."

With an efficiency of motion, he grasped her waist and reversed their positions, bringing her atop him. "Take me inside you, sweeting. Ride me." His features were strained and flushed, the cords of his neck distended with the force of his restraint.

Carried away by renewed passion, Ariana did not protest or question his request. She let instinct guide her. Bending her knees, she took him in her hand and guided him inside her. With a sigh she thrust her hips downward, pressing herself onto the heated tip of him. With a strangled groan, he pulled her to him and kissed her, arousing her with a soul-destroying sweep of his tongue. She quivered and began to move, riding him as he had directed, pleasing herself as well as him by rocking against him as he pressed kisses on her mouth, her throat, her nipples. When the pressure became unbearable, she moved faster, harder, taking him all the way inside her.

With a hoarse cry he exploded high and deep inside her. At first he feared he might have left her behind, but her quivering contractions assured him that she had attained her own pleasure. Then all thought fled as he lost himself in the ecstasy of his climax.

"That was truly amazing, my lord," Ariana said with a contented sigh when her breathing had slowed to a controllable level.

"My sentiments exactly, my lady," Lyon concurred between tortured gasps. "Have I not proved that you are still my wife?"

"You proved that you are an expert in areas where I am a novice. I could not help myself."

"Nor I, sweeting," Lyon admitted frankly. "You are my wife, Ariana. Lord Edric is a fool to think he can have you."

"I do not want Lord Edric. Nor do I love him."

Her candor stunned Lyon. The quiet strength of her tone shook the firm ground of his conviction. It had always been his belief that Ariana loved Edric of Blackheath. He stared at her. The candleglow illuminated her lovely face, though her skin shone paler than normal. Her green eyes carried mysteries of which he had no knowledge. Did she truly not love Edric?

"Do not toy with me, lady. I know you well. You would not run away with Edric if you did not love him. You let him talk you into feeding me poison despite having second thoughts once the deed had nearly ended my life."

"I swear to you on the head of the sweet Virgin, my lord, that I regained my senses in time to prevent you from drinking the wine."

"Lyon, my name is Lyon. I want to hear you say it."

"I did not attempt to poison you out of love for Edric, my . . . Lyon, I did it because you drove me to it, because you are a Norman, because you had stolen my demesne." Her voice shook with emotion. "I ran away because you cared more for Zabrina than you did for me. I know you desire me physically, just as I desire you, but I want more than sexual satisfaction from a husband. I want loyalty, and fidelity, and . . . love. . . ."

Lyon sucked his breath in sharply. "Jesu, Jesu, Ariana, do you love me?"

"I could love you, Lyon. 'Twould be so easy. Yet I cringe with fear at the thought of placing my heart at your disposal. The Lion of Normandy is no protector of a lady's heart."

"You have given me little opportunity, sweeting."

"Did you not bring Lady Zabrina to Scotland to ease the long nights of your journey?"

Lyon thought it was high time he told his lady wife exactly why Zabrina had accompanied him to King Malcolm's lair. " 'Tis not what you think, Ariana. William betrothed Zabrina to Lord Edric before I left Londontown. He commanded me to deliver her to her betrothed and act as witness to their wedding."

Ariana went still. "Zabrina and Edric?" She supposed the betrothal had been hatched by the shrewd William in hopes of bringing Edric back into the fold. It was obvious that William needed Edric's support in the North. It didn't take a genius to grasp William's strategy. "Does Edric know?"

"Aye, I told him."

"What did he say?" She waited with bated breath for Lyon's answer. She had no idea if the annulment Malcolm's bishop had handed down was legal in England, but if Edric was enticed into marriage by Zabrina's wealth, then she had high hopes of remaining Lyon's bride.

"I believe Lord Edric is seriously considering William's proposal. If he accepts, King Malcolm may decide to step in anyway and enforce the betrothal he arranged between you and Edric. You have made a fine mess of things, my lady. I should leave you to find your own solution, but I cannot. Strangely, I find that I care for you." He deliberately avoided using the word love for fear she would laugh at him.

Ariana jerked upright in shock. Had she heard right? Were her ears deceiving her? If Lyon cared for her, it was a beginning. Knowing that, the humiliation of loving him too much would be easier to bear. Mayhap she could turn his caring into love. But she must be sure he spoke the truth.

"Please do not trifle with me, my lord. You need not lie to soothe my feelings."

"I do not lie, sweeting. Lord knows I have little enough reason to care, given the anguish you've put me through, but I cannot control my emotions where you are concerned."

Ariana blinked up at him. "Have I been that unreasonable?"

"You made no secret of your hatred for Normans. You accused me of stealing your land. You called me a bastard, and worse."

"And you left me to rot in a convent," she retaliated. "I hated you long before I really knew you. But now I . . ." She hesitated, still fearful of giving her heart to a man who could break it so easily. "I am confused about my feelings."

Lyon tried to contain his disappointment. He had hoped for more than that, but since he had withheld his own feelings from her, he'd settle for what she offered. Before he could make known his own love, she would have to prove that she loved him more than Edric of Blackheath. So far he'd heard naught to indicate that she felt anything for him but hatred and, aye, lust.

You *will* love me, Ariana, Lyon thought. Aloud, he said, "Sleep, sweeting. We will need all our wits about us if we are to escape this muddle with our hides intact. Malcolm could well charge me with spying and throw me in the dungeon."

"Oh, Lyon, surely not!" Ariana cried, appalled at what she had wrought. If she'd not run away, Lyon wouldn't be risking his life for her.

"Do not worry about it, lady, I was only teasing. I will lie with you until you fall asleep, then I must leave. It wouldn't do for us to be found together. At least not until Edric decides to accept William's olive branch and take Zabrina as wife."

Lyon closed his eyes for a brief moment, enjoying the feel of Ariana in his arms. Unfortunately, exhaustion overcame him and he fell deeply asleep.

Outside the door, Zabrina lurked in the hallway, waiting for Lyon to leave. She had seen him enter Ariana's room earlier. She too had heard footsteps on the stone stairs and cracked open the door to her chamber. She had been lying in wait for Lyon, hoping to lure him into her chamber for a last attempt at seduction.

Then she heard Ariana call out to him and shortly afterward saw them disappear into her chamber. She waited until nearly dawn for him to emerge, and when he did not, she tried the door. Finding it unlocked, she peered inside, not surprised to see Lyon and Ariana intimately entwined in sleep. She returned to her own chamber, her evil smile boding no good for the star-crossed lovers.

The door slammed open with a loud crash. Lyon came awake slowly, still groggy from sleep. Ariana jerked upright, shocked to see daylight streaming through the window and Lyon still lying beside her, both of them gloriously naked. Her gaze flew to the door, where Edric stood glaring at them with murderous intent. Zabrina hovered behind Edric, staring at Lyon's naked body as if she wanted to devour him. Ariana grabbed for the covers, pulling them up to her neck.

"What are you doing with my betrothed?" Edric screamed, reaching for his sword.

Lyon stretched and gave him a lazy smile. "Are you speaking about my wife, Lord Edric? Since when is it a crime to bed one's own wife?"

"Since your marriage to Lady Ariana was annulled."

Lyon scowled. "Until the King of England dissolves my marriage, Ariana is still my wife." He placed an arm around Ariana's shoulders, giving her an intimate squeeze, much to Edric's dismay. "Have you reached a decision yet? If you wed Zabrina, you will become a wealthy and powerful man in England."

" 'Tis obvious Lord Edric does not want me," Zabrina piped up. "Accept the inevitable, my lord. Let Lord Edric have Ariana. Then William will have no argument against a marriage between you and me."

"Have I nothing to say about this?" Ariana asked heatedly. "I do not wish to marry Lord Edric. I would not be in bed with Lord Lyon if I did not consider myself still married to him."

"Mayhap King Malcolm will have something to say about this," Edric contended. "Let us take our leave, my lady," he said to Zabrina, offering his arm, "and confer with the king."

Truth to tell, the more Edric saw of Zabrina, the more he realized how advantageous a marriage to the beautiful vixen would be. But after he had put Malcolm through the trouble of annulling Ariana's marriage, he didn't have the nerve to accept William's generous offer. Jesu, what a coil.

"What do you think will happen now?" Ariana asked, still holding the covers up to her neck.

"I wish I knew," Lyon said, thinking ahead to all the things Malcolm could do to both him and Ariana. " 'Tis best I leave. I'll have a bath sent up to you and meet you later in the hall. By then Malcolm will have been apprised of our indiscretion and we should know soon afterward what he intends to do." He placed a tender kiss on her lips. "Be prepared for anything, my love."

Lyon was summoned to King Malcolm's chambers within the hour. He'd barely had time to bathe and dress before Gunn arrived with the message. Girding himself for the worst possible outcome, Lyon entered Malcolm's chambers in his usual forceful manner, unwilling to bend before the Scottish king who aspired to become ruler of all England.

Malcolm sat at his writing table, perusing a document. Before acknowledging Lyon, he signed the document with a flourish and carefully set it aside. "Sit you down, my lord. It hurts my neck to look up at you."

Lyon seated himself opposite Malcolm, his eyes wary. "You wish to speak with me, sire?"

"Obviously you question the legality of the annulment of your marriage to Lady Ariana of Cragmere. Rest assured that the lady is no longer your wife, my lord. She is to be wed within a fortnight to Lord Edric of Blackheath. Lord Edric and Lady Zabrina demanded an audience this morning—before matins even. What they told me was quite shocking." He fixed Lyon with a baleful glare. "Do you have in your possession a document signed by King William betrothing Lord Edric to Lady Zabrina?"

"Aye, sire," Lyon said without hesitation. Malcolm was bound to find out sooner or later anyway.

"Hmmm." Malcolm stroked his chin thoughtfully. Ever the opportunist, he was eager to turn the situation to his advantage. "Am I to assume you will not willingly relinquish Lady Ariana to Lord Edric?"

"You could assume that, sire." Lyon had no idea what the king was getting at but knew instinctively that he would not like it.

"You have not enough men with you to force the issue," Malcolm warned. "You are entirely at my mercy."

Lyon thought of William, who might even now be marching to Abernethy to confront Malcolm. "Aye, sire, so it would seem."

Malcolm's eyes narrowed shrewdly. "What say you to a compromise, Lord Lyon?"

"A compromise, sire? Know you that I will compromise neither my honor nor my marriage vows."

"That depends entirely on how badly you wish to keep your wife. I could be persuaded to set aside the annulment and restore Lady Ariana to you."

Lyon did not like the tone of Malcolm's offer. "What would it take to persuade you, sire?"

Malcolm sent Lyon a smile that did not reach his eyes. "Very little, actually. Renounce your allegiance to King William and join forces with me. With the Lion of Normandy at my side, I will conquer England and drive the Norman invaders into the sea. Once those Saxon barons who threw their support to William hear you are fighting on my side, they will abandon William and flock to my cause."

"What will it gain me if I agree to your terms, sire?"

"Your lady wife. I will destroy the annulment and nullify her betrothal to Lord Edric."

"For that concession you ask that I betray my king," Lyon said evenly, hanging on to his temper with admirable restraint.

Malcolm shrugged expansively. "If you wish to put it that way."

Lyon's hands tightened into fists. "What you have proposed demands careful thought, sire. You are asking me to choose between my honor and my wife."

"I can be quite generous, my lord. I can give you lands more extensive and richer than Cragmere. Scotland is a beautiful country; you will not regret swearing fealty to me. Once I have extended Scotland's borders, I will give you back Cragmere and any other lands you desire. Think on it, Lord Lyon, and give me your reply tonight. I will await you in my chambers after the evening meal."

Lyon rose, bowed, and took his leave. He feared speaking lest he lose the tenuous hold on his temper. Malcolm had gall, he'd give him that. Did he actually think he'd betray William? He'd find a way, Lyon vowed, to keep Ariana and still remain true to his sovereign.

The moment Lyon walked into the hall, all conversation came to a halt. He felt the weight of dozens of pairs of eyes resting upon him, and he realized that somehow everyone at Abernethy knew of the king's offer. He wondered for a brief moment how it had gotten around so soon—until he saw Zabrina speaking with a group of knights. After an interval the conversation picked up again, and Lyon sat down to break his fast. To his chagrin, Zabrina sat down beside him.

" 'Tis a pretty mess you've made of this, my lord," she taunted. "The whole court knows of Malcolm's offer. Many bets are being wagered. But only I know your answer."

Lyon's brow arched upward. "You know me well, my lady."

"Aye," Zabrina gloated. "I know you intimately, my lord. I know you well enough to predict that you won't forsake William no matter how much you care for that little witch you married. You would see her wed to Lord Edric before you'd submit to Malcolm."

"I fear you are right, Zabrina," Lyon said without hesitation. "I would die before betraying William. We have been through too much together."

" 'Tis just as I thought," Zabrina crowed gleefully. "Edric will marry Ariana, and you will be free to marry me."

"If 'tis God's will," Lyon said, not really meaning it. It would be a cold day in hell before he'd marry Zabrina. An even colder one before he'd stand idly by and watch his wife given to another man.

Unfortunately Ariana could not read his mind. She had entered the hall shortly after

Lyon sat down to eat. She saw Zabrina join him and felt no qualms about intruding. Zabrina had intimidated her for the last time. She had heard their conversation quite by accident as she approached them from behind. She couldn't believe her ears. She certainly did not expect Lyon to betray his king, but neither did she expect him to be so quick to replace her. Yet that was exactly what he seemed to be doing.

"You may marry Lady Zabrina tomorrow if that is your wish," Ariana said, her eyes spitting green flames.

Zabrina and Lyon turned at the same time. Zabrina did not try to conceal her smug grin. Nor could Lyon restrain his groan. Of all the rotten luck.

"Sit down, my lady, and break your fast," Lyon invited.

"I am not hungry, my lord. I do not wish to intrude."

"Please, Ariana," Lyon entreated. "We must talk and I don't know if we will have another opportunity to do so. How much of the conversation between me and Zabrina did you hear?"

Ariana's chin rose at a stubborn angle. "Enough to know that Malcolm offered you a choice between William and me."

"He wants me to submit to him. If I agree he will put aside the annulment of our marriage. If I refuse, he will wed you to Edric within a fortnight. He wants me to join forces with him and dissident Saxon lords who war against William."

Ariana's eyes widened. Even she knew Lyon would never betray his king for a woman. Lyon might care for her, but surely not enough to compromise his honor. He was a proud man. He did not take his oath of fealty lightly. He was loyal to William and nothing would change that.

"I understand," she said slowly. She understood but it still hurt.

"I am glad you understand," Zabrina spoke up. "I think I know Lyon better than you, and he will never submit to Malcolm. He will see you wed to Lord Edric first."

"Leave us, Zabrina, I wish to speak to Ariana alone," Lyon commanded. He knew Zabrina to be a gloating witch who enjoyed causing Ariana pain.

"As you wish, my lord," Zabrina said obsequiously as she rose gracefully and melted into the dark shadows of the hall.

"I cannot submit to Malcolm," Lyon said, staring into Ariana's eyes. "I am to give him my answer tonight. There can be but one answer."

Ariana's gaze fell to her hands, clasped tightly in front of her. "I know. I do not blame you. Malcolm gave you no real choice. You are William's man. Nothing will change that."

Lyon recognized the truth of her words. "Trust me, my lady. I will find a way out of this muddle."

"I fear I will be wed to Lord Edric first, my

lord. Mayhap I do not know you as well as Lady Zabrina, but I am convinced that you are no turncoat. Given a choice between me and your honor, you will choose your honor over me. Now if you will excuse me, my lord, I really am not hungry."

"Ariana . . ." He watched in misery as she fled from the hall.

Chapter Fifteen

"I trust you have decided wisely," King Malcolm said as he faced Lyon later that evening. They were in the king's chamber, and to Lyon's chagrin, Lord Edric was present. "I have asked Lord Edric to attend, for your decision affects him as well."

Lyon sent Edric a fulminating look. He should have slain the man when he first learned how desperately Edric desired Ariana. "My decision was not a difficult one," he told Malcolm. "I am William's man, and naught will change that."

Malcolm pounded his fist on the table and leaped to his feet. "God's blood, man, I have offered to restore your wife to you, whom you seem to hold in great affection. I have offered you wealth and lands, and still you treat my generosity with disdain. Is that your final word?"

"Aye, sire," Lyon said firmly.

"So be it. You may return to England after you have celebrated the wedding of Lord Edric to Lady Ariana. And take Lady Zabrina with you. Queen Margaret does not like her. She fears the woman will cause dissension at court with her flirtatious ways and bold address."

Lyon and Edric rose to leave at the same time. Malcolm, his mood quickly deteriorating, gave them leave with the wave of his hand. They left the chamber together.

"A pity you didn't accept William's generous offer," Lyon taunted. "You and Lady Zabrina would have dealt well together. Now some other fortunate man will control her wealth and lands, not to mention the lady's fiery person. Did you not hear Ariana say she did not want you?"

"Aye," Edric said sourly. "She will come around. She was more than willing to wed me before the Conqueror gave her to you."

"Ariana has been well and truly wedded and bedded by me. Mayhap she carries my child. If she does, nothing on this earth will keep me from claiming what is mine."

"I will cross that bridge when I come to it." Edric sent Lyon a scathing glance. "Mayhap your seed is defective, for there is no indication that Lady Ariana is increasing."

"I could challenge you for that remark," Lyon

said, though he knew he would not. He had to keep his wits about him if he wanted to get Ariana out of this mess, and himself as well.

"Aye, but you won't," Edric said confidently. "If by chance you managed to kill me, Malcolm would put you to death or let you rot in the dungeon beneath the keep." His eyes narrowed, as if trying to make up his mind about something. When he came to a decision, he addressed Lyon once more. "Truth to tell, my lord, under different circumstances I would find a match between me and Lady Zabrina immensely rewarding. But I have already submitted myself to Malcolm."

"Know this, Edric of Blackheath," Lyon vowed solemnly, "you will never have Ariana of Cragmere. She is mine. If any man other than myself touches her, I will kill him." So saying, he whirled on his heel and strode away.

When Ariana prayed for a vision, none came. She was seldom blessed with the Sight when it concerned her own life, but she had hoped for some indication that Lyon was in no danger for refusing to submit to Malcolm. She had stared into space for hours, praying for a vision, but all she received were vague premonitions. A searing pain in the vicinity of her heart warned her that Lyon would rather die than submit to Malcolm.

With a sinking heart, Ariana knew it would be next to impossible for Lyon to sneak into her

Connie Mason

chamber tonight. Malcolm had set a night guard at her door expressly to keep Lyon away. By now Lyon would have told Malcolm that he would not submit to him, and she feared that Malcolm had taken it badly, though she didn't think Malcolm would harm Lyon for fear of inviting William's wrath. And few men were willing to face an enraged William of Normandy.

In fact, Ariana did not know if Lyon even wanted to see her after the way she had walked away from him in the hall. Her pride would not allow her to remain after the conversation she had overheard between Lyon and Zabrina. It sounded to her as if Lyon was eager to be rid of her so he could wed Lady Zabrina. She cursed her damn pride for making her so hot-headed. She could have stayed and listened to his explanation but instead had flounced off in a huff. Last night in Lyon's arms had been an incredible experience. After her temper cooled, she found it difficult to believe he preferred Lady Zabrina. He had asked her to trust him, and she'd let her temper rule her head instead of listening to reason. She was too impetuous, too headstrong for her own good.

Sighing remorsefully, Ariana made ready for bed. She had stripped to her undertunic when she heard a light tapping on her door. With pounding heart she approached the door, which she had bolted from the inside for her own protection. After last night, she would never forget to bolt her door again.

"Who is it?"

"Lyon—open quickly."

Lyon! Ariana's fingers flew to the bolt. Then he was inside, latching the door behind him. He, too, had learned his lesson.

" 'Tis dangerous for you to be here, my lord." Her voice rose. "Where is the guard? I cannot believe he would leave his post."

"He didn't," Lyon grinned. "He merely turned his back while I entered. The man is a mercenary, willing to bend the rules if it profits him to do so."

"And you made it worth his while," Ariana guessed. "Why have you come?"

"We need to talk."

"Aye," Ariana agreed. "I feared for your safety. How did Malcolm take your refusal to submit to him?"

"Badly. His fear of William is all that kept him from doing me bodily harm. He is quite adamant that you will wed Edric of Blackheath in less than a fortnight."

"Lady Zabrina will be most happy. The conversation I overheard earlier leads me to believe you are willing—nay, eager, to wed your leman now that you are free to claim her wealth."

"What you heard was naught but a balm to soothe Zabrina's pride. 'Tis a blow to her to think that neither Edric nor I desire her. Zabrina is a woman who thinks well of herself. She believes no man can resist her charms. Nor refuse her wealth."

"Am I expected to believe that you were merely soothing her pride?"

"I would have explained had you given me a chance. Zabrina is a vindictive bitch. There is no telling what she might do if she thinks no one wants her. You must trust me, Ariana. I won't stand idly by and see you wed to another."

Ariana threw herself into his arms, seeking the comfort he offered. He held her tightly against him, murmuring Norman phrases she did not understand into her ear. He was all heat and hard, virile muscles, and Ariana nearly forgot what she wanted to tell him.

Abruptly she pulled from his arms. "Lyon, mayhap you should subit to King Malcolm." Her words held a note of desperation.

"You know I cannot, Ariana." He gazed at her narrowly. "Have you had another vision? You should know by now that I put little faith in such things."

"Nay, no vision, Lyon, just a premonition. I sense danger but know not whence it comes."

"A knight is always in danger. 'Tis a way of life. I cannot do as you ask, Ariana."

Her eyes grew bright with unshed tears. "Will you stand by and see me wed to Edric?"

"Nay, never! You will just have to trust me, sweeting." He brought her back against him, kissing her lips to stop their trembling.

Ariana melted against him, wanting, needing to feel the comforting beat of his heart against hers. " 'Tis my fault, Lyon. I never should have left Londontown with Edric. I begged him to let me return, but he refused. He even tied me to the saddle and put a guard on my door when we stopped to rest."

Lyon went still. "He tied you?" His eyes grew hard and cold as ice.

"He did not hurt me, truly. Please, Lyon, forget Edric. 'Tis you I fear for."

He kissed her again, hard, then held her away. "I cannot stay, my lady, though my body aches to possess you, to taste your sweetness once again. Do nothing to anger Malcolm. I will find a way out of this coil."

"There is so little time," Ariana said. "Less than a fortnight. I beg you, submit to Malcolm, even if you have to break your vow later. 'Tis such a little thing I ask of you."

"Little thing! Nay, 'tis my honor you ask me to compromise. I cannot do that even for you, Ariana."

Ariana gave a great shudder. "Then go, my lord. There is nothing more to say." Sadness brought tears to her eyes, but she refused to release them. How could Lyon help her when he was but one stubborn man with so few knights?

"I will think of something," Lyon said with quiet determination. Turning abruptly, he let himself out of the room.

Lyon slouched morosely over a cup of ale, brooding over the unhappy events of the past few days. The day following his refusal to submit to King Malcolm, his knights had been rounded up and tossed into the dungeon. Aware of the Lion's reputation as a fierce fighter and powerful leader, Malcolm thought it best to imprison Lyon's personal guard until Edric and Lady Ariana were safely wedded and bedded. It was a devious move, one Lyon hadn't anticipated.

Unfortunately he hadn't enough money to bribe Malcolm's entire garrison, which left him virtually alone in an enemy stronghold. And Lord Edric went to great lengths to make certain Lyon and Ariana were kept apart. Not trusting Malcolm's mercenaries, Edric placed his own trustworthy knights at Ariana's door, thus putting an end to Lyon's nocturnal visits.

The days passed too quickly as the wedding preparations continued under the apt guidance of Queen Margaret. The hall was scrupulously cleaned and polished. Fresh boughs were spread on the floor. Tapestries were shaken and replaced and the entire keep swept from top to bottom. A virtual army of servants were put to work cooking and baking for the celebration.

The eve before the wedding, everyone gathered in the great hall for a prenuptial feast. With burning eyes, Lyon watched Ariana walk into the hall on Edric's arm, clothed in a surcoat of velvet trimmed in precious ermine. The cloth was vibrant green, belted with a girdle of gold filigree. Her pale blond hair was demurely covered with a silken veil held in place with a narrow gold band encrusted with pearls. Her desperate gaze found Lyon, then slid away. She recognized his despair and knew an even greater despair. Nothing would save her now.

It wasn't that Edric was a cruel man, or even a vindictive one. She knew he would treat her with kindness, but she did not love him. And if he'd admit the truth, he did not love her, either. She had seen him seek out Lady Zabrina these past few days, noted the way he looked at her, as if she were a sweetmeat and he dying of hunger. Mayhap at first he had wanted Ariana, but she felt strongly that he wanted her now only to appease Malcolm. She had tried her utmost to convince him that this marriage was wrong for both of them, but he'd refused to listen, stating that it was what both their families had wanted.

The feast was progressing into a proper celebration. The wild Scotsmen raised their glasses countless times to toast the bride. Jugglers and musicians were called in to provide entertainment. Before the night was over, a good many of Malcolm's knights were snoring over the table. Lyon drank little, brooding over his ale like a man condemned to die at dawn. He had searched his brain endlessly for a way out of this coil and had come up blank. With his men rotting in the dungeon, there was little he could do. Of one thing he was certain; he could not let the woman he loved marry another.

Malcolm kept close watch on Lyon, well pleased with his devious method of coaxing the Lion of Normandy into his fold. Now, he decided gleefully, it was time to make a preemptive move. Rising to his feet, he banged his cup on the table and announced grandly, "I've just had a wonderful idea." He found Ariana and Edric in the crowd and motioned them forward.

Ariana stood warily, glancing at Lyon for support. Since the wedding wasn't to take place until tomorrow, she still held to a slim hope that Lyon would somehow work a miracle. Malcolm put an end to her hopes with his next words.

"Send for the priest! All this celebrating should be rewarded. We will have the wedding tonight." He looked down the table at Lyon. Most thought the king was drunk, but Malcolm was too cunning for that. He knew exactly what he was doing. " 'Tis my wish that the Lion of Normandy attend the bedding ceremony." Those sober enough to understand the words cheered loudly.

The priest, disheveled and wiping sleep from his eyes, appeared at Malcolm's elbow. "You summoned me, sire?"

"Aye, Father. 'Tis a perfect time for a wedding. Lord Edric and Lady Ariana are eager to have it done with."

Ariana gasped, drawing the priest's attention. She looked as pale as death and he felt pity for her. "Mayhap we should wait until tomorrow, sire, when we can have a proper mass."

"Nay, priest, tonight. You may begin the ceremony."

"I must get my book, sire."

"Nay, you know the words. Say them and get on with it."

Shaking visibly, the priest began reciting from memory the brief ceremony that would join Edric and Ariana in holy matrimony.

Suddenly Lyon leaped to his feet. Ariana was his! He had lived according to his honor all his life, but without Ariana he would choke on his honor and die a bitter man.

"Hold! Stop the wedding."

Malcolm smiled gleefully, having planned this moment well. It was amazing how low a man could be brought by a woman. "Be still, priest," he ordered curtly. "You wish to speak, Lord Lyon?"

Lyon strode forward, his steps firm, his features hard and determined. "Aye. Stop the wedding now and I will do as you wish. I will submit to you on my knees if you but stop this farce. I am Lady Ariana's legal husband and so I shall remain."

"Sire, what of me?" Edric asked. He had the humiliating feeling that Malcolm had planned this coup from the beginning. Luring the Lion of Normandy away from William was a feat that would be written in the annals of history.

Malcolm waved dismissively at Edric. "I will find you a Scottish heiress. I promise you will be happy with my choice." He turned to Lyon. "Kneel before me, Lord Lyon, and place your hands in mine."

Lyon strode forward, each step bringing him closer to the total destruction of his honor. He hoped William would understand that he did not actually intend to switch loyalty. He would mouth the words, but his heart would know he spoke falsely. Still, just going through the motion was enough to shake him. Swearing an oath was a serious undertaking. It mattered not that he didn't actually intend to honor that oath; swearing falsely compromised his pride. God forgive him. He doubted he'd forgive himself.

Lyon did not so much as glance at Ariana as he knelt before the king and placed his hands in Malcolm's.

"Lord Lyon of Normandy, do you swear fealty to me? Do you promise to come to my aid when I have need of you and submit to me in all things?"

Ariana felt as if her heart were shattering. Because of her, Lyon had to break faith with William and submit to a man he neither liked nor trusted. If only he would look at her, give her some reason to hope he would not hate her for what he was forced to do for her sake.

"I do so swear," Lyon said in a voice so raw that Ariana knew he must be bleeding inside.

"Rise, Lord Lyon, you are now my man." Malcolm's voice rose to include everyone gathered in the hall. "Know you all that I hereby declare the annulment of the marriage between Lyon of Normandy and Ariana of Cragmere invalid. Therefore, the betrothal between Lady Ariana and Lord Edric of Blackheath is also invalid on the grounds that it is an illegal document."

Lyon rose to his feet amidst a chorus of drunken cheers. Malcolm looked quite pleased with himself. He might lose Edric of Blackheath, but he had caught a much bigger fish. He had been pleased to lure Edric to his cause, but

316

the Lion was a man whose very name commanded fear and respect. Lyon was a fierce warrior of great renown and Malcolm was well-satisfied with this day's work, expecting it to greatly aid his cause. His army's ranks would swell and he'd march triumphantly into England to claim new land in Scotland's name.

Lyon finally looked at Ariana. His eyes were dull and empty, as if he were looking through her, not at her. She recognized his anguish but could do nothing to help him.

"Release my men from the dungeon," Lyon demanded as he returned his gaze to Malcolm. "You no longer have reason to mistrust me."

Malcolm was silent for so long that Lyon thought he was going to refuse. He stared at Lyon, searching his face so intently that Lyon felt himself flush. Then abruptly Malcolm summoned Gunn. "Release Lord Lyon's knights from the dungeon and give them whatever they want."

Gunn bowed and hurried away to do his king's bidding.

"And you, Lord Lyon, may now bed your wife with the knowledge that she is legally yours to bed."

His face still grim, Lyon swept Ariana into his arms and carried her from the hall, ignoring the raunchy advice and bawdy comments following in their wake. His steps did not falter as he carried her up the narrow stone staircase and into her chamber. He had spoken not one word to her, nor did she initiate conversation. His expression frightened her; looking into his eyes gave her a glimpse of hell. Once inside the chamber, he set her down carefully and shot home the bolt on the door.

"Lyon . . ."

Ignoring her, he walked to the narrow window embrasure and stared into the inky, star-studded sky.

Thinking he did not hear her, she spoke his name again. A great shudder shook his body, but he neither answered nor looked at her. This was a Lyon she did not know, had never seen before. Troubled by his strange mood, she quickly undressed. When she had stripped to her undertunic, he was still gazing out the window, still as a statue. She approached him gingerly.

"Are you coming to bed, my lord?"

Lyon turned, staring impassively into her eyes, as if surprised to see her there. "What did you say?"

"Are you not tired, Lyon? Come to bed. Did you not hear King Malcolm? We are still husband and wife. What you did for me took courage, my lord. The kind of courage few men possess."

Her words finally seemed to register on him. "Courage! You call losing my honor an act of courage? Nay, Ariana, you witnessed my weakness this night. You are my weakness and my despair." My love and my life, he added silently.

His strong words brought tears to her eyes. He hated her; she could tell by the way he refused to look her in the eye. She reached out to him. "Lyon."

"Don't!"

Her hand came away as if burned. "What?"

"Don't touch me. I cannot bear it."

"Please, Lyon, do not hate me."

"Hate you? Nay, I hate myself. I should have guarded my heart against you. You are my obsession. I am a warrior, trained to live by wits and cunning, not emotion. A knight is taught to love God, king, and country. I am not fit for knighthood."

Even though he did not want to be touched, she touched him anyway. He stiffened and tried to move away, but she did not allow it. Her arms came around his neck and she leaned against him, resting her head on his chest. The tempo of his heart quickened. Suddenly she was in his arms, held so tightly that she could hardly breathe. Then she heard a sound suspiciously like a sob leave his throat as he buried his head in her hair.

"Sweet Jesu! What have I wrought, Ariana? What terrible thing have I done?"

His anguish reached out to her and she could think of no way to comfort him, except to love him. With gentle nudging she eased him over to the bed. The back of his knees came in contact with the edge and he sat down hard, pulling her onto his lap.

"Love me, Lyon," she pleaded in a hushed voice. "Let me ease your suffering."

"How can you ease my suffering when you

are the cause of it?" he charged unkindly. The moment the words left his lips, he wished them back. He could not blame Ariana for his own folly. He cared for her more than he did his honor. How could he ever forgive himself? He started to rise, knowing he could not make love to her, not now, not while his emotions were so raw.

"For the love of God, Ariana, do not ask it of me. My mood is not inclined toward gentleness. I do not wish to hurt you."

Ariana was astute enough to know that the only way to get through to Lyon, to jolt him from his misery, was to turn his mind from it. Before he came to his feet, she threw herself against him, toppling him onto the bed. She clung to him tenaciously, until she felt the tentative signs of surrender in the slackening of his hard body and the softening of his mouth. But it was not enough, for his eyes were still haunted, his face grim.

"You want me to love you, Ariana?" he bit out scathingly. "Very well, but don't say afterward that I didn't warn you. You will not like me this way, I promise."

Ariana started to reply but found her mouth crushed beneath his in a brutal kiss. When she felt him rip her undertunic to get to her bare flesh, she knew a moment of panic. Lyon was a powerful man whose strength was double— nay, triple—hers. In the mood he was in, he could do her serious harm. Realizing her mistake, she tried to pull away. But arousal had come to him on the wings of anger and it was far too late now to cry off.

Stretching atop her, he kissed her until her mouth was swollen, and when he tired of her mouth he found her breasts, tonguing her sensitive nipples roughly. His body was hard and heavy, his staff fully distended and pulsating against her stomach.

He drove her relentlessly toward release, giving her no options, no say in the way he used her. She felt herself spinning dizzily beneath his relentless onslaught and knew it should not be like this no matter that she had urged him on.

"Lyon, wait, not like this."

He lifted his head, giving her a grim smile. "I warned you, lady, but you did not heed me. I am a warrior. Gentleness does not come easily to me."

His hands gripped her hips, lifting her to his mouth as he parted her with his tongue and found her with his fingers. Ariana writhed and cried out, climaxing violently. Then he was over her, thrusting into her, his face contorted into a grimace of pain mingled with ecstasy. Ariana nearly strangled on a sob. She had wanted Lyon to love her, but she hadn't expected this. He hadn't actually hurt her, but she knew he was using her to pound away his lust. She was naught to him but a woman, and he used her to ease the hurt he had done to his honor. He had warned her, but sweet Jesu, she had never envisioned this.

"Lyon—sweet Jesu, Lyon—have pity!"

Something in her tone must have gotten through to Lyon, for he looked down at her as if seeing her for the first time. When he realized what he had done, he dropped his head to her breast and released a heaving sigh.

"Forgive me, Ariana. You are the last person in the world I wish to hurt. 'Tis cruel to punish you for my weakness."

Then he kissed her with all the tenderness at his disposal, rocking back and forth inside her, rousing her with gentle persuasion. To Ariana's utter delight Lyon was once again the tender lover she had grown to love. He brought her slowly to climax, concentrating on her needs as he held his at bay. When he felt her stiffen and vibrate beneath him, he stroked himself to a violent climax. Then he held her until the world stopped spinning around them. He didn't stir for a long time, savoring their closeness and the utter peace their joining had given him. Unfortunately, it was short-lived. With a sigh of regret, he removed himself from the bed and her arms.

He dressed quickly, then stood over her, staring at her dispassionately. "I'm sorry," he repeated. He walked slowly toward the door.

"Lyon, where are you going?" Panic made her voice sharp.

" 'Tis best I brood alone, my lady. I am not fit for gentle company."

"Do not leave me like this. Do not hate me, my lord."

He gave her a sad, somewhat confused smile.

"I do not know how I feel. There is hatred, aye, but 'tis mostly for myself. I betrayed William because I wanted you, and now I don't know if I can ever be a proper husband to you." He felt the agony of his loss, the depreciation of his manhood, the deterioration of who and what he once was, and could not live with it.

Ariana felt the weight of the universe settle upon her slender shoulders as Lyon let himself quietly out the door. The moment the door closed behind him, she burst into tears. Would that she had never met Lyon of Normandy. Because of her, he had betrayed solemn trust and lost his honor.

Chapter Sixteen

The halls echoed with sounds of activity, unusual so early in the morning. Ariana awakened to the certain knowledge that something was amiss. She leaped from bed at the same moment that Lyon burst into the chamber.

"Dress quickly, Ariana. William comes with his army."

Ariana had a dozen questions for him, but he left as quickly as he had appeared. William, she thought, as she flung on her clothes and raced to the window. Her heart nearly stopped in her breast when she saw a veritable army ranged behind the mighty warrior, who approached Abernethy with all the pomp and ceremony of a conqueror. She watched avidly as Malcolm, surrounded by his personal guard, rode out to meet William on the moor. Try as she might, she could not dismiss a nagging fear about William's appearance.

Without waiting to see what happened next, Ariana flew down the stairs, all the way to the inner courtyard, where she had to fight to find a place for herself in the throng of people gathered there. She looked for Lyon but did not see him. Nor could she see over the heads of others to learn what was taking place in the cool, mist-shrouded morning beyond the fortress gates. After what seemed like hours of earnest parlay with William, Malcolm returned to the fortress. He had a look of defeat about him, and Ariana wondered what had transpired between the Conqueror and the King of Scotland. She wasn't surprised to see William following Malcolm into the bailey, surrounded by his personal guard. The main body of his army remained without.

The two monarchs entered the great hall. Ariana pushed inside with the crowd. William removed his helm; his face was stiff with ruthless resolution. To all those assembled, he appeared a hard man in every sense—a ferocious warrior, a harsh ruler, a driving administrator, and a man of vigorous principles. Ariana also knew him as an implacable man whose massive determination and fearsome temper did not tolerate the slightest infringement of his will. He was descended from Viking freebooters and warlords who first plundered and then settled northwestern France, so he came by it naturally.

Connie Mason

William followed Malcolm to the raised dais
and turned to face the throngs filling the huge
hall. Ariana was surprised to see Lyon at William's side, for she hadn't noticed him before.
The chamber grew quiet as everyone waited for
the Conqueror to speak, aware that they were
about to witness an event that would be remembered for generations to come.

William raised his hand and slowly brought
it around to point at Malcolm. "Bow before me,
Malcolm of Scotland! Submit to me or suffer
the consequences. If you refuse, I will lead my
army through your land, visiting death and destruction upon all in our path. With your subjects as witness, I will have your vow never to
march into England with your army. My spies
inform me that you are planning to extend your
borders into English territory, and I will not tolerate it."

Malcolm, unprepared to battle William's
mighty army poised just beyond the fortress,
and fearing the relentless severity of the Conqueror's retribution should he refuse, immediately fell to one knee before an unrelenting
William and swore homage. Placing his hands
in William's, Malcolm submitted to William
and swore to become a vassal of the King of
England.

"As your liege lord, I demand that you deliver
your son Duncan to the English court as hostage for your good conduct. Duncan will not
suffer so long as you remain my man."

Malcolm blanched. "Duncan is my heir, sire."

"Aye, 'tis well you remember that. Where is Lord Edric?"

"Here, sire," Edric said, stepping forward and kneeling before William.

"All your machinations failed to produce the results you wished. What think you of your betrothal to the Lady Zabrina? I offered you more than you deserve." His scowl did not bode well for Edric.

To his credit, Edric did not flinch before the mighty Conqueror. He also did not think twice about his answer. " 'Twas indeed a generous offer, sire, and I accept it with gratitude."

Edric was no fool. He had no choice but to follow Malcolm's example and swear homage to the Conqueror. He had already done so once, and in so doing had earned the right to keep his lands. Would William forgive him for dishonoring his vow? he wondered dimly, or would he demand death as the price for betrayal? He placed his hands in William's and swore fealty.

William searched Edric's face, undecided whether to accept his vassal's homage or order his death. He was angry, but ultimately decided not to act rashly. There might come a time when he would have need of Lord Edric. Malcolm had made a grand show of submitting to him, William reflected, but instinct warned him that he hadn't heard the last of the wily Scotsman.

"You and your knights will return to Londontown with my army," Malcolm commanded, "where I can contemplate your fate at my leisure. Mayhap giving Lady Zabrina to you will be punishment enough," he observed with some amusement.

Bristling indignantly, Zabrina stepped forward. She made a hasty obeisance and said, "Forgive me, sire, but I do not wish to marry Lord Edric."

William brushed her protest aside with a wave of his gloved hand. " 'Tis time you had a husband, my lady. If I decide you will wed Lord Edric, then wed him you shall."

Zabrina's face contorted into a grimace as she turned slightly to glare at Lyon. Ariana looked at Zabrina and saw the face of danger. She held her breath and waited.

"Lord Edric isn't the only man present who has betrayed you. Look well at Lord Lyon, sire, for he is no longer your man."

Lyon stiffened, wishing the floor would open up and swallow him.

William glanced at Lyon, then back to Zabrina. "What nonsense do you spout, lady? No man is more loyal than Lyon of Normandy. He has proven his devotion many times over."

"Your liegeman has sworn fealty to King Malcolm of Scotland. He is no longer your man," Zabrina announced spitefully.

William whirled on Lyon, his rage instant and relentless. He could understand a Saxon such as Edric betraying an oath of fealty, but not one of his own Norman knights. Especially not the Lion of Normandy, a man he'd trust with his life.

"What say you, Lord Lyon? Did you submit to Malcolm? Have you betrayed my trust? I can forgive you anything but that."

Lyon fell to one knee before William. When he spoke, his words were prompted by despair.

"I will not lie to you, sire. I did indeed submit to Malcolm of Scotland." His pride would not allow him to defend his honor with useless explanations. He took full blame for what he had done. He knew instinctively that William was in no mood to listen to excuses. Malcolm had offered him a choice and he had made it, right or wrong. Ariana was still his. Regretfully, his obsession with his own wife had lost him William's regard. For that he could never forgive himself—or her.

William shook his head in disbelief. His expression was a mixture of anger, sadness, and distress. Finally, the stronger emotion of anger banished the others. Since Lyon had offered no excuses or explanations, William saw his action as deliberate betrayal. That a Norman knight would pay homage to any but his own king was incomprehensible as well as contemptible.

"Get you from my sight, Lyon of Cragmere! You will remain in exile at Cragmere until I summon you to Londontown for punishment."

His head bowed, Lyon rose to his feet and backed away from the man who had once considered him a friend and staunch defender. Before he reached the door, he raised his eyes and searched the crowd for Ariana.

Standing nearby, Ariana had heard everything and could not believe her ears. Lyon had suffered William's accusations without offering one word in his own defense. It wasn't fair. No man was more loyal to William than Lyon. He had submitted to Malcolm for her sake, and it had cost him William's trust. Because of her, Lyon's honor had suffered. Her own suffering was nearly as great as his. She had lost her husband. She had never seen such violent emotions on his face—raw fury and blinding pain. She knew instinctively that Lyon's pride was too fierce to permit him to forgive either himself or her.

Bright tears ran down her cheeks when she heard William denounce Lyon and banish him to Cragmere. Consumed with guilt, she watched Lyon back away from the Conqueror. Her breath caught painfully in her throat when he raised his head and looked directly at her. She moved as if in a dream, her feet wooden as she approached her husband, who had summoned her with his eyes if not with his heart. Her shoulders sagged beneath the weight of his despair. Then she was at Lyon's side, lending her support whether he wanted it or not.

"Hold!" William's voice was as harsh and relentless as his unforgiving nature. "The lady Ariana will accompany me to Londontown as hostage to ensure your good conduct. She will remain at court until I decide your punishment."

A muscle twitched in Lyon's jaw, the only indication of his shock. It was as if every human emotion had been stripped from him. He stared at William, offering nothing in his own defense, his thoughts concealed behind hooded eyes.

Ariana's mouth flew open, her gasp conveying her unwillingness to comply with William's edict. If Lyon wasn't willing to defend himself, she would speak for him.

"Sire." Though tremulous, her voice was clear and loud.

William turned in her direction, his brows raised. "You wish to speak, my lady?"

Ariana was at William's side before Lyon knew what she was about. "If you please, sire," she entreated earnestly. "You accuse Lord Lyon unjustly. There is an explanation for my lord's actions."

William scowled, her words impressing him not at all. "Do you speak for your husband, lady? I have never known the Lion of Normandy to hide behind a woman's skirts."

Lyon stepped forward, his face a mask of wounded pride and humiliation. He sent Ariana a scathing look that effectively silenced her. "I am capable of speaking for myself, sire. Forgive my lady wife for presuming to speak on my behalf."

"I am in no mood to listen to excuses, if indeed there are any," William retorted crossly. "When my temper has cooled, I will send for you and mayhap listen to explanations. Naught you can say now will change my mind or alter my decision. Lady Ariana will bide with me at court until I decide otherwise. Fear not—Matilda will take good care of her."

"I will leave at first light," Lyon said tightly. When Ariana started to protest, he sent her a warning glare. Then he turned and strode from the hall. As he disappeared through the door, Ariana felt as if the light had gone out of her life.

Later, Lyon sought the company of his knights in the garrison, nursing a mug of ale and discussing William's punishment. He was still there when a messenger rode through the gates as if the devil were on his tail. His curiosity aroused, Lyon walked to the door, recognizing one of William's men immediately. He hailed the fellow and walked out to meet him.

"What's amiss, Sir Gavin?" Lyon asked, noting with interest the condition of the knight and his winded mount.

"Trouble," the man said, sagging in exhaustion against his destrier. "The Welsh marcher lords have united and are attacking the fortress at Chester. The fortress is in grave danger of falling into the hands of insurgents. King William and his forces are needed desperately to dispel the invaders. William is still here, is he not? God forbid that I have missed him."

"You'll find William in the hall," Lyon said, profoundly affected by the news. If William rode to Chester's defense, it would be the first time he rode into battle without the Lion of Normandy at his side. Then, abruptly, another thought entered Lyon's mind and he returned to the garrison to tell Sir Beltane what he had learned and to ponder the ramifications of William's immediate leavetaking.

"Think you William will ask you to accompany him?" Beltane asked hopefully. As a trained warrior, he hated the thought of being left out of the action.

"Nay, William will not budge from his decision while his temper is still high. Mayhap," he said thoughtfully, "this will work to my advantage."

Beltane's brow wrinkled, unable to follow the direction of Lyon's thoughts. "How so, my lord?"

"Listen well, Beltane, for I'll leave the details to you." As Lyon explained his plan to Beltane, the knight's mouth opened in surprise and his brow lifted. When Lyon finished, Beltane was smiling.

"Leave it to me, my lord. I will see that all is in readiness for a dawn departure."

Lyon nodded and left the garrison. He had no sooner cleared the doorway when William and his men streamed from the hall. Lyon watched from a distance as horses were brought forth and the men mounted. Evidently William was wasting no time in hastening to Chester's defense. Lyon was somewhat startled to see Edric mounted and armored, his knights mingling with William's. He saw neither Ariana nor Malcolm's son, Duncan, leading Lyon to believe that he had been right that William would leave a few knights behind to escort the hostages back to Londontown. When William rode through the gates to join his army camped on the moors, Lyon smiled with grim satisfaction.

Ariana had no idea what was taking place in the bailey. She'd heard the commotion from her room and hurried to the window. Straining to look out the narrow embrasure, she saw William, surrounded by his knights, riding through the gates. Edric was with him, she noted, his mount dancing with impatience as mercenaries and other knights mingled in the bailey before riding out to join the main body of William's army. Though she strained for a glimpse of Lyon, Ariana did not see him among the men riding with the king.

What was amiss? Ariana wondered, alarmed at the thought of being left behind in Scotland. Had William changed his mind about taking hostages back to England? Where was Lyon? Had he already left for Cragmere? Why hadn't he tried to see her before leaving? He had given up so much on her account, she refused to believe he did not care at least a little for her. It hurt dreadfully to think that he blamed her for his loss of honor. The foundation of his pride had been shattered, and unfortunately Lyon could not see beyond that to the love awaiting him if only he'd recognize and accept it.

Turning away from the window, Ariana sighed wearily and sought the bench before the hearth. She stared into the fire, seeing the implacable lines of Lyon's face in the dancing flames and feeling an emptiness far beyond any she had ever known. She started violently at the loud rapping on her chamber door. Her first thought was that Lyon hadn't abandoned her after all, and she hurried to open the panel. Her heart sank when she saw one of William's knights standing on the threshold.

The man bowed and addressed Ariana respectfully. "I am Sir Gwain, captain of the king's guard. My men and I will escort you, Lady Zabrina, and King Malcolm's heir to England. If it pleases you, my lady, we will leave tomorrow after matins. Dress warmly, for 'twill be a long, cold journey."

"I do not understand. What happened to King William? Why did he leave so abruptly? Where is Lord Lyon?"

"An uprising, my lady," was all the captain said. He saw no reason to divulge political information to a woman. "As for Lord Lyon, he is to return to Cragmere as William directed. My men and I will see that he does. After he and his knights depart Abernethy, I will come for you. Is the time agreeable?"

"Aye," Ariana said, choking on the word. She did not want to go to Londontown. She did not want to be parted from Lyon. No matter that he could not be a husband to her, no matter that he blamed her for his loss of honor, she still loved him. She would suffer his anger and his coldness if she could be near him.

She closed the door and returned to her seat by the fire. The days were growing colder now, winter was close at hand, and she longed for the comfort of Cragmere. How she wished Nadia were here to console and advise her. There were times when she had not appreciated the witch's advice, but this was not one of them. Consumed by misery, Ariana did not hear the soft click of the latch or the nearly soundless footstep entering the chamber. What alerted her was the prickling at the nape of her neck as she sensed his presence. Her back was to the door, and she turned slowly.

Lyon leaned against the closed door, watching Ariana as she stared moodily into the dancing flames. She looked so beautiful, the sight of her stole his breath. Her head was bowed. Unruly tendrils of hair drifted around her temples and face, a soft nimbus of silver curls that glowed like a halo in the firelight. And in that moment he knew a hunger that bordered on desperation. A foolish desperation, he thought painfully, for she'd been the cause of his loss of honor. His shattered pride would not permit him to love her. It was his punishment, his cross to bear for following his heart instead of his head. Everything he had, everything he was, he owed to William, and he'd repaid the Conqueror by swearing fealty to another. All because of a woman. Ariana . . .

She turned and saw him.

"Lyon . . ." Her bottom lip trembled as she waited for him to speak.

"My lady." He spoke her name dispassionately. If he pretended a lack of interest, mayhap he could dispel the dangerous heat building inside him, threatening to disrupt his judgment. "Take these," he said, thrusting a bundle into her hands.

"What is this?" She searched his face for a sign of tenderness and saw nothing but cool appraisal in the ice blue of his eyes and the hard lines of his face.

"Clothing, my lady. Chausses and tunic and padded vest. You can wear your own shoes and cloak, a warm one with a hood, if you have it."

"I don't understand. Am I to travel to Londontown dressed as a lad?"

"As a page, Ariana—my page. And you won't be going to Londontown."

"But . . . Sir Gwain told me to be ready to leave after matins."

Lyon crossed to the fire to warm his hands. "I have other plans. I'm taking you to Cragmere."

"Cragmere!" Ariana gasped. "What of William? What of Sir Gwain? Has the Conqueror changed his mind about taking me to Londontown as hostage?"

Finally Lyon turned to look at her, his eyes a cauldron of bubbling emotion. "Nay, William has not changed his mind. He left hastily after learning that the marcher lords were attacking Chester. He is taking his army to Chester's defense."

"What will he do when he learns you disobeyed his orders? What will Sir Gwain do when he finds that I have left without permission? I fear for you, my lord."

He searched her face, hating himself for giving her hope where none existed. He meant what he'd said about never again being a husband to her, but he couldn't bear to leave her in Londontown to be corrupted by a dissolute court that even William could not control. He wanted her with him, even though he knew that her presence would be a constant torture. If he were wise, he would leave her in William's care, out of his sight, out of his reach, where she wouldn't be a constant reminder of his lost honor.

"William will do naught. He is too busy fighting. And Sir Gwain's orders are to take Malcolm's son to England as hostage. They will not tarry on your account. A king's heir is of more importance than a baron's wife. There is also Lady Zabrina to consider. Mayhap," he said hopefully, "William will relent and take me back into his good graces before he discovers you are not in Londontown. I've seen him like this before. His temper is swift and deadly, but once it cools, clear thinking returns."

"I pray you are right," Ariana said doubtfully. She didn't think William's temper would cool anytime soon.

"I will return for you before dawn."

"What if one of William's guards challenges us?"

"They won't," Lyon said confidently. "No one knows except my own men that I have no page. I haven't had one since the young lad in my service was killed accidentally. When we ride from Abernethy, no one will suspect a thing. Sir Gwain's only concern is seeing that William's orders are obeyed."

Ariana gazed at him through a veil of tears. "Lyon, I . . . I don't know what to say. You've lost so much on my account. Why are you doing this? Why?"

Lyon was nearly undone by the sparkling droplets he saw gathering on Ariana's long lashes. "God help me, for I cannot help myself," he hissed through clenched teeth. It wasn't the answer Ariana sought, but it was all he was capable of giving. Anything more would compromise the tattered remnants of his pride, such as it was. Then, as if to give credence to his harsh plea, he pulled Ariana hard against him, kissed her forcefully, then shoved her away. Before Ariana had time to wonder what the kiss meant, he had already let himself out of the chamber.

Ariana had been ready for hours. In fact, she had barely closed her eyes the entire night. Dressed in tunic and chausses and wearing a cloak of dark wool lined in fur for added warmth, she glanced nervously out the window, noting that dawn hovered like a gray ghost on the western horizon. If Lyon were coming, he'd be here by now, she reflected, surrendering to her growing panic.

She started violently when the door opened and Lyon stepped inside. He was dressed in full armor, carrying his helm beneath his arm. A cloak was fastened carelessly over his shoulders. He inspected her person in mute appraisal, nodded his satisfaction, and indicated that she should follow him. She did so silently, unquestioningly, moving through the cold passageway and down the stone staircase into the hall, where men were sleeping on pallets before the massive fireplace.

"Pull up your hood," Lyon said in a hushed voice. Ariana did as he directed, stepping around the sleeping men as they made their way from the fortress into the cold, crisp air.

Their passage did not go undetected. When they entered the bailey where Sir Beltane waited with their horses, Sir Gwain stepped from the shadows into their path.

" 'Tis nearly dawn, my lord."

"Aye," Lyon allowed. "I am leaving, Sir Gwain, as William commanded."

Sir Gwain looked over the dozen or so knights clustered in the bailey awaiting Lyon, then settled his gaze on Ariana. In an effort to disarm Gwain's curiosity, if indeed he was curious, Lyon said, "I had to drag my page from his bed. The lazy lad would sleep past matins if I allowed it."

"Can't blame him," Sir Gwain muttered, pulling his cloak more tightly around him. " 'Tis cold enough to freeze a man's ballocks. Go then, my lord. I wish you Godspeed."

Lyon held his breath as Sir Gwain disappeared into the keep. Then he grasped Ariana by the waist and tossed her upon her waiting mount. He mounted his own destrier and trotted through the gates and past the barbican without mishap. Ariana, surrounded by Lyon's knights, followed close behind. Once on the road, he grasped Ariana's reins and broke into a gallop. Ariana clung to her horse's neck and prayed for the strength to remain upright.

They maintained the hectic pace throughout the morning, stopping briefly to rest the horses and allow them to drink from a stream. The weather grew colder but their luck held, for it neither rained nor snowed. At noon they halted to eat part of the meager rations Sir Beltane had purloined from the kitchens the night before. When Lyon indicated that they should be on their way again, Ariana struggled to her feet. Lyon approached to help her mount.

"We dare not tarry, my lady," he said as he boosted her into the saddle. "I will not breathe easy until we reach Cragmere. I doubt Sir Gwain will follow, but I cannot take the chance. Can you manage?"

"Aye, my lord, do not worry about me. I will not delay you. I am as eager as you to reach Cragmere. I would suffer anything to keep from being taken as hostage to Londontown. I cannot abide that Norman stronghold."

"I pray you will not be sorry," Lyon said by way of warning. She stared deeply into his eyes, their icy depths chilling her to the bone. "Mayhap you'd be happier in Londontown. I can promise you naught at Cragmere but my protection."

" 'Tis enough, Lyon, for now," she whispered

shakily. "Mayhap one day you will no longer blame me for the loss of your honor."

He stepped closer. She felt his heat encompass her and no longer felt chilled. "Ariana, I . . ." Whatever he was going to say died prematurely as he turned on his heel and stalked away.

They camped that night on the moor. After eating a sparse meal, Ariana curled up in a blanket and tried to sleep. But she was so cold that her rattling teeth and shaking body would allow her no respite.

Lying a short distance away, Lyon watched Ariana as she tried to settle into sleep. He saw her shaking beneath the blanket and could not bear to watch her writhe in discomfort.

Ariana's body was numb and shaking violently. She had all but given up on obtaining a moment's rest when she felt a scalding heat at her back. Then Lyon's arms went around her, and heaving a shuddering sigh, she burrowed deep into the curve of his body. Blessed warmth surrounded her, encompassed her, lulled her into a false sense of well-being.

"Go to sleep," Lyon said roughly. "Your shaking is keeping us all awake." The tone of his voice suggested that he'd rather be anyplace but beside her.

Lyon felt Ariana's flesh warm and heard the even cadence of her breathing as sleep claimed her. He blessed all the saints in heaven that she wasn't awake to feel his arousal or suspect the torment he was suffering on her account. Was he destined to suffer untold agony because of this woman he wanted desperately to love but couldn't?

Five miserable days and nights passed before they crossed the border into Northumbria. Cold and nearly beyond caring, Ariana longed for a comfortable bed, a mug of cider, warmed and spiced, and a hot bath. She was so steeped in misery that she barely noticed the towers of Cragmere rising above the Northumbrian hills.

"Ahead lies Cragmere, my lady," Lyon pointed out, hoping to cheer her.

"Home," Ariana said on a breathless sigh. "Home," she repeated as she looked her fill at the graceful towers of her beloved fortress.

A short time later they rode across the bridge and past the barbican in a clatter of hooves and frosty breath. Keane, Tersa, and Nadia were waiting on the steps to meet them.

"Welcome home," Keane greeted them enthusiastically.

" 'Tis good to have you safely home," Tersa said shyly.

"Aye," Nadia agreed, her gaze intent upon the small shrouded figure beside Lyon. "Did I not warn ye, my lady?" Having uttered those cryptic words, she turned and disappeared into the keep.

Chapter Seventeen

Lyon left Ariana standing in the hall greeting her people, who gathered around her in exuberant welcome. He returned almost at once to the bailey to see to his men and horses and Ariana felt sadly bereft at his uncommon haste to be rid of her. The uncompromising tilt of his head combined with the harsh, unrelenting lines of his mouth gave proof of his desire to remove himself from her annoying presence.

Ariana needed time to think, to map out her strategy in regard to Lyon. Her love for him far surpassed even her pride. For Lyon's sake she was willing to do whatever was necessary to win his love.

"My lady, you must be exhausted," Tersa said, aware of Ariana's strange mood. "Would you like to go to the bathing chamber straightaway or would you rather rest first?"

"The bathing chamber," Ariana said without hesitation. "But I do not need your help." She had noticed the way Tersa's gaze returned time and again to the door and knew the maid was eager to see Beltane. "Go greet Sir Beltane. You must be eager to see him."

Tersa smiled shyly. "Aye, my lady. I have not seen him since he and Lord Lyon brought me to Cragmere from Londontown. They left almost immediately afterward for Scotland."

"Then go greet him, Tersa. After you have welcomed him properly, you will find me in my chamber."

"Thank you, my lady," Tersa said, dropping a curtsy before rushing outside into the bailey to find Sir Beltane.

Ariana smiled to herself as she made her way through the kitchens and buttery to the bathing chamber. A servant followed to help with the buckets of water heating on the hearth, and once the huge tub was filled and the temperature to her liking, she dismissed her. Ariana undressed quickly, and with a sigh of contentment sank into the soothing water. She closed her eyes and let the warmth seep into her bones, enjoying the luxury of total immersion instead of making do with a bowl of tepid water. She blessed her father for creating a chamber solely for the purpose of bathing and let her thoughts wander.

Weary to the bone, Lyon pushed open the door to the bathing chamber and froze. He had not expected to find Ariana here so soon. He had assumed she'd be resting in her chamber after so arduous a journey. Her eyes were closed and she appeared to be sleeping. He wanted to back quietly out of the room and forget what he had seen, but his feet refused to obey his command.

The water barely covered the rounded tops of Ariana's breasts. Lyon's gaze penetrated beneath the water, permitting an unrestricted view of her entire body. He saw clearly the pale pink of her puckered nipples, the inviting indentation of her navel, the alabaster surface of her stomach. His gaze shifted downward to the pale silver curls crowning her womanhood, beckoning to him from beneath the water. To his dismay, he grew instantly hard. He had to forcibly restrain himself from tearing off his clothes and joining her in her bath, from thrusting himself into her and stroking them both to dazzling climax.

The water grew tepid. Ariana stirred languorously and reached for the soap. Her eyes widened as they met Lyon's. She could tell by his flushed face that he had been watching her for some time.

"I will be finished directly, my lord," she murmured, noting that he had removed his armor and was wearing only a short shirt and chausses. "There is room for two if you'd care to join me."

Her voice held a huskiness Lyon found highly distracting. He had to clear his throat before he could speak. " 'Tis clearly not advisable."

"Why? Do you fear me? Or do you truly hate me?"

Lyon's lips thinned and his body grew as taut as a bowstring. "I fear no woman. As for hatred"—he shrugged expansively—" 'tis a strong word. I feel naught for you, my lady."

Had Ariana any inkling how dearly those words cost him, she would have been shocked. Even as Lyon uttered the harsh denial, his body reacted violently to her presence.

"Then join me," Ariana challenged. "If you feel naught for me, you have no reason to avoid me."

"Just so," Lyon intoned dryly as he removed his shirt. He knew he was getting himself into dangerous waters, but he could not permit her challenge to go unanswered.

If Lyon expected Ariana to avert her gaze while he removed his chausses, he was disappointed. She stared at him boldly, her green eyes narrowed in speculation. He grew harder, painfully so, but fought the urge to follow his base instincts. Instead, he lowered himself into the tub, taking great care not to brush up against her. But even in that he failed, for his hip touched hers as he settled into the water. He jerked as if scorched.

"Allow me to wash your back, my lord," Ariana said. The slight tremor in her voice betrayed her yearning for this man she loved against all logic.

"Nay, I . . ."

His words fell off as she turned him slightly away from her, took up the cloth and soap, and began scrubbing his back. The pure pleasure of her hands on him brought beads of sweat to his brow. He wanted to groan and bit his tongue to keep the sound from bursting forth. Relief shuddered through him when she finished rinsing off the soap, grateful that his ordeal had ended. To his dismay, he found it had only just begun. Though Ariana's hands were no longer on him, her breasts were pressed tightly against his back, scalding him with her heat. He stiffened and pulled away.

"Are you trying to seduce me, lady?"

"Aye."

"You're wasting your time."

"Please do not hate me, Lyon."

"I feel naught," he repeated. "I am no longer the same man I was before the day I lost my honor because of my obsession for you. I prevented Malcolm from forcing you to marry Edric. I owe you nothing more."

"Jesu, Lyon, must I compromise *my* pride and beg you to love me?"

He turned to look at her then, feeling the stirrings of an emotion he'd tried to deny. "I cannot help the way I feel, Ariana. I cannot be a husband to you knowing I betrayed my king for your sake. How can you expect me to love you when I don't even love myself?"

"Mayhap we both need to try harder." She wanted to shout out her love but was afraid he'd laugh at her.

"Nay."

"Aye." She reached out to touch his face, drawing a finger over his lips. When they softened beneath her touch, she drew his face down to meet hers and kissed him, brushing her lips against his in a sweet, tantalizing caress.

Unable to withstand the raw pleasure of her seduction, Lyon grasped her wrists and held them suspended between them. "Why are you doing this when I do not want you, lady? Have you no pride?"

"At one time I was considered too prideful. If you recall, I hated all Normans, including you. I still bear them little love, but some things have changed. You are my husband. I was forced by William to wed you. You owe me more than lip service."

"Do I indeed? And what do you owe me, lady? I betrayed William for you. No matter how destitute a man may be, he still has his honor. Unfortunately, honor is no longer mine to claim, so I have nothing. If my obsession for you hadn't gotten out of hand, I would still be William's man. 'Tis hard to forgive when a man's pride and honor have been compromised. So tell me, Ariana, what do you owe me?"

"I have only myself to offer," Ariana said, turning away, knowing her love wasn't nearly enough to replace a man's honor.

His hold on her wrists tightened and he pulled her close, closer still, their lips nearly but not quite touching. The look in his eyes was far from reassuring as he brought their mouths together. There was no softening, no tenderness in his kiss.

"Is that what you want, my lady?" he asked. He laughed harshly. "I can give you pleasure if that is your desire."

Ariana drew back in alarm. "Nay . . ."

"Aye." He kissed her again, releasing her wrists and finding her breasts, crushing them beneath his strong fingers. "Do you enjoy this?" He rolled her nipples beneath forefinger and thumb, bringing a gasp to her lips. He released them abruptly and lifted one puckered crown to his mouth, licking it with the roughness of his tongue, then taking her breast into the well of his mouth.

His fingers slid down the slick wetness of her stomach and thighs, finding the glistening pearly folds of her womanhood. Her back arched and the water sloshed over the edge of the tub, flooding the floor. He thrust a finger inside her and she jerked convulsively. His eyes were brilliant shards of blue flame as he watched her expression change with the steady thrusting of his finger.

Ariana felt detached from her body, as if watching from afar as Lyon dispassionately brought her to climax. Suddenly it occurred to her that Lyon intended to deny himself the ultimate pleasure. Detaching herself from what his lips and hands were doing to her, she gathered her wits and tried to dislodge his fingers.

"Lyon, not like this. Come into me, please come into me."

His eyes glittered dangerously as he bared his teeth and growled his refusal. "You wanted this, lady." He thrust deeper, so close to the edge himself that he feared he would expend his seed in the bath water.

Needles of heat slivered through her body. Her back arched, sending rippling cascades of silver hair over the edge of the tub. Then abruptly she was there, gasping his name as spiraling curls of heat wracked her body. When he withdrew his hands and mouth from her, she closed her eyes and summoned forth her anger. When she opened them again, they were blazing with fury.

"Bastard!"

"I've always known I was a bastard, lady."

He hoisted himself from the tub and turned his back on her, but not before Ariana got a glimpse of his erect phallus. Her heart constricted with pain. Did he intend to pound out his lust on a willing maid within the fortress? Or would he go into the village in search of his pleasure?

With stoic acceptance, Lyon suffered the pain of his erection, but the pain didn't compare with the numbing ache within his heart. Ariana had every reason to hate him. He had wanted to punish her for bringing him to this sorry pass, for becoming so indispensable to him that he had denounced his king for her. Mayhap her punishment had been too severe, but it was nothing compared to his own suffering. Aye, he was a bastard, in more ways than one, but when a man no longer possessed his honor, he was undeserving of love and incapable of loving.

Lyon dressed quickly, his hands unsteady as he felt Ariana's eyes on him. "I'll not bother you again, my lady."

Ariana felt keenly the piercing agony of his words. He stood in the shadows of the room, so tall, so strong, so broodingly handsome that he stole her breath away. He had hurt and humiliated her, but if he bedded another woman she'd die. He could deny it all he wanted, but she knew he cared for her. If he didn't, he would have allowed her to marry Edric and left with his honor intact. Why would he risk William's wrath if he cared naught for her?

"Who *will* you bother, my lord—some willing serving wench?"

He spun around to glare at her. "Would you care? Am I not a Norman bastard?"

"Aye. I have never been more aware of that, my lord. Mayhap you have forgotten that we spoke vows before a priest, promising to forsake all others. I intend holding you to those vows, Lyon of Cragmere."

"So," Lyon said harshly, "you would have me live the life of a monk." Truth to tell, he had no desire for another woman. No woman save Ariana appealed to him. But he'd be a fool to confess to such emotional sentiments when his shattered pride lay between them.

" 'Tis not necessary for you to live like a monk," Ariana said, gazing at him from behind lowered lashes. "I am your wife."

"My wife!" Lyon lashed out. "How could I forget when I surrendered my honor for you? You have bewitched me, Ariana. You have reduced my mind to mush and my body to quivering need. I despise everything you've done to me and what I've been forced to do for your sake."

His impassioned words rendered Ariana speechless. His verbal acknowledgment of how deeply she affected him was not an avowal of love. For all she knew, he hated the sight of her, for it reminded him of his loss of William's affection. But at least she knew he was emotionally involved, and that wasn't a bad thing. He was so complex, this man she had married against her will but had come to love without reservation.

Ariana plunged herself into the running of Cragmere. There was candlemaking to undertake, meat to be preserved by either salting or smoking, and the last of summer's bounty to be preserved. In addition, Ariana undertook a thorough cleaning of the castle, and servants moved about industriously under her supervision.

During all this activity, Lyon spent as much time as possible in the tiltyard with his knights or out hunting game for their table. Then there was archery practice, seeing to the harvest of late crops, and inspecting the village. Lyon often accompanied the bailiff on his rounds to collect taxes, making adjustments where needed. At the evening meal he sat at his customary place beside Ariana, brooding silently, drinking too much, devouring her with his eyes but saying little. Ariana had no idea where he spent his nights, for he never sought their bed.

Two weeks after their return to Cragmere, Ariana realized that she was carrying Lyon's child. She woke up one morning and vomited violently into the chamber pot. As if that weren't proof enough, Nadia arrived shortly afterward to confirm Ariana's suspicion. It was the first Ariana had seen of the old woman since the day of her return from Scotland.

When Ariana lifted her head from the chamber pot, she found Nadia standing beside her, offering a cup of cool water and a cloth to wipe her face. Ariana took them gratefully, by now accustomed to the witch's mysterious comings and goings.

"Does the Lion know he's going to have a cub?"

Ariana was not surprised that Nadia knew she was going to have a child almost at the same instant she'd come to the realization herself. "I did not even know myself until just now. Besides, I doubt if Lyon will even care. As you well know, I've seen precious little of him since our return to Cragmere."

"The Lion is a proud man, my lady. Ye present a danger to him. He does not understand his feelings. He only sees what caring for ye has wrought."

"Dangerous? Me? Nay, Nadia, I am nothing

to Lyon. He lusts for me—he's admitted as much—but he is determined to deny that which his body craves. He wants me not. How can I tell him about the babe when he rejects the mother?"

"What will ye do? The Lion will find out soon enough."

"I will go to the abbey," Ariana said with sudden insight. "They will not turn me away if I deed a section of land to them. I will take the veil and raise my child at St. Claire's."

"Bah, 'tis a foolish notion. Ye cannot deed land that belongs to yer husband, and the abbess will not welcome ye if ye cannot pay for yer keep. Nay, my lady, ye will abide with the Lion in his den and raise his cub."

Ariana thrust her jaw out stubbornly. "Not if he doesn't want me."

Nadia's mouth grew slack and her eyes glazed over. "My visions reveal many things, my lady. A dark specter threatens Lord Lyon. Ye must cheat death before ye find true happiness," she prophesied, her eyes focused on something beyond Ariana's vision. "But 'ware, Ariana, for I see great danger lurking on a distant battlefield. I see death. Aye, death, but ye have the power to cheat the grim reaper."

The witch's prophesy both frightened and puzzled Ariana. How could Lyon face death on the battlefield when he'd been banished to Cragmere and was not likely to take up arms anytime soon?

When Nadia spoke again, her voice had returned to its normal tone and her eyes had lost their unholy luster. "Tell Lord Lyon about his cub, my lady. If ye wait, it may be too late."

"You sound like a purveyor of doom," Ariana scoffed. "My Sight has revealed none of the dire events of which you speak."

"Has it not, my lady? Think back, to that first day the Lion appeared at yer door."

Ariana blanched, recalling vividly the vision she'd perceived of Lyon shadowed by the specter of death.

Nadia nodded sagely. "I knew ye'd remember. I have warned ye. 'Tis all I can do."

"I have not had a vision in many weeks," Ariana temporized. "I've had vague premonitions, but nothing that came to me in vivid detail. Think you I've outgrown them?"

"What I think does not matter. 'Tis what I see that counts. I wish ye a pleasant day, my lady."

Ariana blinked her eyes and when she opened them Nadia was gone. Damn the woman! She came and went at will and appeared only to impart dire warnings or predict doom. Would that the witch had something pleasant to report once in a while. Or spoke in something other than riddles.

Dragging herself from bed, Ariana spent the next half-hour dry-heaving into the chamber pot. By the time Tersa appeared with a pitcher of fresh water and a cup of ale, Ariana was as weak as a kitten.

Tersa took one look at her mistress and flew to her side. "Oh, my lady, what is it? Are you ill?

Should I summon a healer?"

Ariana shook her head, summoning the words to set Tersa's mind at ease. " 'Tis nothing, Tersa—a slight upset only. I'm feeling better already."

Tersa sent her mistress a doubtful look. "Are you sure, my lady? Is there anything I can do for you?"

Ariana managed a weak smile. "Nay, nothing. Except mayhap tell me how it goes between you and Sir Beltane."

Tersa's mouth widened into a sunny smile, making her appear beautiful instead of merely attractive. "Beltane is going to ask Lord Lyon's permission to marry me. I pray he will offer no objection."

"I know of no reason why Lord Lyon would object to the match," Ariana said with less confidence than she felt. Lyon's mood had been so foul lately that she never knew what to expect from him.

"I hope you are right, my lady, but even Beltane isn't so sure Lord Lyon will agree. He may think Beltane is too good for me. But I love him, my lady. I beg you, speak to Lord Lyon and implore him not to refuse Beltane's request."

"I doubt my words will hold any weight with my lord husband," Ariana said frankly. Her hand brushed the empty bed beside her.

"Please, my lady," Tersa pleaded, "I know he will listen to you. Beltane says Lord Lyon is besotted with you."

Startled, Ariana stared at Tersa in disbelief.

Lyon besotted with her? Wherever did Beltane get that idea? More like he couldn't stand the sight of her. "I will do what I can," she finally said, unwilling to disappoint the maid who had served her so well.

"Thank you, my lady. Can I help you dress now?"

"Nay, I will rest in my chamber a while longer."

Tersa tried not to show her surprise. Ariana was not one to linger in bed. There was so much to do in the castle that her mistress usually flew from one task to another without respite. Tersa left a short time later, her expression thoughtful.

Lyon rose stiffly from his makeshift bed beside the hearth and moved to the table. A servant appeared at his elbow with a mug of ale.

"Good morrow, my lord."

"Good morrow," Lyon mumbled stonily, wondering what was good about it. Nothing had changed. Each morning he lingered in the hall as long as possible, eager for the sight of his wife, hungering for her touch, for a mere glance from her green eyes. And each night he forcibly restrained himself from bursting into her chamber and making love to her. His self-hatred and disgust grew in leaps and bounds as it became harder and harder to stay away from the woman who had bewitched him, the woman who was the cause of his fall from the king's grace. And still he wanted her.

He took another gulp of ale and slammed the mug down on the table. It was immediately refilled. When a serving wench brought a trencher of cold meat and cheese, he shoved it aside. It slid the length of the table and fell to the floor.

Where was she? Lyon wondered dully. By this time he could usually catch a glimpse of Ariana as she crossed the hall to the chapel or went about her duties. Then, from the corner of his eye he saw a movement by the stairs. He turned slightly and saw Tersa enter the hall. He waited a moment, and when Ariana did not appear, he indicated that he wished to speak with Tersa.

"How may I help you, my lord?" Tersa asked shyly. Had Beltane spoken with Lord Lyon already? she wondered excitedly.

Her hopes were dashed when he asked curtly, "Where is your mistress?"

"Still abed, my lord."

"In bed? Is she ill?" Alarm colored his words. He had never known Ariana to lie in bed when there was work to be done.

Tersa pondered her answer. She didn't know for sure that Ariana was ill, but if she was, her husband had a right to know. Everyone in the castle knew things were not right between them. They did not even share a bed. If she did not tell Lord Lyon about her mistress's illness, he might become angry with her. She dropped her gaze beneath the probing intensity of his eyes.

"I asked you a question, Tersa. Is your mistress ill?"

"If my lady is ill, she did not acknowledge it."

Lyon relaxed visibly. But the look in Tersa's eyes gave him little reassurance. "Tell me the truth, Tersa."

"Mayhap my lady was a bit pale this morning," Tersa admitted. "She said 'twas merely a stomach upset. Is there aught else, my lord?"

"Nay, go back to your duties."

Tersa hurried off, leaving Lyon mulling over her words. If Ariana was ill, he wanted to know. He decided to wait until eventide, and if Ariana appeared ill he would summon a healer.

Ariana's usual humor and robust appetite returned by midday. She ate heartily of lunch, wondering where Lyon was and if he was eating properly. But as the day waned, so did her spirits. By vespers her stomach felt somewhat unsettled, and she hoped she wouldn't embarrass herself at table tonight before Lyon and his knights. By the time she entered the hall, she was feeling better and looking forward to a hearty meal. She also remembered her promise to Tersa and intended to speak to Lyon concerning Sir Beltane's desire to wed the maid.

Lyon's dark mood hadn't lifted through the day. If anything, it had grown worse. He wouldn't be satisfied until he saw Ariana for himself. When she entered the hall, he felt as if a great weight had been lifted from him. She looked as she always looked, so beautiful he could hardly keep his eyes from devouring her.

She wore a rose-colored surcoat tonight, with

a jeweled broach at her shoulder. Her silver hair was caught up in a gold net and covered with a veil the same color as her surcoat. When she took her place beside him, he rose politely, carefully averting his eyes lest she bedazzle him more than he already was. After she had settled into her chair, he noticed her unusual pallor.

They ate in silence for a time, sharing a trencher as was the custom. When she indicated that she was full, he turned and searched her face. "I trust you are well, my lady." His voice was politely inquiring.

"Do you care, my lord?"

"Only a monster would not be concerned about the state of his wife's health. I was merely inquiring."

"As you can see, I am well," Ariana replied.

"Aye, so it would seem. I am pleased to hear it."

"Has Sir Beltane spoken to you about Tersa?" she asked, abruptly changing the direction of their conversation. There was no time like the present to broach the subject, she decided.

"Aye, just today."

"What did you tell him?"

"Nothing yet. I am considering his request. Sir Beltane is of noble lineage while Tersa is merely a freeman's daughter."

"I think we should discuss this before you come to a decision," Ariana insisted. "I promised Tersa I would speak in her behalf."

Lyon skewered her with a piercing glance. "And so you have." With a calmness that enraged her, he returned to his meal.

Sparing him a disgusted look, Ariana rose abruptly. "I suddenly find I am exhausted. Good night, my lord."

Lyon hadn't meant to be so abrupt with Ariana. It wasn't that he didn't want to discuss Beltane and Tersa. He had already decided to give his blessing to their marriage. It was the foul mood he'd been in of late that made him surly. He regretted not telling Ariana his decision about Beltane and Tersa and decided to do just that after fortifying himself with more of the excellent wine from Cragmere's cellars. An hour passed before he rose unsteadily and marched up the stairs to Ariana's bedchamber.

Ariana undressed to her sheer undertunic after leaving the hall and stood now before the blazing fire, waiting for Tersa. She had no idea what to tell the maid concerning Lyon's decision, for he'd given no indication of what he intended. He'd been stubborn and uncommunicative on the subject. Ariana had been somewhat surprised by his concern over her health, but once she told him she was well, he had promptly ignored her. Dimly she wondered how he'd react to the news that he was going to be a father. Given his foul disposition of late, she doubted he'd remark on it at all. For all she knew he didn't want children by her, the woman he held responsible for his loss of honor.

The nearly noiseless scrape of the door ended

Ariana's silent ruminations. Thinking it was Tersa, she did not turn around, motioning Tersa inside with a careless wave of her hand.

"I am sorry, Tersa, but I was unable to sway Lord Lyon one way or another. He has little respect for my opinions."

"Not so, my lady."

Ariana gasped and whirled, surprised to see Lyon standing behind her. He was so close, she could reach out and touch him. "Lyon, I . . . I thought you were Tersa."

"I met Tersa in the hall on my way up here. You will be pleased to know that I gave her my blessing to wed Sir Beltane. She went off immediately to inform Beltane of my decision. I took the liberty of telling her that you would not need her services tonight."

"Th-thank you for telling me," Ariana said gratefully. "I'm sure they'll both be very happy."

His gaze slid over her greedily, devouring her with his eyes. The firelight behind her rendered her undertunic nearly transparent, revealing every delicious line and curve of her body. He could see her nipples clearly, poking impudently against the material of her undertunic. And the tempting indentation of her navel. His gaze dropped lower, to the shadowy place between her legs. His mouth went dry and he swallowed the groan that rose from his throat. His loins tightened painfully as he felt his phallus rise and harden.

He was staring at her so intently that she began to tremble. She licked her lips and his intense gaze followed the movement of her tongue with uninhibited pleasure. Ariana's trembling increased. When she could no longer bear the intensity of his gaze, she took a hesitant step forward and reached out to him.

"Lyon . . ."

The sound of her voice brought Lyon abruptly to his senses. Jesu, what was he thinking of? "Good night, my lady. I came merely to tell you that your entreaty on Tersa's behalf was unnecessary, for I had already decided to allow the marriage."

He turned slowly, reluctantly, as if leaving her was causing him great anguish. He walked to the door, his legs wooden, his movements stiff and disjointed. Ariana held her breath as he reached for the doorknob. Her breath came out in a trembling sigh when he paused and turned abruptly. He was beside her instantly, sweeping her into his arms, branding her with his scalding heat.

"Damn you, Ariana!" he gasped between clenched teeth. "You've bewitched me, lady. God help me, for I cannot help myself!"

Chapter Eighteen

Bearing her down to the bed, Lyon made a sound deep in his throat—a groan or a curse, it was difficult to tell—and his lips took hers. The fierceness of his possession stunned her, plunging her deep into a river of desire. His body slanted across hers, his mouth devouring hers, his tongue lashing relentlessly in a frenzy of taste and touch. The trembling need ruling his body rivaled the thunder of his heart. Grasping the neckline of her undertunic, he rent the garment in half, baring her to his greedy mouth and hands.

He lifted himself away from her long enough to shed his tunic and chausses, and when he returned she felt the hardness of his body and sensed the hunger building inside him. Then all thought ceased as he plied his mouth to the silky flesh of her breasts while his fingers sought the wetness between her thighs. He kissed and licked her rounded breasts, his tongue playing havoc with her nipples before moving downward to tease the hollow of her navel. Grasping her hips with both hands, he parted her legs with his knees and lifted her into the moist heat of his mouth.

Ariana gave a shuddering sigh as his mouth explored her inner thighs, coming just close enough to the bright delta of curls to send a thrill of apprehension shivering along her spine. He nipped and tasted the sweet silkiness of her thighs until she could stand it no longer, grasping his dark head and placing it where she wanted his mouth to roam next. With a feral growl, his mouth took undeniable possession of the glistening folds of her womanhood.

Each wet lash of his tongue drew a soft hiss of pleasure; each calculated pull of his lips made her legs tremble and her body vibrate. Her back arched and she lifted herself more firmly into his wicked caress, denying him nothing, gripping his dark hair and gasping his name. Shimmering spirals of heat wracked her body with each scalding thrust of his tongue. Suddenly she was there, cresting the brightest peak with breathless cries and moaning sighs, her hands restlessly skimming the tangles of soft, thick hair crowning his bent head.

Tiny contractions were still shuddering through her when Lyon lifted his head and slid upward until he hovered above her, his blue eyes blazing into hers with burning hunger. Ariana felt no compunction as she pulled his face to hers, eagerly opening her lips to the sweep of his tongue as her hands skimmed over the sculpted muscles of his back and shoulders and into the soft, thick hair that covered his chest. His naked body felt warm and hard as he pressed her down into the surface of the bed. His palms caressed her breasts, cupping the supple flesh as he drew it into his mouth and suckled her nipples. The points were puckered and ripe and eager for plucking, and his rod reacted violently to the knowledge.

Ariana arched into his mouth, feeling the hot tug of his lips on her nipples clear down to her toes. His turgid heat was resting between her thighs and she felt her own melting wetness gathering in anticipation of his entry. She wanted him inside her, would die if he didn't come into her now, and she grasped his shoulders and tilted her hips, entreating him closer with urgent little whimpers. He teased her mercilessly, sliding against her glistening heat, again and again, denying himself, denying her, until both were panting with the need for consummation.

"Lyon . . ." His name fell from her lips in a gasping plea.

"Aye," Lyon growled fiercely. "I know what you want, lady. 'Tis this, is it not?" He flexed his hips and buried himself deeply inside her, stunned by the heat and tightness squeezing around him, shouting with the joy of it.

Ariana's hands trembled where she grasped his shoulders. She felt him swelling, growing harder, plunging, pushing himself to his full potential, plowing new depths, deeper . . . deeper . . . until he filled her completely. Her cries fired his blood, driving him powerfully, every muscle straining, his breath harsh. Her body quickened against him as he braced himself above her, his body crying out for release, his hips pumping furiously, his lips moving in silent entreaty as he fought to nurture his pleasure and hers as long as humanly possible.

Ariana closed her eyes, flung her arms and legs around him, and stiffened convulsively through shimmering waves of intense, sustained ecstasy. She felt her soul leave her body as he continued to pump vigorously with the fierceness of his impending climax. His eyes closed, his neck arched, his breath came in choppy gasps and his body gleamed wetly beneath a film of perspiration. He shouted and thrust one last time, letting the pleasure roll over him, overwhelm him, bursting white-hot into the violent thrashing of Ariana's prolonged orgasm.

Pulsating heat and damp, steamy flesh melded as they rocked together, flushed and panting. Ariana seemed unwilling to let him go as her legs locked around him, still beset by tiny tremors and bursts of liquid heat. She felt his incredible fullness diminish within her, then his restless movement. Then he left her. Ariana felt keenly his abrupt withdrawal, sadly aware that he regretted his inability to control himself where she was concerned and that he blamed her for turning his noble intentions into a mockery.

He fell on his back beside her, his hand flung over his eyes. He looked so vulnerable that she wanted to reach out and comfort him, to smother him with love. His hair was stuck to the dampness of his neck and she felt the tension in his body, sensed his struggle with his conscience. Removing his hand abruptly from his eyes, he turned to stare at her. She flushed beneath his harsh scrutiny, wishing she knew what to say to appease him. She wanted desperately to tell him about their child, but something in his eyes warned her that now was not a good time.

"I hope you're happy, lady," he said with scathing contempt. "I gave you what you wanted and lost what remained of my pride."

"You wanted it as much as I, my lord."

Lyon grimaced as if in pain. "Aye, I cannot deny it, much to my regret. I resisted your subtle seduction as long as I could, but I am not made of stone. If I am to resist temptation, mayhap I should leave Cragmere."

"You cannot," Ariana said, clutching his arm in alarm. "William banished you to Cragmere."

"So he did," Lyon grumbled, rising to his feet. "In the future I'll not tempt myself by seeking your company in private."

The glowing candle provided just enough light for Ariana to see the outline of Lyon's powerful form as he dressed with uncommon haste. It was both torment and pleasure to watch him, knowing that his body welcomed her while his mind utterly rejected her. She got out of bed on shaky legs, reaching out to him in mute appeal. He backed away, steeling himself against the mesmerizing power of her allure. If she touched him now, it would strip him of the last shreds of his dignity. When she would have followed, he held out his hand to stop her, a hand that shook visibly with the effort it was taking to resist her.

"Lyon . . . ?"

"Come no further, Ariana. I have nothing more to give you."

Ariana's soft intake of breath effectively conveyed her hurt and anger. "Go then. I want naught from you," she muttered in ominous undertones. "You use me at your whim and give naught in return but your lust. I can live without that kind of attention. Get you from my sight, Lyon of Cragmere."

Lyon closed his eyes briefly to hide his anguish. When he opened them the coldness had returned, along with his resolve. "Gladly, my lady." He sketched a mocking bow and left the chamber.

Ariana paced her room, sequestered with her thoughts and her rage. Unfortunately, no amount of pacing seemed to provide any answer to her dilemma. She loved Lyon with all her heart, but he was making it difficult for their relationship to survive. If he continued in this way, there would be no relationship left to save. Weariness finally forced her to bed, and sheer exhaustion sent her into a restless sleep.

The following morning Ariana awoke feeling sluggish and dull. After emptying the contents of her stomach into the slop jar, she lay back down to wait until the sickness passed. By the time Tersa arrived, she was feeling much better. But when Tersa spied the slop jar which Ariana hadn't been completely successful in hiding, the maid cried out in alarm.

"You were ill again, my lady. Does Lord Lyon know? Has a healer been summoned?"

"There is no need," Ariana said dully. Keeping her pregnancy from Lyon was one thing, but trying to fool her maid was another entirely. "I know what ails me, Tersa."

The tone of Ariana's voice and her bleak expression brought the truth crashing down on Tersa. "You're going to have the Lion's babe!" She clapped her hands, accepting the news with eager anticipation. "Lord Lyon must be thrilled."

"I haven't told him yet."

"Oh, my lady, you . . ."

"Nay, Tersa, you do not understand. Lyon wants nothing to do with me. He blames me for his loss of honor. I suppose Sir Beltane told you what happened in Scotland." Tersa nodded. "Lord Lyon submitted to King Malcolm to save me from Edric."

"He will relent, my lady, once he learns about his child." She sighed wistfully. "He must love you greatly to give up so much for you."

Ariana laughed harshly. "Nay, Tersa, the damage to his pride has made him bitter and resentful. He hates me."

Tersa looked skeptical, especially when she saw the rumpled bedclothes and the imprint of Lyon's head on the pillow beside Ariana's. She did not have to reveal her thoughts to Ariana, for her expression spoke more eloquently than words.

" 'Tis not what you think, Tersa. Lord Lyon cares nothing for me. He is a man of enormous appetites and comes to me only to assuage his lust. Afterwards he can bear neither himself nor me. 'Tis a terrible burden. I do not want him if he wants me merely for the sake of our child."

"I will speak to Beltane. Perhaps he—"

"Nay! You will tell no one, including Sir Beltane. Do I have your promise, Tersa?"

Tersa gave reluctant agreement. "I promise, my lady, but I like it not."

Lyon did not appear for the evening meal. Ariana saw nothing of him for two days. On the third day he took his place beside her at the high table and nodded politely. He gave no hint of the passion and fire they had shared a few short nights ago as he ate with little interest in his food. When Ariana attempted conversation, he answered in disjointed syllables and she soon gave up all pretense of sociability. She retired to her chamber shortly afterward.

Lyon watched her leave through narrowed lids, admiring the gentle curve of her back, the subtle sway of her hips. He wanted her. For the past three nights, he'd slept in the garrison with his men in order to escape the sweet allure of her special scent that wrapped itself around him whenever he chanced to cross her path. He wanted her. He ached with it and hated himself for it. He stared morosely into his empty wine cup, held it up to be refilled, and drank deeply. When it was empty, he held it up again and emptied it quickly.

"My lord, mayhap you should go to her," Beltane advised as he joined Lyon. " 'Tis not good to brood so over a woman."

"You know naught, Beltane," Lyon complained bitterly. "You still have your honor. Go to your woman. Let me know when you wish to wed and I will arrange it with the priest."

Realizing that Lyon did not wish to discuss his problems, Beltane took himself off, grateful that the relationship between him and Tersa was less complicated, less volatile than that of Lyon and his lady wife.

Lyon drank two more cups of wine, then slammed the empty container down with a resounding bang. Resolutely he pushed himself away from the table and stormed up the stone staircase.

Ariana lay in bed sound asleep. She did not hear the chamber door open, or the soft tread of footsteps, or the whisper of clothing falling to the floor. She was not aware of the tall man staring down at her through blurry eyes, or the weight of a body joining her beneath the covers.

She sensed nothing until his hands found her body and his lips located her mouth. She awoke with a start, murmuring a protest that was lost in the hot depths of his mouth.

He loved her with wild passion, wordlessly. He left her before dawn, while she was sleeping, and the following day he gave no indication of having visited her chamber at all—or of loving her with silent hunger. His nocturnal visits continued with increasing frequency. They existed as passionate strangers, each seeking comfort in the dead of the night, unable to resist the sweet urgency driving them into each other's arms.

Each night Ariana listened for his footsteps, and when he did not appear, she cursed herself for a fool. Lyon did not want her; it was her body he craved. Yet when he did appear, she did not reject him, instead welcoming him eagerly, praying this would be the night she could tell him about their babe. But it did not happen and her secret still lay beneath her heart.

Dismal, driving sleet heralded the arrival of the king's messenger. He clattered across the bridge and past the barbican, demanding that the gate be opened in the king's name. Lyon ordered the gate to be raised immediately and stood out in the stinging sleet to greet the exhausted messenger, who had to be lifted from his horse and literally carried into the hall to thaw out before the roaring fire. A mug was thrust into his hand as he handed a sheet of rolled parchment to Lyon. Moving closer to the light, Lyon read the message through twice before tossing it into the consuming flames.

Beltane watched his liege lord expectantly, waiting to be told what the king had deemed urgent enough to send a messenger racing halfway across England in such foul weather. When Lyon raised his head, his eyes gleamed with suspicious moisture, and Beltane averted his gaze to the blazing fire. When Lyon spoke, his voice held a note of pride that had been lacking since William had exiled him to Cragmere.

"William has need of me in Chester. The marcher lords have gained control of the fortress and are threatening the town. His temper has cooled and he forgives me everything, including bringing Ariana to Cragmere. He begs me to hasten with my knights to his aid." A wide smile stretched his lips. "I am in William's favor again, Beltane. My king needs me. My honor has been restored. Alert the men and recruit villeins from the village who know how to handle a weapon. We ride at dawn."

Ariana stood behind Lyon, having arrived in time to hear his words. Her heart sang with joy, knowing how much this meant to Lyon, how deeply William's faith in him affected him. Yet she couldn't help thinking what this would mean to their own tenuous relationship. Lovers by night, strangers by day. The paradox of the situation was appalling. She knew she could delay but a short time before telling Lyon about the babe, and she didn't want to tell him if he still felt nothing for her but lust. She wanted him to love her as much as she loved him.

Lyon turned abruptly and saw Ariana standing nearby. He didn't have time to analyze what William's forgiveness meant in terms of their marriage, but he couldn't help smiling at her.

"You're going to the king's aid." It was more of a statement than a question.

"Aye, you heard?"

"You go to do battle," Ariana said, suddenly realizing that she could still lose him to death.

"William has forgiven me everything. 'Tis what I've prayed for. I know him well. His temper is fearsome but quickly cools. He misses my strong sword arm protecting his back."

Recalling Nadia's warning, Ariana's senses reeled, rendering her mute with fear. Nadia had known Lyon would be going off to war and had foreseen his death. But the witch had also said that she, Ariana, had the power to save his life. How? What could she do to prevent Lyon's death short of telling him not to go? She knew he would not heed her no matter how desperately she begged him.

"Ariana, did you hear me? I leave at dawn. Come, I would speak with you in private." Grasping her arm, he gently pulled her up the staircase to their bedchamber. By the time he turned and closed the door behind them, her eyes were glazing over, oblivious to all but the vision closing in on her.

She saw Lyon in the center of a battlefield, wielding his sword with a vengeance, protect-

ing William from the onslaught of wild Welshmen. He fought like a demon. She screamed
aloud when she saw an enemy's blade pierce an
unprotected place in his armor, felling him with
one vicious thrust. She watched in horror as
Lyon fell to his knees, taking another thrust before dropping facedown to the frozen earth. He
lay as still as death. Then the mist closed
around him and Ariana knew no more.

Lyon watched in growing horror as Ariana
slipped into a trance before his eyes. Her eyes
were wide, staring sightlessly past him. She
screamed and he grasped her shoulders, shaking her gently to bring her out of her spell. Her
eyes rolled inward and she spiraled slowly to
the floor. He spit out a curse, caught her deftly,
and carried her to the bed. When she did not
awaken to his voice, his alarm escalated into
raw panic.

"Tersa!" His summons was loud enough to
bring the maid running into the chamber.

"What is it, my lord?" She was out of breath
from rushing up the flight of stone stairs. When
she saw Ariana lying lifelessly on the bed, she
let out a startled cry. "Oh, my poor lady. What
happened?"

"I do not know," Lyon said harshly. "Find the
witch. She's the only one who can help my
lady."

"I'm here, my lord." Once again Nadia appeared on the threshold at a crucial moment,
startling Lyon.

"Jesu, woman, are you always lurking about?"

Nadia drew herself up indignantly. "I do not lurk, my lord. I know when I am needed. If my timing startles ye, 'tis because I see things others cannot and am able to appear even before I am summoned." She hurried to the bed, where Ariana lay limp and wan.

"What is wrong with my lady wife, witch?" Lyon asked harshly.

Nadia found Ariana's pulse, then placed her ear to her heart. When she raised her head, her eyes betrayed her worry. "Her heart beats but faintly, my lord. I have never known my lady to remain insensate so long once the Sight has left her."

When Lyon would have questioned her further, she waved his questions aside and spoke briefly to Tersa. The maid nodded and hurried off. A few moments later Tersa returned with a feather. Igniting the feather in the candle flame, Nadia waved it beneath Ariana's nose. Not even the pungent odor brought Ariana to her senses, and Nadia's frown turned grim.

Lyon's fear turned to panic. What he had just seen defied logic. All his life he'd refused to believe in anything that opposed God's teachings, but Ariana's gift of Sight could not be denied. He wondered what she had seen this time to cause such a violent reaction.

"Will she recover, woman?"

"Ah, look, my lord, she is coming around," Nadia said with heartfelt relief.

Lyon bent close, anxious to see for himself that Ariana was well. He breathed a mute prayer when she opened her eyes and stared at him. At first she appeared not to know him, but as she slowly came to her senses, he was relieved to see recognition dawn in the green depths of her eyes.

The first person Ariana saw upon awakening was Lyon. She attempted a shaky smile and failed miserably. Her vision was still too fresh in her mind for levity. She must warn Lyon and quickly. Reaching out, she touched his cheek. He grasped her hand, holding it firmly in place, surprised to find it cold and shaking beneath his.

"What did you see, Ariana?" he asked in a hushed voice.

Ariana's reply was a moaning sigh.

"Ariana, tell me what distresses you."

Did she dare tell him that she had seen his death? He would not believe her, let alone listen to her. William had restored his honor by calling him to arms and not even the certainty of death would prevent him from going to his king's aid.

"Promise me you will take care, my lord," she whispered with desperate urgency. "Watch the enemy at your back."

Lyon frowned, aware that there was more to Ariana's strange warning than she was admitting. "I am always careful, Ariana. But if I die on the battlefield, it will be with my honor and pride intact. I thank God that William finally realized I would never submit to another without good reason and is ready to accept my explanation. The knowledge that he has forgiven me has restored my life to me."

"What has it done for me, my lord?" Ariana asked, awaiting his answer with bated breath.

Realizing that they were not alone, and that every word spoken between them would spread like wildfire through every part of the fortress, Lyon ordered Tersa and Nadia from the chamber. Tersa went quickly and without protest, but Nadia glared at Lyon and stood her ground.

"What is it now, woman?"

"A warning, my lord," Nadia said. "Ye'd do well to listen to yer lady wife. Watch yer back, though I do not think it will matter. Yer fate has been decided by a power far greater than mine."

"Nay!" Ariana's cry echoed hollowly in the room. "You said 'twas in my power to save my lord. What must I do?"

"God's blood! What in all that's holy are you talking about?" Lyon bellowed.

Nadia ignored him, scrutinizing Ariana's frightened features with dark intensity. Her eyes gleamed with unholy light as she bent her head and whispered into Ariana's ear. "Aye, ye do have that power, my lady, but 'twill do you no good if ye know not how to use it. Sometimes I do not see things as clearly as I would like."

"If you will not enlighten me, witch, get you from my sight!" Lyon ordered harshly. He had so much to do and so little time. He feared there was not enough time to tell Ariana how he truly felt about her, or explain the feelings he'd buried deep within his heart while he was too steeped in misery to think of anything save his loss of honor.

Unmoved by Lyon's anger, Nadia took her time following his orders. Her back bent beneath her great age, she shuffled to the door. Before she stepped into the dark passageway, she imparted one final word of advice to Ariana.

"Tell him now, my lady. Tell him now, for if ye don't ye may never have another opportunity." Then she was gone.

Lyon stared after her in consternation, unable to decipher her words. Not so Ariana. She knew exactly to what Nadia was referring.

"The woman talks in riddles," Lyon grumbled crossly. "Do you know what she was talking about?"

"Sometimes not even I understand her," Ariana lied, refusing to look into his eyes lest he see that she was being less than truthful.

She was still lying on the bed, and when she tried to rise, Lyon reached out a helping hand. She accepted gratefully, finding herself not quite as steady as she would like. She grasped his hand, finding his strength and warmth comforting.

"You know what Nadia was referring to," Lyon persisted, "I can see it in your eyes. Did you both have the same vision?"

Ariana studied her hands in abject misery. She had already warned Lyon to take care.

What more could she say? That he was going to die on the battlefield? Nay, it would be cruel to make him worry about something that might never come to pass. And since she had heard nothing yet to suggest that his feelings for her had changed, she wanted to wait before telling him about the babe. Yet he expected something from her, and quickly. She chose the easier of two paths.

"You are correct, my lord, the vision I had was frightening, but not necessarily a prediction of the future."

Lyon grasped her hands and led her to a bench, kneeling beside her on the floor as she sat on the edge. "Tell me, Ariana."

"I saw you suffer a fatal blow on the battlefield," she whispered, her gaze turning inward. " 'Twas a mortal wound. I saw you fall and lie motionless."

Lyon went still. "What else did you see?"

She shook her head. "Nothing."

"Did the witch see my death also?"

"Aye, but Nadia saw something I did not," Ariana was quick to add. "She said it was within my power to save you."

"You?" Lyon's voice was thick with doubt.

" 'Tis indeed puzzling, but if Nadia has seen it, it must be true." Suddenly her face lit up. "I know, I will go with you to Chester! I will protect your back in the same way you protect William's." She leaped to her feet. "Hurry, Lyon, we have no time to waste if we are to leave at first light."

Ariana's brave words caused Lyon's heart to swell with an emotion he wouldn't have recognized a week ago. He had never known love before he met Ariana, didn't even believe in it.

But Ariana was like no other woman. She was courageous and stubborn, passionate and loving. He needed her with the same clawing intensity that he craved food and water. He knew of no other woman brave enough to take up arms in defense of her man. Yet that was exactly what this feisty scrap of a woman was willing to do for his sake. Despite his burgeoning pride in his lady wife, he couldn't allow such a needless sacrifice when he was perfectly capable of protecting himself.

"Nay, Ariana, your offer is admirable but unnecessary. I have been protecting myself for many years without your help. You will *not* go to Chester. You will remain here at Cragmere where you'll be safe."

Ariana whirled on her heel, impaling him with the green fury of her gaze. "How dare you mock my good intentions! My gift of Sight may not always be reliable, but 'tis dangerous to disregard it altogether. Nadia says I am the only one who can save you. You have no reason to deny my right to do so."

"I have every reason in the world, Ariana. You are my wife. I care what happens to you. If I must die, I will do so knowing you are safe within the walls of Cragmere. But all this conjecture is unnecessary, for I have no intention of dying. I suddenly find I have too much to live for. Wait for me, Ariana. When I return we will talk about things I've just recently discovered. Things I've foolishly neglected to admit to anyone, including myself."

He grasped her waist, bringing her into the circle of his arms. He spoke earnestly, his expression giving hint of his anguish.

"Promise me you won't try to follow me," he said, his arms tightening around her. "Promise you won't do anything foolish. You do indeed have the power to save me, just as Nadia said. You can do it by giving me peace of mind."

Ariana withheld her promise for so long that she thought Lyon was going to explode with the waiting. She resisted the urge to weep and bemoan the fact that he'd rejected her help. He carried enough on his shoulders without that kind of unnecessary emotional baggage. In the end she gave reluctant agreement, praying she wasn't making the biggest mistake of her life. Once her promise was given, Lyon appeared to breathe easier. That was the moment Ariana decided to tell him about their child. It would be cruel of her to let him go off to battle without knowing he was going to be a father.

"Lyon, before you go, there is something you should know. Something I hope will please you."

"You already please me," Lyon said, reluctant to spoil this moment which had brought them closer than they'd been at any time during their marriage.

"But I think you should know . . ."

"Nay, Ariana," he said, placing a finger against her lips. "Save it for when I return. Both of us have much to forgive, and 'tis better left for another time. My men await my orders. There are weapons to dispense and provisions to gather. William needs me and I must make haste."

"You're right, of course. It will keep. Go to William, my lord. I will wait most eagerly for your return."

"I *will* return, my lady, believe it."

His conviction did little to ease her fears, but she tried not to show them. When he pressed her close and kissed her hungrily, she wanted to believe all would be well, but her vision kept intruding. When he lowered her to the bed, her flesh rose up to meet him, and for a pitifully brief interval his passion gave her a deceptive feeling of well-being.

Chapter Nineteen

"Don't get up," Lyon whispered when Ariana attempted to arise from bed with him two hours before dawn. "This is how I want to picture you when I'm gone. In our bed, waiting for me, your face flushed from my loving and your lips swollen from my kisses. There is so much I want to say and no time in which to say it."

"Why did you wait so long?" Ariana asked curiously. "All these weeks could have been wondrously happy if you hadn't allowed your anger to rule your heart."

"You are not a man, Ariana. You have a name and family. The whole of my life I've had naught but my pride and my honor. I earned them on the battlefield, fighting beside my king. Then you came along. I didn't want to marry but did so to appease William. Not that I didn't appreciate Cragmere; the demesne has earned a place in my heart.

"Then suddenly I found my honor in jeopardy, threatened by a woman who scorned me. You've never made any secret of the fact that you hated all Normans. Yet despite that, despite everything, when it came down to letting Edric have you or submitting to Malcolm, I chose a woman over honor. You can't begin to imagine what that did to me."

"I did not ask you to do it," Ariana reminded him.

"You did not have to. I did it for myself. That's what made it even more devastating. Even when I wanted to, I couldn't resist you."

"Lyon, I . . ."

"Nay, my lady, there is no time. I must leave. We will speak of these things when I return."

"Aye, when you return," Ariana said bleakly. *If you return.*

She watched him dress by candlelight, admiring his legs as he fastened his chausses and drew on the tunic and padded vest that went beneath his chain mail. She knew his armor awaited him in the garrison, where Sir Beltane would help him don all the trappings of battle and choose his weapons. When he was ready to leave he turned and stared at her for a painful moment. Then he dropped to one knee and kissed her hard. A sob left her lips when the door closed softly behind him.

"Go with God, my love," she whispered into the empty room.

* * *

Two hours later Ariana stood huddled against the icy wind on the rampart, watching Lyon and his knights ride through the gates. He looked massive in his armor. Massive and invincible, yet strangely vulnerable in the cold clear light of a forbidding dawn. She thought she saw him turn once and look up at her, but she couldn't be sure. Her hand went to her still flat stomach and she groaned aloud, wondering if her child would ever know his father. She prayed for her Sight to come upon her and show her how she might save Lyon, but when she wanted it most, it failed her.

" 'Tis cold out here, my lady. Ye must think of yer child."

Ariana started violently at the sound of Nadia's voice. "You are forever creeping up on me, Nadia. What is it this time? Have you come to tell me how I may save Lord Lyon?"

"Ye will know when the time comes," the old crone said cryptically. "Meanwhile, ye must think of yer son. The Lion's cub will inherit this land and must be protected at all costs."

Ariana stared at her in consternation. "How do you know the child will be a boy? No one can predict that."

Nadia gazed into space. "Ye will have a son, my lady, and he will be a great man in his time. Aye, men will respect the Lion's cub, just as they respect the Lion." She took Ariana's arm and led her toward the stone staircase leading down into the keep. "Come, my lady, get ye out of the cold."

Ariana resisted, turning toward the old woman and asking, "What about Lord Lyon, Nadia? Will he be here to raise his son?"

Nadia shrugged her hunched shoulders. "If God wills it, my lady."

As the days passed, Ariana felt the crushing responsibility of the fortress pressing down on her. Her morning sickness was still with her. Without Lyon to take charge of the everyday running of Cragmere, she depended heavily on Keane and his innate good judgment to guide her. Having Tersa's company helped somewhat, but the maid was as lonesome for Sir Beltane as she was for Lyon, and not a day went by that they did not worry about the men they loved.

She feared the terrifying vision her Sight had revealed and prayed nightly for Lyon's safe deliverance. She couldn't wait to tell him about their child. It didn't even matter if he didn't love her as much as she loved him; her heart told her he cared for her in his own way. He had almost admitted as much last night, but there had not been enough time. What little time they had together was spent in joining their bodies in the timeless way of lovers.

Ariana had no idea how long Lyon would be gone, or if William's campaign against the marcher lords would be successful, but nothing was as important as his coming home alive. The longer she thought about what her Sight had revealed, the more frightened she became. If not for Nadia's warning about keeping her child safe, she would disregard Lyon's wishes and go to Chester. If she were with him, mayhap she could protect him against the unnamed assassin of her vision.

Eating and sleeping for the sake of her child, Ariana existed in a near void, wondering if Lyon missed her as desperately as she missed him.

Lyon reached Chester in good time, finding William's welcome heartening. The king displayed little of the rage he had exhibited toward Lyon in Abernethy now that his temper had cooled and he'd had time to think about what Lyon had done and why. And once Lyon had satisfactorily explained his reasons for submitting to Malcolm, William forgave him everything and expressed gratitude for Lyon's haste in coming to his aid.

"If someone threatened to take Matilda from me, I might have done the same," William admitted grudgingly. "I forgive you, Lord Lyon, because I need you, and because 'tis not the same without you riding beside me in the heat of battle. These accursed Welshmen have tried me sorely. I have been unable to pry them out of the fortress. The cowards leave their stronghold in the dead of night, riding out to strike at my army without warning. Then they ride back within the safety of the walls before we can retaliate. They're a wily lot."

"What are your plans, sire?"

"Lay siege to the countryside. Destroy everything for miles around. Houses, crops, churches, entire villages if need be, until they surrender or see their homes destroyed and their land laid waste as far as the eye can see."

Lyon blanched. He was well aware of William's ruthlessness; he'd witnessed it firsthand. He'd participated in the Conqueror's sweep of terror through England. William would do whatever it took to bring the marcher lords to their knees.

"Come," William invited. "Join me in my tent and tell me how your lady wife fares. Is she breeding yet? My Matilda has given me four fine sons. I expect no less from Lady Ariana, who doubtless wishes to please you with an heir for your good care of her."

"I have given my lady wife little reason to please me," Lyon admitted. "After submitting to Malcolm, I could not bear the loss of my honor and blamed her for what I did in the name of . . ." He paused, his lips twisting wryly at the word that came to mind. ". . . love."

"It pleases me to hear you admit that I chose well for you." William grinned. "Do you still lust for Lady Zabrina?"

"Lust is hardly the word I would use in describing what I feel for Zabrina," Lyon said bitterly. "She is a troublemaker and a shrew. I'm surprised I never noticed it before. Do you still propose giving her to Lord Edric?"

"Lord Edric has become useful to me in your absence," William mused thoughtfully. "Once he relinquished all hope of rebellion, he's proven his value in many ways. Yet I cannot forgive him entirely for conspiring with Malcolm and fleeing north with your bride. Mating him with Zabrina is a fitting punishment for his crimes against the crown. What say you, my lord?"

Lyon gave a shout of laughter. "Aye, sire, 'tis a punishment I would wish upon few men. But if 'tis all the same to you, I'll withhold my judgment of Lord Edric until he's safely wed and no longer a threat to my marriage. 'Tis no secret that my lady has always preferred her own countryman over a Norman bastard."

When Lyon rejoined his own men a short time later, he explained the standoff at Chester as told to him by William. Beltane wanted to storm the castle, another knight suggested digging a tunnel under the wall, while yet another wanted to build a catapult to send stones crashing through the curtain wall. All were good suggestions, but ultimately it was William's decision to make.

In the end it was the marcher lords holed up within the fortress who decided their own fate. From the parapets of the fortress they watched in growing dismay as William's army began a thorough destruction of the land—burning, pillaging, and laying waste to everything within their path. They saw their people fleeing before William's army with nothing but the clothes on their backs and finally realized how determined William was to bring the rebellion to an end.

Their rage brought them riding from the fortress when nothing else could.

Shortly after dawn one morning, they marched out en masse to meet the enemy. William knew instinctively that this was no strike-and-retreat tactic. Nay, this would be hand-to-hand combat. The marcher lords meant to drive him back to Londontown in defeat.

The Welshmen had chosen a most advantageous time to attack. The bulk of William's army had been deployed over the countryside, blazing a path of destruction that rivaled York. Only a handful of seasoned fighters remained with William, including Lyon and Edric. As the Welshmen marched from the fortress toward the battlefield where William had elected to wait for them, Lyon marshaled men and arms in defense of his king.

The marcher lords were the last to resist William's sweep across England, and once they were defeated there would be none left to raise arms against him. England belonged almost totally to the Conqueror now, and he was determined to put down this last pocket of resistance once and for all. Only then would the Norman conquest of England be complete.

The two factions met on a flat plain between a river to the north and a ridge of hills to the south. Without the support of his main army, William was slightly outnumbered, but he'd fought against overwhelming odds before and triumphed. With Lyon at his back and Edric at his side, and his own strong sword arm, he entertained no thought of losing the battle.

Lyon joined in the fighting with grim anticipation. For his own peace of mind he wanted to vindicate himself in William's eyes, and fighting valiantly was his way of reaffirming his loyalty. Fighting at William's back now, deflecting lethal blows from the enemy, Lyon thought of Ariana and how desperately he wished he had admitted that his feelings for her had grown into love.

Lyon feared Ariana could never love a Norman bastard like him, but he intended to change her mind. He felt certain she cared for him on some level, for she'd shown it in many ways. And she definitely felt lust for him. Their lovemaking was both wild and uninhibited and as necessary to their well-being as the air they breathed. That was a start he could build upon, until she learned to love him too.

Lyon glanced at William, noting that the king was defending himself against two burly Welshmen, who were whirling battle axes in the air, ready to launch them at William's head. Giving no thought to his own safety, Lyon made swift work of his own opponent and whirled to engage William's attackers. He saw that two more Welshmen had joined the others and all four were closing in for the kill. Lyon lunged forward to deflect a blow that would have proved fatal to the king, deftly dispatching the enemy to hell.

William had no time to convey his thanks, but Lyon knew the king had taken note of his timely intervention. It was just like old times, Lyon thought, fighting at William's back, protecting his king. Then suddenly all thought ceased as Lyon concentrated his efforts upon the cunning Welshman who was intent upon killing the Conqueror.

From the corner of his eye he saw a man rushing at William, brandishing a sword like a wild man. By the time Lyon rid himself of his own attacker, it was too late to disarm or kill the man lunging at a vulnerable place in William's armor. Thinking not of himself but of the king, Lyon threw himself in front of William, taking the thrust meant for the king. The broadsword found its mark beneath Lyon's arm where his armor was the weakest, piercing through the padded vest beneath and into his flesh.

The thrust went deep, and Lyon fell to his knees, the searing, gut-wrenching pain twisting his innards. With bloodlust upon him, the Welshman gave a shout of triumph, withdrew the sword from Lyon's flesh and prepared to thrust again, this time at a place even more susceptible than before—Lyon's exposed neck.

Lyon saw the thrust coming but did not close his eyes. He wanted to be aware of the exact moment when his soul departed his body and he went to meet his maker. His eyes glazed over, but he refused to relinquish his grasp on life. He felt the blade at his neck, felt the sour taste of death spurt against the back of his throat, and called out Ariana's name.

He did not feel the pressure against his neck ease. Nor was he aware that Edric had deflected the swordsman's aim and dispatched the Welshman. The only thing Lyon knew was that his death was imminent. With a prayer on his lips, he finally accepted his fate and closed his eyes, waiting for God to claim him.

Ariana cried out and doubled over in pain. The searing agony had nothing to do with the child she carried. She knew that immediately. She cried out again, holding her middle and rocking back and forth. Everyone in the hall was staring at her, wondering what was happening and uncertain what to do. Fortunately Tersa was nearby and rushed to Ariana's aid.

"My lady, what is it? Are you in pain?"

"Fetch Nadia. Hurry, Tersa, bring Nadia to me."

"I will fetch her directly, my lady, after I help you to your chamber."

"I will take my lady to her chamber," Keane said, taking Ariana's arm and escorting her from the hall. "Go fetch the witch as my lady wishes."

The pain coursed through Ariana in increasing waves. There wasn't a part of her that didn't hurt. Reluctant to leave her alone in her chamber, Keane watched her closely, at a loss to know how to help her. He breathed a sigh of relief when Tersa appeared with Nadia. He left most gratefully when Nadia motioned him from the room. One did not argue with a witch.

"What is it, my lady?" Nadia asked worriedly. "Is it the child?"

"Nay," Ariana gasped as the pain crested and ebbed within her. " 'Tis Lyon. Can you not feel it? Did you not see it in a vision? He is dead, Nadia. The Lion of Normandy is dead. Jesu, Jesu, Jesu, I cannot bear it."

Tersa cried out and staggered into the nearest chair, while Nadia frowned at Ariana in consternation. "Are ye sure, my lady?"

"I know the exact moment Lyon was struck down," Ariana claimed, squeezing her eyes shut against the renewed pain. "Can you not feel it?"

"Ye are the only one who can feel it, my lady, the only one who loves him enough to perceive his death. I will tell ye, though, I do not believe the Lion is dead."

"Jesu, I want to believe you, Nadia, but the pain is too fierce to deny. I must go to Chester and see for myself," Ariana said, clearly distraught. "I thought you could help me. I thought you of all people would know what has happened at Chester. You have ever been free with your advice and knowledge of things no one else could possibly know. Why can't you tell me what has happened to Lyon?"

For once Nadia was at a loss for words. She knew the Lion faced death at Chester and had warned Ariana. But she did not perceive his death now.

"Ye must remain at Cragmere, my lady," Nadia said earnestly, "for the sake of yer child. The third month is the most dangerous to the babe."

"Is that all you can tell me, Nadia?" Ariana cried out.

"I can tell ye that the Lion is not dead. Mortally wounded, mayhap, and near death, but still breathing."

"How can I save him when he is so far away? You know more about medicine than I."

"Yer medicine is stronger than mine, my lady. Ye will understand when the time comes. I cannot help ye."

"Jesu!" Ariana cried out in anguish. "What can I do?"

"Naught but wait," Nadia replied.

"My lady, you must not fret so," Tersa said, worried over Ariana's delicate state. " 'Tis not good for the babe. We have had no word from Chester. You do not know that Lord Lyon is wounded or lies near death. Mayhap the babe is playing tricks with your mind."

Ariana did not reply, knowing full well that it was more than the babe that had caused her pain. She turned back to Nadia, wishing to question her further, but to her chagrin the witch had disappeared.

During the following days Ariana existed in a state of anxiety. Soul-grinding fear gripped her and refused to let go. She still felt pain, though not as severe, and existed in a void, waiting for God knew what. She slept little and ate even less. Of Nadia she saw nothing. The witch was suspiciously absent during these trying days. Though Ariana prayed for a vision, or a miracle, none appeared.

Each day Ariana climbed to the rampart to stare into the empty horizon, until the cold drove her back inside to the warmth of the hearth. One day, as Ariana stared into a heavy gray mist blanketing the moors, her eyes blurred with weariness and the cold seeped into her bones. She was about to turn away and seek the warmth of the fire when she saw several riders outlined against the dull gray sky. Her lips formed a prayer as she watched them approach. When they neared the bridge, Ariana hurried down the winding staircase to order the gates opened.

Wringing her hands, she stood in the bailey as six riders clattered over the bridge and into the yard. One of the horses carried a double burden. Ariana knew immediately that the man slumped over the horse's neck was Lyon. Beltane rode behind him, holding him in place. When the men removed their helms, Ariana was surprised to see Edric among Lyon's men.

"My lady," Beltane said in a strangled voice as he dismounted and lifted Lyon from the saddle. "I am sorry."

Ariana stifled a cry of dismay as she saw the blood staining Lyon's tunic. Someone had removed his armor and applied a crude bandage, but obviously the efforts were those of an amateur.

She stared at Beltane, fearing to ask the question uppermost in her mind. Beltane answered her silent plea. "He lives, my lady—barely."

"Carry him to his bed," she ordered shakily.

"Someone summon Nadia." Keane hurried off to do her bidding as Ariana turned and followed Beltane and another knight, who bore Lyon's body between them into the hall and up the stairs. "Gently," she admonished, fighting to control her emotions lest she break down before Lyon's men.

She wasn't aware that Edric followed until they were inside the sleeping chamber. "I did what I could, Lady Ariana," Edric said, "but I am no healer."

Surprised, Ariana asked, "You treated Lyon's wounds?"

"Aye. He is grievously wounded, Ariana. I am surprised he lived this long. We rode night and day to bring him home to Cragmere."

"Home to die, you mean," Ariana said bitterly.

Edric did not dispute her words. " 'Twas William's wish that Lord Lyon be carried home. He saved the king's life."

"I expected no less from him. His courage was never in doubt."

She worked over him quickly, frightened by his grave condition. The ride from Chester had done him no good. His face was ashen, his chest barely moving. He hadn't so much as lifted an eyelid since he was carried into the keep. He lay as still as death and Ariana wanted to weep and wail and curse. When she uncovered his wound, she swayed and nearly swooned. The gaping hole was deep, festering, and raw, running from beneath his armpit and curving around his ribcage. The enemy's sword had pierced deeply into the upper section of his chest, entering beneath his right arm. Another wound on his neck, not as deep or as serious, caught Ariana's attention and she dabbed at it with a cloth as she waited for Nadia to arrive.

The witch appeared a few moments later, carrying a basket with her healing paraphernalia. She placed it on the bedside table and set to work immediately. She called for hot water, and Ariana, reluctant to leave Lyon's side, asked Edric to fetch it.

Nadia shook her head gravely. " 'Tis serious, my lady. I will do what I can."

"Will he die?" Ariana asked in a hushed voice.

"I cannot say."

"He must live! He cannot die. He doesn't even know about his child."

"I warned ye, my lady," Nadia chided. "Ye should have told him before he left. Hush now, while I treat his wound."

Ariana hovered at Nadia's elbow as she cleansed the wound thoroughly with a potion made by pouring hot water over certain herbs. When she squeezed the pus from the festering wound, Ariana turned her head away and gagged. When as much infection as possible was removed, Nadia placed fresh dill seeds in the open wound and sewed the jagged edges together. Then she placed a poultice on the wound. She covered the hole with a clean cloth.

As Nadia worked over him, Lyon gave no indication that he felt anything. Next Nadia examined the wound on his neck, declared it not life-threatening, and covered it with a healing salve made from marigolds.

"I can do no more," she said, rocking back on her heels.

"He's barely breathing," Ariana whispered fearfully. "Is he in pain? Why doesn't he awaken?"

"Mayhap he never will, my lady. He has gone too long without proper treatment; the infection is most fearsome and festers within him."

Ariana's eyes widened and her chin rose stubbornly. She would not allow Lyon to die! Nay, by sheer dint of will she'd keep him alive. *"He will not die, Nadia*. Do you hear me? *He will not die*! I will remain by his side and fight for his life. If it's in my power to save him, I will do so, by whatever method may be at my command."

Nadia did not look Ariana in the eye lest she give her false hope. "I will brew a tea from valerian root and send it to ye. 'Tis a powerful tranquilizer. He will sleep and feel no pain. Ye must feed it to him a little at a time so he does not choke. If fever sets in, I will brew willow tea to ease his suffering. Other than that I can do nothing. Ye must use yer power to coax the Lion from death's door."

"I have no power!" Ariana screamed the words, distraught over her inability to understand what was needed to save Lyon.

"Think on it, my lady. The power ye possess 'tis the most potent known to man. I go now, but I will know if ye need me."

Ariana knelt beside Lyon, taking his limp hand in hers and holding it to her breast as Nadia slipped out of the chamber.

"What was the witch babbling about, my lady?" Edric asked. "What is the nature of the power you possess?"

Ariana started violently. She'd had no idea Edric was still in the room. "Alas, I have no power. If I did, I would use it to restore my lord to health."

"You look exhausted, Ariana. Why don't you rest? Let one of the servants sit here with Lord Lyon."

Ariana raised hollow, purple-smudged eyes to Edric. She had slept little since that day she'd felt the pain of Lyon's wound and perceived his death. She'd worried and fretted and eaten only for the sake of her child. Now that he was here, so close to death, she wouldn't leave him.

"Nay, I cannot. I want him to see me when he opens his eyes."

"If he opens his eyes," Edric amended ominously. "I will remain at Cragmere to lend my support."

"Thank you, Lord Edric," Ariana said distractedly. Right now it was difficult to think of anything save Lyon and how helpless she was to save him despite Nadia's words to the contrary. Why was the woman so cursed vague?

Edric left and the night wore on with little noticeable change in Lyon's condition. Ariana removed the poultice and replaced it with another, which Nadia had sent along with other medication. She spooned valerian tea into his mouth and massaged his throat until he swallowed involuntarily. She placed her ear over his heart and listened to the weak beat, finding hope in the steady thumping. She cried, she prayed, she searched her mind endlessly for the elusive power to save him. She called on God and all the saints. She cursed and ranted and raved at the injustice of it all. Then she fell asleep with her head on his chest.

The voices around him flowed and ebbed, and Lyon emerged from the depths of darkness to listen. He thought he heard angels and wanted to open his arms to welcome them, but he could not move. He tried to open his eyes but his lids were glued in place. Strange, he thought, he'd never perceived death as being a place where he'd lack free movement or sight. He'd always thought he'd greet God in a brilliant flash of heavenly light, with angels singing and cherubim carrying him aloft on wings of gold. There was a dampness on his face, soft and strangely comforting. He smiled and slid deeper into unconsciousness.

Chapter Twenty

Ariana's tears bathed Lyon's face. When Tersa returned to the sickroom she found Ariana kneeling at Lyon's bedside, her head resting upon his chest.

"My lady, you must rest. 'Tis doing your babe little good sitting here without rest or food."

"I cannot eat, Tersa, not while my lord lies so near death."

"Then you must rest. I will sit here with him and call you the moment he opens his eyes."

"Nay, I will not leave him."

"Then I will bring you a tray of food. You cannot go on like this." She turned to leave, then paused. "I almost forgot. Lord Edric wishes a word with you."

Ariana frowned. She had all but forgotten

that Edric remained within the keep. "I do not wish to see him now."

"Did you know Lord Edric saved Lord Lyon's life?" Tersa asked. "Beltane told me that Lord Edric saw Lord Lyon fall and killed his attacker scant seconds before the man thrust his blade into Lord Lyon's neck. The blow would have surely killed him."

Ariana recalled the neck wound inflicted upon Lyon. It could have been fatal. If it had, Beltane would have brought home Lyon's corpse instead of a man who still breathed. She owed Edric a huge debt of gratitude.

"Tell Lord Edric I will see him. Send him here to me, for I will not leave my lord."

"Aye, my lady. I will fetch a tray of food for you while you speak with Lord Edric."

A few minutes later Edric walked into the chamber and approached the bed. Ariana rose to greet him. She managed a weak smile and held out her hand to him.

"I understand that I have you to thank for saving Lord Lyon's life."

Edric took her hand between his, looking deeply into her eyes. "Do not thank me yet, Ariana. I may have prolonged Lord Lyon's life, but only God knows for how long. 'Tis obvious he lies near death."

Edric's devastating words released all her pent-up grief, sending a flood of tears streaming down her cheeks. "Oh, Edric, I fear Lyon will die. What will I do without him?"

Reacting to her distress, Edric pulled her

against him, offering her the comfort of his arms and a shoulder to cry upon. His hands consoled and soothed as Ariana gained control of her grief.

"Do you love him so much?" Edric asked with a hint of sadness. It had taken him a long time, but he'd finally come to the realization that Ariana truly loved her husband. He had always considered Ariana his, ever since they were children and the contract for their marriage was signed and sealed. If not for the Conqueror and his penchant for arranging marriages to suit his political purposes, Ariana would now be his wife.

"With all my heart and soul," Ariana sobbed against his chest.

"I did not know. I always thought that you and I . . . That's why I brought you to Scotland and insisted upon our marriage. If the Conqueror had not given you to Lord Lyon, would you have been content with me as a husband?"

"I would have been content, Edric. We were friends as children. You were the only one who remembered me during my years behind convent walls, the only one who cared what happened to me. But that was before I knew Lyon and grew to love him. Had he insisted I become a wife to him at the time of our marriage, while I was still a child, I would have hated and resented him for the rest of my life. He must have known that and realized I would be better off at the convent. Fortunately, I've grown up and

407

my hatred for Normans has been tempered by reality."

"No matter, I will not abandon you, my lady. I will remain at Cragmere. If Lord Lyon does not survive, you and I will marry before William can give you to another."

Lyon stirred restlessly. Voices intruded into the void of his subconscious. He struggled to listen, to open his eyes. For a brief, lucid moment his senses sharpened and his eyes opened into narrow slits. When the film over his eyes cleared, he saw Ariana in Lord Edric's arms. Edric was speaking. Concentrating with the last vestige of his strength, Lyon heard Edric tell Ariana that they would marry after Lyon's death.

The pain was more than Lyon could bear. Ariana had ever wanted Edric, he thought dully, and she would have him now, for he sensed that his death was imminent. On that thought his will to live deserted him and he closed his eyes, waiting for the grim reaper to claim him.

It took Ariana a moment to react to Edric's words. Then, abruptly, she pulled from his arms. "Nay, if I cannot have Lyon, I want no man. I will never love another man the way I love Lyon. His child grows inside me."

Stunned, Edric stared at her. "You carry the Lion's child?"

"Aye. 'Tis a boy. If God takes Lyon, I will raise his son and mourn Lyon the rest of my days."

"A child needs a father. Marry me when—if," he corrected, "Lord Lyon dies, and I will raise his son as my own. I vow this on my honor."

This talk of death did not sit well with Ariana. She would not, could not, think of Lyon's death, not as long as a breath remained in his body— or in hers.

"Lyon will not die!" she proclaimed in a voice that did not bode well for anyone who dared to disagree with her. "He will not," she repeated, this time less vigorously. "I will not let him. I thank you for saving Lyon's life, Edric. I will not forget it."

When Ariana turned back to the bed, Edric left quietly, stunned by the depth of Ariana's love. If love alone could save Lyon, he would surely survive.

Ariana returned to her vigil at Lyon's bedside, crying out in alarm when she noted the grayness of his complexion and the shallowness of his breath. Clearly he had taken a turn for the worse. She rushed from the chamber, calling for Tersa. When the maid appeared, she sent her racing for Nadia. After what seemed like hours Nadia appeared, huffing and puffing as if she'd run all the way.

"What is it, my lady? Is Lord Lyon worse?"

"Aye, Nadia, I fear he is close to death. Look at him. He barely breathes and his face is drained of all color. His body shakes with chills while his head burns like fire."

Nadia's brow furrowed. "I do not understand. The Lion's condition was grave when he arrived at Cragmere, but he was not as close to death as he is now. What has happened?"

"Naught. Lord Edric was here and we spoke

together for a few moments before he left. When I turned back to Lyon, his condition had worsened in those few minutes. What can I do, Nadia? I cannot let him die. Tell me how to save him."

Nadia stared at Ariana, her eyes vacant. When she spoke, her voice held a glimmer of enlightenment. "Ah, I begin to see more clearly now, my lady. Ye must look deeply within yerself for the power to coax Lord Lyon from death's door. Search yer heart for the answer. Ye are the only one who can do it. Ye must instill in him the will to live. I have done all I can do. He needs something more powerful than medicine to save him."

"Jesu, help me!" Ariana cried, dropping to her knees beside the bed. "Give me the power to save my husband." Her head fell upon Lyon's breast, her lips moving silently in fervent prayer. When she looked up a moment later, Nadia was gone.

Ariana closed her eyes, looking deeply within herself as Nadia suggested. At first she saw and felt nothing but her sadness, her grief. Then she felt uncontrollable fury. She cursed fate for giving her someone to love, then taking him away. With tremendous effort she pushed aside the nearly insurmountable barriers of sadness, grief, and fury and confronted the inner core of her emotions.

Love.

Pure love. Simple love. Everlasting love.

She opened her eyes and smiled through a mist of tears.

She smoothed an errant strand of Lyon's hair from his damp forehead and realized that he did not know how much she truly loved him, for she had never told him. She intended to remedy that lack immediately. Somehow she knew he could hear her words as she whispered into his ear, telling him all the things that she had withheld in the past.

"I love you, my lord. You are my heart and my soul, my very life. I cannot live without you. I want you in bed beside me at night. I want to see your face first thing every morning and last thing every night. I want to bear your children and grow old with you. Come back to me, my brave Lion. I need you to make my life complete."

Lyon gave no indication that he heard Ariana's passionate words. His eyes remained tightly closed, his breathing labored. Ariana refused to give up. The only power at her command was the strength of her love. Was it enough?

"Lyon, hear me," she implored earnestly. "I am carrying your child. Your son needs a father. Would you leave me to raise your cub alone? He was conceived in love, my lord, and deserves better than a fatherless existence. If you can hear me, Lyon, blink your eyes. Give me some sign that you will fight to get well."

Lyon wished the noise in his ear would go away. It was disrupting the peaceful transfer from one world to the next. He was nearly there; he knew it because he could feel the benevolent light of God shining upon him. He had but to step over the boundary to leave behind all his suffering and pain. And Ariana. She was the only thing preventing him from crossing over into sweet everlasting. Thoughts of her were potent enough to make him pause on the threshold of eternal sleep.

The noise in his ear transmitted itself into a voice. A soft feminine voice rising on a note of panic. Willing himself to listen, Lyon concentrated on the words being whispered into his ear. He recognized the voice. It belonged to Ariana. His attention sharpened. He heard her say she loved him, that she needed him, that she couldn't live without him. He heard Ariana tell him she was carrying his child. His soul lurched back from the brink, turning toward the voice, retreating abruptly from death, which had seemed so desirable only moments before.

Ariana felt the flutter of his heart against her palm and jerked upright, staring intently into his face. She gasped aloud when his lids fluttered. It was the first sign of life she had seen in him since Beltane carried him home.

"Lyon, can you hear me?"

His mouth worked soundlessly and she leaned close, listening, hoping, praying that he was trying to speak. Then his eyes opened and he stared at her. Tears of joy fell unrestrained upon his face, and he lifted his hand as if to brush them from her cheek, but he was still too weak. She grasped his hand and brought it to her lips. He curled his fingers around hers, his eyes moist with his own tears.

"Ariana . . ." The sound was a hoarse croak, scarcely recognizable. But Ariana read his lips and knew he spoke her name. Her tears fell harder.

She placed a cup of water to his lips, lifted his head, and helped him drink. He took a sip, swallowed painfully, then took another. When she set the cup down on the table and turned back to him, he was staring at her strangely.

"Do you love me more than you love Lord Edric?" This time his voice was stronger, though barely above a whisper.

"Aye, my lord, I love you with all my heart, and Edric not at all. You must get well for my sake."

He tried to reassure her. One corner of his mouth lifted in a brief parody of a smile. "How can I not when I have a son to look forward to? You did say a son, did you not?"

Ariana smiled through her tears. "Aye, a son. You heard?"

"Aye. You were most insistent. No matter how much I wished it, I could not escape your incessant chatter."

"Thank God," Ariana breathed gratefully. "I hope you are pleased. About the babe, I mean."

He closed his eyes, weary from his brief journey back to the world of the living. He had ventured so close to death, so very close. "Immensely pleased."

"You're tired," Ariana said, stroking his brow. "Sleep, my love. We'll talk later."

He opened his eyes. "Your power is awesome, my lady. You called me from death's door and I heard." He wanted to tell her that from the moment he heard her voice, his heart and mind had acknowledged his love for her and embraced it fully, without reservation or question, but words failed him.

Suddenly Ariana knew what Nadia meant when she said that only Ariana possessed the power to save Lyon. The healing power of love was stronger than any medicine. Because she loved Lyon more than life, she had been able to get through to him. "The power I possess comes from the love I bear you."

"A love returned full measure," Lyon replied. Exhaustion had reduced his voice to a mere whisper, but it was loud enough for Ariana to hear and take heart.

"You love me? Truly love me?"

A reply was beyond Lyon, for he had fallen into a healing sleep. His face had regained a little color and his forehead felt cool to the touch. Ariana rocked back on her heels and offered a prayer of thanksgiving.

"Ye have yerself to thank, my lady."

Ariana gasped in surprise. "You frightened me, Nadia. How long have you been here?"

"Long enough."

"He loves me, Nadia. Lord Lyon loves me."

"It took ye both long enough to discover that simple truth. Yer love saved him. Without it he would have passed beyond our grasp. He was close, my lady, very close."

"I know," Ariana said on a trembling sigh. "Will he be all right?"

Nadia shuffled to the bed, making a swift inspection of Lyon's wound and general condition. "His fever is gone, and there's no sign of infection, my lady. Ye have given him a reason to live, and his own strength and will to recover will do the rest. He will live," she pronounced grandly. "And ye had best rest yerself if ye expect to bring a healthy babe into this world."

Lyon was on the mend, yet just when Ariana thought all her problems were solved, another presented itself. Two weeks after Lyon came out of his stupor, Lady Zabrina arrived at Cragmere. Word had reached Londontown that the Lion of Normandy had been mortally wounded and lay near death, and she had rushed to Cragmere to comfort him. William had not yet returned from Chester, so she secured her own escort and traveled north with all haste. None of the servants had been able to stop her from storming up the staircase and searching each room until she found Lyon.

Ariana was resting in another bedchamber. Now that Lyon was recovering, she could leave him for short periods without fear of his dying in her absence. Tersa, who had been sitting with Lyon, had gone to the kitchen to fetch broth to spoon into him as soon as he awakened. As luck would have it, Lyon roused from sleep moments after Tersa left and was awake when Zabrina burst into the chamber.

"Lyon, oh, Lyon, I knew you could not be dead," Zabrina crooned, bending over him, nearly smothering him with her cloying perfume. "I have come to nurse you back to health, my love."

"You should not have bestirred yourself, Zabrina," Lyon said with a hint of amusement. "My lady wife is more than capable of seeing to my needs. If I recall, we parted on less than friendly terms at Abernethy."

"I am sorry for the distress I caused you, Lyon. I love you. I've always loved you. You were mine for more years than you were hers."

"Not so, Zabrina. I married Ariana long before I met you."

"But you did not bed her," Zabrina reminded him. " 'Twas I who gave you comfort and pleasure."

"Aye, and 'tis over, Zabrina. Accept that I love my wife. I would be dead but for her."

It was at that point that Ariana walked into the room. She stopped dead in her tracks when she saw Zabrina with Lyon. "What are you doing here?"

"I heard Lord Lyon was dying."

"As you can see, he is recovering. Mayhap you should turn around and return to London-town."

"Are you refusing me your hospitality?"

Just then Tersa entered the chamber, carrying a bowl of broth. She was more than a little surprised to see Zabrina in the sickroom.

"Show Lady Zabrina to an empty chamber, Tersa," Ariana said grudgingly, "and see that she is made comfortable. I will see to Lord Lyon's food."

Zabrina left the room wearing a smug smile. Muttering to herself, Ariana sat down beside Lyon and patiently spooned broth into his mouth.

"Enough," Lyon said when he'd had his fill.

"You look much improved after your nap." Ariana pointedly avoided mentioning Zabrina's unwelcome appearance.

"So do you." His eyes followed her as she moved about the room, performing mundane chores easily left to servants. "Ariana, cease your fidgeting and come here. I wish to speak with you."

"You should rest, Lyon. You are still very weak."

"I wish to know what Lord Edric is still doing here."

"He came with Beltane and your personal guard. You owe him a debt of gratitude, Lyon."

"A debt of gratitude," he asked, frowning. "How so, my love? For waiting around for me to die so that he may have my wife? For trying to seduce you with fine words? Do you think I did not see you in his arms?"

"You saw me?" Ariana gasped. "You were unconscious. If you had been awake, you would have heard me tell Edric I wanted only you, that I loved only you, that no other man would ever do for me, whether you lived or died. Edric is my friend, nothing more. He knows it and accepts it. Besides," she explained, "Edric saved your life."

Lyon looked confused. "Explain yourself, my love."

"Beltane said Edric pulled the Welshman from you and killed him seconds before his blade would have pierced your neck. Edric was the one who treated your wound and stopped you from bleeding to death. Mayhap it was crudely done, but it served until Nadia could treat you properly."

"If what you say is true, then I owe Lord Edric a great deal. But I do not owe him my wife. You're mine, Ariana, and I will give you up to no man. I love but once in my lifetime." He looked pointedly at her stomach. "How fares our child?"

Ariana gave him a brilliant smile. "Our babe rests easily, my lord, now that you are recovering. We are a perfect match, you and I, for I am a jealous wife. One love in a lifetime is all I can handle. You're my only love, my life."

He sighed blissfully. "I don't think I'll ever tire of hearing those words."

Suddenly reality intruded upon Ariana's happiness. "What are we going to do about Lady Zabrina?"

A hint of amusement colored his words. "Do? Why, nothing, my lady. William confided that he is serious about wedding Zabrina to Edric. When William returns from his campaign, I'm sure he will see the thing properly done. Now come closer so that I may place my hand upon the place where my child grows."

Ariana moved to stand beside him, blushing prettily when he lifted her surcoat and undertunic and placed his hand on her stomach. It amazed her that he could exert himself even that much given his grave condition a few short days ago. But she had underestimated his strength. The wicked gleam in his eye told her that he was thinking about things he shouldn't be, considering his near brush with death. True, his wound was healing, but it still caused considerable discomfort. When his hand slid down to cup between her legs, she sucked in her breath and retreated.

"Lyon, you're not well enough for that. Get well, my love, there is plenty of time for . . . for *that*."

"But *that* is what I want to do," Lyon pouted as he made a grab for her. The stretch proved beyond him as he grimaced and dropped his arm. His groan of pain brought Ariana rushing back to his side.

"I told you you were in no condition to exert yourself. Now, if you're ready to settle down, I'd like to discuss Tersa and Beltane's wedding. They would like to be married in the chapel as soon as you are able to attend, if that's agreeable to you."

"I have no objection," Lyon said grumpily. He wasn't a man given to inactivity. Being restricted to his bed made him a less-than-ideal patient. Besides that, he wanted his wife fiercely and hated the fact that he could do nothing about it. Or could he? "When does the witch think I'll be able to leave this cursed bed?"

"You still have several weeks of recuperation before you're well enough to move about freely."

"Several weeks! Nay, Ariana. I will not lie here on my back any longer than necessary. One week more, that's all."

Actually, Ariana was glad he'd agreed to another week. She'd expected him to tell her he would leave the bed tomorrow at the latest. "We will see how strong you are in another week."

"If you'd feed me something besides broth and pap fit for babes, I'd regain my strength much faster. A thick slice of venison and freshly caught trout drenched in dill sauce would do for a start."

"Mayhap 'tis time you sampled solid food again," Ariana acquiesced. "I'll see to it."

She started to walk away, but Lyon was loathe to let her go. Reaching out, he grasped her arm, dragging her down on the bed beside him. Ariana cried out in dismay, startled by his strength. "Lyon, let me go. You'll hurt yourself. Your wound will reopen."

" 'Tis healing nicely. I think I'm capable of kissing my wife without doing myself irreparable harm."

Ariana grew breathless. Even ill, Lyon was a formidable man. She could feel the heat of his body, his hardness, his determination, and grew dizzy with yearning. It had been so long since she'd been physically intimate with her husband, and the memory of his absolute command over her body left her trembling with fear and anticipation. She feared he would hurt himself, yet she shivered with excitement at the thought of his kisses.

Her mouth was softly yielding as his lips closed over hers, commanding the focus of her entire body. Her flesh constricted, and her stomach churned as his tongue entered her mouth, lashing her with slow, evocative strokes. A ragged groan greeted the pressure of his hands as he cradled her hips and pulled them against him. Scalding heat coursed through her limbs, making her weak and witless. His moan reminded her that what he was doing must be causing him considerable pain.

"Lyon, you must not."

"Aye, I must."

Jesu! He had not expected a simple kiss to leave him palsied with the tremors of an untried youth. He had not anticipated that she would respond so sweetly or taste so delicious, or that his flesh would ache with need despite the throbbing pain of his wound. The thundering rush of blood to his loins brought another kind of pain that had naught to do with his wound.

"Help me, Ariana," he whispered urgently. "I cannot do this alone."

"You cannot do it at all," Ariana warned, trying to extract herself from his grip.

"I can and I will. Hike up your skirts and climb atop me."

Her lips, swollen and wet from his kisses, quivered slightly as she panted to steady her rising passion. "Nay."

Undaunted, he tugged her surcoat and undertunic up to her waist. "If you do not help me, I will doubtless hurt myself trying to make love to my wife." He lowered the sheet, exposing the extent of his hunger. He was big, his thickness stretching even larger as she stared at him.

"Please," he whispered urgently.

Recognizing defeat, Ariana rose to her knees, balanced herself on the bed and carefully straddled Lyon's hips. She lowered herself onto him, gasping in pleasure as he came deeply inside her. Lyon moaned. It was all he could do to keep from spilling immediately. He felt no pain, only rapture—deep and enduring, consuming him with devastating pleasure.

Ariana moved slowly, the solid length of him piercing her deeply, fearing she would hurt him. She felt his fingers tug at the laces holding her clothing together, freeing her breasts to his hands and lips. Because he could not lift himself to her, he pulled her down until her breasts dangled within reach of his lips. He took a nipple into his mouth, suckling the rosy tip into an erect bud. Her pregnancy had made it ultrasensitive to his manipulation. She cried out and tightened around him as his thrusts pounded into her.

She tried to gentle his thrusts, fearing he

would tear his stitches, but the pleasure was too shattering, too intense to hold back. The tug at her nipples combined with the friction below triggered a violent response. Her ragged gasp of warning brought Lyon's mouth over hers, swallowing her hoarse cries of ecstasy.

Lyon felt her begin to convulse around him and he fed the stunning, pulsating force of her climax with ever deeper strokes. The tempest of his own rapture consumed him as he erupted inside her. He held her suspended above him, swallowing her cries as he writhed and undulated beneath her, moving with each of her mewling cries until the last shuddering heartbeat of pleasure subsided. Ariana regained her senses first, guilt-stricken over her loss of control. She had known better than to let Lyon have his way. He was in no condition for this kind of activity.

"Are you all right?" she asked breathlessly. Her hands flew over his bandaged chest, searching for signs of damage. She dared to breathe again when she saw no fresh bleeding against the snowy bandage.

"Better than all right, sweeting." He grinned.

Finding herself suddenly free, she rose shakily and put her clothing in order. She had just managed to pull the sheet over Lyon when the door opened and Beltane burst inside. Ariana nearly fainted when she realized how close she and Lyon had come to being discovered in an embarrassing position.

Beltane took one look at Ariana's flushed face

423

and Lyon's foolish grin and realized that he had interrupted at a most inappropriate time. But there was no help for it. Lord Lyon had to be apprised of the latest development.

"I regret interrupting, my lord, but there are riders approaching Cragmere."

Lyon became instantly alert. "How many?"

"A small army," Beltane informed Lyon. "From what I could see of them, they were neither Scotsmen nor Welshmen."

Ariana had moved to the window embrasure in hopes of catching a glimpse of the approaching army. She saw them outlined against the sun on the distant horizon. Suddenly one man broke away from the main group and rode toward Cragmere ahead of the others.

"An outrider comes!" she cried out.

"I will greet him," Lyon said, trying unsuccessfully to rise from bed. The bout of lovemaking had taken more out of him than he was willing to admit.

"Nay," Ariana said in a voice that brooked no argument. "You will not. I will go with Sir Beltane."

"I like it not," Lyon grumbled as he settled back against the pillows, but since there was nothing he could do about it, he offered no further protest.

A few minutes later, Ariana stood in the inner bailey, waiting to greet the messenger. The gates were lifted and the rider entered the bailey, stopping before Ariana and Beltane in a clatter of hooves. He dismounted and lifted his helm. Ariana gasped aloud when she recognized King William. When she dropped to her knees before him, he grasped her hands and lifted her to her feet.

"Nay, my lady, I come not to receive your homage but to mourn my courageous liegeman, who lost his life in my defense. Lord Lyon fought bravely at Chester, disregarding his own danger. He saved my life. The moment I saw his grave injury, I sent him home to Cragmere to die. Once the uprising was broken, I rode directly to Cragmere to mourn the passing of my most faithful liegeman and pay my respects to his widow. I loved the Lion of Normandy like a son."

Ariana was stunned beyond speech. Evidently William thought Lyon had perished from his severe wounds.

"Sire," she said, once she regained the ability to speak. "I am most happy to inform you that Lord Lyon lives."

Chapter Twenty-one

King William, the Conqueror of England, raised his eyes to heaven and wept unashamedly. When he looked back at Ariana, his face was transformed with joy. She could tell by his stunned expression that he had considered Lyon's wounds so serious that his chances for recovery were nil. He had come to pay his respects to a fallen comrade and instead found a reason to rejoice.

"Lyon lives," he repeated numbly. "What miracle have you wrought, my lady?"

Ariana gave him a sweet smile. " 'Tis no miracle, sire. I simply refused to let Lyon die. He would be here greeting you now, but I would not allow him to leave his bed. He is a terrible patient. His wound is not yet healed and he wants to cavort like a . . . a . . ." Her words slid to a stammering halt, suddenly aware of how they sounded. "I'm sure you know what I mean, sire," she finished lamely.

William stared at her in bemusement. "Indeed, lady, I know exactly what you mean. Take me to my liegeman. I would see him immediately."

Ariana ushered William into the hall. The Conqueror seemed surprised when he spied Edric of Blackheath. He stopped, motioning Edric forward. "Lord Edric, I am surprised to find you still at Cragmere. Are you not needed at Blackheath?"

"I remained to lend my support to Lady Ariana during Lord Lyon's illness," Edric said blandly. "For a time we did not know if he would live or die."

"I see," William said astutely. "Do not leave yet. I would speak with you after I have properly greeted Lord Lyon."

"Aye, sire," Edric said, sketching a bow. "I will await your pleasure."

William continued on his way when suddenly he caught a glimpse of Zabrina standing in the crowd. His dark frown hinted at his displeasure. He had not expected to find Zabrina at Cragmere.

"Lady Zabrina," he said loudly, summoning her with a beckoning finger. "By all that's holy, what are you doing at Cragmere? Did I not order you to remain in Londontown?"

Zabrina hurried forward, smiling beguilingly at the king. "Aye, sire, 'twas in Londontown that

427

I learned Lord Lyon lay near death. As you well know, Lord Lyon and I were . . . uh, very close at one time. In view of our longstanding relationship, I felt the need to come to Cragmere."

"I imagine Lady Ariana appreciates your concern," William mocked dryly.

"I will leave at once if you wish it," Zabrina said, not wishing to earn William's wrath. Besides, she realized now that coming to Cragmere had been a mistake. What she and Lyon once had no longer existed. She liked it not, but she accepted it.

A crafty look came into William's eyes. "Nay, stay. I have plans that include you. They can be carried out here as well as in Londontown."

"What kind of plans?" Zabrina asked curiously. She did not like William's arranging her life.

"We will speak of it later, after I have seen Lord Lyon." He dismissed her with a wave of his hand and motioned for Ariana to precede him to Lyon's chamber.

Lyon had no idea what was taking place below in the hall. No one had seen fit to tell him. An enemy could have invaded the keep for all he knew, and here he lay as helpless as a newborn babe. Well, maybe not so helpless, he thought, grinning wickedly as he recalled the passionate bout of lovemaking he'd participated in a short time ago. He had nearly convinced himself to venture downstairs when the door opened, admitting Ariana.

" 'Tis about time," Lyon grumbled crossly. Then William stepped into the chamber and Lyon lost the ability to speak. He started to rise, but William shook his head.

"Do not rise, Lord Lyon. You need pay me no homage. You have proven your loyalty on the battlefield. But for you, I would be lying in a cold grave. I came to Cragmere with the intention of paying my respects to your widow. My joy was boundless when I learned you still lived. Not only do you live," he said with a hint of amusement, "but your lady wife tells me you are recovered enough to cavort in bed."

Aghast, Lyon stared at Ariana. Surely she hadn't told the king they had been making love shortly before his arrival, had she? For the first time in his life, he blushed.

"My lord, nay, I did not . . ." Aware of Lyon's assumption, Ariana was at a loss for words.

William lifted his head and roared with laughter. Laughter was so rarely seen in the king that both Lyon and Ariana gaped at him in astonishment.

"Be at ease, Lord Lyon," William said, wiping mirthful tears from his eyes. "I but jest. I couldn't be happier for you and your lady wife. 'Tis a miracle that Lady Ariana still has a husband and I a faithful liegeman. With your leave, I will remain at Cragmere until after the wedding."

"Wedding?" Ariana and Lyon asked in unison.

"I was surprised to find both Lord Edric and

Lady Zabrina at Cragmere. Their presence here serves my purpose well. If it meets with your approval, their wedding ceremony can be held at Cragmere instead of Londontown."

"We will be most happy to have the wedding at Cragmere," Lyon said. "If it meets with your approval, we will celebrate the wedding of my man Beltane the Bold and the freewoman Tersa at the same time."

"So be it," William said agreeably. "The weddings will be held tomorrow at noontide. I go now to inform Lord Edric and Lady Zabrina of my decision. Then I will seek my rest. 'Tis a long journey from Chester."

"I assume you were victorious," Lyon said.

"Aye, the Welshmen were routed from the fortress and sent back whence they came."

"I pity Lord Edric," Ariana said when William had left. "He deserves better than Lady Zabrina."

"I think they will deal well with one another if Lord Edric puts Zabrina in her place before they are wed."

Ariana sent him a withering glance. "I prefer not to be reminded that you know Zabrina better than most. If you will excuse me, there is much to be done before the ceremony. I must speak with the kitchen staff about the wedding feast and order the hall cleaned for the occasion."

He sent her a guileless smile and reached for her. She slipped from his grasp and gave him a saucy grin. "You've had enough activity for one day, my lord." With a toss of her head, she left the chamber. Lyon's frustrated groan followed her from the room.

"I have spoken to Lord Lyon, and he is agreeable to holding your wedding at Cragmere tomorrow," William said as he faced Edric and Zabrina a short time later. He had chosen a small antechamber off the hall to impart the news of their forthcoming marriage.

"Tomorrow?" Zabrina gasped, darting a furtive look at Edric. "Can we not wait for a more propitious time, sire?"

"The time is ripe now," William contended. "Even as I speak, my scribe is making a list of all the properties, monies, and manors that will pass into Lord Edric's possession upon your marriage. 'Twill be a double celebration, I'm told. Sir Beltane and the freewoman Tersa will also wed tomorrow."

Edric watched Zabrina closely. Since he could not have Ariana, he was not averse to taking a wife of Zabrina's wealth and beauty. But if she thought she could rule him with her feminine wiles, she was mistaken. And the sooner she learned that, the better chance their marriage had for success. He would not tolerate infidelities such as she'd been practicing since her widowhood, and he intended to set her straight on that score immediately.

A man of few words and little tolerance for disobedience, William took his leave abruptly. When Zabrina attempted to leave seconds later,

Edric grasped her arm and pulled her back into the room.

"Stay, my lady. I wish to speak with you in private."

Zabrina sent him a look that spoke eloquently of her repugnance for this marriage. "I have nothing to say to you, my lord."

"How can you say that when you are the woman William has chosen to bear my name and my children? Very soon we will share a bed and other intimacies too numerous to name."

"You speak of things that most likely will never come to pass, my lord."

"They will happen, my lady, you can count on it. And make no mistake—when our children are born, there will be no speculation about the identity of their father. I will not tolerate infidelity. If I have to keep you behind locked doors, I will do so. But mark my word, Zabrina, from this day forward no man but me will sample your sweet charms."

Zabrina looked into the glowing depths of Edric's dark eyes and did not doubt him. Having her freedom curtailed did not sit well with her. She had become accustomed to more than one lover. She had grown to appreciate men like the Lion of Normandy, whose prowess in bed was legendary. Edric was an unknown entity, and she feared facing the future with a man she couldn't control. She was contrary enough to resist his strict edicts and speak out against them. She would give up none of her freedom without a fight.

"I do not follow orders," she said haughtily.

Edric knew she was testing him and welcomed the challenge with a tingling anticipation he had not experienced in a long time. "You will, my lady—oh, aye, you will. I will not play the cuckold. But fear not, you will not lack the pleasures you have grown accustomed to. I intend to bed you regularly, be it night or day or whenever the mood strikes me. No one will be able to accuse me of neglecting my wife."

Zabrina's mouth went dry. Had she misjudged this man? She studied him from beneath slitted lids. He was a handsome and well-built man, young but obviously quite capable of satisfying her in the manner to which she'd become accustomed. But she certainly wasn't going to let him know she found him pleasing to the eye. She deliberately turned her back on him.

"You think well of yourself, my lord Edric. If I am to judge properly, I require proof."

Edric took that as an invitation. "You want proof, Zabrina? You shall have it."

He grasped her arm and whirled her around to face him. Her mouth opened in surprise, and Edric found the sight of that little pink tongue darting out to moisten her lips too heady to resist. Before she had realized what he was about, Edric seized her lips in a bruising kiss. His tongue found hers, dueling with it within the sweet cavern of her mouth. His hands located her breasts, finding their size perfect, neither too small nor too large. She moaned aloud when he slowly raised her skirts and thrust his fingers into the clenching moistness between her legs. He grinned delightedly when she seemed to explode beneath his bold caress.

"Jesu! You're a hot little piece. But I will tame you, my lady. Once you have become a dutiful wife, we will enjoy one another to our heart's content. But not now." Abruptly he removed his hand and set her away from him.

Breathing hard, her violet eyes dilated with desire, Zabrina stared at Edric as if he'd just lost his mind. "Why did you stop?" she gasped breathlessly.

His eyes gleamed mischievously. "I want to leave you with something to anticipate on our wedding night. Until tomorrow, my lady," he said, sketching a graceful bow.

"Don't you dare leave me like this!" Zabrina screeched in dismay. "You will pay for humiliating me."

Edric's lips curved upward into a mocking grin. "I'm counting on it, my lady."

The next day dawned cold and clear. Tersa and Beltane were married at noontide. Tersa looked lovely in a silk tunic Ariana had given her in honor of the occasion. Beltane was splendidly garbed in velvet and fur. Both looked happy beyond belief. King William smiled benevolently as the couple spoke their vows. A few moments later, Edric and Zabrina took their place before the priest.

Edric had sent to his manor for his clothing

the day before and was resplendent in a short tunic of silver cloth trimmed in ermine. His chausses hugged the shape of his strong thighs and his shoulders appeared huge beneath the material of his tunic, inviting admiration from the ladies present.

Lyon had negotiated the stone staircase with Ariana's help and viewed the ceremony from the dais, with Ariana seated on one side and William on the other. He wore a smug smile as his rival was wed to his former mistress. It might not be a wedding made in heaven, but it certainly put Lyon's mind at ease. With both Edric and Zabrina out of their lives, he and Ariana could settle down to await the birth of their first child without interference.

A sumptuous wedding feast followed the ceremonies. After an indecently short interval, Edric approached the king and asked permission to take his bride home to Blackheath. Lyon thought Zabrina looked uncharacteristically subdued and wondered what Edric had done to bring about such a change. But he quickly forgot the couple as he noted tears in Ariana's eyes.

"What's amiss, my lady?" he asked, fearing that her tears were for her lost love.

Ariana sighed wistfully. "Naught is amiss, my lord. I was just recalling our wedding day. 'Twas not at all auspicious, if you recall. I would that we could do it over."

Lyon brushed a wayward tear from her cheek. "There is no need, sweetheart. I love but once in my life and wed but once in my life. Our

435

wedding may not have been auspicious, but it gained me a treasure beyond my wildest imagination."

Ariana's heart swelled with love for this Norman she'd vowed to hate but had grown to love beyond measure. She smiled at him sweetly and said, "Are you not tired, my lord? Mayhap you should return to your bed."

He gave her a startled look. He wasn't at all tired. The celebration had just begun and he wanted . . . Slowly comprehension dawned. The glowing spark of devilment in Ariana's eyes gave emphasis to her subtle meaning. Suddenly he felt in desperate need of his bed, but certainly not to rest. The wanton minx beside him would see to that.

"Aye, my lady, mayhap you're right. Bed is exactly what I need right now. I will make our excuses to King William and then you may help me to our bedchamber."

Color rose in Ariana's cheeks as Lyon whispered into William's ear. Ariana was grateful that her long skirt covered her quaking knees. Just the thought of Lyon's hands and mouth on her sent a thrill of anticipation up her spine. Would William suspect the reason for their hasty departure?

William's eyebrows rose to his hairline and he stifled a smile as he heard Lyon's explanation for their abrupt leavetaking. Then he nodded and sent Ariana a look of complete understanding. He could not hide his amusement as he dismissed them with a wave of his hand.

"See to your husband's comfort, my lady," he advised. "When your babe is born, name him after me."

"You told him!" Ariana hissed as they made their way slowly from the hall.

"Aye," Lyon grinned foolishly. "I don't care if the whole world knows you are carrying my child. Now, what's this nonsense about my being tired?" he asked, once they were inside their chamber. "You were quite insistent about putting me to bed. I hope you intend to join me."

"Would I suggest it if I didn't?" she asked archly. "I fear Lyon's bride is nearly as bold as the Lion when it comes to her pleasure."

"My passionate little vixen," he murmured, taking her in his arms and kissing her nearly senseless. "I would have you no other way. Thank you for loving me when I did not deserve it. How can I repay you for all the pain I've caused you?"

"You can love me, my lord."

"I do, my lady, I do."

Dear Readers,

I hope you enjoyed my first medieval romance from Leisure. I love writing in that time period, and if you liked *The Lion's Bride* I may be tempted to write another . . . or two.

Expect to find a ghost in my next offering from Leisure. I call it *The Graystroke Legacy*. My hero, Jack Warwick, impoverished cousin of the Earl of Graystroke, is visited by the family ghost, who leads him most reluctantly to a lady in distress. Lovely Moira soon becomes a pawn in one of rogue Jack's games. But it is Moira who has the last laugh, with the help of Jack's ghostly ancestor.

I love hearing from readers. For a bookmark and newsletter, write me in care of Leisure Books. For a prompt reply include a stamped, self-addressed, legal-sized envelope. I'm anxiously awaiting your response to *The Lion's Bride*.

All My Romantic Best,
Connie Mason

COMING IN JANUARY 1996!

**THE GREATEST ROMANCE STORIES
EVER TOLD BY ELEVEN OF THE MOST
POPULAR ROMANCE AUTHORS
IN THE WORLD!**

MADELINE BAKER

MARY BALOGH

ELAINE BARBIERI

LORI COPELAND

CASSIE EDWARDS

HEATHER GRAHAM

CATHERINE HART

VIRGINIA HENLEY

PENELOPE NERI

DIANA PALMER

JANELLE TAYLOR

*ALL PROFITS WILL BE DONATED
TO THE LITERACY PARTNERSHIP!*

LEGACY OF LOVE

From the Middle Ages to the present day, these stories follow the men and women whose lives are forever changed by a special book—a cherished volume that teaches the love of learning and the learning of love!

JOIN US—
AND CELEBRATE THE LEARNING OF LOVE AND THE LOVE OF LEARNING!

ALL PROFITS WILL BE DONATED TO THE LITERACY PARTNERSHIP!

COMING IN JANUARY 1996!

MADELINE BAKER
"To Love Again"

Madeline Baker is the author of eighteen romances for Leisure. Her novels have consistently appeared on the Walden and B. Dalton bestseller lists, and she is the winner of the *Romantic Times* Reviewers' Choice Award. Her newest historical romance is *Apache Runaway* (Leisure; March 1995).

MARY BALOGH
"The Betrothal Ball"

With more than forty romances to her credit, Mary Balogh is the winner of two *Romantic Times* Career Achievement Awards. She has been praised by *Publishers Weekly* for writing an "epic love story…absorbing reading right up until the end!" Her latest historical romance is *Longing* (NAL Topaz; December 1994).

ELAINE BARBIERI
"Loving Charity"

The author of twenty romances for Jove, Zebra, Harlequin, and Leisure, Elaine Barbieri has been called "an absolute master of her craft" by *Romantic Times*. She is the winner of several *Romantic Times* Reviewers' Choice Awards, including those for Storyteller Of The Year and Lifetime Achievement; and her historical romance *Wings Of The Dove* was a Doubleday Book Club selection. Her most recent title is *Dance Of The Flame* (Leisure; June 1995).

LORI COPELAND
"Kindred Hearts"

Lori Copeland is the author of more than forty romances for Harlequin, Bantam, Dell, Fawcett, and Love Spell. Her novels have consistently appeared on the Walden, B. Dalton, and *USA Today* bestseller lists. Her newest historical romance is *Someone To Love* (Fawcett; May 1995).

CASSIE EDWARDS
"Savage Fantasy"

The author of fifty romances for Jove, Zebra, Harlequin, NAL Topaz, and Leisure, Cassie Edwards has been called "a shining talent" by *Romantic Times*. She is the winner of the *Romantic Times* Lifetime Achievement Award for Best Indian Romance Series. Her most recent title is *Wild Bliss* (Topaz; June 1995).

HEATHER GRAHAM
"Fairy Tale"

The author of more than seventy novels for Dell, Harlequin, Silhouette, Avon, and Pinnacle, Heather Graham also publishes under the pseudonyms Heather Graham Pozzessere and Shannon Drake. She has been celebrated as "an incredible storyteller" by the *Los Angeles Times*. Her romances have been featured by the Doubleday Book Club and the Literary Guild; she has also had several titles on the *New York Times* bestseller list. Writing as Shannon Drake, she recently published *Branded Hearts* (Avon; February 1995).

CATHERINE HART
"Golden Treasures"

Catherine Hart is the author of fourteen historical romances for Leisure and Avon. Her novels have consistently appeared on the Walden and B. Dalton bestseller lists. Her newest historical romance is *Dazzled* (Avon; September 1994).

VIRGINIA HENLEY
"Letter Of Love"

The author of eleven titles for Avon and Dell, Virginia Henley has been awarded the *Affaire de Coeur* Silver Pen Award. Two of her historical romances—*Seduced* and *Desired*—have appeared on the *USA Today*, *Publishers Weekly,* and *New York Times* bestseller lists. Her latest historical romance is *Desired* (Dell Island; February 1995).

PENELOPE NERI
"Hidden Treasures"

Penelope Neri is the author of eighteen historical romances for Zebra. She is the winner of the *Romantic Times* Storyteller Of The Year Award and *Affaire de Coeur's* Golden Certificate Award. Her most recent title is *This Stolen Moment* (Zebra; October 1994).

DIANA PALMER
"Annabelle's Legacy"

With more than eighty novels to her credit, Diana Palmer has published with Fawcett, Warner, Silhouette, and Dell. Among her numerous writing awards are seven Walden Romance Bestseller Awards and four B. Dalton Bestseller Awards. Her latest romance is *That Burke Man* (Silhouette Desire; March 1995).

JANELLE TAYLOR
"Winds Of Change"

The author of thirty-four books, Janelle Taylor has had seven titles on the *New York Times* bestseller list, and eight of her novels have sold over a million copies each. Ms. Taylor has received much acclaim for her writing, including being inducted into the *Romantic Times* Writers Hall Of Fame. Her newest historical romance is *Destiny Mine* (Kensington; February 1995).

SIERRA

Connie Mason

Bestselling Author Of *Wind Rider*

Fresh from finishing school, Sierra Alden is the toast of the Barbary Coast. And everybody knows a proper lady doesn't go traipsing through untamed lands with a perfect stranger, especially one as devilishly handsome as Ramsey Hunter. But Sierra believes the rumors that say that her long-lost brother and sister are living in Denver, and she will imperil her reputation and her heart to find them.

Ram isn't the type of man to let a woman boss him around. Yet from the instant he spies Sierra on the muddy streets of San Francisco, she turns his life upside down. Before long, he is her unwilling guide across the wilderness and her more-than-willing tutor in the ways of love. But sweet words and gentle kisses aren't enough to claim the love of the delicious temptation called Sierra.

_3815-3 $5.99 US/$6.99 CAN